# *Dark Changeling*

## *Margaret L. Carter*

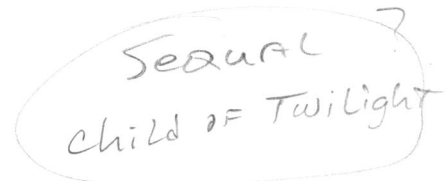

## Hard Shell Word Factory

I received information on matters forensic and psychiatric from Thomas G. Gutheil, M.D., and D. G. Goldberg.
Their help is gratefully acknowledged.
Any errors, of course, are my own.

Annapolis appears more or less as it existed in 1979-1980, allowing for artistic license. Any resemblance to real people is purely coincidental.

This novel is dedicated to Elaine Bergstrom, whose talent and achievements have been an inspiration to me.

© 1999, Margaret L. Carter

ISBN: 0-7599-0096-5
Trade Paperback
Published June 2001

Ebook published June 1999
Ebook ISBN: 1-58200-121-9

Hard Shell Word Factory
PO Box 161
Amherst Jct. WI 54407
books@hardshell.com
http://www.hardshell.com
Cover Art © 1999, Dirk A. Wolf
All electronic rights reserved.

This is a work of fiction. Any resemblance to persons known or unknown, is strictly coincidental.

## Prologue

***Boston, August 1979:***

HE WORE THE night like a black cloak.

Shrouded in an illusion of emptiness, he knew any human eyes would slide past him as if invisible.

From the shelter of an alley between a pair of deserted office buildings, Neil scanned the front of the movie theater and the small, gravel-surfaced parking lot next to it. The stink of garbage and auto fumes filled his nose. From nearby streets he heard the rumble of cars, the occasional sigh of brakes. At this hour little traffic turned down the dingy side street where the cinema was located. Bored with waiting, he let his eyes drift over the marquee, reading "OUBLE FEATUR," followed by the titles of two recent slasher films. Appropriate.

Neil grinned above his shaggy, copper-red beard when a young man and woman appeared beneath the overhang in front of the theater. He'd expected to loiter until the second show let out. Too bad the girl wasn't alone. What the hell, he could handle both of them.

The parking lot's single floodlight cast a halo on the girl's blonde, shoulder-length hair. She wore sky-blue flared slacks and a matching sweater against the nip of the March night. Her aura glowed with the indignation echoed in her shrill voice and the staccato tap of her heels. "What the hell is the matter with you, anyway? How could you be so stupid, bringing liquor into a movie? I've never been so embarrassed in my life!"

The watcher noticed, beneath the young man's open brown leather jacket, the bulge of a flask in the hip pocket. "What's the big deal? So we got thrown out. The flick was lousy anyway." His abundant chestnut hair, brushed into an exaggerated bouffant and curling at the back of his neck, framed a delicately handsome face distorted by a pout.

"Oh, yeah? It was your idea to see those stupid second-run axe-murderer films in this crummy neighborhood."

"Forget it, let's go for a ride." He slipped an arm around his date's waist to pat her on the bottom.

The air crackled with her anger. "Are you nuts? I wouldn't ride around the block with you!" She squirmed away from his touch.

Staggering, he groped for her, then steadied himself against the smudged bricks of the nearest wall. "Come on, Lisa, the night's young." Judging from his lopsided smile, he considered that remark urbanely witty.

"My mother was right, for once," said the girl, her heels clicking on the sidewalk as she strode away from him. "I shouldn't have gone out with you in the first place, M.I.T. honor student or not. What do you get honors in, Party 101?"

When her date made another grab for her arm, she whipped around and smacked him in the diaphragm with her purse. He doubled over with a whoosh of breath. "Well, screw it! You can just walk home!" He stumbled across the lot to his car. Neil, still watching from across the street, heard the crunch of gravel and the boy's labored breathing.

Neil's own breathing was none too steady, either. The girl's anger stung his nostrils like ozone. He fought to quiet the rasping of his lungs and concentrated on veiling himself from the young people's eyes. Not that he had much to worry about, since they were too caught up in their fight to spare a glance in his direction. The boy's Corvette roared out of the lot and weaved down the narrow street. Brandishing her purse, the girl screeched after him, "Go ahead and kill yourself! I'm calling a cab."

Neil's tongue flicked over his dry lips. This encounter was working out better than he'd hoped. Now he could catch her alone and, with luck, away from the movie theater's lights. Sure enough, she threw one glance at the closed entrance of the theater and headed for the phone booth at the gas station next door instead.

Gliding soundlessly, he kept pace with the girl's hurrying steps. If she happened to look his way, her eyes would slip over him unseeing. Even consumed with lust, he easily maintained that much psychic control.

Her hair swung in rhythm with her rapid strides and her disjointed mutters of, "Stupid jerk -- macho airhead --" In the empty parking lot of the deserted gas station, Neil watched her lean into the phone booth and fumble through the directory with hands that shook from anger. She dropped a coin into the slot, listened to the receiver, frowned, and jiggled the coin return. After trying once more, she spat a curse and slammed the phone back into its cradle.

*Out of order! Great!*

She checked her watch and started walking back toward the theater. He decided to make his move now.

In a fluid blur he crossed the street to block her path. At the same instant he dropped the illusion that kept her from seeing him.

With a gasp, she froze. Her surge of panic went straight to Neil's head like a triple shot of hundred-proof rum. His hands clamped onto her arms. Her throat closed on the scream she ached to expel.

Already high on her impotent terror, Neil forced himself to quell it, for it didn't want to deal with panic just yet. Gazing into her eyes, he soothed her with wordless murmurs. Gradually her fear melted away, until she stared at him in mindless docility.

"You need a ride," he said softly. "Come along, I'll take you home."

She nodded. Entwining his arm with hers, he guided her around the corner to his car. A quick scan of the area assured him that the street lined with shabby small businesses was safely deserted at this time of night. He opened the back door of his drab compact wagon, neither new enough nor old enough to attract notice, and shoved Lisa in. She landed on a threadbare Army blanket he'd picked up at a thrift shop for just this purpose. She stared at him with wide, empty eyes like Disney's cartoon Snow White lost in the woods.

*Too easy! Damn it, they're all too easy!*

But for now he had to accept her submission as an advantage. "I'm taking you home," he said in the same gentle murmur as before. "You sit back here and stay perfectly quiet. Understand?"

Again she nodded.

Neil drove to an elementary school in an lower-class neighborhood. Here, if he decided to indulge in the pleasure of letting her scream, nobody would come to her rescue. Pulling up beside the playground, well outside the circle of the nearest street lamp, he walked around to open the back door. He coaxed his victim, loose-jointed and half-asleep, out of the back seat.

At that moment he heard the growl of a defective muffler and glimpsed the headlights of a car turning the corner in his direction. Instantly he pulled the girl into his arms and crushed her to him. When the car's lights swept over them, Neil was kissing her with grinding force. His teeth cut her lip, and he tasted blood. Electricity rippled from his mouth down to his groin, sparking along every nerve.

The fire in his gut wouldn't let him wait any longer. As soon as the car vanished, he held the girl away from him, his hands squeezing her upper arms, and dropped the mental vise that had paralyzed her will. Her eyes snapped awake, bottomless wells of terror to drink from.

"You want to run away," he said in a mockingly soft voice. "All right. You can't scream – you can't make a sound – but you can run." He relaxed his grip.

When she tried to dart past him, he blocked her. "No," he said. "The other way."

She wheeled around and ran through a gap in the chain-link fence into the playground. On the blacktop her mid-height heels clomped awkwardly. In her panic she didn't pause to kick them off. Neil gave her a head start, watching her lurch under the metal frame from which two broken swings dangled. She threw a wild look over her shoulder. Blundering into one of the poles, she tumbled on the ground. Still he didn't follow. She scrambled to her feet and hurried on, limping now.

Neil lunged after her. The wind of his own headlong charge lashed him in the face. He halted a few yards from Lisa. Sobbing deep in her throat, she fell face-first on the blacktop. She barely managed to catch herself, scraping her palms on the rough surface.

Neil pounced. His full weight landed on the girl. For a few seconds he savored the way she writhed, helpless, beneath him. He smelled fear-sweat and fresh blood. Easing the pressure just enough to allow maneuvering room, he flipped her onto her back.

Her terror poured over him in searing waves, like an eruption of lava. Delirious, he feasted on it, his body convulsing in ecstasy.

His teeth ripped into the soft flesh of her neck.

Not that he couldn't be subtle, when the occasion demanded. But subtlety bored him. He found this way far more satisfying.

Afterward, he wrapped the girl's torn body in the blanket and carried it back to the car. It amused him to taunt fate by discarding his leftovers in conspicuous places. Tonight he'd thought of a deliciously outrageous location.

## Chapter 1

THE SMELL OF blood congealed around Roger like a coppery fog.

He stared down at the blonde girl slumped on the brick pavement, her head lolling to one side. He watched the glow of her body heat seep away into the night air, along with the blood from the gash in her neck. Crouching over her, he felt the glare of her sightless eyes boring into his chest. Did he know her? Surely not – so why did the spectacle of her death paralyze him?

*Why are you accusing me? I'm not your killer!*

Then why were his hands sticky with clotting blood? Why did the taste of it linger in his mouth?

Roger cast a furtive glance around the courtyard. Behind him loomed the equestrian statue of Paul Revere, adding its stern judgment to the victim's silent reproach.

A voice in a remote corner of Roger's brain screamed for him to run. Instead he leaned closer, until his lips touched the wound.

The wail of a siren lanced through his head. Leaping up, he whirled to face a dozen pulsing lights that spurted crimson beams. The siren shrieked louder, until the pain of it forced him to his knees.

It woke him.

Slowly Roger sat up on the damask-covered couch where he'd fallen asleep. The wan light that trickled between the drapes signalled the shift from day to evening. As he stretched out a hand to steady himself, he brushed the folded newspaper he'd been reading.

*No wonder her face looked familiar – here it is.*

He picked up the second section of the paper and gazed at the high school graduation portrait of the blonde girl in his dream. No problem interpreting this dream; no need to search for some obscure symbolism or deeply buried conflict.

*Buried, hell, it's right on the surface.* Like a lump of rock jutting up through thin soil.

He'd read the article with morbid curiosity, rationalizing that the unidentified psychopath made an interesting case study. Fourth in a series of similar killings, this one featured the usual hints of unspecified "mutilation" and "unexplained volume of blood loss," rumors that the paper reported with the disclaimer that police spokesmen refused to comment on the details. This last murder differed from the others only in its brazenness, with the victim's corpse found outside the tall wrought-iron gates of the Old North Church.

Catching himself crumpling a corner of the newspaper in one hand, Roger loosed his grip and stood up to pace the dim living room. Why should he identify, even in nightmares, with a homicidal maniac like hundreds of others in casebooks and sensational tabloids?

*Damn it, I'm not like that! I'm not.*

He started for the bedroom, hoping to catch another hour of sleep before nightfall made that impossible.

The phone rang.

*Blast – should have turned on the answering machine.*

The caller turned out to be Detective Lieutenant Kevin O'Toole, an acquaintance of Roger's in the Boston Police Department's homicide division. He got right to the point. "You read today's paper yet, Doc?"

"Yes. You're talking about last night's murder, aren't you?" On several occasions Roger had acted as a psychiatric consultant to the police, as well as providing expert witness services to the District Attorney in alleged insanity cases. So it wasn't hard to guess what the lieutenant wanted.

"Yeah." Roger visualized O'Toole running his fingers through his thinning shock of sandy hair, as he often did when perplexed. "So what do you think of this vampire killer, as they're calling him now? Friggin' newspapers!"

*Think of him? I try not to.* "It's a complex topic to handle over the telephone. Have you made an arrest?"

"No such luck. But there's something you could do for us. We could use a psychological profile – you know, what kind of creep we should be looking for. How about it?"

Roger sank into the nearest chair, conscious of the way his heartbeat had accelerated since the beginning of the conversation. *Damn, this is the last thing I want to get involved with!* But if his unique perspective could lead to the criminal's capture, he felt obligated to accept the assignment. "Yes, I'd be glad to work up something, if you could send over a precis of the outstanding features of the various cases, along with the medical examiner's reports. I'll check some references and put together a written evaluation as soon as I can." Not that he would need to do much research, for he'd gathered material on blood fetishism for years, in a vain attempt to understand his own problem.

"Say, would it do you any good to see the latest body? I could get you a pass for the morgue, no sweat."

"No!" Roger forced himself to continue in a level tone, "The post mortem findings will tell me all I need to know about their – condition."

"Thanks. Anything to get a handle on this guy – and I'm betting he *won't* be turnin' himself into a bat," said O'Toole in the rich Irish accent he sometimes affected to throw suspects off guard. In fact, as Roger knew, the detective stood four generations removed from his immigrant ancestors.

"You have some evidence that it's a man?" Roger said.

"Not really, except that he – it – has to be one strong bastard, judging from broken bones on a couple of the girls. Anyway, I can't imagine a woman –" His voice echoed Roger's own revulsion at the murders.

"There was Countess Elisabeth Bathory, in late medieval Hungary."

"Countess, huh? With a castle and the whole nine yards?"

"Yes. In fact, she was imprisoned for life in a chamber of her own castle, after she was convicted of slaughtering hundreds of young women to bathe in their blood."

O'Toole gave a grunt of disgust. "What the hell did she do that for?"

"Supposedly she believed it would keep her young."

"Some beauty treatment! But isn't it rare for a woman to do crazy shit like that?"

"You're right," said Roger, "this is apt to be a masculine type of paraphilia." Shifting the discussion to a more general level distanced the subject enough to let him ask about a point left unmentioned in the newspapers. "Have any of the victims been raped?"

"No, it's like the crimes aren't sexually motivated."

"But there is no demonstrable connection among the victims, is there?" Roger asked.

"Not that we can find." Roger heard the weary perplexity in the detective's voice. "Looks to me like they were just unlucky enough to be in the wrong place."

"Opportunistic crimes." Roger nodded to himself. "Then it's probably sexual, simply not genital sexuality."

"You mean he gets off on the blood itself?"

"Probably." The immediacy of the crude phrase undermined Roger's precarious calm. He understood that aspect of the crimes all too well. "The fact that you haven't found semen on – or inside – the bodies doesn't necessarily mean the perpetrator doesn't ejaculate."

"He might jerk off later, you mean," the detective said. Roger's keen ears picked up a scratching sound – O'Toole's ballpoint pen taking notes.

"Or he might suffer from ejaculatory incompetence and not be capable of, or even desire, that kind of release." The conversation was hitting too close to home again. "Listen, I can't possibly diagnose the case in a vacuum, and I'm sure you're too busy for this. Send the documents to my office, and I'll get on it right away."

"Okay, will do. Thanks, Doc."

After hanging up, Roger dismissed the idea of lying down again. That conversation destroyed any hope of sleep – at least, sleep without nightmares.

At forty years of age, Roger Sean Gallagher Darvell, M. D., stood at the apex of his professional prime, and his patients were driving him crazy. This one, for instance, a slim brunette of only seventeen, with unblemished skin and naturally curly hair, dressed in a halter top and a snakeskin-tight pair of designer jeans. Through the partly open venetian blinds, the sun cast a barred pattern on her face, eyes glazed in hypnotic trance. The rest of the office lay in shadow, curtained by heavy forest green drapes that matched the deep-piled carpet. Seated on the leather-upholstered chair next to the couch where the patient reclined, Roger bent over her.

It wasn't her neurosis that disturbed him; it was the temptation she presented. His life would be much simpler if his secret obsession fitted into some currently fashionable pigeon-hole. Numerous treatment programs existed for alcoholics and drug abusers. Even a weakness for conventional sexual harassment of female patients might conceivably be cured. Not this "weakness," though.

So he had to fight the urge awakened by his last patient of the afternoon. Showing up for her weekly appointment, the young woman had burst in babbling about an argument with one of her teachers. After hearing her out for almost half an hour, Roger had eased her into trance. He often used that method to calm agitated patients, much as it strained his self-control. The girl's vulnerability enticed him.

*It's been so long, and this would be so easy!*

As he stroked her forehead, deepening the trance, her skin seemed to burn his cool fingers. Her breathing and the throb of her pulse roared in his ears like waves on rock. The glow of her aura made the rest of the room fade into a gray fog. He leaned closer, his fingertips drifting to the warm hollow of her throat.

He shuddered in a spasm of disgust at his own behavior. *No! I swore I would not do this again – not here!*

Less than a month before, he had succumbed to this temptation with another patient, and his office partner, Matthew Lloyd, had blundered in and practically caught him *in flagrante*. He mustn't repeat that risk. As it was, even Lloyd's shallow intuition had picked up the stress Roger couldn't completely hide.

Pulling back from the girl on the couch, he drew several deep breaths to steady his heartbeat and subdue the tumult of his desire.

He closed his eyes and fought to silence the imaginary whis-pers in his head. He visualized the speakers as a pair of imps, demon and angel, like the figures perched on the shoulders of a cartoon character.

The tempter with the horns and pitchfork murmured, *You're not doing her any harm. A few cc's, she'll never miss it.*

*The amount is irrelevant,* the haloed angel said. *This is perverted, abominable.*

*It's no more than you owe yourself for the hours you devote to these people. A supplement to your fee, that's all it is. Like an old country doctor taking his pay in farm produce instead of cash.*

The angel's wings quivered in outrage. *It's no different from sexually molesting her while she's under hypnosis.*

*It is different – it's different because you need this. You're half out of your mind with needing it, aren't you? She'll never know what you took, and you'll repay her for it with pleasure. Even if you can't let her remember.*

*That's disgusting!*

*By whose standards? Even old Doc Lloyd comments on how fast your patients improve,* the demon insisted in its taunting voice.

*The ends never justify the means,* the angel retorted. *And have you forgotten how you almost got caught last time?*

*You won't get caught, not if you're careful.*

The angelic figure played its trump card. *Never mind that, what about the Hippocratic Oath?*

Roger opened his eyes, banishing the actors in his miniature psychodrama. As usual, the internal debate temporarily quenched his ardor. Now that he'd regained control, he once more leaned over the patient, his fingertips lightly touching her temples. He infused her with suggestions of serenity and self-confidence, reinforcing the trigger word he'd taught her to use for therapeutic self-hypnosis. He then woke her to full consciousness and sent her away.

*Friday afternoon, thank God!* Left alone, Roger packed the day's notes into his briefcase, locked his office, and walked out through the waiting room. He found the receptionist already gone and Dr. Lloyd also on his way out.

"It's five o'clock on Friday," said the older therapist, his florid, mustached face showing the vague concern that had Roger censoring his every word and gesture in Lloyd's presence. "Why are you still here?"

"I could ask you the same," said Roger, feigning a light response to the joke Lloyd's remark pretended to be.

"Touche," said Lloyd, pausing at the outer door. "But I'm not the one taking work home every night, weekends included."

"I find it easier to concentrate away from the distractions of the office." He couldn't mention his main reason for taking work home, to fill the sleepless hours between nightfall and dawn. A respectable resume of journal articles had grown out of his unconventional sleep rhythms.

"Every weekend, though? Good Lord, man, do you have a social life at all?"

"As it happens, I'm going to a party tonight." No need to mention that it was strictly a "duty" engagement – and why couldn't Lloyd mind his own business, anyway? The man's persistent solicitude made Roger feel swathed in an itchy blanket.

*I'm not being fair to him. He thinks he's showing friendly interest.* But that awareness didn't reduce the irritation.

"Good, you should try that more often. Look, if you need a break, you know I can cover for you in case of emergency. Why not take a few days off?" He stepped closer and laid a hand on Roger's shoulder.

Roger stiffened. Uninvited touch always felt like an attack to him. Striving not to show his annoyance, he said, "I'll get that `break' when I make the transfer I'm planning." And it couldn't happen soon enough, a fresh start with a colleague who had no excuse for probing into his personal life.

Lloyd's smile faded. "Yeah. Too late to talk you into stay-ing, I guess. You've got things practically settled with that lady psychiatrist in Maryland, haven't you?" He let out a long sigh. "Her gain, my loss.

You're flying down to meet her – when?
Oh, yeah, Monday, how could I forget?"

Roger was sure Lloyd hadn't forgotten and was only making the remark for effect. The man was creeping toward retirement but far from senile. "Yes – if we get along as well in person as we have through the mail, we'll sign the contract, and I'll start preparing for the move." He eased away from Lloyd's touch and shifted his grip on his briefcase, his other hand poised on the doorknob.

"Hate to see you leave."

"You know I've spent my entire life in Boston. I feel that staying here is no longer conducive to personal growth." That sort of reasoning always appealed to his partner. He couldn't admit the other motive, his hope that in a new environment he might find the strength to curtail or even overcome his compulsion. "Not that I don't appreciate all you've done for me over the years." That was true enough; he owed the older man gratitude for accepting him as an associate straight out of his residency and giving him a solid start in private practice.

"Well, maybe you do need a change. We all tend to get a little stale after too long in one place."

Roger couldn't take any more of Lloyd's informal diagnosis today. *Next, I'll have to listen to another lecture on "burnout."* Furthermore, the other man's body heat and pulse stirred the craving Roger thought he had managed to suppress. He said a curt goodbye and strode briskly to the elevator, gratefully shaking off his colleague before they reached the parking garage.

When he eased his black Citroen down the ramp and into the street, the late afternoon sun hurt his eyes even through dark glasses. Fortunately his condo, in a high-rise just off the Southeast Expressway, was only a couple of miles from the office. While his senses and emotions whirled in confusion, a detached segment of his brain maneuvered along the taxi-clogged downtown streets, darting through holes in traffic where a less skilled driver wouldn't dare risk the large, expensive car. His reflexes, operating on automatic, avoided several potential collisions without conscious awareness, while his mind dwelt on his unsatisfied need. Nausea roiled in his stomach. To make matters worse, he'd promised to attend that Harvard fund-raising concert tonight, followed by a party in Cambridge. He saw no way to get out of the commitment, since the hostess was a relative of his late mother.

Once inside his air-conditioned apartment, with curtains closed and chain and deadbolt secured, Roger at last felt free to relax. Maybe he could fit in a decent nap before the evening's ordeal. He expected to enjoy the concert; the thought of the party, though, plunged him into depression. He would much rather spend the night reading a new Martha Grimes mystery or even working on case files. After removing coat and tie, he poured himself a tall glass of milk. As an afterthought he added a shot of brandy. Not for the first time, he wished it were easier for him to get drunk.

In the dim living room he put a Bach cassette on the stereo and sat in an Ethan Allen wing-backed armchair, sipping the milk. Though a staple of his diet, it was a poor substitute for what he really craved.

Human blood.

He turned hot with shame at the recollection of how he'd almost slipped this afternoon. He was as enslaved to his need as any heroin addict. Otherwise he wouldn't have considered using a patient again. Abstaining for so long -- over three weeks -- must have clouded his judgment. Guilt impelled him to hold off as long as possible between victims.

*That's illogical, you know,* he chastised himself. *If drinking blood is wrong, the wrongness doesn't depend on the frequency.* Even the rigidly traditional pre-Vatican-II Catholic Church in which he'd been reared hadn't endorsed such a mechanical, score-keeping approach to sin.

*But I don't hurt them. I've never done any permanent damage, much less killed.*

The rationalization didn't convince him any better than it ever did. To head off another round of self-flagellation, Roger leafed through the mail he'd deposited on the claw-footed end table on his way in. Two professional journals, an American Express bill, a supermarket ad – and an envelope postmarked Annapolis, Maryland.

Good – a letter from his prospective partner, Dr. Britt Loren. He added businesslike promptness to the list of virtues her correspondence with him had already revealed. Her letter confirmed their meeting in Annapolis the following Monday.

Right now, he had to get some rest to fortify himself for the evening. He downed the rest of the drink and retreated to the bedroom. Maybe the milk would enable him to sleep despite the void inside him that screamed to be filled. *Look on the bright side,* he reminded himself. *I've held out for over three weeks. Maybe next time I can go for an entire month.* Perhaps he could eventually condition himself to do without it altogether.

No violence haunted his dreams this time, just murky, half-formed visions that faded immediately upon waking. Wrenched awake at seven by the beep of the digital alarm clock, he stumbled through a cold shower, then went to the kitchen in search of something to damp down the fire in his gut.

He contemplated tossing a quarter pound of raw ground sirloin into the food processor with a can of beef broth. His stomach protested at the thought; he needed a stronger elixir to help him face crowds of people without losing control. Blood from live animals sometimes worked, an indulgence he had no time for tonight.

From the freezer he extracted a second-rate substitute, a container of cattle blood. Filipino and Vietnamese markets kept him supplied with the stuff, normally used as an ingredient in pudding-like recipes; he simply took care not to buy too much from any store at once. In the microwave he defrosted the package gradually, on a low setting, then warmed it to body heat. To dilute the viscosity and mask the dead taste, he whirled it in the blender with a cup of burgundy.

Pouring the concoction into a mug, he drank it at the living room window. He surveyed the view of the Charles River and the skyline of Cambridge until the setting sun began to strain his eyes. In the kitchen he rinsed out the cup and blender, contemplating the dregs with distaste. Thawed beef blood muted the craving but didn't satisfy. He needed the real thing.

Perhaps Mrs. Bronson's party would offer possibilities. Among all the women present, surely he could find an unattached one who would accept a ride home. *Better than violating the doctor-patient boundary. Even if not much better.*

He brushed his teeth to clean out the stale taste and dressed with his usual efficient speed. Knotting his tie, he examined himself in the bathroom mirror, relieved to note that his agitation didn't show on the outside. His silver-gray eyes gave him back a cool stare that could easily be mistaken for self-assurance.

*The stereotype of an omnicompetent healer,* he jeered at himself. *Too bad it's an illusion.*

## Chapter 2

*FIRST, DO NO harm.* The vow echoed mockingly in Roger's brain. *Hippocrates never had a problem like this.*

But a peaceful summer night in Cambridge, he told himself, was no time to brood on his own depravity. Nor to brood on the burning in the pit of his stomach, when he could slip away to do something about it. Martini in hand, he lurked in a corner of Mrs. Bronson's living room, fighting the queasiness induced by an atmosphere thick with aromas of powder, soap, cologne, smoke, overheated flesh, and assorted food and drink. Worse, though, was the emotional static buzzing in his head. Worst of all was his own ever-present doubt as to whether this "static" was a figment of his own imagination. The clash between the psychic caco-phony and the audible cocktail party chitchat affected him like a TV with the picture tuned to one channel and the sound to another.

He especially disliked the topic dominating the conversation at the nearby buffet table – the recent outbreak of murders in the area. "Drained of blood – do you believe that?" "Nah, sounds like something the papers would make up to sell copies." "You'd think the police would be able to find him, slaughtering people in the middle of downtown Boston." "Hell, the police can't find their –" "Now even the *Globe's* started calling him a vampire." "Why does everybody keep saying `him'? Couldn't it be a woman?" "Women don't commit violent crimes like that. Ask our resident expert on abnormal psychology, if you don't believe me." "Yeah, Roger, what do you think of –"

The moment he picked up a hint that he might be asked for an opinion, Roger drifted in the other direction. He would almost rather deal with people who insisted on telling him their dreams. He flinched away from a white-coated waiter who thrust a plate of garlic-scented canapes under his nose. Checking his watch, he decided he'd done his duty as a loyal Harvard alumnus for this occasion. He drained his glass, set it down, and began an unobtrusive glide through the eddies of conversation toward the front hall and the stairs.

A respected member of the medical profession shouldn't be stalking his hosts' twenty-year-old daughter, but Meg, in bed convalescing from a cold, made too good an opportunity to pass up. As soon as he'd learned of the girl's indisposition, he had decided to visit her instead of launching a tedious and risky seduction of one of the female guests.

He was dismayed to see Mrs. Bronson herself, with a young woman in tow, cutting a path in his direction through the clustered guests.

*Oh, Lord, not another matchmaking scheme!*

Since the deaths of Roger's parents, nearly twenty years before, Mrs. Bronson had never ceased trying to "fix" his bachelor status. Despite her diminutive, softly rounded exterior, on this topic she displayed the persistence of a hungry shark on a crowded beach. "Now, Roger, what are you doing hiding over here again?" she said, tugging on the hand of a dark-haired woman who looked as lukewarm toward the introduction as Roger felt. "You should try to enjoy yourself more. You work too hard."

*Dear lady, if you'll let me escape, I fully intend to start enjoying myself.*

"Don't worry about me. No one could possibly have any complaints about your parties." He bent an appraising stare upon Mrs. Bronson's sacrificial maiden. Her aura, he noticed, held a peculiar streak of deep purple.

"Sylvia LaMotte, Roger Darvell," said Mrs. Bronson, relinquishing the girl's hand. "You have something in common. Sylvia's a Radcliffe graduate, class of '78. Sylvia, dear, Roger took his pre-med training and his M.D. at Harvard. His mother was a cousin of mine." Her cheeks grew pink as she completed this speech in a breathy Marilyn Monroe voice that belied her social-dragon personality. "Roger, Sylvia doesn't know anyone here. Be a dear and take her under your wing for a few minutes."

With a nod to his fellow victim, Roger said, "Ordinarily I'd be delighted, but I was about to say goodnight. Headache."

"Oh, I suppose your allergies must be acting up again. You've always had trouble with parties, what with other people's perfume and cigarette smoke, haven't you? I do hope you feel better soon." Mrs. Bronson squeezed his hand in farewell and forged on.

Roger's first thought about Sylvia was that she was too young. She might be a couple of years older than the average woman only a year out of college, but no more. Mrs. Bronson must be scraping the bottom of the matrimonial barrel. Still, he preferred this offering over most of her choices. For one thing, Sylvia was tall, her gray eyes meeting

Roger's almost level.

*Maybe that's why our hostess decided to match us. There aren't many men this woman could look up to.*

"Well, what's your verdict?" Sylvia interrupted his reverie, tossing her long, black hair back from her shoulders. "If you want to part like ships hooting in the fog, I won't tell on you."

Probing the surface of her mind, he encountered an intriguing opacity. He'd never met a woman whose emotions he couldn't read instantly. *Assuming I'm not imagining the whole thing to begin with, aura and all,* he reminded himself for the thousandth time. Clasping her hand, he noticed that her skin felt cool in spite of the stuffy, overcrowded room. "I assure you, if it weren't for my – headache, I wouldn't think of passing you in the fog," he said as he gave her a more leisurely inspection.

She wore an Empire gown of pale lilac that echoed a violet tint in her gray eyes. She was pale, small-breasted, thin, almost emaciated, yet with no symptoms of ill health, except the puzzling hue of her aura. Roger fixed his eyes on hers, willing her response to the mesmeric talent he'd exercised for years before studying hypnosis during his psychiatric training. She merely stared back with bold curiosity.

"I didn't know the Bronsons had any cousins named Dar-vell," she said. "Doesn't sound like a Boston Brahmin name."

Nor was it. He was adopted, a circumstance the family didn't hold against him. He deflected the probe with a question of his own. "And you, Miss LaMotte? Are you a `Brahmin'?" Her very use of the word made that seem unlikely, but why else would she have been invited?

"No way," she laughed, a sound like icy water over rock. "Call me Sylvia. I think we have something more in common than dear old Harvard Yard. I don't think you're any happier to be here than I am." Her pronunciation of the R's in "Harvard" confirmed her non-local origin. She gave him an expectant, faint-ly puzzled stare, as if he'd failed to return a secret password. Roger caught the fragrance of her hair, unadulterated by any perfume. Her scent, like her aura, tingled with an unfamiliar sharpness, an almost metallic quality.

*Losing my grip – must need it even worse than I thought.*

He trained his eyes upon her again, casually grazing her bare shoulder with his fingertips. She responded to his silent overture only with another quizzical stare. The rhythm of her breathing and heartbeat didn't alter. "I'm here because my professional status obligates me. What about you?"

Sylvia shrugged. "My – guardian – knows Mrs. Bronson. He asked her to invite me to a few social affairs, and he *strongly* urged me to accept. I'm not sure why he insisted, but it beats sitting at home in the evenings. Though not by much."

"You're not from this area yourself, then?" Beneath the conventional gambit, he continued to dig at the smooth surface of her mind, intrigued by her lack of response.

*What would it take to crack her shell? Or would it be more like peeling an onion?*

"I grew up in Nevada," she said. "Wonder why Mrs. Bronson shoved us together? Maybe we shouldn't disappoint her." She punctuated the sentence with a sly smile, inviting him to conspire with her against their hostess.

*Enough – why am I pretending I have some Svengali power over women? She's living proof that I don't. Good God, Darvell, at least try to maintain a nodding acquaintance with reality!* He retracted what he thought of as psychic tendrils and responded to Sylvia's flirtatious gambit: "Ah, but are you Catholic? If not, it would never work."

For the first time she looked disconcerted. "I don't go to church." Her eyes slid away from his.

Roger smoothed the awkward moment with the remark, "Unfortunately, we're not likely to meet again anyway. I expect to be moving out of state within a month or so." He broke off the conversation and resumed his original course. As he shouldered his way to the front hall, he felt Sylvia's eyes upon him.

His pulse quickened at the thought of Meg unknowingly waiting for him. Her cold virus wasn't serious enough to incon-venience Roger. He never succumbed to minor infectious diseases. Moreover, her condition would disguise any aftereffects she might suffer from the "donation."

But she wouldn't suffer; he would see to that. He would exercise caution, rein his appetite – and reward her with deep, peaceful sleep afterward. Better than any over-the-counter drug.

*Oh, why don't you stop rationalizing? What you're doing is bad enough, without lying to yourself in the bargain!*

He reached the deserted upstairs hall unobserved. Striding silently along the carpeted floor to the dark, unoccupied guest bath, he ducked inside and stood, listening. His hyperacute hearing confirmed that he was alone on this floor, except for the sleeping girl. Emerging into the corridor again, he followed the rise and fall of her breath to her closed bedroom door. After one last look around, he opened the door, stepped through it, and soundlessly closed it behind him.

He leaned back against the wood panel, struggling to slow his own respiration. The girl in the bed didn't stir. The satin sheet, tangled around her legs, left her upper body bare except for a buttercup-yellow cotton gown, damp with sweat. Her platinum hair spilled over the pillow. Except for an automatic precautionary glance at the window, he didn't bother noticing any other details. Being able to see the unconscious object of his quest was enough.

Where did he get his keen night vision? For that matter, where did the rest of his anomalous abilities come from? For all he knew, they might be delusions. He might be as disconnected from reality as the narrator of Poe's "Tell-Tale Heart," who imagined he could hear his victim's pulse reverberating through-out the house.

As Roger could hear Meg's pulse now.

Reality or delusion, he was past caring. The sound set his own heart racing, and his throat went dry. Swallowing the excess saliva that flooded his mouth did nothing to alleviate the distress. He moved to the bedside and sat down.

He laid a hand on Meg's warm forehead. Immediately she sank from normal sleep into a trance from which she wouldn't wake until he released her. He planned to rouse her just enough to evoke a dreamlike erotic response, the emotional nourishment he needed for full satisfaction. Afterward he would lull her back into the dreaming phase, with no memory of his visit.

As he bent over the girl, the door opened.

He sprang to his feet. Sylvia LaMotte darted in and shut the door.

They glared at each other. In his alarm Roger thought he glimpsed a red spark in Sylvia's eyes but dismissed it as an optical illusion. "What are you doing here?" he whispered. His heart raced, making him lightheaded. He fought off the threatened panic. *Got to take the offensive – I can't let her guess what I'm up to.*

"What do you think? I assumed you wouldn't mind sharing."

"What in the name of –"

She said with a puzzled frown, "Maybe I read you wrong, downstairs. What *are* you in here for?"

Passing over Sylvia's incomprehensible babbling, he said in a more normal tone, though still keeping his voice low, "I have a right to be. I'm not only a relative, I'm a doctor. Why shouldn't I check on my cousin?"

"Didn't I hear somebody say you're a psychiatrist? And what would Mrs. Bronson think of Cousin Roger 'checking' on her daughter in the dark?"

Roger's head throbbed with tension, but he fought to keep his voice steady long enough to placate and dispose of the intruder. "I wouldn't want to disturb Meg unnecessarily. But that's none of your business. What's your excuse? Are you a debutante kleptomaniac, perhaps? Or just a garden-variety snoop? Don't try to claim you were looking for the powder room." His throat felt clogged with fear. *She's not buying it; I can't control her.*

Her mind was no longer unreadable; its surface roiled with anger. Yet she suppressed her rage and spoke quietly. "Deal, Roger – let's both go downstairs and forget this happened. I won't tell if you won't. I don't mind keeping your guilty secret."

"I don't make deals in circumstances like this. Shall I call Mrs. Bronson and tell her I caught you rummaging in Meg's jewelry? Which of us do you think she'll believe?" An imperfect solution at best, for anything that drew attention to his presence in this room risked exposing him.

"Damn you, Dr. Darvell –" She scurried across the room to him, her natural grace hampered by her narrow skirt. "I don't know what you want, but I don't see why I should leave you alone with her when it's obvious you're lying."

"You're in no position to speak – you certainly aren't inno-cent." Why was she gazing down at Meg instead of looking at him? Sparing a glance for the girl in the bed, Roger noted that the trance he'd imposed on her still held firm.

Suddenly his attention was diverted by masculine footsteps in the hall. "Now look what you've done," Sylvia whispered.

"What I –!"

A tap sounded at the door. "Meg? You need anything?" Mr. Bronson. Sylvia clutched Roger's sleeve in unthinking appeal. The man's voice continued, "I thought I heard something in there. Not keeping yourself up with the radio, are you, Honey?"

Roger heard a hand close on the doorknob. "Closet," he mouthed. He ducked into the walk-in closet, not caring whether Sylvia followed. She was right beside him, though, and they had the door shut before Meg's father entered the bedroom. They listened to his puzzled muttering as he checked the sleeping girl. After he'd walked down the hall and descended the stairs, Roger said, "It's not safe to stay here now. I'm leaving, and you are coming with me." Frustration displaced his fear. Sylvia's oddities no longer mattered. She was available, and she would damn well compensate him for what she'd interrupted.

"If I don't want to?" she whispered as they crossed to the bedroom door.

"I can still inform on you to the Bronsons. They know me a lot better."

He felt Sylvia's smoldering anger, but she docilely followed him out of the house. She balked only when he led the way down the circular drive to his black Citroen. "I'd rather take my own car."

His hand clamped onto her arm. "You can pick it up tomorrow. I'm not letting you escape until we have this out." He sensed her debating whether to fight him and rejecting the idea. Though she was tall for a woman, he was taller and outweighed her. He shoved her into the passenger seat, then got in on the driver's side and leaned across her to fasten her belt and lock the door. She watched him speculatively as she accepted these indignities. He sensed her anger yielding to curiosity.

He roared out of the driveway in a shower of gravel. Beside him, Sylvia wedged herself against the far door, subdued by his display of temper. After skirting the perimeter of the M.I.T. campus, he headed north out of Cambridge. Thankful for the late-night dearth of traffic, he didn't slack off the accelerator until they came to a scenic turnoff on Route 1A several miles out of town. The car swerved off the road and squealed to a stop.

Sylvia gave Roger a wary look. "Are we getting out?" She scanned the marshland beyond the low wall of unworked stone, as if evaluating its suitability as a refuge. Roger gripped her shoulders and jerked her around to face him. "What is this, rape?"

"Not exactly." His inflamed thirst left him with no patience for hypnotic seduction. He'd rely on physical force and wipe her memory later. He came down upon her.

Her resistance astonished him. Rather than overcoming her easily, he had to use all his strength to keep her immobilized. She kicked and squirmed in his grasp, twisting her neck away from his mouth, her own teeth bared as she tried vainly to retaliate. But she had no chance against him. Pinning her legs with one knee, he bit into her throat with a roughness unusual for him.

When her blood began to flow, she relaxed, not cooperative, but resigned. The taste was cool and tart, not the hot richness he expected.

Despite Sylvia's residual excitement, satisfaction eluded him. He felt no outpouring of vitality from her, only an emptiness like his own. Baffled, he finally drew back, still unappeased.

She gazed at him, heavy-lidded, and pressed her palm to the oozing gash on the side of her neck. "What's the matter with you? Don't you know we can't get nourishment from each other?'

His rage dissipated by the struggle, Roger offered her his folded handkerchief, resisting the impulse to apologize for the red flecks staining her gown. "What do you mean, 'we'?"

Sylvia wearily dabbed at her wound. "You mean you don't know? That's impossible." Her eyes probed his.

He sat up straight on his side of the car. "What are you raving about?"

"Come off it! With that strength, and your psychic power – you have it, I felt you trying to manipulate me –and those teeth? You're my kind. I wasn't sure until just now, because you feel somehow human, too, but you are."

He stared through the windshield, his fingers cramping on the wheel. He felt overheated in his suit jacket, stifled by the knot of his tie; he envied Sylvia's lightweight clothes. "Human? What else could I be? What do you mean, your kind?"

Again she projected bewilderment. "Maybe I did read you wrong. You don't feel right – but you don't feel human, either."

*The woman is schizophrenic, and I'm listening to her.* "Are you saying that you're not human?"

She forced a humorless smile. "You don't believe me."

"Do you expect me to?"

*What about the things she mentioned, though? Especially the quasi-telepathy?*

Well, what about it? Some educated and otherwise rational people did believe in auras and paranormal perception. Stipulate that the power was more than delusion, that he did possess an empathic passkey to other people's emotions. If he met a woman who shared not only that power but the same perversion he suffered from, it made sense that they would be drawn to each other. Perhaps the power to read emotions predisposed to an obsession with blood. That didn't mean he had to accept Sylvia's proposed *folie a deux*.

"Can't you decide about having me committed later?" she said. Her shoulders twitched, and he glimpsed the tautness of her nipples through the rippling *crepe de chine* of her dress. She hugged her arms to her chest. "You've got both of us needing it in the worst way."

His own nerves vibrated in sync with the thirst she projected. Regardless of her mental balance or lack thereof, she certainly shared his obsession. "What do you suggest?"

"Drive," she said through clenched teeth.

He pulled onto the highway and floored the accelerator. After a few minutes she said, "Better slow down, or you won't be able to stop in time."

He noticed her eyes darting from window to window in a restless circuit of the visual field. "What are you looking for?"

"Hitchhikers."

"At this hour?"

"You'd be surprised." She didn't pause in her scan of the roadside. Over twenty minutes passed before she pointed to a figure standing on the shoulder. "There. Pick her up."

Roger slowed to a stop next to a teenage girl in a denim jacket, holding a crayoned sign that read "Cape Cod." "She's a bit young, isn't she? And what's the matter with her? Doesn't she know she's begging for assault or murder?" he said to Sylvia.

"Yes, isn't it lucky for us that people are such idiots?" she replied. Opening the door, she leaned out and beckoned to the hitchhiker.

When Sylvia slid to the middle of the seat, the girl hefted an oversized backpack and climbed in. "Gee, thanks, I never thought anybody would stop this late."

Sylvia patted the girl's hand. "Aren't you worried about what could happen to you on the road at night?"

"Well, sooner or later we're all going to die of living, aren't we? Anyway, I'm careful. Like, I knew it was safe to get in this time, because you're here. What could happen with another woman in the car, not much older than me?"

"Right, we women have to stick together," Sylvia said with her ice-water laugh. "But I'm older than I look. See, it's all in the way you use makeup." The passenger automatically turned to look at Sylvia's face. Sylvia's long, sharp-nailed fingers curled around the girl's chin. Within seconds of feeling that touch and meeting Sylvia's eyes, the victim lapsed into trance. Sylvia's free hand unsnapped the jacket, while she murmured, "You don't need this, it's much too hot. You must be tired after standing for so long – just close your eyes and relax – that's it." Her hand wandered over the front of the girl's blouse, while her mouth grazed the parted lips.

After a minute or two Sylvia said in a strangled tone, "She's ready. Pull over."

Not waiting for a legal stopping zone, Roger complied. He stared straight ahead as Sylvia completed the seduction she'd begun. He might as well have watched, since the lapping sounds of Sylvia's tongue and the soft moans from the victim tied his stomach in knots. On top of the bloodlust, his head reeled with the illusion that he'd stepped into a falling elevator that would never hit bottom. *She's actually drinking blood. And she does it exactly the same way I do. What in God's name is she?*

When Sylvia turned to face him, licking her lips with catlike daintiness, the girl was slumped with her head lolling against the leather-covered seat back, her eyes closed. Sylvia climbed over the girl's lap and pushed her toward Roger. Embracing the limp body, he found that it still quivered with semiconscious response at the light touch of his lips. He drank. His flesh quivered with echoes of the victim's arousal.

A few miles further on, they woke their passenger and let her out. Though groggy, she had nothing to show for her unwitting donation except a neat, painless quarter-inch cut that, given Sylvia's mind-clouding influence, she probably wouldn't even notice before it healed.

Watching the girl's shambling gait, Sylvia remarked, "You really were hungry, weren't you?"

Roger switched on the ignition and eased the car onto the highway again. He felt as if a hurricane howled around him, with gusts of hundred-mile-per-hour winds that threatened to knock him flat. It was all he could do to reply in a steady voice. "Hungry? You make it sound like a legitimate biological need."

"It is," Sylvia said with a contented stretch of her slender arms. "We'd better start back to Boston. I don't know about you, but I need to get some rest."

"Don't tell me – you sleep during the day." He took the next turnoff and circled around to return the way they'd come.

"Whenever possible. Don't you? How else are vampires supposed to live?"

*She isn't just play-acting. She believes this nonsense!*

"I do dislike sunlight, and I do find it almost impossible to sleep after dark," he admitted. "But that word – Sylvia, it's sheer tripe. Superstition. I wouldn't insist you're laboring under a delusion, not on such short acquaintance. But you have to admit that vampires do *not* fit into our culture's consensus reality."

"So much the worse for consensus reality. There are plenty of things it doesn't know. Consensus reality used to believe the sun revolved around the earth." She bared her teeth in a feral grin.

"You don't look like a walking corpse, and I certainly am not."

"I didn't say either of us was. But can you think of a better word for a night-prowling creature that lives on blood?"

THE WOMAN WAS psychotic, no doubt about it, Roger told himself when he awoke the following afternoon. If she'd been referred to him for treatment, he would have diagnosed her with an encapsulated delusional disorder, mildly paranoid. He imagined labeling her with a code from the *DSM III,* the therapist's "bible" of diagnoses: Psychotic disorder, NOS II, R/O Borderline Personality Disorder. Peculiar, how a person who embraced such an elaborate and systematic delusion could function so well in daily life.

To his own dismay, on some level he longed to believe her. Perhaps that was why he had no intention of losing touch. Dropping her at her apartment, a high-rise in downtown Boston not far from his own, he'd made an appointment to meet her there tonight.

Since this was Saturday, Roger detoured to his church, a Gothic structure in the North End, on the way to Sylvia's place. He saw no reason to break his lifelong habit of frequent con-fession, no matter what this new generation of priests advocated.

Now, kneeling in the third pew, with the stained glass windows muting the glare of the setting sun, he was bludgeoned anew by the fact of his cowardice. His bloodlust was either a sin to be repented and abandoned or a disease to be cured. Seeing it mirrored in Sylvia brought that truth home to him. Yet he knew he would never turn himself in. As usual, he mentally rehearsed the confession he planned to make, translating his predation into coded terms intelligible only to himself and the Almighty: "I sexually abused one of my patients." "I picked up a young girl on the highway and used her to satisfy my lust." "I tried to molest a friend's daughter." Whether the absolution he received for these incomplete admissions was theologically valid, he couldn't be sure.

Attempting to soothe himself with the familiar smells of varnished wood, dusty carpet, and leatherbound missals, he waited until the other penitents had left before taking his turn in the old-style confessional. This relic was one reason he'd chosen this parish. As often as he deceived people to feed his bloodlust, he drew the line at looking a priest straight in the eye and lying by omission under the seal of a sacrament. A barrier between them made the lie marginally easier. He knelt, crossed himself, and began in a rapid, uninflected voice, "Bless me, Father, for I have sinned. My last confession was two weeks ago...."

## Chapter 3

TWILIGHT WAS closing in when Roger arrived at Sylvia's apartment. She met him in the lobby and introduced him to the doorman, whom she favored with a sultry smile before walking Roger around to the parking garage where he'd left the Citroen. "I want to drive this time," she said. "Let's swing through Cambridge for my car, and I'll drive you back to pick up yours before we go home."

"What are your plans for the night?" he asked as he held the car door for her.

"Well, we want to talk, and we could cruise at the same time. You know, hunt." She put on a pair of sunglasses whose large frames accentuated the informal look of her white, backless sundress.

"So soon?" he said.

"Why not? How often do you, usually?"

His chest tightened as he considered the question. Wrestling the car through traffic across the Charles River, he answered, "Once every couple of weeks."

"Good grief, how can you stand it?"

"That isn't the kind of thing one would want to do any more often than necessary. If it's necessary at all."

"You still think I'm nuts, don't you?" She seemed unperturbed by that judgment.

"Frankly, yes. And I should either persuade you to go into therapy or refuse to see you again." By "hunting" with her, he was acting as an enabler, colluding in a bizarre codependence.

"You won't, though, will you?"

"No, God help me," he said. "I want to know more about you – no matter how much it sounds like complete drivel."

"You don't have much time to dissect my brain, if you're moving soon. Or was that just an excuse you invented to get rid of me?"

"No, it's true. I'm planning to relocate to Maryland within a few weeks." He wondered what his prospective partner would think of Sylvia. Dr. Loren had mentioned in her letters that she took an interest in psi phenomena and had once participated in a series of ESP trials. Still, Rhine cards were a far cry from delusions of vampirism.

They'd almost reached the Bronsons' neighborhood before he nerved himself to question Sylvia further. "You used the expression 'my kind.' Please explain."

"I've been thinking it over, since last night, and I've figured out what you are," she said. "You're a changeling, brought up by ephemerals, ignorant of your real identity. Roger, it's downright romantic!"

Sourly amused by her enthusiasm for her hypothesis, he said, "It doesn't seem romantic to me, living it. Brought up by what?"

"Ephemerals. You know, short-lifers."

"What does that make you? Immortal?"

"Close enough. We can't die; we have to be killed."

"Oh, and I suppose you claim to be hundreds of years old."

She laughed. "Don't be silly, I'm twenty-nine, just a kid." Signalling for him to pull over, she said, "There's my car."

Sylvia's car, a white Mustang, sat unmolested where she'd left it, parked under a tree about a block from the site of last night's party. *So that's the theory she uses to justify her behavior – she belongs to a higher species,* Roger thought. *Ingenious, if nothing else.* "Do you really expect me to believe there is a subculture of – of vampires – lurking in the shadowed corners of human society?"

"Believe what you like." She seemed more entertained than annoyed by his skepticism. Since darkness was falling, Roger and Sylvia both removed their sunglasses as they switched to the other car. She gave it a pat on the fender before slipping into the driver's seat and rolling down her window. "As a matter of fact, there's another one in Boston right now. You wouldn't want to meet him, though. I've stayed away from him since I found out how rough he plays."

"Rough?"

She said with a humorless laugh, "Would you believe he's that serial killer the papers are full of? Leaving bodies around is strictly against the rules."

Her flippant tone chilled Roger. "You know who he is, and you haven't informed the police?" *That settles one thing – I have to keep seeing her. If there's the slightest chance she really does know the killer, it's my duty to get that information for O'Toole.*

She paused with her hand on the ignition key. "Are you out of your mind?" He felt her outrage like a slap in the face. "Never mind, you don't understand," she said, revving the engine. "You were brought up human."

Roger didn't waste time insisting again that he *was* human. "If you think I'm one of your race, you should tell me about them."

"It's not my place to give out information that might betray the group. I can answer general questions and tell you about myself, but not about anybody else." Sylvia gave him a sidelong smile as the Mustang inched through the Cambridge streets toward the freeway. "I've already said too much – for some reason you rattle me, Doctor. Maybe because I keep thinking you want to get me on your couch."

For a second he suspected an intentional *double entendre*, but her surface emotions carried no indication of that. Yes, he did itch to psychoanalyze her, just as he wanted to worm information about the supposed vampire race from her.

"As for believing you are or aren't a vampire –" She held up a hand to cut off his automatic protest. "Yeah, I know, you think the word is unscientific nonsense. But, heck, you even look like one of us. I noticed that before I picked up on the color of your aura."

"How so?" He told himself he was humoring her to be polite. After all, he couldn't very well psychoanalyze a person who rejected the whole idea of therapy.

"Your height, for one thing. You're – how tall? Definitely over six feet."

"Six four," he said.

"And lean – not an ounce of extra fat. Gray eyes, almost silver; aquiline profile; black hair with no sign of middle-aged baldness and only a dash of gray at the temples."

Despite the roar of confusion in his brain, the tenuous nature of her "evidence" amused him. "Those traits could describe any of a hundred thousand men."

"We all have hair of either black or some shade of red." She stretched her right arm across the back of the seat to brush her fingers over his hair. "I'll bet that distinguished-looking sprinkle of silver makes you a real lady-killer."

Roger shifted away from her hand, his lips tightening in distaste at the pun.

She gave him a sly grin, clearly amused by his reaction. "Not that you need it. Haven't you noticed how women gravitate toward you when you're hungry?"

He refused to admit aloud that he'd sometimes imagined they did. "Sounds like blatant wish-fulfillment to me."

"When you tried to feed on me, I felt your strength and the

coolness of your skin. Along with the tint of your aura, that's plenty of proof for me that you're not human."

He clutched the armrest, battling the sensation that he was sinking ever deeper into the quicksand of her delusional construct. "Sheer fantasy."

"Oh, yeah? Then how do you explain your hypnotic powers, your sixth sense for emotions, the way you can hear the slightest noises, even people's heartbeats –"

"If that last is anything more than my imagination," he said, "some neurological abnormalities involve hyperacute sensory perception. I have an eidetic memory; the two conditions may go together, for all I know."

"Aha!" She thumped the dashboard as if scoring a point. "Photographic memory is another trait all our people have."

"You're reaching, Sylvia." How conveniently she mani-pulated every piece of data to fit into her world-view. "For all I know, most of what I think I perceive could be imaginary."

"Even seeing auras? You have confirmation from me on that."

He flashed her a grim smile. If he could dissociate the topic from his own lifelong self-doubt, he could almost enjoy debating with her. "That's assuming I accept your testimony as reliable."

"Oh, yeah, I keep forgetting. According to you, my elevator doesn't go up to the penthouse." Once on the open highway, she weaved in and out of traffic until suburban congestion fell behind, leaving her a clear road. "Roger, I have never met such a stubborn, rock-skulled – I give up! If you don't think you're a vampire, what do you call yourself?"

"A blood fetishist, of course, though I've never found a case in the literature exactly like mine." Speaking that diagnosis aloud to another person for the first time in his life gave him an unexpected sense of relief.

"And you won't trust me. Oh, well, speaking of blood –" With a feline smile she gunned the engine to top speed, the wind whistling through her hair.

"How many points have you got on your license?" Roger said.

"Zero," she shouted back over the wind.

"Don't you get stopped?"

"All the time. I want to." A few minutes later, a siren wailed in the rear. Sylvia flashed Roger a grin as she braked. "Here comes dinner."

"That strikes me as an unjustified risk."

"Roger, you aren't much fun, but I like you anyway." She opened her door and stood up, watching the highway patrolman bring his car to a stop behind the Mustang. Sylvia walked over to the patrol car, her skirt fluttering around her long, slim legs. When the officer got out, she leaned toward him, resting one hand on his forearm. Though they stood outside the headlights' glow, where no passing driver could see more than the dark outline of their bodies, Roger's keen night vision allowed him a clear view. The wind blew Sylvia's words away, but the tilt of her head made the pleading character of her speech obvious. A moment later her arms were around the policeman's neck, her lips nibbling at his ear.

She left the officer sitting, dazed, in the front seat of his vehicle and returned to her own car. "Want him?" she asked Roger.

"Certainly not. I don't have any homoerotic tendencies."

Sylvia got in and restarted the motor. "Those distinctions don't mean much to us. Don't you ever take men?"

"Not if given a choice," he said. In the absence of sexual polarity, male victims could be no more than a tepid substitute for what Roger considered the real thing.

"I can't blame you much," Sylvia said, accelerating to just above the speed limit. "Human males can be disappointing. They don't last; there's a physical limit to how long they can maintain that excitement we feed on. Women have a lot more stamina. I guess that's why we female vampires indulge in more – homoeroticism – than our male cousins do."

He had to grant Sylvia more honesty than he possessed, for she wasn't afraid to apply the word "vampire" to herself. He reluctantly admired the coherence of her delusional system, too; she so conveniently avoided all guilt, by relegating her victims to a biologically inferior status.

He almost wished he could do the same, for then his sleep wouldn't be haunted by blood-drenched dreams.

AFTER AN UNSETTLING weekend with Sylvia, Roger felt positive relief in tackling the chore that faced him on Monday – flying to Maryland to check out the practice he expected to buy into. On a pragmatic level, he was glad he'd thoroughly appeased his blood-need Sunday night. For this interview he had to be clear-headed.

Dr. Loren had arranged matters at her end with admirable efficiency. She'd provided Roger with a reservation at the downtown

Annapolis Hilton and a xerox copy of a local map, with the locations of the hotel and her office circled in red ink. This forethought, along with her precise, legible handwriting, further predisposed him in her favor.

Meeting her, at ten thirty the morning of his arrival, produced a few surprises. He wasn't surprised to find her office, in a three-story building two blocks from the Navy football stadium, as meticulously neat as her correspondence. True, the enlarged "Peanuts" cartoons that shared wall space with her diplomas from the University of Maryland and Johns Hopkins weren't conventional decor, but doubtless she used them to put patients at ease. He had expected her tailored three-piece suit and the tightly disciplined coil of her hair. He'd also expected the briskly businesslike handshake with which she greeted him.

He hadn't anticipated her flaming titian hair, her flawlessly creamy redhead's skin, or the sharp green eyes that assessed him as if she could read him as easily as he read her. Nor had he anticipated his own reaction when their hands touched – a desire to continue touching, to enjoy the flutter of her pulse against his fingertips, as if he couldn't hear her heartbeat from across the room anyway. The tiny hairs in the center of his palm tingled at the contact.

*What's wrong with me? Why am I thinking about a professional colleague that way when I'm not even in need?* The roseate shimmer of her aura fascinated him; he had to concentrate hard to keep his mind on what she was saying.

Dr. Loren wasted little time on ritual pleasantries. As soon as they'd introduced themselves and commented on the humidity outside, she said, "Well, Dr. Darvell, what can you tell me about your reasons for relocating?"

Thoroughly prepared for this question, Roger delivered his rehearsed account of a "midlife crisis" with all the persuasiveness at his command, short of exercising his hypnotic skill. Their association would have to spring from free choice on both sides. Using any coercion on Dr. Loren would backfire in the long run. After all, he couldn't keep her under control every hour of the working day, nor would he want a partner on those terms.

As quickly as possible, he transferred the burden of explanation to her by inquiring about the practice's financial status. She replied at length, elaborating on what she had already told him in her letters and making no attempt to soft-pedal her situation. Because her former partner had unexpectedly been forced into early retirement by a cardiac condition, she needed a new associate as soon as possible. She couldn't afford to carry the practice alone.

By imperceptible degrees the conversation shifted from business matters to the theory and technique of psychoanalysis. As a Jungian, Dr. Loren stood close enough to Roger's basically Freudian orientation that they could put up with each other, but not close enough to preclude disagreement. Over an hour raced by in theoretical argument. At the conclusion of a spirited wrangle about dream symbolism, Dr. Loren said, "You don't sound like a conventional Freudian."

"Only in modified form," said Roger. He shifted in the chair to avoid the sunlight filtering between the curtains. "I use a psychodynamic approach, with a combination of methods."

"Then our styles will mesh – good. What about medication? I don't see you as the type to reach for the prescription pad first thing."

"Certainly not." He was glad to note that, judging from the tone of the question, she didn't overuse drugs, either. "Meds have their place, of course, especially when long-term therapy is out of the question for most patients. Nowadays nobody wants to spend years in analysis, even if the insurance companies would allow it. I suppose if pinned to the wall, I'd have to consider myself eclectic."

"Aren't we all – nowadays?" Her smile caused an odd quiver in Roger's diaphragm. "You're not above using a spot of behavioral modification?"

"Not so long as it isn't a substitute for tracing the roots of the problem."

She nodded agreement. "And I hope you don't believe in vaginal orgasm or penis envy?"

"Really, Doctor, I'm not blind to the fact that our field has made some progress in the past eighty years!"

"Wonderful. I couldn't risk being saddled with an archaic-minded male chauvinist for a partner." A broad smile took the sting out of the remark. She stood up. "I think we'll suit, Dr. Darvell. I've got an appointment set up with my attorney for this afternoon, to sign the contract. I definitely want you for an associate."

*And I want you, Dr. Loren – but it's out of the question, so kindly maintain that professional persona you do so well.*

Good God, what was he thinking of? When she offered her hand to seal the bargain, he clasped it as briefly as politeness allowed. Glancing at her watch, she announced with an air of mild surprise that it was past lunchtime. Roger declined her invitation, pleading fatigue from his trip, and instead returned to the hotel for a futile attempt at a nap.

Dr. Loren picked him up early for the meeting with the lawyer. Apparently she wanted leisure to pursue their morning's conversation. Pulling away from the Hilton, next to the city dock with its view of a sailboat-clogged inlet, she said, "If you don't mind satisfying idle curiosity, why did you become a psychiatrist?"

Caught off guard by the unexpected question, Roger told the truth. "Morbid inquisitiveness about the workings of the human mind. Besides, I discovered early in my medical training that hospitals made me ill, and I reacted badly to the sight of blood."

Dr. Loren said with a throaty laugh, "If you'd claimed you went into the field out of a deep yearning to help suffering humanity, somehow I wouldn't have believed you."

"Why did you choose this specialty?" he countered.

"Partly the same as you," she said. "People's thought processes fascinate me. Every human being is unique – though you might not guess it from the sheeplike way some of them behave – and I enjoy helping them discover and cultivate their uniqueness. Watching a person waste energy lugging around the baggage of the past when he or she could be living a fully creative life drives me up the wall." She added with a self-deprecating smile at her own intensity, "Sometimes I want to grab them and give them a good shaking. Probably a byproduct of growing up as the older of two sisters. There's a lot of truth in those theories about family dynamics, even if they've been oversimplified in the popular press. Are you a firstborn, too?"

"Only child," Roger said.

"Aha – QED!"

Both to divert the conversation from personal matters and to appease his curiosity, he asked about the psi experiments she had mentioned in her letters.

"Inconclusive," she said. "And I can't afford time off to pursue those bypaths on my own. I keep an open mind on the subject, though."

"How open?" This speculative field seemed odd for such a levelheaded woman. "Do you accept the whole gamut of paranormal phenomena – clairvoyance, telepathy, past life regression, psychokinesis, astral projection –?"

She finished, "Not to mention psychic healing, sympathetic magic, and human spontaneous combustion? I don't –accept' any of it, in the absence of concrete proof. But some of the anecdotal evidence is highly suggestive."

By the time he had made his disdain for anecdotal evidence perfectly clear, they'd reached the attorney's office. The lawyer was a woman, no surprise to Roger, who had noticed the faded E.R.A. bumper sticker on the back of his new associate's car. The front bumper, urging the reelection of President Carter, branded her a liberal on other issues, too. Roger decided he could live with that aberration, considering her numerous good qualities. A third sticker, proclaiming, "Places to Go, Heads to Shrink," he decided simply to ignore.

On the way out of the attorney's West Street office, Dr. Loren said with a grin, "Well, we're stuck with each other now. How about a nice relaxing tour of historic Annapolis?"

"Relaxing" wasn't the word Roger would have chosen. He might have enjoyed the drive up the narrow, brick-paved Main Street and around Church Circle, with its colonial church at the center of town, if she'd conducted the tour after sunset. As it was, he had to endure the glare of the afternoon sun while chugging along tourist-choked streets in a Volkswagen beetle with inadequate leg room. "How many months a year does your weather stay like this, Dr. Loren?" he asked as they inched past the city dock a couple of minutes later. From there, they turned onto the shady campus of the Naval Academy, providing a slight break in his discomfort.

"Missing New England already? Don't try to con me – I've met your mosquitoes, and your summers are as muggy as ours. Yes, if you're partial to winter, we get our share. Even snow." She gave him a sidelong glance as she stopped the car near the chapel to make way for a squad of jogging midshipmen. "And since we're starting a long association – we hope – how about calling me Britt?"

Well aware that the gesture was a meaningless social amenity, Roger nevertheless felt warmed, a minute later, when she spoke his given name in her rich alto. The tingle at the roots of his teeth reminded him that he had to keep her at a distance. Indulging his appetite with a coworker would invite catastrophe. He began by politely refusing Britt's invitation to join her at dinner to celebrate their contract. He claimed a health condition that restricted his diet (true enough), insisting that he wasn't hungry (by now, an outrageous lie) and would dine alone later.

He did exactly that after the hotel quieted down for the night. Crossing to the other wing of the Hilton, he prowled until he found an unaccompanied woman just unlocking the door of her room. It took him only seconds to catch her eye with a casual remark, then lull her into a trance. He followed her inside, took what he needed, and put her to sleep with a command to forget the encounter.

In the morning he met with a real estate agent before heading to the airport. When he made the move, scheduled for Labor Day week, he wanted to spend as little time as possible stuck in a hotel. The return flight, though only a short hop from B.W.I. to Boston, affected Roger as badly as airline trips usually did. Being trapped in a vehicle over which he had no control, with a pack of nervous, sad, or exuberant people, taxed his undeveloped psychic barriers. He had never learned to shut out such stimuli, except by ingesting heavy doses of alcohol.

After several drinks he managed to fall into a shallow, dream-haunted doze. This time, however, he suffered neither his usual amorphous anxiety dreams nor the violent nightmares he dreaded. Instead, he plunged into a lurid vision of Britt Loren lying in his arms, her magnificent red-gold hair unbound, a single scarlet drop adorning the smooth whiteness of her neck. He awakened with his jaws aching and his heart hammering in frustration.

*Too many of those over-romanticized vampire movies,* he decided, calling the flight attendant for another Scotch. *What is the matter with me today? I'm not even hungry.*

Noting the word that he'd unthinkingly used brought him up short. *Hungry? I'm already thinking like Sylvia. That young woman is dangerous!*

Yet he knew he wouldn't break with Sylvia; she intrigued him too much, and she provided something he'd never had be-fore – one person with whom he could freely discuss his secret. As for his reaction to Britt, his longing for her must be a tem-porary aberration. Nobody fell that fast, that hard. Since the desire couldn't be consummated, the sooner he crushed it, the better.

He returned home to an additional stress, the folder of case notes and medical examiner's reports O'Toole had sent him over the weekend. Roger forced himself to study the black and white copies of autopsy photos, with their images of torn throats and lacerated breasts. When he read the reports, two anomalies, in addition to the corpses' low blood volume, struck him. The only clue to the attacker's identity, the saliva in the wounds, made no sense; analysis of the saliva collected from the earliest victim – admittedly a small amount, hence vulnerable to laboratory error – revealed no recognizable blood type. Furthermore, not only did the autopsies turn up no semen samples, they recovered no specimens of the killer's skin or blood from the girls' fingernails. At least one of the victims should have managed to claw her attacker before dying. It looked as if the girls hadn't struggled, none of them.

Could they have been killed by someone they all trusted, catching them off guard? Unlikely, since investigation had revealed no connection among the victims. Perhaps the murderer had solicited trust in some other way, such as wearing a uniform. Or perhaps he used hypnosis, like Roger.

*No! There's no resemblance!*

"Liar," Roger said aloud into the silence of his home office. He shifted his attention to another oddity of the cases. In each instance, the pattern of post mortem lividity revealed that the girls had not died where the bodies had turned up. So the perpetrator, at increased risk to himself, had transported his victims away from the murder sites after death. To make sure they would be found distant from some location that could be linked to him? Or to flaunt his contempt for the authorities by leaving the evidence in conspicuous places? Abandoning that young blonde in front of the Old North Church certainly looked like a gesture of defiance.

*If he's that bold, sooner or later he'll give himself away.* From the file cabinet next to his desk, Roger pulled out a thick file of xerox copies and notes on blood fetishism. A few of the classic cases resembled the current series of murders. He glanced at and dismissed his material on John George Haigh, the "Acid Bath Vampire," for some authorities suspected Haigh of commit-ting his crimes solely for profit, inventing his tales of blood-drinking in support of an insanity plea. Roger also set aside the cases in which ingestion of blood served as a prelude to rape rather than a substitute for it.

Krafft-Ebing's account of Vincenz Verzeni, a nineteenth-century Spanish serial killer, more closely paralleled the Boston murders. Instead of raping his victims, Verzeni had experienced sexual release in the mere strangling and biting of women, and he had claimed a total lack of interest in – indeed, ignorance of – female genitalia.

Roger paused to consider whether he might be reading too much into the sketchy information provided by O'Toole, projecting his own lusts onto the killer. Certainly the resemblance between himself and the unknown criminal did not extend to their *modus operandi*. Roger's morbid introspection had never unearthed impulses within himself that reflected the unknown's obvious delight in pain and death.

On the other hand, intuition told him he wasn't imagining the similarities in their sexual preferences. Roger's libido had expressed itself atypically – *be honest, why don't you, abnormally!* – from the beginning. Unlike O'Toole's shadowy killer, who seemed to crave negative emotions, Roger fed on erotic arousal.

Sylvia claimed she knew the murderer. Had she simply read about the crimes and appropriated them as part of her fantasy? Or could she, properly approached, offer a solid lead?

## Chapter 4

SATURDAY NIGHT Roger again hunted with Sylvia in the Cambridge area, this time in his own car. At her request, he picked up another teenage girl for her, a Radcliffe student in search of a lift back to the dorm. Before Sylvia lulled her into a trance, the girl remarked that she was a freshman, not yet turned eighteen. By getting out of the car and walking around until Sylvia finished, Roger resisted the temptation to share this prey with her.

Afterward he asked Sylvia, "Why do you tend to pick on such young victims?" He didn't completely abstain from girls under twenty, but they weren't his first choice.

"I wish you could hear yourself, Roger," she said with a contented wiggle. "You sound like the father in a fifties sitcom scolding his daughter for staying out past midnight. I take teenagers, when I can, because their emotions are so intense. I get a fantastic charge out of those bubbling cauldrons of hormones."

Silenced by his distaste for her blatant hedonism, Roger drove across the Longfellow Bridge to Sylvia's downtown apartment. For the first time, she invited him to come up for a visit. They greeted the uniformed doorman, walked through the lobby past a wall of mirrors, and rode the elevator to her floor. Although the building itself screamed "money," he found no Wedgewood and crystal here. Braided rugs and beanbag chairs covered the apartment's living-room floor, horror movie posters the walls. The thousand-dollar Japanese stereo system shared department-store metal shelves with stacks of paperback books, which also colonized the rug in wobbly mounds.

Scanning the room, he said, "So this is your lair. Where do you keep the coffin?"

"Ha, ha." Sylvia plucked a plaid shawl off the only solid piece of furniture in the room, a low divan, and slung the garment onto one of the chairs.

Roger accepted the implied invitation and sat down, avoiding a heap of newspapers and a copy of *Analog* that had been hidden by the shawl. How could anyone live in such clutter? Aside from a little dust, though, the place was clean. The only taint in the air was a not-unpleasant animal scent.

Its source stalked around the corner from the adjoining kitchen. A black Persian cat. She circled Sylvia's legs and emitted a meow of greeting. "You got fed before I left," Sylvia said, "so don't try to snow me with any of that 'hungry' stuff." Picking up the cat, she joined Roger on the couch. "Meet Katrina. She's a pet, not a snack."

"Good grief, what kind of barbarian do you think I am?"

"Sorry – after all, I don't know much about you yet." When Katrina squirmed, Sylvia loosened her hold, and the cat minced toward Roger. Instead of hissing and running, as he'd expected, the cat sniffed his hand, then placed her front paws on his thigh, whiskers twitching. She stretched up to bump against his shoulder and allowed him to rub her chin. "Strange – animals don't like me."

"Most of them don't like me, either," Sylvia replied. "Katrina's different because I raised her from a kitten. She's weird – can't stand ephemerals, likes vampires. More evidence that you're one of us."

"More likely she senses you approve of me." Dropping the argument, Roger gave himself up to the unaccustomed pleasure of smoothing the silky fur over lithe muscles.

"I'd like to have a human pet someday," she said, "but the addiction risk scares me."

Instead of getting sidetracked by the concept of a human being as a "pet," he asked her about the term "addiction."

"If we use the same person too many times," she said, scratching under the cat's chin, "we can get fixated on them. It's not just psychological; it's a chemical thing."

He marveled at the complexity of the background she'd imagined for herself. "Not something I have to worry about," he said. "I don't – drink – often enough for that to happen."

"How about now? Are you sure you're all right?" Sylvia asked. "I don't feel any need in you, but maybe you're just good at hiding it."

Roger didn't care for the vulnerability of being read with such ease. "Since you are the first person I've met who's claimed any degree of clairvoyance, I've never learned to hide it. I'm fine, but I could use a glass of milk."

Sylvia went into the kitchen, leaving him with Katrina, who had homesteaded his lap. Roger flipped through the magazine and scanned the opening page of a Spider Robinson story. He heard the beep of a microwave oven, and a moment later Sylvia returned with two earthenware mugs. "I thought you'd prefer it warm. I always do."

"Yes, thank you." He sipped the milk. Body temperature. He didn't dwell on the coincidence that she shared his taste in late-night drinks. "If you insist you're a vampire, I suppose blood and milk make up your entire diet."

She smiled at his transparent attempt to catch her in a contradiction. "No, I drink beef broth, too, sometimes with ground meat in it. How about you?"

"I've found that suppresses the – hunger – up to a point. So does animal blood from butcher shops."

She grimaced. "I resort to that myself if I have to. Yuck – like an ephemeral eating frozen TV dinners."

"Then you don't take human blood every night?"

Seated next to him, she said, "Of course not. I hunt live animals, too."

"So do I – better than preying on people."

"You take this guilt thing seriously, don't you?" She sipped her milk. "For some things animals really are better than human prey. With a rabbit or a deer, you can let yourself go, enjoy the chase and the kill, gorge yourself. We need that release some-times. You can't do that with people unless you want to end up like our cousin the serial killer."

"No cousin of mine!" Roger took a long drink of milk to settle his stomach. "Do you think he feeds on – human prey – every night?"

"I wouldn't be surprised. Every other night, at least, I bet. The cops don't find all his kills, only the ones he doesn't bother to hide." She tucked her legs under her on the couch and offered her mug to the cat, who lapped at the surface of the milk. "I'm sure he has no trouble luring victims. Ephemerals can't resist us when we focus on them. And as you've noticed yourself, when we're hungry they flock to us even if we're not trying."

"I never admitted to noticing anything of the sort." The way she picked up subtle cues in his behavior and speech, feeding them back to him as "facts," struck him as uncanny. She would make an outstanding therapist – or con artist.

"Yeah, right, you're totally human. Drinking warmed-over blood for midnight snacks doesn't mean a thing."

"However, I also eat solid food. Face it – I'm an ordinary man with a few peculiar habits." His mouth twisted in a wry smile at his own understatement.

"And those allergies Mrs. Bronson mentioned? I bet they include sunlight and garlic."

"Along with a tedious list of other things," he said. "You're selecting the data that fit your hypothesis and ignoring all the rest."

"Have it your way," Sylvia said. "Care to listen to some music?"

"I can't stay long. I have to get a nap between now and church tomorrow morning."

"You really go to church? And participate?"

"Why not? I was brought up Catholic." He would have laughed if her consternation hadn't been so deep; she stared at him as if he'd confessed to drinking a cup of hemlock every day for breakfast. "Sylvia, you aren't afraid of crosses, are you, like the vampires in those idiotic films?" He gestured toward a blown-up photo of Bela Lugosi, black cape billowing, on the opposite wall.

She nodded, avoiding his eyes. "I know there's no objective danger, but I can hardly stand to look at one. If a cross touched me, I'd freak."

"But that's ridiculous. You're letting a lot of superstitious tripe have psychosomatic effects on you. We both know you're not a corpse reanimated by the Devil, so how can you believe religious symbols have power over you?" He cut the lecture short; as a psychiatrist, he ought to know the futility of trying to talk someone out of a phobia. "You know, that problem might be curable." *I should be urging her to get therapy for more than just the phobia. But that would mean admitting I need the same treatment, wouldn't it?*

"No, thank you, Doctor! I don't need to have my head shrunk."

"That's a matter of opinion." He consoled himself that, while she might not be quite so harmless as the fellow in the movie who claimed to hang out with a six-foot invisible rabbit, in any rating of dangerous psychotics she scored pretty low. Finishing his milk, he let his eyes roam over Sylvia's slender curves. Despite the smallness of her bosom, her long-legged, feline grace gave her an erotic appeal no man could fail to notice. Still edgy from watching her seduce her victim, Roger almost wished he had ignored his scruples and joined her.

"You want something from me," she said. "What is it?"

*Damn, I'll have to learn to shield my emotions better.* Her keen perception made him feel naked. He set his cup on the floor, and Katrina leaped down to lick at the dregs. Roger put his arm around Sylvia, who purred – that was the only word for it – deep in her throat and reached up to stroke his cheek.

Clasping her hand, he brushed his lips across it to confirm what he thought he'd felt. "You have tiny hairs in your palm."

She laughed softly. "So do you." He caught his breath when she captured his free hand and tickled the sensitive center of his palm with her thumb. "Cilia, really – or vibrissae, like a cat's whiskers. And you still think you're not like me?"

"I still haven't decided which of us is psychotic – or possibly both." He didn't want to deal with the implications of this discovery right now. After all, the strange trait, though rare, fell within the normal range of human variation. "But I can't help thinking of that first night, when I – took – from you. It felt different from anything else I've experienced."

Sylvia rubbed her head, catlike, against his shoulder. "And you want another taste? All right, I don't mind. We sometimes share blood with our own kind, in friendship or mating. Just don't mark my throat again."

He flushed when she offhandedly unbuttoned her blouse. Her willingness to be "marked" at all surprised him, but he co-operated when she drew his head down on her breast, her fingers twined in his hair. She sighed with pleasure as he lapped blood from the superficial incision his teeth inflicted just above her bra line. How could she enjoy this now, after fighting so furiously the previous time? He told himself to stop being so relentlessly analytic. Now that he knew what he could and couldn't expect from this union, he enjoyed it, too.

Careful not to take enough to weaken her, he withdrew after only a few minutes. He had no urge to go further. Not that contact with Sylvia didn't ignite a tingling warmth in his loins, but he felt the same heat throughout his body, radiating from the point where his mouth touched her skin. Nor did Sylvia show a desire for anything more intimate.

Nevertheless, curiosity impelled him to ask, "You mentioned mating?"

"Oh, we can't do that. I'm not in heat – I'm a little too young for it." Before he could question this bizarre statement, she added, "We can still play around, though."

She kissed him, licking her own blood off his lips. Then her mouth wandered down to his neck. He went rigid, his hands tightening on her arms. She looked up to meet his eyes. "What's wrong?"

"I thought you were –"

"I was. Don't you want –?" His shuttered gaze answered her. She pulled free of his grip. "You'd better get going. Didn't you say you needed to get to bed early?"

A chill reflecting surface rebuffed his attempt to read the emotion behind her sudden aloofness. "If I've offended you, it wasn't intentional."

"I know." She forced a smile. "Don't worry about it. You'll understand later. Now go."

IN THE NEXT couple of weeks Roger enjoyed Sylvia's companionship without any progress toward unraveling the riddle she presented. She played the guitar, he learned, singing songs by sixties folk-rock performers. Her favorites were selections from the Kingston Trio. She delighted in tormenting Roger with "M.T.A." and the saga of poor old Charlie.

"That song doesn't even make sense as humor," Roger once protested. "His wife can't have handed him a sandwich through the window; those windows don't open."

"Oh, Roger, can't you just relax and enjoy a joke?" She switched to "The Ballad of Lizzie Borden." After five choruses on the impropriety of dismembering one's parents in the state of Massachusetts, he was ready to do anything to shut her up. *Including "hunt,"* he thought. *So much for my plan to cut back on blood-drinking.* He decided to view these few weeks as a carnival before the fast he resolved to impose on himself once he settled in Maryland.

She maintained her "vampire" persona with remarkable consistency; never once did he see her eat. He had read articles about people, obsessed with that novel by Anne Rice, who claimed to be "real" vampires, avoiding daylight, dressing in black, and consuming blood. But never had he heard of anyone who lived the pose as thoroughly as Sylvia did. On Friday and Saturday nights, and often in mid-week as well, they cruised the highways north of Boston in search of victims. Sometimes they prowled coffeehouses, choosing their prey from among students listening to folk singers and poetry readings.

More often than not, he remained a detached spectator of what he considered Sylvia's gluttony. He knew that on week nights, when he was usually too tense and exhausted to be a stimulating companion, she hunted alone, feeding every other night. Roger, who functioned more or less contentedly on a biweekly ration, viewed that indulgence as dangerously reckless. He didn't even care for the term "feeding," which seemed like an evasive euphemism to him.

"So what would you call it?" Sylvia asked him when he raised that objection one evening at her apartment. "Sometimes we refer to it as 'scoring.'"

"I like that even less," he said.

She poured two glasses of Chablis and handed him one. "Okay, how about `making love'? I have a feeling you'd really hate that one."

"You're absolutely right. It would be sheer hypocrisy."

"So? Aren't most homo saps – ephemerals – being hypo-critical when they use it that way?"

"I had no idea you were a cynic at heart."

Sylvia shrugged. "Love is a human concept. I have only the foggiest idea of how to recognize it. So you categorize our feeding as some kind of perversion – maybe the right term should be `getting a fix.'"

"That may be accurate," he conceded, "but I'm coward enough not to want to think of it that way."

"The trouble with you," she said, folding her arms in exasperation, "is that you don't want to think of it at all. You might as well just say 'doing it,' like a teeny-bopper talking about sex." She raised clinked her glass against his. "Here's to 'it' – as often as possible."

Later that same night, with one of her Joan Baez tapes playing in the background, Sylvia asked him when he had first realized he was different.

"For as long as I can remember, I perceived auras – or imagined I did. By the age of six I learned not to mention the colored lights I saw around people. My parents accused me of 'making up stories.' After a while I doubted the evidence of my own eyes. After all, nobody else could see those haloes of light."

"Well, I can, so quit doubting yourself," she said briskly. "What about sensing emotions?"

"From childhood, I could tell when people were lying. I embarrassed the hell out of Mother and Dad several times before I learned to keep my mouth shut."

Sylvia giggled, "I bet you did."

"But I didn't start feeling other people's emotions intensely – or imagining them – until I was about fourteen. It came on gradually."

"Okay, that's the normal age for it. And then we develop the need to absorb life-force from ephemerals by, you might say, soaking up strong emotion. That happens before the bloodlust hits. How about you?"

*Damn, how does she do that?* With Sylvia's uncanny guesses, it was all too easy to forget that most of what they were discussing had to be pure fantasy. "Soaking up strong emotion – interesting way to put it.

Yes, I did – still do – have experiences like that. It started with girls, when I began dating."

"No surprise there," she said.

"I've never had sexual intercourse." The embarrassment he felt at confessing that lack surprised him. "At that age I was capable of ejaculation, but good Catholic boys didn't 'go all the way' with nice girls. And the brothers in charge of my prep school made sure we didn't have much chance to meet the other kind."

Sylvia shook her head. "A vampire at a parochial school – I'm having a lot of trouble with that picture. So if you didn't go all the way, what did you do?"

Roger smiled reminiscently. "Nice girls, under the right conditions, could indulge in heavy petting – a concept you're probably too young to remember."

"I've heard of it. I wasn't allowed to associate with humans until my teens, but I'm not *that* out of touch with their culture."

"It happened the first time at one of those ghastly dances they arranged for us . . . ."

Roger had been fifteen. He'd felt no urge to taste the girl's blood, but neither had he felt a drive toward the acts the older boys bragged about.

He'd been at a dance hosted by the girls' finishing school down the road. Too young and introverted to have a date of his own, Roger had gone stag, like most of the boys in his grade. If the headmaster hadn't required all the students to attend the dance, as part of their education in the social graces, Roger would have stayed away. Already his empathic powers had developed enough that crowds made him uncomfortable. Suf-fering through the evening in the stuffy room, redolent of nervous sweat and heavy cologne, he took his turn at dancing with a succession of unattached young ladies.

Eventually he found himself waltzing with a petite brunette who wore less perfume than the others and hadn't nibbled on the garlic-flavored salami hors-d'oeuvres whose odor nauseated him. By that time, after ten, he began to feel downright sick from the crowding and the smells. Sensing emotions was still new to him, and he had none of the precarious control he'd later developed. The barrage of alien passions sometimes made him suspect he was losing his mind. After his parents' response to his other odd perceptions, he knew better than to mention this new problem.

He persuaded his dancing partner to step outside for a few minutes of fresh air. Sensing the blend of amusement and nervousness in her, he guessed, from what he'd overheard from his more experienced peers, that she suspected him of ulterior motives. More from curiosity than lust, he'd kissed her. The memory of her mint-flavored lips, the fragrance of her corsage, and the silken fabric of her powder-blue evening gown came vividly back to him.

He'd drawn back from the kiss to gaze into her eyes, half expecting her to retreat in alarm or indignation. Instead, she stared dreamily at him for a full minute – and then, standing on tiptoe, wrapped her arms around his neck to pull his face down to hers.

Suddenly her arousal flooded over him. *So this is what the fellows were talking about!* Instinct guided his hands over her body, tracing a fiery path from one erogenous zone to the next, guided by her burgeoning excitement. His lips never left hers while his fingers discovered the core of her feminine heat. His whole being echoed the cataclysmic vibrations of her climax.

As soon as they caught their breath, he escorted her inside and handed her over to another partner. The girl didn't speak to Roger, behaving as if she were floating in a daze. He found, to his surprise, that the throng around him had become bearable. He felt refreshed, energized. Even if he had been more outgoing, he would have known better than to tell any of his classmates about the experience. Upon reflection, he recognized that it differed from the sexual exploits the other boys reveled in trading at their locker-room bull sessions . . . .

After he told Sylvia about this incident, she said, "With all that going on, you didn't have a clue that you weren't an ordinary teenager?"

"Don't you understand?" Given her obtuseness about so many everyday facets of social interaction, he could halfway believe she wasn't human, after all. "I couldn't tell anyone about those incidents, so I had no reality test. For all I knew, I was losing my mind. That fear, in fact, was what first got me interested in psychology."

"So what about drinking blood? I'd have expected you to feel that need within a year or two."

"No, it didn't happen until my early twenties, during my residency at Mass General." Even now, the memory made his stomach knot with anxiety. "It was – terrible. I denied the urge as long as possible, tried to convince myself it was anything but – what it was. I stuffed myself with raw meat, bone marrow, anything to stifle that craving for – whatever."

Sylvia stared at him, wide-eyed. "I can't imagine how awful that must have been. I always knew what I was, and when my bloodlust started, it meant I was growing up."

Recalling the turmoil he'd suffered, Roger almost wished he could share her fantasy of vampirism.

"About the same time, I lost the capacity for – sexual release. Not that I noticed it right away, being an exhausted, overworked resident –" He smiled grimly. "But when I finally re-alized I had become inexplicably and permanently impotent—"

"Now, that part I can't understand at all. I mean, ephemerals have to settle for short, localized climaxes. Why would you want to be limited that way? For us, it's so much *more.*"

Her words roused an unwelcome heat in the pit of his sto-mach. He poured himself a fresh glass of wine and gulped half of it at once. "Well, I didn't know about the – compensations — at the time. And I can't share your belief that it's all perfectly natural."

"It's natural for us. You aren't some kind of depraved pervert; you're just taking what you need. As for the human-type sex, have you missed it?"

"Well –" He had to concede that the rush he enjoyed when he tasted the blood of a properly stimulated victim far surpassed his memory of masturbating to climax. On the other hand, how well could he rely on that memory?

"See what I mean?" She raised her glass with a triumphant flourish. "Why do you keep fighting your nature, trying to set new records on how long you can go without? You're driving yourself crazy for nothing. After all, ephemerals were made to feed us. Why else would they taste so delicious?"

The appeasement of Sylvia's voracious appetite left many hours unaccounted for, hours spent hiking through the woods or driving up the coast to walk over deserted seaside beaches at midnight. They spent one weekend exploring rural Maine, searching, as Sylvia put it, "for Stephen King landmarks. Wouldn't it be neat to stumble across 'Salem's Lot?"

"No, thank you," Roger said. "I read that book, too – the vampires were cremated *en masse*, remember?"

"In real life we know better than to make ourselves that conspicuous."

"Real life?" He arched a skeptical eyebrow at her. "Odd choice of phrase. Stipulating it's true, for the sake of argument, where do vampires congregate in real life, if not in small New England towns?"

"Mostly we don't. Congregate, that is. We're solitary predators. Give up, Roger, I'm not allowed to talk about it." Sylvia consistently met Roger's questions with similar non-answers or light retorts. He clung to the assumption that her unwillingness to provide him with specific data masked the fact that no real data existed.

"Introduce me to your former friend – the other vampire you claim is haunting Boston," he challenged her on one occasion.

Sylvia immediately turned serious. "You don't want to meet him. I wasn't lying when I said he'd committed those murders. He's an outlaw." Not another word would she volunteer. Roger wished he could persuade her to speak more freely; suppose she actually did know the killer's identity, even if she harbored delusions about his nature? *But if I got a name from her, how could I explain it to O'Toole?* First things first; get the information, stop the slaughter, and then figure out how to handle the detective.

The only other source of tension between them was Sylvia's unfulfilled wish to taste Roger's blood. Though she didn't ask outright, he knew she wanted it. She had allowed him to drink from her, enjoyed it. Why couldn't he reciprocate? He saw the silent question in her eyes and had no answer for it, even in his own mind. He knew only that the fathomless need he sensed in her frightened him; he felt if she opened his veins, she would drain his life away.

A new shock hit him the night she talked him into experimenting with his psychic powers. "There's so much more you should be able to do," she said, curled up next to him on her living room couch. "Reading emotions and controlling people's minds is just the beginning."

"What do you have in mind?" said Roger, stroking Katrina, who sprawled limply across his knees. "Telekinesis? Levitation? Walking through walls?"

"Go ahead, laugh it up," she said. "I want to teach you how to – I guess you'd say, create a psychic disguise. It's an extension of the mind-control you've mastered on your own. Projecting an illusion can be not only useful but fun. And since you do have the hypnotic talent, you should be able to pick this up."

"How do you mean? Like a hologram?"

"No, no, I mean making *yourself* look different." She stood up, facing Roger. "It's a self-protective technique, like camou-flage. I can make people see me as a wolf, a panther –" she smiled sardonically – "even a bat. But the easiest is what you might call psychic invisibility." Her outline blurred. She rippled like an image on water and vanished.

## Chapter 5

*JESUS, MARY, and Joseph! She disappeared into thin air!* Roger almost crossed himself before he remembered that would upset Sylvia. *This can't be literally supernatural, but it's as close as I ever want to get.*

He watched in stunned silence until she reappeared. "Good God – how in the name of all that's holy –?"

He felt her delight in his astonishment. "I just made you see me differently. You should be able to handle that – go ahead, try. I'd love to see what you're capable of." She lifted the cat out of his lap.

*Is that why the legends say vampires can dissolve into mist?* "How?"

With a frown Sylvia said, "I don't know how to teach you, not the way my advisor taught me. If we were bonded –" She stood up. "You need feedback from another person. You wouldn't see your own reflection fade from the mirror." For a moment her eyes clouded. "I used to, but I got over that. Now all that's left is the fear of crosses."

When she beckoned him to stand opposite her, he complied. "Look into my eyes, Roger. I'll be your mirror. Try to feel what I feel when I do it." She faded into transparency again. Now that Roger was expecting the illusion, he could almost penetrate it; a faint outline of her form teased his vision. Sylvia shimmered back into view and said, "Now you."

He imagined weaving a curtain around himself to deflect rays of light, shaping a pocket of opacity to veil himself from her eyes. He fixed his gaze on those red-gleaming eyes, seeking confirmation of his skill. For a second he fell into a whirlpool of double vision, viewing Sylvia's half-naked body, outlined by the glow of her aura, yet simultaneously seeing himself through her eyes, his body enveloped in shadow. His eyes smoldered back at hers.

"Yes – yes!" she whispered. "Oh, Roger, that's outstanding for a first try." She groped for his hand. When their fingers brushed, he felt the illusion dissolve.

He clutched her fingers like a drowning man. "Thank you – I think. If I really did what you claim you saw. As you said, I can't see myself vanish." When the initial shock faded, he flashed on an image of the crowd cheering for the nude Emperor's "new clothes." "For all I know, you're convincing me I can do this for your own purposes."

"Oh, come on, Roger! Why would I lie? What possible rea-son could I have for working a scam on you?"

True, he couldn't think of a plausible motive. She had plenty of money and didn't need anything from him. "All right, maybe there's something to all this. Maybe we share some obscure con-genital syndrome. We might even be distantly related."

She laughed at his desperate attempt to cling to his skepti-cism. "I keep telling you, we are. But not the way you think." She let go of his hand and rearranged her clothes. "That's kind of draining the first time, isn't it? If you've worked up an appetite, let's get out there and score."

Roger was surprised and not quite pleased to find that the trick came easily to him. His hypothetical kinship with Sylvia cast doubt on what he'd always considered his unpardonable guilt. Could a spider be damned for trapping flies? A cat for devouring mice?

*So should I adopt Sylvia's notion that I'm a superior being, and humanity is my lawful prey? This is progress?* Only natural that he half wanted to believe her – fantasies of glamorous origins, indulged in by most children, were especially common among adoptees. As a Freudian, he should be particularly aware of that tendency. He needed expert help, and not from a medical expert. From the Church.

He wouldn't consider, however, unfolding the truth to his own parish priest. The seal of confession would prevent the pastor from revealing Roger's secret and compel him to act as if he'd forgotten it, but nothing could keep him from viewing Roger differently thereafter. On the other hand, the idea of picking a priest at random from the phone book repelled Roger. A quick scan through his mental card file turned up a suitable confessor. Some months back, he had attended a weekend psychiatric conference in Providence. While there, he'd heard Mass at a small nineteenth-century church near Brown Uni-versity. The pastor, an older man near retirement, had made a favorable impression on him.

Telephoning the Providence parish long distance, Roger arranged a Saturday afternoon appointment. Enduring the loss of half a day's sleep and a long drive in daylight would be worthwhile if he got some answers.

ARRIVING IN Providence with a pounding headache from the sun,

Roger walked for a few minutes under the shade of the hundred-year-old oaks in the small churchyard, contemplating sculpted cherubs and lilies on headstones, postponing the moment of confrontation. The afternoon sun made him over-heated in the coat and tie he wore to underline his solidly professional status. The discomfort drove him into the cool dimness of the church. Bas-reliefs of the Stations of the Cross lined the side walls, while up front a life-size grouping of the Holy Family brooded over a bank of votive candles. Roger lit one on principle, though the only petition that came to mind was the missal's prayer for examination of conscience.

*I confess myself in the dark as to my own failings; my passions blind me, self-love flatters me, presumption deludes me . . . remove every veil that hides my sins from me, that I may be no longer a secret to myself.*

Kneeling at the altar rail, he heard the creak of a side door and the pad of feet on the carpet. He sprang up to face the priest.

"Dr. Darvell?" The man was slightly plump, with a fringe of sandy-gray hair. "I'm Father Hale. Shall we go into my office?"

*Too late to back out now.*

"You don't use the old-fashioned confessional?" Roger glanced at the carved mahogany doors to one side of the nave.

"Sometimes those little boxes could be a device for evasion, I'm afraid," said Father Hale, leading the way through a dusty back hall to the office. His blue eyes flashed a challenge at Roger. "Do you think I'm wrong?"

"I think you're all too right." He followed the priest into a room dominated by a wide desk that barely left space enough to navigate between bookshelves and overstuffed chairs. Father Hale tugged a *prie-dieu* from a corner and placed it in the one clear spot on the braid rug.

Roger knelt stiffly upright as the priest donned his stole, murmuring the familiar prayer. "Shall we begin, my son?"

*No escape – no barriers.* Roger recited the customary opening phrases and ground to a halt.

"Please go on," Father Hale softly prompted. "You made your last confession less than two weeks ago, yet today you come here, to a parish where you're unknown. There must be a particular reason. What is it?"

Unable to think of any smooth lead-in to his revelation, Roger blurted out, "Father, I drink human blood." For a few seconds he felt dizzy with relief at getting the words spoken.

Aside from an acceleration in his heartbeat, the priest showed no reaction. His face remained expressionless. The man was as good at his job as Roger had hoped. "My son, are you confessing to murder?"

"No, I don't kill."

"What, then? Perversion?"

"I'm not sure. I thought so at first, but now I'm reconsidering." With the critical words spoken, Roger found he had no further trouble discussing his problem. "Living on blood is abnormal for human beings. Suppose I'm not human?"

Father Hale gave a single start of astonishment, instantly suppressed. "What else could you be?"

"Could you accept the possibility of another intelligent species – humanoid but not truly human – created to feed on blood?"

"If they existed, wouldn't we know about them?"

"Not if they carefully concealed themselves, as they certainly would." Noting the priest's continued skepticism, Roger added in a more insistent tone, "Father, I've met one. She claims that she isn't human – and she believes I belong to her species."

After a moment of thoughtful silence, the priest said, "You're a physician. If someone came to you with a story like this, what would your scientific training tell you?"

"This woman has shown me – things – that suggest she may be telling the truth. And it's not scientific to ignore the evidence of one's senses."

Father Hale shifted uneasily in his chair. "I can see you believe this. I haven't experienced your 'evidence,' though. Can you give me any reason to believe?"

Roger bowed his head on his hands. How could he demonstrate his paranormal talents in any way that would convince a skeptical observer? Any use of hypnosis would be recognized as just that – and hypnotic illusion proved nothing. He looked up to meet the priest's eyes. How easy it would be to bend Father Hale's will, force him to believe. An act that would subvert the whole purpose of making this confession. "No, I can't," Roger said. "I only know that I'm going out of my mind, living a lie, not sure what I am."

"Are you prepared to give up consuming blood?"

"Don't you understand what I'm getting at?" Roger snarled. "I can't give it up. I'm asking you to show me how to live with it."

With no trace of fear, only sorrow, the priest said, "You know I can't absolve you of a sin you don't repent and have no intention of stopping. When was the last time you –?"

"Sunday night." The question reminded him of his growing hunger, which would drive him to satisfy it before the weekend was out. *I was tapering off, before. Why is it getting worse now?*

"And you perform this act frequently?" To Roger's silent acknowledgement, he continued, "For how long? How many years?"

"Almost twenty," said Roger.

"You see what I mean, my son? If you remain willfully incorrigible –"

Roger got wearily to his feet. "Then what do you advise me to do about it?"

Father Hale, too, stood up, removing the sacramental stole. "I suggest you see a psychiatrist."

Roger swallowed the obvious reply that leaped to mind. Instead, with a bitter smile, he turned and walked out.

SOON AFTER HIS confrontation with Father Hale, Roger received an unexpected call from Lieutenant O'Toole. "Doc, we have ourselves a suspect in that serial murder case."

Roger sat up straight in the padded leather office chair where he'd been dozing when the telephone had interrupted his lunch break. "Excellent. How did you manage to track him down?" He wondered whether the profile of the hypothetical killer that he'd assembled from the police reports and a rereading of Krafft-Ebing's *Psychopathia Sexualis* had been of any help.

"Didn't. It was pure dumb luck." O'Toole sounded dis-gusted. "He confessed, for God's sake!"

"Not unheard of," Roger said. "The 'stop me before I kill again' syndrome. Some criminals commit their crimes precisely in order to be punished. On the other hand, irrational guilt can drive people to confess crimes they didn't commit." Catching himself lecturing, he stopped short. O'Toole knew as much as he did about false confessions, maybe more.

"Yeah, we get the crazies. That's exactly why I called you. The details this guy gave us fit the murders, but we can't be sure." He emitted a nervous cough. "Plus, his lawyer's bringing in a consultant to pass on the suspect's competence to stand trial. So the D.A.'s going to ask you to check him out for the pro-secution. That okay with you?"

"I'd be glad to." Roger's hand, clenching the phone receiver, began to ache; he deliberately relaxed his grip. So he would finally get to meet Sylvia's supposed "outlaw vampire." *Maybe. Or maybe it's a false alarm, after all.* Nevertheless, his mouth went dry with excitement.

"Great! The D.A.'s office will contact you later today to set it up, probably for tomorrow sometime. I just wanted to touch base with you first."

"Can you give me a general idea of why his competence is in question?"

"Personally, I think the lawyer's laying the background for an insanity defense." Over the phone, Roger heard the detective tapping a pen against the receiver. "But I have to admit the guy is a little weird. He didn't want a lawyer; his married sister practically forced one on him. He hasn't given the cops one minute of trouble. He doesn't react to anything much, sits around staring at the walls like he's in a trance. Only thing that got him worked up was the mention of bail. Said he didn't want to be let out, can you beat that?"

"Oh? Did he say why?" The whole profile didn't fit Sylvia's claim of a serial killer vampire. Nor did this behavior sound much like the human psychopath Roger had postulated in his report. He reminded himself that the chance of a false confession was better than even.

"Said he wouldn't be safe on the outside."

"What's the suspect's background?" Not that he needed to know any of that to evaluate the man's mental balance, but he couldn't suppress his curiosity. He wanted to know how closely this self-confessed murderer matched Sylvia's hints.

"Security guard at M.I.T., name of Albert Warren, age fifty-two, not married," said O'Toole, again tapping his phone as if the sound stimulated his thought processes. "Usually works the night shift. He managed to give us some on-target times and places for the crimes, and being he lives alone, he doesn't have anybody to alibi for him, but he doesn't really fit that profile you worked up. Of course, that's just your statistical average, right?"

"True, this kind of prediction is far from an exact science," Roger said.

"Listen, if you find out anything useful when you examine the perp, you'll let me know, right?"

"Of course. I'll call you immediately afterwards, either way." Roger hung up, his thoughts drifting to Krafft-Ebing's examples of subjects addicted to "infliction of pain during the most intense emotion of lust." *Is that what they've got locked up downtown? Or do they have something even less human?*

Shoving aside these futile speculations, he considered whether to tell Sylvia her "vampire" had been arrested. No – why upset her until he was certain the suspect had indeed committed the murders?

THAT NIGHT, driving with Sylvia through downtown Boston, he found her in an unusually communicative mood. She asked him whether he hadn't been lonely before the two of them had met.

The question touched too closely upon memories of his childhood that had sprung to mind while reviewing the case histories of blood fetishists. Roger had to spend several minutes sorting out his thoughts before he could reply. Sylvia waited quietly, with uncharacteristic patience.

"If I was, I didn't know it," he said, rolling down his win-dow to let in the summer night breeze. "As the only child of parents well into middle age – Mother and Dad were in their late forties when they adopted me – and a pretty strange child at that—"

"Strange?" He could almost see Sylvia's ears perk up.

"I was a solitary introvert, with no idea how to relate to other children." *But not "hypochondriac" and "neurasthenic" like those pathetic specimens in the textbooks.* Aside from his food allergies and sensitivity to sunlight, Roger had never been ill in his life. "Even at a Catholic high school run by Jesuits, an academic overachiever with no social skills doesn't score high in popularity. My strength and reflexes didn't help, since I couldn't stay out in the sun long enough to apply them to something useful, such as football." He smiled at the memory of the day his more athletic classmates had taunted him too far, causing his temper to break out with devastating effect. Being left alone from then on had been well worth the demerits he'd received for fighting.

"You didn't mind that?"

With a shrug Roger said, "I came to terms with it. Maxi-mized the things I did well, won Latin competitions for the school and so forth. I enjoyed the company of older people and had easy successes with the young ladies from the girls' academy down the road – surprised me almost as much as it must have annoyed my rivals. No, I didn't miss having a more 'normal' up-bringing. I assumed that was the only way to live. Wishing for something different, even later, as an adult, would have been like –" he flashed her a self-mocking smile – "wanting to change into a bat. It never occurred to me."

The car inched along clogged streets past Quincy Market, with its open-air stalls selling everything from produce and flowers to fish and meats. Even after dark, shoppers crowded the sidewalk between the rows of displays. Aromas of fruit, fish, fresh-ground coffee, and the occasional nauseating whiff of garlic scented the air. Among the storefronts that lined the alley, Roger glimpsed a butcher shop with a sign in the window, "Fresh-killed goat, whole or half." *And people think buying fro-zen blood is peculiar!*

Sylvia wrinkled her nose at the flood of odors. "You must have wondered about your special powers. Other teenage boys didn't see auras, read emotions, or seduce girls with a look and a touch."

He shrugged his shoulders as if the memory weighed on him like a poorly balanced backpack. "Of course I did. I learned quickly to use them – and hide them. And naturally I wondered why I was – strange. But as for not being human – my imagi-nation didn't run wild to that extent, and it still doesn't." *Not quite true. If I weren't entertaining the idea, I wouldn't have gone to Father Hale.* The priest's rejection still left a bitter taste in his thoughts. He braked, waiting for the traffic light to change.

"That's where we differ," she said, still unusually serious. "I always knew what I was, and I had a family that understood my needs – even if not exactly what ephemerals would call a family. Going to Radcliffe, then living here after graduation, I've missed that companionship. Meeting you has helped." That was the most she'd said at one time about her background, whether real or fan-tasized. With an impish grin she added, "Even if you are incre-dibly square."

"So you did have a childhood?" he said, hoping to take advantage of her willingness to talk.

She gave an impatient sniff. "Of course we have a child-hood. We just don't have the same family structure homo saps do." She stretched and wiggled in her seat. "Have you been practicing that disappearing act?"

"Once or twice. I'm almost afraid of it," he confessed.

"You still doubt your own sanity, don't you?" She sounded both impatient and incredulous. "Look, I can prove one thing – we both see auras. It's not your imagination or mine." She dug a pen and pocket notebook out of her purse. "Choose a couple of people on the street. I'll write down what I see in their auras and then give you my list. You tell me if you picked up the same things."

"Well – I have to admit that's a sound scientific approach."

"Gee, thanks," she said with her wolfish grin. "And I trust you to answer truthfully when I hit the target. Go ahead, pick two people at random."

He glanced over the throng of pedestrians and said, "All right, how about the plump woman at the flower stall and that black man crossing the street?"

"Fine." After staring at each of the two subjects for a few seconds, Sylvia jotted in her notepad. "Here." She handed him the list.

Not bothering with the dome light, Roger read her notes in the glow from nearby street lamps: "Woman – dull yellow with muddy gray blotches around the chest area – sick with some-thing, maybe breast cancer. Man – deep reddish pink, with darker vermilion swirls around his head – probably has a headache – high blood pressure?"

Roger exhaled a long breath and gave back the paper. He felt as if he'd plunged into water over his head, and the undertow was dragging him out to sea.

"Well?" The teasing lilt in Sylvia's voice proved that she sensed his stunned reaction. "Do your observations agree, Doctor?"

"You know they do." *I'm not deranged. I actually do have some kind of ESP.* "I suppose I should thank you."

"After you get over the shock? I won't hold my breath."

They headed into the heart of the North End, where the cooking smells from scores of Italian restaurants forced Roger to roll up the window and turn on the air conditioner. Just as well, since he heard thunder in the distance, and a sprinkle of raindrops spattered onto the windshield. Shortly the car turned in front of the courtyard in front of the Old North Church. A wind sprang up, plucking a few leaves from the trees to whisk them across the brick pavement.

Roger couldn't help recalling the girl whose body had been found here. The memory of his nightmare made a sour taste rise in the back of his throat. "Fighting traffic isn't my idea of a pleasant evening," he said. "Why did you suggest we come down here?"

"Just cruising. You know I like to pick up tourists." She glanced toward the plaza just ahead. "Hey, look over there."

The Citroen's headlights illuminated a skinny teenager slouched on a stone bench under a tree near the equestrian statue of Paul Revere. The boy looked up as the car slowed at the curb.

"Stop a minute," Sylvia said. "Maybe he wants a ride."

"You can't be serious. He's only a child."

"I'm going to check him out anyway. If he's old enough to be interested, he's old enough."

"Didn't you get all you needed last night?"

"Oh, Roger, don't be so stuffy." She unlatched her door and leaned out, as he resignedly put on the brakes. The boy stood up and took a couple of steps in their direction. "Need a lift?" Sylvia called.

He bent over to peer past Sylvia at Roger. "Uh – sure, that'd be cool."

She scooted over. "Well, get in. This is my Uncle Roger, and I'm Sylvia."

Uncle? Sylvia must have decided to drop her age a few years.

"Thanks, man," the boy said, leaning forward again to address Roger. "Name's Rico." Raindrops beaded his hair. He wore a T-shirt, slashed off at mid-chest, with a picture of the rock group Kiss. If the outfit was an attempt to look tough, it hadn't succeeded. His curly, over-long black hair and delicate features made him look more like Hawthorne's Marble Faun than an extra from *West Side Story.*

"Where are you headed, Rico?" Sylvia brushed his finger-tips lightly with hers.

"Home. My cousin picked up a girl and ditched me. I have to catch the T."

"No problem, we'll drop you at the station," she said.

Taking the hint, Roger put the Citroen in gear, circled around to a southbound street, and headed toward Faneuil Hall while Sylvia had her way with their passenger. The musk of arousal tinged the boy's sweat. By the time they'd reached the subway entrance, Roger's head throbbed from clenching his jaws. The combined aromas of blood and sexual excitement in the confines of the car formed an irritant he still hadn't learned to deal with.

When Sylvia brought the boy out of trance, he said, "You're something else. How about giving me your phone number?"

"I'm too old for you," she said, her right hand still playing with the hair at the nape of his neck.

"Don't go putting me on! Couldn't be more than a couple of years' difference!"

Giving Sylvia a sidelong glance, Roger realized that dressed as she was, in jeans, a halter, and sandals, she did indeed look no older than eighteen, rather than her actual late twenties.

"How old are you, Rico?" she asked.

"Seventeen."

*Small for his age,* thought Roger. *Probably something of a misfit in his subculture.*

When Sylvia showed no sign of yielding, Rico persisted, "Come on, who cares about a year or two? I never ran into anybody like you before. You make me think of that poem, you know, 'She walks in beauty, like the night.' I'm not trying to lay any big moves on you. We could meet in the park and, you know, ride the swan boats, or whatever."

Quoting Byron? Definitely a misfit.

Sylvia laughed, "All right, I give up. I don't go out in the daytime much, but you can visit me tomorrow night." She delved into her purse on the floor, tore a sheet off the notepad, and scribbled her address.

Rico glanced at it, shoved it into his side pocket, whooped, "All right!" and jumped out of the car, slamming the door on the way. Roger noticed that his legs wobbled as he meandered toward the MTA station.

Following Roger's gaze, Sylvia said, "Quit worrying. I didn't drink that much. It's the energy drain. He'll be fine in a couple of hours."

A car honked behind them. Shifting into gear and driving away, Roger glared at her in speechless indignation. Impulsive though she was, he'd never known her to do anything this foolish.

"If I'd been alone with Rico," she said, "I'd have let him come. But I knew that would annoy you. Oh, well, maybe next time." She licked her lips.

"'Annoy' is hardly the word!"

She refastened her seat belt with a sensual undulation of her hips. "You disapprove," she mocked. "You think I'm greedy, immoral, reckless, and a total airhead."

"I wouldn't use such unprofessional language, but I do think you've set yourself up for trouble. How could you even consider giving a victim access to your home? What has got into you?"

She leaned back, hands clasped behind her head. "I think I'm drunk."

"Impossible."

"Because it's outside your uptight experience?" she said. "You can't imagine how refreshing that was – how different from older men. As for taking them home, don't you ever do that?"

"It wouldn't be safe."

"Why not? You just make them forget afterwards. And in your own place you can relax, create the proper atmosphere."

"Atmosphere?"

"Candles, music, maybe satin sheets or an embroidered quilt or other special decorations. Look, you know a feeding isn't complete without emotional satisfaction. You have to plan for that. Grabbing a quickie in a car or an alley isn't always enough."

He shook his head. *Might as well try to deliver a moral lecture to a cat.* "Sylvia, you're a shameless hedonist."

"Now you're catching on." She didn't attempt to justify herself further. On the way home she gazed out the window and sang an obscure Elton John song about a wistful revenant named Lady Samantha.

## Chapter 6

The next day on his lunch hour, Roger caught a cab for the short trip between his office and the Charles Street Jail. The antiquated gray building with its barred windows bore a depressing resemblance to a medieval fortress. As always, Roger braced himself before he stepped inside, but no amount of preparation really cushioned the shock.

When he entered the vast central atrium with its seven-story-high ceiling, a torrent of noise crashed over him. From the multi-leveled tiers of cells, the cacophony of hundreds of voices bounced off the bare walls. The racket seemed to drill straight into the center of his skull. Odors of urine, vomit, and disin-fectant oozed from the very walls.

Still worse, the emotional atmosphere made him feel suffocated — so much anger and fear packed into such an overcrowded space. The negative emanations from prisoners and staff alike clotted around him like smog on a hot, windless day. Behind the thunderous din of too-loud voices, he heard a man alternately sobbing and cursing, someone else pounding on a wall in monotonous cadence. He forced his breathing to a slow, even rhythm.

A guard showed him to the cubicle where he would interview the suspect. The walls, wood on the bottom and glass at the top, didn't reach all the way to the ceiling. To Roger's hypersensitive ears, the noise was hardly muffled at all. *I've done this before and survived the ordeal,* he reminded himself with a hint of sarcasm. *So I may as well quit whining and concentrate on the job.* He took a seat and waited several minutes, until he heard two pairs of footsteps approaching the door. The prisoner's feet shuffled, to the rattle of the ankle chains that shackled him.

Roger took out a notepad and pen. Thanks to his eidetic memory, he could have functioned without notes, but he thought it best to keep a written record, just as he did with his own patients. The guard guided the prisoner, handcuffed as well as shackled, to a chair across the small table from Roger. Clad in the blue-gray prison coverall, the suspect slumped into the chair and stared at nothing, his cuffed hands motionless in his lap. The guard stepped outside and shut the door, remaining there with his back turned.

Roger's first reaction mingled disappointment and relief. This lean, middle-aged man of average height, with brown hair turning gray at the temples, didn't resemble Sylvia. Albert Warren had sun-weathered skin and brown eyes. Moreover, his aura showed none of the electric violet-blue streaks that distinguished hers. Nor did the odor of his sour breath and sweat-stained clothes bring to mind Sylvia's crisp, metallic scent.

Roger suppressed a smile, realizing how close he'd come to believing Sylvia's fantasy of a vampire race. The man not only looked nothing like a vampire; he didn't look like a murderer, either. Appearances meant little, of course. Psychopathic killers didn't bear any obvious stigmata, even to the eyes of an empath.

Pulling his straight-backed chair closer to the table, Roger said, "Mr. Warren, I'm Dr. Darvell. Do you know why I'm here?"

The man raised his head, gazing over Roger's shoulder instead of meeting his eyes. "To find out if I'm crazy." He sounded unconcerned about the prospect.

"I wouldn't put it quite that way. I've been retained by the District Attorney to assess your mental condition. There are a few things I need to make sure you understand before we begin."

Warren gazed at him without response.

"First, this interview is not confidential. I may pass on anything you tell me to the prosecution or to investigating officers. Do you understand?"

A slow nod.

"Although I'm interviewing you on behalf of the prosecution, my testimony won't necessarily hurt your case. It may also help your case or have no effect one way or the other."

He waited for Warren to acknowledge the statement with another nod. The man wasn't simply maintaining a stoic mask; he projected no emotion at all.

"You aren't legally required to answer my questions," Roger said, "but if you don't, I'll make note of that fact and include it in my report. Do you understand?"

"Sure. I don't mind answering questions. But I already told those detectives all about it."

"I need to hear the story directly from you. First, though, do you know where you are?"

Warren looked faintly puzzled at the question. "In jail. Charles Street."

"Do you know today's date?"

"August twenty-something. I kinda lost track."

"What is the year?"

Throwing Roger an "I may be crazy but I'm not stupid" look, the prisoner said, "1979."

*Oriented to time and place*, Roger noted. *Now, down to business*. "Mr. Warren, can you explain why you turned yourself in to the police?"

"Like I told them," said the man in a flat tone. "I killed those girls. I need to be locked up." He raised his hands in a half-hearted gesture, and the cuffs clinked as he let them fall back to his lap.

"Why did you suddenly make that decision at this particular time?"

"I been thinking about it, that's all. It's not right, me running around loose." He didn't meet Roger's eyes as he spoke. He radiated no guilt; in fact, he still projected no feeling whatever. He sounded like an amateur actor reciting an imperfectly learned script. *Tranquilized?* No, Roger had asked the assistant D.A. about medication, and none had been prescribed. The absence of sedation made the emotional flatness more puzzling.

Roger regarded the patient with a puzzled frown. Lack of affect characterized sociopaths, but Warren didn't feel like other specimens of that class Roger had examined. He tried a different angle. "Can you tell me why you killed the women? What did you want from them?"

"I don't know. Felt like I had to." Nothing seethed behind that statement. No suppressed compulsion fighting to break out.

"Did you hate the victims?"

Warren reacted to that – mild confusion. "No. Heck, I didn't even know them."

"Was there sexual feeling associated with them?" Normally Roger wouldn't approach that question head-on so early; this man baffled him, driving him to provoke some positive response.

"I don't think so. Don't remember."

Roger stood up. This line of attack wasn't getting anywhere. "Mr. Warren, I want to try something that may help me understand you better – and may help you get out of here. You want that, don't you?"

Alarm flickered in the brown eyes. "No! It's safe here."

Safe from what? Roger's professional antennae quivered. Safe from his own guilty impulses? Or from some outside force he imagined to be forcing him into the violent acts? "Mr. Warren, I want to hypnotize you. Will you cooperate?"

A shrug. No resistance, at least.

Roger used hypnosis more than most therapists, for the technique suited his peculiar talents. No subject could lie to him for long. Now he stood up, moved to Warren's side, and laid a hand lightly on the prisoner's shoulder. "Look at me, please." Roger needed no glittering object as a focal point to compel the subject's concentration. His gaze and touch did the work.

Warren raised his eyes to Roger's. Instantly his apathy dissolved into an open-mouthed stare of panic. His heart racing, he tried to squirm out of Roger's grasp. Both of Roger's hands tightened on the man's shoulders and wrestled him to stillness. Choked with terror, Warren struggled to emit a cry for help.

Staring him down, Roger said in a low voice, "You will be quiet. You will not scream. You'll answer when I speak to you, and that's all. Understand?"

A jerky nod. Soothed by the circular strokes of Roger's thumbs on his collarbone, the man's heartbeat and breathing gradually slowed. "I'm not going to hurt you. You're safe here, remember? Now, what are you afraid of?"

"Your eyes," the man whispered.

The air in Roger's lungs turned icy. "What about them?"

"Like his. Red – they glow –" Warren paused to gulp a breath. "He told me to forget –"

"Now *I* tell you to remember," Roger said. "Who is 'he'?"

"Grabbed me one night at work," said Warren. "He bit me – here." The man raised both arms in a vague wave, pointing with his chin toward the left one. "Told me I killed those girls, and I better give myself up. Explained to me how each one died, so I wouldn't get mixed up when I told the cops."

"This man ordered you to confess to the murders?"

Another nod. "Then told me to forget he'd talked to me."

"He made you believe you'd actually done it." Roger fixed Warren's attention with a steady gaze. "You didn't kill anyone. You are innocent. You'll forget the details of what this man did to you, but you will remember that." Would he? A single hypnotic session didn't always do the trick. At least Roger had the truth on his side; restoring true memory had to be easier and more reliable than imposing a false memory. "When the police learn that you're innocent, they'll release you."

Fear leaped in the man's eyes again. "No – he'll kill me for this."

"The criminal will be arrested, Mr. Warren. You'll be safe." Roger tightened his mesmeric grip. "Tell me who this man is. What is his name?"

Warren's mouth twisted as if trying not to vomit. At last the words spewed out. "Neil – Sandor."

"One of your co-workers?"

"Yes." Warren let out a shuddering breath and closed his eyes.

"Tell me about him."

"Janitor – works nights. I never ran into him much until he—" Warren gulped and shivered. Roger lightly stroked the man's shoulders to calm him.

*Nights, eh? Could this be Sylvia's 'vampire'?* The mention of "red eyes" made the hypothesis plausible. "What does he look like?"

"Red hair, beard, kind of scruffy. Real tall."

"How tall, compared to me?"

Warren craned his neck to look up at Roger. "About the same. Maybe a little bigger." He started trembling again and whined, "Don't let them send me home. He's out there – he'll kill me –"

"That's up to the police and your attorney," Roger said. He lulled Warren into trance once more. "Remember, you didn't kill those victims. You are innocent. Forget what Sandor did to you. You don't have to be afraid."

Finally the prisoner sank back into slack-jawed passivity. Roger had heard enough. He knocked on the door for the guard to return Warren to his cell.

During the cab ride back to his office, Roger's brain simmered with the implications of the interview. *Maybe Sylvia really does know the killer; maybe he's related to her. An extended family with an exotic set of powers and weaknesses?* In the office, he telephoned O'Toole as promised.

"I'll be sending the usual written report to the District Attorney, of course," said. "I need to talk to you about the case right away, though. In my opinion, Mr. Warren isn't competent to assist in his own defense. However, I also believe he's not your murderer."

O'Toole's voice sounded like a bulldog's growl. "Hell – we're back to square one?"

"Not at all," Roger said. "He gave me some information you may find useful, which I'd rather not go into over the phone. Can you drop by my office later today?"

"Sure, if that works better for you." The detective sounded puzzled, no doubt wondering why Roger didn't just deliver his "information" without further ado.

The main reason was to ensure that O'Toole believed in Sandor's guilt and would push for an immediate arrest. For that, face-to-face application of hypnotic influence was necessary. "How about five o'clock," Roger said, "right after my last patient?"

O'Toole agreed. When he showed up at five, to the unex-pressed curiosity of both Dr. Lloyd and the receptionist, Roger led the Lieutenant directly into his office.

As soon as the door was safely shut, Roger said, "Mr. Warren is covering for someone I believe to be the real perpetrator, a man by the name of Neil Sandor who works on the custodial staff at M.I.T."

"Man, that was fast work!" O'Toole's grin faded as he con-sidered the implications. "You telling me Warren's an accessory? The two of them in a serial murder conspiracy?"

"No, Warren isn't an accomplice. He needs therapy, not punishment. I suspect psychotropic drugs may have been used to convince him of his own guilt." That explanation would work better than opening a discussion of whether hypnosis could make a person act against his own best interests.

"You seem damn sure of all this." O'Toole stood up, took a few paces across the limited floor space, and jingled the change in his pockets. "So you think Warren isn't the killer. But couldn't accusing Sandor be another fantasy he dreamed up? Oh, hell, at least it's a lead."

"My intuition suggests that this time Warren is telling the truth." He caught O'Toole's eyes and administered a firm psychic shove. "If you check out the two men's work schedules, I have a feeling that Sandor's hours will dovetail with the times of the murders better than Warren's."

"It's worth a try." He still sounded dubious.

"I'm certain of it," Roger said, increasing the mental pressure. "How soon can you get a warrant? You'll want to bring the man in for questioning before he gets suspicious and bolts."

"You're right, we can't take any chances. I'll check with the D.A.'s office and talk to a friendly judge." O'Toole brightened up and shook Roger's hand. "Thanks, Doc! I knew you'd come through for us."

*What have I done, though?* Roger asked himself as he struggled home through downtown traffic. Sylvia would say he'd betrayed one of his own kind. Again Roger wondered whether to tell her what he'd learned. Though aware of his own cowardice in evading the confrontation, he decided to wait until the police ar-rested the supposed vampire. Until then, what he'd discussed with O'Toole was confidential. Smiling grimly at this ration-alization, Roger pigeonholed the subject.

LIFTING A CORNER of the living room curtain, Sylvia stared at the figure under the street lamp three stories down. Roger, curse him, was right; she never should have given Rico her address. When the boy had come to her apartment, they'd shared a delicious hour together. Excitement tingled through her at the memory. She had brought him to climax three times. No older man, even goaded by the stimulus of her hypnotic seduction, could do that. The third time, she had allowed Rico to penetrate her, a new experience for both of them. No danger of pregnancy existed, since Sylvia hadn't reached her fertile stage.

Thinking of Rico's lovemaking made her lightheaded. Too bad she had to blur his memory of the union, for her own safety. After that one encounter, she had ordered him to stay away. The order hadn't stuck. If she'd had better sense, she knew, she would have wiped her address from his mind. In the four nights since then, the boy had shown up each evening promptly at sunset. At first he had lingered in the lobby to waylay her. When the doorman evicted him, he turned to skulking outside.

Watching Rico, Sylvia pressed the back of her hand to her mouth to stifle a moan. *Dark Powers, I want him so badly!* She'd been warned about this kind of addiction but never experienced it before. Its intensity took her by storm. What made this boy different from other donors? Because he pursued her with such abject devotion? Poor child, she was his first sexual partner, and he thought he was in love with her. Sylvia felt hollow inside, and the idea of stalking some other victim made her queasy. Imagining the joy that would burst from Rico if she invited him in demolished the last of her judgment. Even from this distance she felt the tug of his passion. She allowed it to draw her down to him.

When she reentered the lobby, holding Rico's hand, the doorman frowned as they walked past. The man disapproved of Sylvia's allowing "riffraff" into his domain. Well, this was one intruder she didn't want protection from.

Upstairs, she led Rico to the couch and wrapped her arms around his waist, her hands massaging his chest under his T-shirt. His flesh seemed to scorch her palms. Already she couldn't restrain herself from nibbling his earlobes, licking his face and neck. *What's wrong with me? Slow down, girl, what's the rush?* Four nights was a long time to go without, but she shouldn't be starving quite yet.

Just before she submerged him in an erotic waking dream, Rico said in a voice hoarse with arousal, "I'm getting hassled a lot by Tony – you know, my cousin, he lives with me and Mom— he keeps bugging me about where I go at night."

Half drunk on Rico's lust, without having tasted a drop of his blood, Sylvia took little notice of the remark. "What did you tell him?" she asked unconcernedly, working Rico's arms out of his shirt.

"Nothing." The boy sounded faintly offended. "Hey, what do you think I am? You're special – I wouldn't go shooting off my mouth about you. But Tony, he's worried, he thinks I'm still a little kid."

"Well, you certainly aren't that!" She silenced Rico with a kiss, and within minutes neither of them had energy to spare for talking.

THE SIGHT OF the man looming in her doorway hit Sylvia like a blow to the chest. "How in the name of – how did you get up here?"

The tall, broad-shouldered, red-bearded man laughed, "You think I couldn't handle that uniformed clown in the lobby? Well, are you going to let me in, or risk your neighbors hearing this?"

She retreated a step. "Oh, all right, come in." After closing the door, she said, "Neil, I told you in no uncertain terms that I never wanted to see you again. I don't like the way you operate."

"Not liking it is your privilege. Turning me in is something else." No longer laughing, he radiated anger like heat from a furnace.

"What on earth are you talking about?" She sat down. Neil didn't; he paced around the room, narrowly avoiding her books and stereo equipment, as he raged at her.

"I'm talking about losing my home – losing my *car,* for hell's sake – going underground! You think you can drive me into hiding and get away with it?"

Sylvia clutched the edge of the sofa to keep from trembling. "I haven't done anything to you. All I wanted was to stay as far away from you as possible."

He bared his teeth at her. "You expect me to believe that?"

"It's the truth. Why would I suddenly betray you, after all this time?"

"The cops came to get me four days ago. I was asleep, I barely woke up in time, I had to *fight* them!" His fist slammed into the nearest wall. "They saw me, they know what I look like! I've had to hole up in abandoned buildings." The scent of his anger made her stomach lurch.

Noting the hairline crack in the plaster where he'd hit the wall, Sylvia armored her mind against the fear seeping through her vitals. In a hand-to-hand struggle she would have little chance against Neil, older, larger, and more experienced. "Sit down and take it easy. If you'll just listen to me –"

"Listen!" He whirled to face her. "All right, little one, if you didn't tip off the police, who did?"

"I don't know. We're the only ones in Boston." A sudden thought struck her. *Roger – who else?* She couldn't guess how he had stumbled across Neil's identity, but that had to be the answer.

Neil's quivering alertness showed that he had caught her shift of mood. "You do know something. Who is it?"

Sylvia reinforced her psychic shield. Older than she, Neil could probably force Roger's name out of her unless she kept her guard up. "I don't really know. I have a good guess."

Neil bent over her, his hands pressing on the couch on either side of her head. "So tell me. Why won't you let me read your emotions? What are you hiding?"

Sylvia sat rigidly still, visualizing those hands compressing her skull. "I won't say any more. I wouldn't turn you in to the police, but I certainly won't betray him to you, either. Especially when I'm not sure."

Neil straightened up. Sylvia couldn't help letting out a relieved breath. "I think you're lying. You're inventing this third person just to make me believe you're not a traitor. If there were another of us in Boston, I'd know."

Sylvia said nothing.

His eyes bored into her. "Then open up to me." When Sylvia shook her head, he said, "Just give me a name – then I might believe you're not guilty."

Standing up, she said, "Neil, this conversation is over."

He relaxed the pressure on her mind and headed for the door. "The conversation may be over. What I'm going to do to you sure as hell isn't."

## Chapter 7

In the passenger seat of Sylvia's car, Roger stole wary glances at her. Since leaving her apartment earlier that night, she'd hardly spoken to him. Nor had she stopped to claim a vic-tim. He felt her anger but couldn't guess the reason for it.

Finally, on an expressway deserted except for the speeding Mustang, Sylvia said, "I guess I'm cooled off enough to talk now. Roger, does the name 'eil Sandor' mean anything to you?"

He went cold. "So you really do know him."

"What I'm asking is, how do you know about him?" Her anger felt like an ice pick between Roger's eyes.

"I helped the police in their investigation of the serial murders, as a consultant to the prosecution."

"So somehow you unearthed his name – and you *gave* it to them!" She gunned the engine. "How in the name of all the powers of darkness could you do something so stupid?"

Now that the jolt of hearing her mention Sandor had re-ceded, Roger felt indignation rising in him. "Stupid? Turning in a murderer? What would you expect me to do, shield the man?"

*"Yes!"* She screeched the word, and her fingers worked spasmodically on the wheel. Calming herself, she said, "You never, never betray one of us to ephemerals, no matter what he's done."

In no mood to cater to Sylvia's fantasy, Roger said, "You know I don't believe there is an 'us.' And even if there were, I'd feel no obligation to protect a killer."

"You still need convincing? Well, stand by to be convinced." Taking an off-ramp two exits further along, she drove into a rural area, unlit two-lane back roads overhung with trees. She cruised with the headlights off. Some twenty minutes after leaving the freeway, she pulled the Mustang off the road into an open field. "Looks good and deserted." She killed the ignition and stepped out.

Roger followed her a few hundred yards through damp weeds. "Pleasant night for a walk, but I don't see the point of it."

"Just watch." She lifted her face to the sky, spreading her arms to test the wind. With her back to Roger, he could see her muscles undulating beneath the skin as the outline of her body blurred and reformed. The glow of her aura intensified, and the energy she radiated ruffled the hair on Roger's arms. Her skin color darkened from white to glossy blue-black, sprouting velvety fuzz.

Petrified with disbelief, burrs clinging to his trouser cuffs and gnats buzzing around his head, Roger stared at what unfurled from Sylvia's back.

She had wings.

Veined like newly-budded leaves, they spanned over ten feet from tip to tip. When she spread them to full extension, they quivered in the cool breeze. She glanced over her shoulder and laughed at his astonishment. He noted that her ears had become pointed, her face more feline than human. She took a running start for a leap into the wind that reminded Roger of a child trying to launch a kite twice her own size. She kicked off her sandals as she left the ground.

Catching an updraft, Sylvia glided toward the trees, her body arched like a bow. She barely skimmed the highest branches before attaining a safe altitude. Not much of one, around fifty feet. In a gradual spiral she managed to ascend another twenty or thirty. Recovering his powers of observation, Roger noticed that the motion was more of a glide than birdlike flight. The wings flexed only to restore balance or to steer.

After a few minutes she spiraled down, drifting to the ground a few yards from Roger. Her aura crackled with energy, as if she'd absorbed electricity from the atmosphere. She combed her tangled hair back from her face with both hands, arching her neck with a wordless purr of delight.

Her elation infected Roger. He stepped up to her and gave her an exuberant hug, half disappointed that the change was already reversing. Holding her at arms' length, he gazed into her glowing eyes. *They're red, like live coals!* "My God, that would be worth a lifetime of lurking in the shadows!"

Pulling away, she said, "You should be able to do it, too. If you're like me –"

"Give it up, Sylvia." Momentarily his head swam with vertigo. At the thought of changing – dissolving – like that, and breaking loose from the earth, he felt as if he were falling into an interstellar void.

"You're afraid to let me teach you."

He shook his head, snapping the world back into focus. "If it'll satisfy you once and for all, you may try."

Her blazed with eagerness. "Wonderful! Look at me, concentrate." He allowed her to lure him with her eyes, draw him into the maelstrom of energy spinning around her. The wings erupted from her back. When she clasped his hands, hers burned his skin like dry ice. "Now, Roger," she whispered. "Come with me, soar with me!"

For an instant his vision misted over, and he lost all awareness of Sylvia's touch and the ground beneath his feet. A second later, the dizziness faded, and he saw and heard only the mundane spring night. Again Sylvia looked fully human.

Her disappointment pressed on him. "Try again," she urged.

"No, thank you, once is enough. Accept it, Sylvia, this knocks out your assumption about me." He felt a grim satis-faction in the failure.

She withdrew her hands from his. "Let's go back to my place. We need to talk."

"Yes – we certainly do. Why did you choose to show me that now?"

"Because I was fed up with your stubbornness, thinking I was crazy. You see where it got us?"

In the car, easing it back onto the pavement, she remarked, "I can't figure out why you don't have the power."

*Maybe because this notion that I'm like you is a friendly piece of wishful thinking.*

"No human being can do that," said Roger.

Sylvia shrugged. "I'm not human. When are you going to admit that you aren't, either? Our psi powers include limited control over our physical forms. We can shift our molecules into an alternate configuration, a shape that's – imprinted on the genes, I guess – for a brief time. Except for the oldest ones, it takes a pretty big expenditure of energy. What the observer sees partly depends on what he expects to see. Oh, Roger, I can't explain it, not the way one of the elders could. Can't you just accept, for once?" Accelerating down the highway, she launched into a falsetto crooning of "Little Old Lady from Pasadena."

A few minutes later she said, "I think I know why you couldn't change. You don't want to badly enough."

"You're fantasizing again." The subject made him physi-cally uncomfortable, constricting his lungs with anxiety. "Would wanting to be a fish make me able to breathe water?"

Back at Sylvia's apartment, Roger felt her mood shifting to grim apprehension. He asked, "How did you know I'd turned Sandor in?"

"He came here," she said, handing Roger a glass of wine and

sitting on the floor with her own drink. "First time I'd seen him in months. He had a clash with the police and barely got away."

"I know about that," Roger said. "The detective in charge told me about the suspect escaping." O'Toole had described one arresting officer's broken neck and the multiple fractures sustained by the other. "He said they later found Sandor's car abandoned a few miles south of the city." The Lieutenant had also told him about Albert Warren's hysterical terror upon being told of his imminent release. The judge had committed Warren for a ten-day period of psychiatric evaluation, probably for the best with Sandor on the loose.

"Neil threatened me." Roger sensed Sylvia's fear. "He thinks I gave him away. I guessed it must've been you, but of course I didn't tell him that. I have a few principles."

That stung. "How could you expect me to adhere to the ethics of a group I didn't know existed?"

Sylvia bristled. "I told you often enough. You should have listened. Anyway, you know now."

"I know that you are something – not human. It seems plausible that Sandor belongs to the same species – though his habits are radically different from yours – if there is a species. For all I know, you might belong to a family group carrying a unique complex of mutations."

Putting down her wine glass, Sylvia plunged both hands into her hair. "I give up – I absolutely give up!"

"Am I supposed to take your word for all this? Prove it by introducing me to your people." He didn't know whether to hope or fear that she would take him up on the dare.

"After what you've done? I told you, I'm not allowed to pass out indiscriminate information – and you are a menace!"

"What do you think Sandor will do? If he's on the run, maybe he won't have time to harass you."

Sylvia hid her face in her hands for a moment before staring up at Roger. "There's no telling what he might do. He's a renegade; rules don't mean anything to him."

"Renegade? Then surely your group - if there is a group – doesn't approve of his crimes."

"Killing ephemerals conspicuously is against the rules," she said. "Betraying one of our own is a *crime*. The worst thing any of us can do, besides murdering one of our kin." She tossed her head, brushing tangled hair out of her eyes. "But you don't think any of that applies to you."

Roger finished his wine, fortifying himself for what he intended to say. "Sylvia, I know this isn't worth much, but I apologize for doubting your – difference."

"My inhumanity, you mean. Thanks, I guess."

"May I – would you demonstrate that shapeshifting again? I was too shocked to notice the details."

"All right." He felt himself blushing when she peeled off her sundress. Amused at his discomfort, she turned her back to him. "You'll get a better look this way, and I can change more fully. I'm nowhere near advanced enough to include clothes in the transformation."

Again Roger sensed the air around her vibrating with elec-tricity. Here she hadn't space to extend the wings completely. They were as light as parachute silk, yet aglow with the vitality of her aura. "I still don't believe what I'm seeing," he murmured. "I've had to accept some forms of ESP, but changing the very shape of your body – that's a whole different order of impossibility."

"Not so much as it seems," Sylvia replied. "My mass and internal organs don't change. It's all on the outside."

He ran a fingertip along the satiny surface of one wing. A velvet layer of hair covered it, as well as her shoulders and arms.

She started, with a hissing intake of breath. "Careful – when my molecules are in flux, I'm super-sensitive."

"I won't hurt you." He lightened his touch but didn't break contact. The membrane's delicate strength fascinated him. It quivered under his caress as it had in the night wind. Sylvia's breathing and heartbeat quickened. Turning to face him, she reached up to grasp his wrists, but if she'd intended to remove his hands, the will to do so deserted her. She leaned against his chest as he continued stroking her wings, his arms encircling her. Now her whole body trembled – excited, he sensed, by his touch on her transformed flesh. Their lips met. The cool caress of her mouth titillated without violently arousing him. He broke off the kiss when her nails dug into the nape of his neck. "Sheath your claws."

"They really are claws if I don't clip them often enough," she said, her breathing ragged. "You still taste strange – almost human, but not quite."

"You have a rather interesting flavor, too." He nuzzled her neck.

Suddenly her embrace lost its playful quality. Melting back into fully human shape, she flung her arms around his neck and fastened her mouth to his neck with desperate intensity.

Instinctively reacting as if to an attack, he raised his hands to ward her off. Recovering, he stiffly put his arms around her again.

"Sorry," she gulped. "The last few days have been terrible. I keep having nightmares. Or should that be 'daymares'?"

"That's one of the sillier neologisms I've ever heard." He led her to the couch and fitted her half-empty wine glass into her hand. "Care to talk about it?"

"I dream about Rico," she said. "And our kind aren't supposed to dream frequently or vividly at all. I'm on the verge of taking him, and he suddenly grows fangs and attacks me. Stuff like that." She sipped her drink and said with more animation, "Don't bother trying to analyze it, Doctor."

"You already know what I would say."

"Okay, on this one thing you were right, and I was wrong. I shouldn't have told Rico where to find me."

"So you regret your cradle-robbing already?"

"Don't rub it in." She hunched her shoulders, trying to dislodge the arm he'd draped around them. "The kid came to visit me the night after we picked him up, and he's been hanging around the building ever since. He won't take no for an answer. The doorman threatened him with the police, so now he loiters across the street as long as he can get away with it."

"I can understand you don't want that kind of attention focused on you," said Roger. "But surely he'll give up sooner or later?"

"Sure, if I don't encourage him."

"You wouldn't have any reason to do that."

She set her glass on the coffee table and looked up at him in wide-eyed appeal. "But I already have. It isn't a matter of reason. Roger, he's so – It's no use, I can't explain why I want him. Help me."

What did she expect from him? Noticing the washed-out hue of her aura, Roger said, "You haven't had anyone in several nights, have you? That's unusual for you."

She grabbed his hand, her nails gouging his wrist. "I need what you can give me."

"Sylvia, you'll have to explain more clearly." But he sus-pected, with dismay, that he knew what she meant.

She wrapped her arms around his neck and kissed him, a hard, grinding pseudo-caress. He had to force himself to return the embrace and stroke her head and back, gentling her until her mouth softened under his. Her body temperature seemed lower than usual, her taste like crisp, chilled white wine. She snuggled into his lap, burrowing under his shirt and raking his back with her nails. Her bared teeth skimmed his cheek and throat without quite breaking the skin. He felt her trembling with the effort of restraint.

He perceived her need as a whirlpool sucking him under. With gentle firmness he dislodged her and placed her a few inches from him on the sofa. "As you yourself told me, we can't get that from each other. What you need is human prey. Whether it's right for me or not, it obviously is right for you."

"Not when I'm wanting that boy this badly. It's an addiction – and maybe you could help me break it, if –" She gulped a couple of deep breaths. "Let's drink from each other."

"No, don't ask that," said Roger, feeling her bristle at his rejection but unable to accept her advances.

He sensed the effort it cost her to speak quietly. "Listen, Roger, I know you're moving away. Soon, isn't it?"

He nodded. "Around Labor Day." He'd already done most of his packing and had accepted a farewell steak dinner from Matthew Lloyd and his wife.

"Then it may be a long time before we see each other again. Do this for me before you go – as kind of a parting gift."

"Sylvia, I just can't – Believe me, I'll do anything else to help."

Her lips curled back from her teeth. "Easy to say – after you're taken from me twice."

"Not by force, the second time." He clenched his fists at his sides to combat the impulse to shake sense into her. "And I apologize."

"Not good enough. I don't know much about how human boys are trained, so I can't imagine what you picked up in prep school. But I was taught not to tease. And that's exactly what all this – this heavy petting amounts to."

Her anger felt like an iron band tightening around his forehead. "I simply don't see what you could expect to gain from such an exchange."

"That's exactly it. You don't understand. You never will understand, unless you trust me and take that step. I'll be damned if I'll try to explain. Not with your skeptical, analytical, super-rational – oh, forget it!"

When she tried to retreat, Roger pinioned her arms with his own. The desperation in her voice knifed through him. He couldn't refuse to assuage it. "If that's truly what you want, I'll cooperate."

Fierce need flamed in Sylvia's aura. With no preliminary caresses, she sank her teeth into Roger's throat. Though the pain made him wince, he didn't fight. He endured the initial gush of blood in passive silence. After a few seconds, however, his vision misted over, and he felt as if his life were pouring away into a black hole. Sylvia's thirst seemed to turn him inside out, scraping him hollow, like a starfish dissolving and absorbing its prey.

Then he felt her creeping, oozing into his mind. No – ripping into it. Tearing out his consciousness by the roots, to clear space for her own. *God, she's inside me!*

"Get out!" He didn't know whether or not he screamed aloud. He threw her out in a convulsion more like a visceral heave than a voluntary act. At the same instant, he tore free of her hands and teeth. He found himself looming over Sylvia as she knelt on the couch, her mouth smeared with crimson.

She staggered to her feet, automatically wiping her lips on her forearm. "Monster – human? – you're colder than any of us!"

He reached for her, the gesture dying halfway through.

"Go away!" she gasped. "Go – and stay away!"

He went out into the night.

SHADOWED BY a gnarled two-hundred-year-old tree, Sylvia sat on a bench next to the pond in the Public Garden and waited for Rico. The doorman's suspicious glances had convinced her to stop inviting the boy to her apartment, but she couldn't make herself stay away from him. Well aware that the more times she drank from Rico, the worse she became hooked on him, and painfully conscious of his pale skin, violet-smudged eye sockets, and growing fatigue, she couldn't stop. Only night before last she had met him here, determined to send him away once and for all, and yielded to his begging for yet another rendezvous.

Sylvia raised her eyes from the reflection of the moon on the pond and scanned the park. Her night vision picked up no sign of human life. Why was Rico late? If anything, she would expect him to show up early, as he had for their last meeting. The thought of his naive ardor brought a smile to her lips despite her worry. He'd be shattered when she broke off with him, as she had to sooner or later. *It had better be sooner, if I want him to survive.* She'd never killed a donor and never intended to.

Her skin prickled, not from chill, but from nervousness. Folding her arms across her bosom, she got up and started walking slowly around the pond on the footpath. Disturbed by her passage, a duck quacked under a bush. No other sound. Sylvia raised her head to sniff the air. The night breeze shifted, carrying a trace of a scent that scraped on her nerves. Following it, she turned away from the pond and catfooted along a winding walkway. Now she heard the murmur of a man's voice on the far side of the pond, mingled with a wordless coo in a woman's tones. *Tourists, she* thought. Locals knew better than to walk here after dark. After a second to assure herself that the lovers weren't headed in her direction, Sylvia continued on her course.

Approaching the boundary of the park, she heard harsh breathing. When she slinked closer, a bearlike growl rasped on her ears.

She caught sight of a feeble glow at the foot of a tree. Residual heat, distinct from the pale blue auras of insects and frogs. At the same instant, the smell filled her nose. Blood – dead blood, but freshly spilled.

A shape loomed above the heap of cooling flesh. A lurid aura, the crimson glow of vampire eyes, and a mouth smeared with red. *Neil!*

She broke into a trot. The attacker vanished into the night. No point in pursuing, for he'd veiled himself and sprinted out of her reach. Huddled against the tree trunk lay Rico's body. Sylvia needed no touch to tell her he was dead. The last vestiges of warmth seeped out of his flesh. There was a dark gash under his chin. Her stomach churned with the scent of his blood.

*So this is what Neil meant!*

Much worse than attacking her directly! He'd violated her property rights, slaughtered her human pet, and branded her with the same stigma of violence he wore.

Sylvia threw back her head and wailed.

AFTER RICO'S murder, Sylvia half expected Neil to show up at her door again to gloat over his revenge. That didn't happen. Instead, when she alighted from the elevator on the ground floor of her building the following night, she found a young man strange to her arguing with the doorman. The latter threw a harassed glance at Sylvia.

"Miss LaMotte, I been trying to tell this punk you don't want to see him." He turned back to the intruder. "You leaving, or do I have to call the cops?"

The visitor, who looked around twenty years old, wore jeans and a leather jacket. Along with the black hair that grew below his collar, the clothes reinforced the "punk" stereotype the doorman had pinned on him. Though this boy stood taller and broader than Rico, Sylvia saw something in his profile that reminded her of her murdered "pet." Chest heaving, the young man said, "Oh, so that's her! Lady, I've got a few things to say to you!"

The doorman grabbed his arm. "That does it, you –"

Sylvia hurried over to them. "Wait a minute." The two men froze. "Who are you, and why do you want to see me?"

"Rico ever mention his cousin Tony?"

"Yes, he told me about you. I'm terribly sorry about what happened – I saw it in the paper." Catching Tony's eyes, she focused her hypnotic power. If she could calm him here and now, he might leave without creating further trouble.

Tony relaxed in the doorman's grasp. Only for a second, though; then he stiffened again and said, "Yeah, I bet you're sorry! He told me some of what you did to him."

"We were friends, that's all." She brushed her fingertips over his arm, trying to reinforce the compulsion of her gaze.

Jerking away from her, Tony said, "That's not how I heard it."

Hopeless, Sylvia decided. To have any chance of manipulating him, she had to work on him in private. Here, depending on how much Rico had remembered and passed on, Tony might blurt out the word "vampire" within earshot of the doorman and anyone else wandering through the lobby.

"It's all right," she said. "Tony can come up to my apartment. You'd like that, wouldn't you?" she said to the young man. "We can talk about Rico."

"That's what I'm here for." With a defiant glare at the con-fused doorman, he rubbed his arm and followed Sylvia to the elevator.

Upstairs she let him into her living room, bolted the door, and turned on the overhead light. The prosaic atmosphere didn't calm her uninvited guest. Tony reeked of grief and hate, as well as a more palpable miasma of nervous sweat. He feared her, Sylvia realized. How much of the truth had he gleaned from Rico? She wished her advisor were here to help. *Dark Powers, I wish anybody were here – even Roger, the idiot!* She hadn't spoken to him again before his departure from Boston, and now she regretted cutting herself off from that comfort, inadequate though it was.

*Stop that! I'm too old to expect constant protection. Powers of night, I'm practically a mature woman!*

"Can I get you something to drink, Tony?" she said, determined to seize control of the situation. "Maybe I could make a pot of coffee."

"I wouldn't drink with you if I were dying of thirst." He planted himself on the couch like a soldier defending a hill.

Her attempt to treat this intrusion as a normal social call wasn't working too well. "Listen, Tony, I liked Rico. It was a terrible shock to read about his death. Why should you be mad at me?"

"Don't give me that bull!" Tony's voice was hoarse with stifled tears. "He got his throat ripped up – I had to go ID him!"

"What do you think that could possibly have to do with me?" She sat on the couch, as far from Tony as possible.

"I know damn well you had something to do with it. I seen Rico go nuts over girls before. He didn't get sick and sleep all day and hook school – or come out with this jive about drinking blood."

So Rico had started to remember. Sylvia tensed, prepared to pounce if Tony made a threatening move. "That simply doesn't make sense. Are you suggesting I tore his throat to get his blood?" She feigned a tremulous laugh, as if the idea were too silly to mention. "Look at me – a skinny girl is going to kill a guy with her bare hands? Anyway, haven't you read about all the other murders like this? Rico was just another victim."

"Crap! The others were women." He leaned forward, tucking a hand inside his jacket. "Maybe most girls wouldn't be able to do that to Rico, but from what he said, you're different. Vampires have super strength, don't they?"

She suppressed a gasp. "I can't believe you're spaced out enough to accept that!"

"It sounds pretty wild, all right. So let's see –" He pulled a rosary out of his jacket and lunged at Sylvia.

Involuntarily she cringed back, arms raised to guard her face. His grin of triumph showed Sylvia her mistake. At once she recovered, forcing herself to fold her hands in her lap and ignore the cross less than a foot away. But it was too late to erase the impression made by her initial retreat.

"This sure does the job on you, all right," said Tony.

"Don't be ridiculous," she said, taming the quaver that tried to creep into her voice. "You startled me, so of course I jumped."

"I don't buy that. You're scared! I never believed in vampires before, but the way Rico looked, and the way you're acting –" He jabbed the cross at her and smirked when she flinched.

"What now?" she said, staring into his eyes. If she could keep him talking long enough, she ought to be able to hypnotize him out of his vindictive mood.

Fumbling in his side pocket, Tony pulled out a knife and unfolded it one-handed.

"Oh, I see," she said. "You're going to cut my throat because you have some fantasy about me killing your cousin."

"Shut up!" Again he thrust the cross at her. This time it touched her bare arm.

The cheap plastic seared her like hot iron. With a scream she leaped up. Tony crowded her toward the bookcase, training the cross on her like a gun. His eyes flickered to the red welt on her arm. "Well, son of a bitch, it works!"

"Look at me, Tony," she pleaded in a whisper he had to strain to hear. "I liked Rico, I never would have hurt him. Go home and forget all this." For a few seconds he gazed into her eyes, his hostile stare softening. "I know how upset you are about his death. I can feel your sorrow. Let me help you, Tony, let me take the hurt away."

He let her take a step closer to him. The arm holding up the rosary drooped a little. She reached up, her fingers almost brushing his cheek.

Abruptly he jolted back to full alertness. He took a swipe at her with the knife, which she barely dodged. "Don't touch me, monster!" He brandished the cross between them.

Now she understood that Tony's faith in the symbol armored his mind against her. She had no hope of controlling him as long as he held the cross.

Again she backed up, pretending even more fear than she felt. She gathered her psychic energy, shaping it in her mind as a child's hands might shape a snowball, ready to throw. Her muscles coiled tautly. She reached behind her to grope in the bookshelf. Tony, focused on the cross that sustained his courage, didn't notice. In a blur of motion human eyes couldn't track, she pitched a heavy book at him.

He involuntarily ducked. At the same instant, Sylvia activated her psychic veil. To Tony's sight, she knew she appeared to vanish. She darted behind him. Her right hand slammed down on the nape of his neck. He collapsed to the floor.

He lay face down, the knife next to him, the rosary still beneath his limp fingers. Sylvia lifted his hand off the thing but couldn't work up the nerve to move it. Even without Tony's will charging it, the religious symbol frightened her. She was ashamed of the feeling but powerless to fight it. She had to get the rosary out of his reach. He wouldn't stay unconscious long.

After a minute's thought, she summoned Katrina with a soft mewing call. The cat padded into the room from wherever she'd been resting. "You managed to miss the riot, didn't you?" Sylvia said. She knelt beside Katrina to stroke the fluffy head. Gazing into the cat's eyes, Sylvia silently delivered her command.

Her erect tail twitching, Katrina stalked over to the unconscious boy. Fastidiously she snagged the rosary beads between her teeth. Holding her head high, the beads dangling, she minced into the kitchen. Sylvia followed, to watch her leap to the window left open for access to the balcony. Familiar with this route, Katrina climbed out to the balcony as confidently as ever. Through the window Sylvia watched her slink to the rail and drop the rosary between the bars.

Sylvia let out a sigh of relief. She hadn't known for sure that the trick would work, for she'd never given the cat such a complex command before. Calling Katrina back to the kitchen, she bestowed a "Good girl" upon her and opened a can of tuna.

When she returned to the living room, she found Tony stirring, emitting muffled groans. After switching off the light, she rolled him over on his back and sat astride his chest. The second he opened his eyes, her own captured him. In the dark, she knew, he would see her eyes glow red.

He swallowed, choked with terror.

"Now you will listen to me, Tony," she whispered. "I did not kill Rico. I couldn't have killed him, because I'm just an ordinary woman, nowhere near strong enough. I never hurt Rico. Do you understand that?"

She stared at him until he gave a jerky, puppet-like nod. "You're confused from the shock of the murder. I understand how you feel; I won't report this assault to the police. Thank me for that, Tony."

"Thanks," he parroted.

The response pleased her, not because she cared about the meaningless apology, but because it proved her mind-control was working. "You aren't feeling well. You're sick from all this stress. You need to go home and rest for a few days. After that you'll feel better. You'll be at peace, and you'll forget all this stuff about me being a killer. Won't you?"

He nodded. "Rest."

"Yes, that's exactly what you need." She smoothed his shaggy bangs back from his forehead. "Where do you live?"

He recited an address.

"Very good. Now I'm sending you home. You're feeling sick, so lean on me, and don't say a word."

"Okay."

After tucking the knife into his pocket, she led him to the elevator. In the lobby she told the doorman, "The poor boy is ill. That's why he said all those things earlier. Get him a cab." She repeated Tony's address and handed the doorman a couple of twenty-dollar bills.

"Sure. Thanks, Miss LaMotte."

She didn't go upstairs until she'd seen Tony safely dispatched. Would the hurried hypnotic treatment permanently blot out his conviction that she was a vampire? She doubted that. However, it would hold long enough for her to pack, break her apartment lease, and get out of Boston. She saw no alternative. To that extent, Neil had won.

## Chapter 8

**Annapolis, October, 1979:**

RAIN FELL in a heavy downpour. At his computer keyboard, Roger listened to the rush of water outside. He heard a distant grumble of thunder in the night.

Glad, for once, of an excuse to interrupt his work, he saved the file and switched off the computer. Why waste a magnificent night like this fiddling with case notes? He welcomed the storm, which provided a break in the Maryland humidity. The cool rain tempted him to go for a run through the trees, perhaps track down a raccoon or deer for a late supper. His townhouse condo, in the St. Margaret's area across the Severn River from Annapolis proper, was conveniently surrounded by unimproved woodland. Pushing the chair back from the desk, he toyed with the question of whether the pleasure of hunting would be worth the inconvenience of dealing with wet clothes afterward.

With a luxurious stretch, he stood up. He decided to change into shorts and a T-shirt and take that run. On the way to the stairs, his contented mood was fractured by a knock on the front door. He frowned in puzzlement. No one ever visited him except salespeople and the paper boy, and it was too late for either of those. The only acquaintance who might conceivably drop in was Britt, and she would call first. Nor could he think of a reason why she would do so, instead of waiting to speak to him at the office in the morning.

He strode to the door, probing for the psychic emissions of whoever waited there. The moment he touched the knob, the vibrations resonated through him.

From the other side of the door he felt something that could emanate from no ordinary visitor – a sensation of pressure, as if the air were about to implode around him. "Who's there?" He detested the harsh tone that betrayed his apprehension.

"Sylvia." The thickening tension in the atmosphere vanished at once, like a bubble popping. "Let me in, Roger."

Astonished at hearing her voice, Roger opened the door. "Come in." He stepped aside for her. She said nothing while he closed and bolted the door.

Physically she hadn't changed. Her black hair, now dripping wet, still flowed wild over her shoulders. She wore black slacks, with a matching sweater plastered to her breasts by the rain. Just before she stepped into the dim light of the living room, her eyes flared with pinpoints of red. Her aura, however, looked pale from stress, and she moved like a skittish cat. Her lips curled back from her teeth as she glared at him. "Doing all right for yourself, Roger? Are you nicely settled? Not going hungry?"

Her bitter sarcasm bewildered him. By now, he would have expected her anger to cool. And why would she make a visit, after the lapse of a month, just to snarl at him? "Won't you sit down and talk calmly, Sylvia? I have to admit I'm glad to see you – I only wish that were mutual."

"Calmly!" She flung her arms wide in exasperation, scattering raindrops. She did stalk over to the fireplace, though, and plant herself on the couch. "You don't have the slightest idea what you did!"

"No, I don't. I'm sorry for the way I mishandled my part in Sandor's case, but I did what seemed right, considering what I knew at the time." He recalled the police officer murdered in the attempted arrest. "I had to try to stop him. How could I just ignore what I knew?"

"Oh, Roger, you sound so damn self-righteous!"

He stood facing her, his arms folded. "Why are you here?" The turmoil of her emotions gave him shooting pains behind the eyes. "Let me get you a drink – brandy, perhaps."

She nodded, some of her tension fading. "I came straight here from the Holiday Inn – stopped just long enough to drop off my luggage. Get me that drink, and I'll tell you exactly what you did."

When Roger emerged from the kitchen with a pair of brandy snifters, he found Sylvia leaning back on the couch in a more relaxed position. She even moved over to make room for him. After a swallow of the brandy, she said, "Not what I really want, but it'll do. I've left Boston permanently."

"What?" A fresh pain stabbed his forehead. "You're moving here?"

She gave him a wry smile. "Don't like the idea of sharing your territory? I can't blame you. Don't worry, I'm not planning to settle down. Just a few weeks, to rest – if I can. I've been a nomad for the past month."

"Since I left?"

"Not long after that, and it's your fault." Her anger flared again, quickly squelched. "Sure, you didn't know what you were doing, so I shouldn't be so hard on you. But I'm the one who's being hounded."

Roger took a long drink of his brandy. Its fire did nothing for the anxiety that roiled within him. "By whom? What in Heaven's name are you talking about?"

"Neil Sandor," she said.

He stared at her, beyond surprise. "That is my fault?"

Sylvia's shoulders twitched irritably. "I told you, he thinks I turned him in, forced him into hiding. Remember Rico?"

"The boy you were obsessed with. Of course."

"Neil killed him – in a very messy way." Roger felt acid rising in his throat. "Ever since, I've been running from Neil. I can't stay in one city more than a few days. He shadows me, sticks to my trail – and kills most of the donors I've used. Roger, he killed Katrina! Just to prove he was serious!" She almost sobbed the words.

Her desperation lashed Roger like an icy wind. He clasped her hand, projecting a cloud of warmth as he would for a human sufferer. "Sooner or later, he has to give up, doesn't he? There must be a limit to his revenge."

Sylvia shook off Roger's hand. "You don't know him. I used to hunt with him, before I found out what he's like. This kind of thing *amuses* him. Even if he got over hating me for what he thinks I did, he'd keep this up for the fun of it."

"I simply can't fathom that."

"Of course you can't! You're too human – in all the wrong ways! Well, I came here to make bloody certain you know precisely what you've done to me! Not to mention all those people who've been killed, which you probably consider more important."

With guilt twisting like a snake in his vitals, Roger tried to protest. "If he hadn't chosen them, it would have been someone else. From all you've said, it sounds as if he's addicted to vio-lence."

"Brilliant diagnosis, Doctor." She abandoned her half-finished brandy to pace across the room and back. "Frankly, I don't care about his addiction. All I want is for him to satisfy it somewhere far away from me."

The offhand remark chilled Roger. "Human lives mean nothing to you. You only want security for yourself."

She leaned against the fireplace, her gaze challenging him. "You're beginning to catch on. That upsets you, doesn't it? Well, it isn't completely true. I do care about some ephemerals – my pets, like Rico. I didn't want him hurt. But, yes, my own safety comes first."

Standing up, Roger glared back at her. "So you led Sandor here. You led him straight to me."

"Not intentionally," Sylvia said. "I may have shaken him – I hope so. There's a chance he didn't follow me this far. Under-stand, Roger – I still like you, for some crazy reason. I won't betray you to Neil. Dark Powers, I could have saved myself all this trouble by giving him your name a month ago."

Roger sensed that she spoke the truth. "Then what are your plans?"

Sylvia shrugged. "Open. I came to Maryland to, well, accuse you, but also to warn you, just in case. Now that's done. After a few weeks here, or longer if Neil doesn't catch up with me, I'll decide where to go next. Maybe Baltimore or Washington, close enough so we can be friends without crowding each other." Her smile hinted at memories of their nights together in Massa-chusetts, and Roger caught himself smiling back. If nothing else, Sylvia provided something he'd lacked all his life, a companion with whom he didn't need to guard his secret.

Abruptly her expression turned grim. "But understand this, too. I won't shield you at the risk of my own life."

ROGER'S PALE, slender fingers drummed impatiently on his notebook as he half-listened to the ramblings of the man seated in front of him. He forced himself to stop; it wouldn't do to show nervousness. The patient, a Navy Commander with close-trimmed brown hair, sitting tensely upright on the couch, deserved Roger's professional attention. Still, he had trouble imagining that Commander Ford's midlife crisis equaled his own in stress level.

Sylvia's arrival had thrown him into turmoil. Was Sandor still following her? Or was that her fear talking? After all, a vampire could just as well suffer neurotic fears – look at her religious phobia! – as a human being could. Roger turned cold inside at the thought of the killer's stalking his new home.

He decided to cut the session short; after all, it was Friday afternoon. A light touch on the wrist and a few whispered words eased the Commander, preconditioned by many previous sessions, into trance immediately. His muscles went limp; his breathing slowed. Roger picked up the rhythm of the man's heartbeat. He caught himself bending closer, until his face was only inches from the patient's. Despite years of practice, exercising his mesmeric power never failed to rouse his appetite. It would be so easy to close the gap –

No. Since the move, he had kept to his self-imposed discipline. He wouldn't spoil his record.

Roger drew back until the tumult of his need subsided. After regaining control, he filled the patient's mind with suggestions of tranquil self-confidence. A moment later the man left. Before locking up for the weekend, Roger spent a few minutes in relaxation exercises, which forced the knots out of his limbs without touching more than the fringe of his mental agitation.

In the reception room he ran into Britt, also on her way out. "I noticed Commander Ford leaving," she said. "Remarkable improvement in so short a time. How do you do it?"

"Black magic," Roger snarled.

"Not feeling well?" she asked in an impersonal tone, though her green eyes scanned him with more than casual interest.

"I'm fine, damn it!" Roger caught himself, realizing this touchiness encouraged further curiosity. "Sorry, Britt. I'm just tired – long week." "Tired" was always an acceptable excuse for bad temper; a reply of "hungry" would provoke unanswerable questions. He wondered why he didn't resent Britt's friendly inquiries as much as he had Dr. Lloyd's. *Because Lloyd was a sixty-two-year-old man with hypertension and a scraggly mustache*, he reminded himself, not a beautiful woman almost my own age, in perfect health.

Since Marcia, their receptionist, had already left, Roger and Britt locked the suite. Roger heard silence from behind the other closed office doors as they walked down the dusty hall. He was anxious to get out of the building without further conversation, but his associate wanted to ask his advice on a new case. "This probably isn't the time to discuss it," she said, "but this particular patient shows some fascinating variations from the classic pattern."

"Of what?" Roger said automatically as they boarded the elevator. Remembering his resolve to discourage conversation, he corrected himself. "No, don't tell me now. Better wait until Mon-day at lunch." Lunching together to discuss their work wasn't un-usual, though it was generally Britt's work, not Roger's. Despite his vow to keep her at a distance, when she made the overtures, he usually proved too weak to resist.

Emerging from the building into the late afternoon sun, Roger donned polarized sunglasses and headed for his car. Only Britt's aging

VW bug still shared the parking lot with the Citroen. For a moment he watched her retreating figure, wondering (not for the first time) how her titian hair would look released from the tightly coiled knot in which she wore it, to harmonize with dress-for-success three-piece suits. Decidedly unprofessional of him, he reflected, and probably sexist as well. Not to mention lethal to his peace of mind.

After turning on his ignition, he sat for a moment waiting for the car's air conditioner to relieve some of the accumulated heat. Glancing over at Britt's beetle, he noticed she hadn't driven away either. Instead she stood in back of the car with the hood up and scowled at the exposed engine. Roger sighed. This wasn't the first time he'd seen her clash with the VW's cranky temperament. Now that she'd finished paying off her med school loans, why didn't she buy a vehicle worthy of her professional status?

He got out, leaving the motor running. When he walked up to Britt, she said, "The generator died. Knew I should have put the darn thing in the shop last week." She glanced down at the engine, waves of heat shimmering around it, with a wry smile. "And why am I staring at this contraption as if I knew what to do about it?" She banged the hood shut. "I'll have to unlock the office to call triple-A and a cab. Well, I wasn't doing anything this evening anyway." She started for the building.

Though Roger did have an appointment, one he wouldn't break, that wasn't until nine. Eager as he was to get home, out of the sun, he could hardly leave his associate stranded. Catching up with her, he said, "Never mind the cab. I'll wait with you and drive you home. It's not far out of my way."

In the elevator he asked, "Why don't you trade in that superannuated pregnant roller skate? It's more trouble than it's worth, surely."

"You won't laugh? It's a matter of security. I don't *like* getting used to a new car. I don't even enjoy shopping for one – too much of a muchness of choices." She tilted her head, watching his reaction with a half-smile. "After all, I'm entitled to my little neurotic quirks. We all have them."

"If that's all it is, I'll help you shop. Meanwhile, make your calls so we can get out of here."

"I'll second that." They'd reached the office by now. After Britt had finished her arrangements, they went back downstairs to wait for the tow truck.

Unable to avoid looking directly at her, Roger noticed a pin on the lapel of her cafe-au-lait jacket. It announced, "If you're not part of the solution, you're part of the precipitate."

"Where on earth did you get that? It doesn't quite go with the ensemble."

"From a teenage patient who picked it up at a science fiction convention," she said. "In fact, the very boy I wanted to discuss with you. Roger, I think I may have found a genuine poltergeist."

"Still dabbling in that lunatic fringe research?"

She laughed, unperturbed, as usual, by his rudeness. "When the impossible is eliminated –"

"Spare me Sherlock Holmes! I much prefer Lord Peter Wimsey, anyhow. You'll have to go to considerable lengths to convince me you really have eliminated natural causes. Fraud or hallucination would be the rational person's first hypothesis."

"Meaning I'm irrational? That's just why I want you for a sounding board; you're such a hidebound skeptic. The ideal Devil's advocate."

Roger knew very well that Britt's enthusiasm for psychic research didn't make her credulous. She would exhaust every natural possibility before resorting to the supernatural. Never-theless he was about to fling out another provocative remark, just for the pleasure of listening to her rebuttal, when the tow truck pulled up. He was relieved, for his eyes ached from the sun despite the tinted glasses.

After the auto club's truck had left with Britt's crippled vehicle, she said to Roger as they got into the Citroen, "How about letting me reward you with dinner? I've got filet mignon in the freezer, and it's just as easy to thaw two as one."

Having dropped Britt off the last time her car was in the shop, he needed no directions. He drove down Ridgely Avenue and turned left on Taylor toward the Naval Academy. His first impulse was to refuse the dinner invitation. At nine a young female patient, acting under post-hypnotic suggestion, would arrive at his townhouse. He wouldn't risk missing her. On the other hand, Britt offered a way to kill that uninviting stretch of hours until then. "All right," he finally said. "We can hash over your `poltergeist' case." *So much for not socializing with my partner. Turning into a world-class rationalizer, aren't I?*

"You mean you plan to slice it into gory fragments," she said. "You may not find that so easy."

By the time they reached Britt's condo, billed as a "luxury flat" in a renovated turn-of-the-century building in the historic district just outside the Academy's Maryland Avenue gate, Roger's daylight-driving headache had grown to maximum intensity. He followed his companion up to the second floor, breathing an audible sigh of relief upon stepping from the unseasonably warm fall afternoon into the cool dimness of the apartment. When Britt started to open the drapes, he said, "Could you leave them, please? I've got a bit of a headache."

"Of course. Care for a drink?" She deposited her briefcase and shoulder bag on the nearest chair and headed for the wet bar.

"Dry martini," he said, not because he particularly cared for the flavor, but because that drink was strong enough to have some effect on him, however slight. In his present mood he wanted to dull his senses a little.

After handing him a martini and mixing herself a wine cooler, Britt transferred two steaks from the freezer to the micro-wave. "How do you like yours?" she asked from across the semi-circular counter marking the borders of the free-standing kitchen.

He sipped his drink and settled on the couch. The living room furniture, though too armless and angular for his taste, had a restful color scheme of pastel blues and greens. His headache began to fade. "Very rare – barely charred around the edges."

"Oh, you want it to bleed."

He took a larger swallow of the chilled drink. "Precisely. And no seasonings, please, except a little salt. Especially not garlic – violent allergy."

Britt took a chair across from him. "And an unusual one. You've mentioned your food sensitivities before. It must be limiting sometimes."

"Not necessarily. I'm comfortable as long as I avoid the things that trigger my problems."

"Sunlight, too?"

Roger's startled reaction barely escaped tipping the martini onto his lap. "What?"

"Well, I can hardly miss noticing those sunglasses, even when it's pouring rain." She got up in response to the microwave's beep. "What else shall we have? Baked potato and salad are quick."

"Nothing but steak for me," he said. "I can't handle fiber."

Britt paused to replace one of the two potatoes she'd picked out of a basket next to the refrigerator. "That *is* an interesting complex of sensitivities. Your problem with sunlight – some variety of xeroderma pigmentosum?" After a moment's thought, she answered her own question. "No, it can't be XP, or you couldn't go out during the day at all, or even face full-strength indoor lighting."

Blast – he should have realized Britt wouldn't leave a medical topic alone. She had a disconcerting ability to draw him out. "It might be a less severe variant of the syndrome, for all I know. But my parents weren't able to learn much about my condition, medically. They discovered the optimum treatments mostly by trial and error." That summary was more or less true, anyway.

Her piercing green eyes followed him while he emptied his glass and mixed another drink, then leaned on the counter to watch her assembling lettuce and other vegetables for her salad. "I'd love to hear more about it, but obviously you don't want to talk." Her tone suggested that she was tabling, not abandoning, the subject. "Can you drink orange juice?"

*Not my first choice.* "Yes, that would be fine. I'm afraid I'm not an interesting dinner guest." He glanced at his watch. "And I can't stay long tonight. I have a – prior commitment."

Britt paused in her methodical slicing of tomatoes. She gave him a mildly surprised look across the counter, her eyes nearly level with his. "A date – you?"

"Not exactly." Why didn't he want her to think he was involved with anyone? It wasn't as if he could risk becoming intimate with her.

"Oh, Roger," she laughed, "don't you ever loosen up?"

"In my own way," he said, as stiffly as before.

"Catholic or not, at heart you're a dyed in the wool Boston Puritan. I know that `Haavuhd' persona impresses the patients, but you don't have to *live* it. I think I've guessed the secret of your therapeutic success – you terrify the people into health."

He could think of no adequate reply to this remark. *If she only knew.*

"Before I forget," she said, "I don't think we've talked about Thanksgiving week."

"What about it?"

"I always close the office for the entire week, because I spend the Saturday before Thanksgiving through the Sunday after at my sister's. She's in Long Beach right now. I've told you about her, right? – husband in the Navy."

Roger nodded. "I'd just as soon keep my regular schedule through Wednesday of that week."

She poured oil and vinegar on her salad and tossed it. "Up to you, of course."

"Well, I'm not going anywhere, and I'd rather work than sit at home. Food-centered holidays don't have much appeal for me."

"No family to visit?" she said.

"Only a few second and third cousins."

Britt, obviously sensing his lack of enthusiasm for personal conversation, changed the subject. "About that boy I've started treating," she said as she set the table, "not only is he unusual as the focus of poltergeist phenomena – the catalyst is more often a pubescent girl – the somnambulism doesn't fit, either. Also, his episodes seem to include flashes of demonstrable precognition."

"Demonstrable as anything but reading back present knowledge into past ambiguous remarks? You actually believe in that sort of thing, don't you? As a youthful aberration, it's excusable, but I'd think that a professional in her mid-thirties would have outgrown it." He saw no contradiction between exer-cising his own powers and disbelieving the phenomena popularly called "supernatural." The very fact that he could control those powers demystified them for him.

He watched Britt placing the steaks under the broiler. For a few seconds he toyed with the fantasy of slaking his thirst here and now. The allure of a mind like hers – But it had to remain a fantasy.

Setting out her salad and Roger's juice, Britt motioned for him to join her at the table. "Just because I don't have time for research in private practice doesn't mean I've given up. If I could be the one to produce objective, repeatable verification of psi phenomena, wild talents –"

"By its very nature, doesn't that sort of thing tend to be non-repeatable?" He sipped the orange juice, particularly unappealing while blood-hunger nagged at him. "It's a faint hope, anyway, since all the most interesting 'supernatural' events in the literature have been exposed as fraud or, at best, honest confusion. Look at Bridey Murphy."

"Not conclusive," Britt retorted. "Besides, I don't specialize in reincarnation."

"Surprising, what with your belief in collective memory. Your readiness to pay attention to this tripe obviously springs from your unfortunate theoretical orientation. Mystical Jungian mumbo-jumbo."

"More humane than your Freudian mumbo-jumbo." The exchange, repeated countless times, had already jelled into a ritual.

Britt broke off the duel to serve the steaks. With an exaggerated flourish of her wine glass, she said, "Laugh all you like. They laughed at Galileo – they laughed at Columbus –"

Roger eagerly attacked the nearly raw meat. "And they were right. His calculations were off by several thousand miles."

Britt went on to explain in detail her presumptive evidence for authentic poltergeist and precognitive events. Roger was almost sorry when the meal – topped off by vanilla ice cream drizzled with creme de menthe – ended. Close contact with a superior mind was delightfully stimulating. Almost too stimu-lating.

After dinner Britt persuaded him, against his better judg-ment, to linger on the couch with a cup of strong coffee. "Then again, speaking of psychic powers," she said, "what do you think of mosquitoes?"

"I seldom do. They seem to find me unappetizing." Perhaps bloodsuckers didn't prey on their own kind.

"Lucky you – they love me. I must have delicious blood."

*I'm sure you do.* He took a long swallow of the hot coffee, wishing it could scald away his thirst.

"My point is that some people positively attract mos-quitoes," Britt said.

He gave her a puzzled look. "If there's a connection with Fortean `wild talents,' I'm missing it."

"Haven't you ever met people who seem to materialize the little beasties out of thin air, when nobody else notices them at all?"

He smiled indulgently. "So?"

"I theorize that these individuals project a subliminal force that draws biting insects – perhaps causing them to teleport from distant locations. A kind of psychic pheromone." Only the sparkle in her eyes revealed that she was joking. "Think of it as a negative talent. What I need to do is set up a statistical study of the number of mosquitoes per victim, corrected for age, sex, state of health –"

"And you'll discover that the attraction factor is a purely physical pheromone," Roger said, going along with the joke.

"To rule that out, I'll have to seal the subject in a sterile room, so when a swarm of mosquitoes appears out of nowhere, like the cloud over that man in `Li'l Abner' –" She trailed off into giggles. In spite of his physical discomfort, Roger laughed with her.

Frowning at the coffee she'd sloshed into her saucer, Britt set the cup and saucer on the table. She leaned back to stretch an arm across the top of the couch, her fingers lightly grazing the nape of Roger's neck. "Too bad you have to rush off. How un-breakable is that date of yours?"

His spine tingled at her touch. "Set in concrete." If only it didn't have to be that way.

Britt edged closer to him. Roger held perfectly still, to avoid making any move she might read as encouragement. "How's the headache?" Her fingertips massaged the taut muscles of his neck and shoulder blades.

He hadn't given it a thought for the past hour. "Better."

Her mouth quirked in amusement at his curt reply. "Then stop looking as if you're about to be tortured on the rack."

Had she no idea what she was doing to him? Of course she did – an experienced woman like Britt wouldn't flirt without full awareness of consequences.

How experienced? An unexpected flash of jealousy seared through Roger. Ridiculous – he knew Britt had no intimate male friends and, in fact, restricted her social activities mainly to career-related events. Anyway, he had no right to speculate about her private life.

Somehow she had inched so close that her breath tickled his cheek. He smelled mint, vanilla, coffee, and her unique scent, enhanced by only a whisper of Chanel. (He'd firmly impressed on both Britt and Marcia his allergic reaction to heavy perfumes.) *I could have her right now.* What he'd pigeonholed as impossible suddenly loomed before him as a live temptation. If she desired him, too –

*No! She is not prey!* He mentally rehearsed all the reasons why he could neither take her unaware nor – unthinkable! – tell her the truth.

Meanwhile, Britt's eyes searched his for cues. Interpreting his hesitation as consent, she closed the gap and brushed his lips with hers. Electricity zapped through him. He didn't dare re-spond. Losing himself in the kiss would overturn his self-control like a rowboat in a storm-lashed river. Yet he couldn't force himself to pull away, either. He put one arm lightly around her and passively accepted her exploratory nibbles.

When Britt's tongue probed the corners of his mouth, he knew he had to stop her. Suppose the razor edge of his teeth nicked her tongue, and he tasted her blood? He wrenched himself out of the loose embrace and checked his watch. "I must go now." He hoped she couldn't hear the unsteadiness of his breathing.

Britt sat back, hands locked behind her head, coolly gazing at Roger. "I don't interest you?"

*Interest!* What a feeble word for how she affected him! "That's beside the point." He stood up before she could renew her attack. "We work together."

Britt, too, got to her feet, smiling ruefully at what she clearly considered a lame excuse. "Have you forgotten we run the office? Not to mention that we have only one employee? Why should we enforce fraternization rules against ourselves?"

"Any – intimacy – would make a professional relationship too difficult." He started for the door.

"Has anyone ever told you how exasperating you are?" He felt indignation sizzling beneath her calm surface.

"Now and then, yes." Safe on the threshold, he said, "Thank you for dinner. I'll see you Monday."

"Fine." Her green eyes glinted dangerously. He could almost hear her thoughts: *We're not finished with this!*

Twilight was well advanced when Roger's Citroen crept past the Naval Academy and turned toward the Severn. Traffic became lighter and faster-moving, only to grind to a halt at the old Severn River bridge. The blasted drawbridge stood open. Roger gritted his teeth in frustration. No sailor himself, he felt no sympathy for the boating hobbyists and considered it an outrage that their frivolous pastime was allowed to disrupt the serious business of the town.

*Calm down,* he told himself. *There's still plenty of time until nine. Good grief, I might as well be begging for ulcers and hypertension!*

After the bridge traffic unclogged, he made it to his condominium near St. Margaret's Road without further delay. The developer had let plenty of trees stand untouched around the semicircular townhouse complex, built well back from the narrow, winding side road. The quiet and shade began to quell Roger's irritation as soon as he pulled into the parking lot. While unlocking his door he felt a sudden prickle of uneasiness, like eyes focused on the back of his head. He turned to scan the parked cars and the surrounding woods. Nothing. With a shake of his head he stepped inside. No unfamiliar scent hung in the air.

Yet he couldn't cast off the impression that something was about to go wrong. He ordered himself to stop thinking nonsense. As he had told Britt, he didn't believe in premonitions. Simple tension, that must be his problem.

After a cold shower, he dressed in a royal blue lounging jacket and poured a glass of milk. The more bulk nourishment he consumed before the assignation, the more easily he could hold the his donor's blood loss to a minimum. He had to force himself to sit down and drink the milk slowly rather than prowling around the house in a fever of impatience. Next he drew out as long as possible the routine of preparing the bedroom – red satin throw cover on the bed, fresh candles on the dresser to shed a muted, eerie glow.

He'd adopted Sylvia's suggestion about "atmosphere." Experimentation had proved her right; the decor did enhance his satisfaction, allowing him to take a smaller fluid volume from a donor. Still, he felt like an idiot in this setting. Why not go all the way and wear a Bela Lugosi cape?

He knew he would forget his self-consciousness the moment his visitor walked into the room. He'd chosen Alice Kovak, a twenty-year-old community college student under treatment for depression. She lived at home with her parents and older brother, who viewed her lively imagination with stolidly blue-collar suspicion. At present she was between antidepressants, so her blood would taste pure. She would park about a mile away and walk to his condo. After a delicious half-hour, she would return to her car and drive home, remembering only vague restlessness assuaged by a long, solitary ride. He salivated at the thought.

He loaded a Wagner cassette into the stereo and paced around the living room, hardly aware of the music. What could be keeping the girl? Glancing at his watch, he found it was only two minutes after nine. Seemed later. *This has got to be the last time with her,* he admonished himself, *so I'd better make it good.*

He hadn't planned to prey on patients here at all, but he hadn't yet learned his new territory very well. Ordering a patient to his home under post-hypnotic suggestion seemed the safest course, until he developed fresh hunting strategies. *That excuse has about worn out, hasn't it? Next time I'll feed on a stranger.* He reminded himself that this would be only the second time he'd consumed human blood since leaving Boston. Maybe his tapering-off program would succeed.

He circled the room a few more times, then strode to the window to peer between the drapes. There she was, finally. A slim blonde, Alice wore a pale pink dress, swirling around her knees, and clutched a shawl around her neck. *Funny, it seems too warm for that.* Watching her cross the road, Roger was struck by something odd in her gait. She almost staggered. When she came closer, he noticed that her aura was faded and murky.

As soon as she reached the door, he opened it and clasped her free hand to draw her inside. The other hand kept the shawl tightly wrapped around her shoulders and neck. Trance glazed her eyes – an unexpectedly deep trance. The perfume of fresh blood wafted from her.

"Alice?" He gently pried her fingers away from the shawl. At that touch she let it drop. Under it she wore a scarf – soaked bright red.

Roger abruptly released her. Fumbling at the scarf, she pulled it off and at the same instant crumpled to the floor.

Her lacerated throat bled copiously. Roger dug a handkerchief out of his pocket and pressed it to the wound. Too alarmed to think of his own thirst, he gazed into her eyes. The hypnotic bond compelled her. She relaxed, and the direct pressure slowed the bleeding. Given a prompt transfusion, she might live. Whatever had slashed her throat had missed the jugular and carotid.

He slid the shawl beneath her and lifted her to the couch, propping her feet on a cushion. "Alice, who did this?" Her eyes stared unresponsively, her consciousness slipping away. "Answer me!"

He picked up an emotion, a blend of lust and terror, not directed at him. "Don't know his name," she whispered. "Eyes –like yours."

Astonished, Roger let her fall into unconsciousness.

He had no time to analyze the implications, for Alice needed hospitalization. Imagine this happening in his living room! Yet in this case he owned no guilt. He had to hang onto that fact. What would he do if he were equally innocent in thought?

Examine her, then call for an ambulance. He drew a deep breath to steel himself for the ordeal. Why should the police suspect him, after all? Wasn't it natural for Alice, when attacked, to turn to her doctor for help? And if she lived, she would testify that Roger wasn't her assailant.

He picked up the phone and punched 911. After completing the call, he turned off the music and put the candles back in a bedroom drawer. He didn't want to leave any evidence that he'd been expecting a visitor.

WITHIN LESS than an hour the ambulance and police had come and gone. The IV had revived Alice enough to enable her to give a sketchy account of how she'd been driving around "to think things over," had stopped for a stroll in the woods, and had been attacked by a man whose face she couldn't recall. She'd set out for Roger's house, since she knew he lived close by. She claimed to remember nothing else.

As far as Roger could tell from analyzing the police of-ficers' reactions, they accepted his "innocent bystander" pose. He expected no further trouble. *That was damn close, though!* he reflected, his hands shaking as he poured a fresh glass of milk, liberally laced with brandy. Though his stomach protested the additional burden, he forced down the concoction for its tran-quilizing effect.

His head still reeled between pity for Alice and rage at her attacker. To rip out her throat and leave her to die! The atrocity, touching someone he knew, stirred Roger more deeply than the other assaults had. He felt responsible for the girl's condition, since her link with him must have drawn the ravisher. *Sandor – who else? Sylvia was right.*

And she had brought him here!

Meanwhile, on top of his major crime, the renegade had disrupted Roger's schedule. Roger frowned at his empty glass. His system still cried out for what it had been denied. He wouldn't risk taking a victim at random, not so close to home. Instead he went out to hunt animal prey. Several hours of strenuous hiking through the woods, along with the blood of a few rac-coons or opossums, might relieve his tension enough to let him rest the following day.

LATE SATURDAY afternoon the telephone's ring broke into Roger's sleep. Sometimes he wished he hadn't trained himself to wake at that stimulus. With a muttered curse, he picked up the receiver.

"Hello, Dr. Darvell," said a male voice. "How did you like last night's entertainment?"

Roger sat up. "Who is this?"

"Have you already forgotten what you did to me in Boston?" The voice didn't display anger; instead, it gloated.

Roger felt as if an icicle were stabbing through his temples. "Neil Sandor."

"And I thought it was little Sylvia! I should have known she didn't have the guts."

"What are you after, Sandor?"

"For now, just to watch you squirm – take my time and have fun with you."

Roger struggled to rein his anger. Losing control wouldn't help. "By attacking an innocent woman?"

"Innocent?" Sandor made the word sound like an obscene joke. "How was it? Didn't you enjoy my present? I got her primed and ready for you."

"I didn't –" Roger shut up, revolted at the thought of dis-cussing his habits with this psychopath.

"Not even a sip? Then you must be in bad shape by now. You've got a lot to learn if you actually passed up that luscious little –"

Roger slammed the phone down.

Trembling with fury, he dressed in a blind rush and stormed out of the house to the car. He didn't realize where he meant to go, until he found himself pulling up to the Holiday Inn near Route 50 in Annapolis. He needed answers from Sylvia – right now.

## Chapter 9

WHEN HE KNOCKED on the door of Sylvia's motel room, she mumbled a protest in a voice thick with sleep.

"I don't care how early it is," he said through the door. "Let me in, if you don't want me to shout it in the middle of the corridor."

Her sluggish footsteps approached. "You wouldn't. You're the one who has to keep living here." But she was already unfastening the bolt.

Sylvia let him in and offered him a chair. Draped in a sheer nightgown, her hair a tangled mane, she curled up on the bed. "Did it take you this long to think up a rebuttal to what I said the other night? And if so, couldn't it wait until after dark?" She yawned.

"Sandor is here."

She froze in mid-stretch. "What happened?"

"He almost killed one of my patients." Roger narrated Friday night's events and repeated Sandor's message verbatim.

Staring at the wall, Sylvia murmured, "So he believes me now."

Roger felt like shaking her. "Why the devil wouldn't he? You came straight to me the moment you arrived here, so he must have followed you and then started watching me. If his paranormal perception is anything like yours, it couldn't have taken him long to discover my – oddity."

Sylvia focused on him. "Yes. And it must have been your – well, your shadow, you might say – on the girl that led Neil to attack her. We can tell when someone has served as a donor – it shows in the aura. And people who've been touched are awfully attractive. Maybe he mesmerized your girl and found out she belonged to you."

"And that made her fair game? Is that how your kind think?" Even now, he didn't think "our kind." He wasn't like Sylvia; he couldn't sprout wings and levitate.

"Only for an outlaw. Taking somebody else's prey is taboo. That's why Neil would see it as the perfect revenge." Stripping off her gown, she stepped over to an open suitcase and picked out a selection of garments. "Roger, I'm sorry he's done this to you. On the other hand, I won't deny that I'm glad he isn't after me anymore."

Roger lunged across the room, grabbed her by the shoulders, and spun her around. "Not good enough, damn it! You *led* him to me! I've had more than enough of your evasiveness."

Dropping the clothes she was holding, Sylvia placed her hands lightly on his chest. "All right, Roger. What do you want from me?"

"I can't deal with this in a vacuum, and you claim you aren't allowed to give out information. Very well – put me in touch with the other vampires."

She projected a flare of resistance, instantly quenched. "So now you believe they exist?"

They had argued that point too much already. "Introduce me to them."

She slumped in his grasp. "Only fair, I guess. Listen, Roger, I can't do it on my own. But I suspect, from the way my advisor reacted when I mentioned you, that the elders do know about you already. I'll contact my advisor and pass on your request."

"Tonight."

He sensed her complete surrender. "Yes, tonight."

DRIVING AWAY from the motel, Roger shook with pent-up frustration. Sandor, damn him to hell, had been right about one thing. Roger's body, accustomed to regular "doses" of human blood, was in violent revolt.

*I can handle it. I've abstained longer than this many times.*

That reminder didn't ease the burning in the throat and the cramps in his stomach. For an hour he drove the crisscrossing back roads of the county, ignoring speed limits. He almost hoped for a confrontation to discharge his aggression, but, ironically, no radar trap netted him. Finally he returned to Annapolis and parked downtown at the city dock. He knew resorting to a casual pickup so near home was dangerous. For once, though, need overpowered caution.

It didn't take long to find a solitary woman who responded to his practiced seduction technique. Together they walked away from the crowded, brightly lit tourist district to a thicket of trees on the Naval Academy campus, where Roger lulled her into a sensual dream. He drank deeply and went home satisfied.

HE OPENED HIS eyes upon dense gray fog. He lay, not in bed, but on mossy ground. Above him spread the branches of a decaying, hollowed-out tree. Alice Kovak stepped out of the fog, a bloody hole gaping in her neck. She raised a pointed stake in her clenched hands. He tried to leap up. Someone held both his arms pinned to the ground. Looking wildly from side to side, he saw Sylvia at his right, the woman he had just drunk from at his left. The woman's neck, like Alice's, bled copiously.

"Why?" he tried to scream. The word came out as a faint whisper. "I didn't do that to you."

"He's lying," Sylvia growled. "He's a traitor – kill him!"

The stake swept down to pierce his chest.

ROGER WOKE TO the ringing of the phone. For once he welcomed the interruption. He checked the clock. He'd gone to sleep between four and five a.m., and it was now six thirty.

When he answered the phone, Sylvia's voice said, "All right, I made that call, and I'm waiting for an answer. I should hear before tonight. Want me to come over then?"

"Yes, please do." The dream was already dissolving, except for a confused miasma of guilt and terror.

"I can hardly believe what my advisor told me." Sylvia sounded almost childlike in her excitement. "He said I'd be getting a call from Lord Volnar."

Her awed tone reminded Roger of the way his late mother would have spoken about an audience with the Pope. "I gather that's something special?"

"Lord Volnar is – well, you'll find out. He spent a lot of time with me when I was growing up, almost a co-advisor, but he's very busy, and I hardly ever see him now." Roger didn't need empathic contact with Sylvia to guess that she had, in human terms, a crush on Volnar. "I never expected him to take a personal interest in you. Roger, there must be something important about you that I've never suspected."

Roger discounted that suggestion. Sylvia was jumping to conclusions with little more data than he himself possessed. Besides, even if true, "importance" wasn't necessarily a good thing. In this context, "important" could mean "dangerous." Roger didn't dare assume this Lord Volnar's attitude toward him would be favorable.

"LORD VOLNAR will contact you sometime in the next few days." Sylvia paused to lean against a tree, absent-mindedly shredding a pine cone. She and Roger were strolling together in the woods behind his townhouse. "I can't say exactly when. He's the oldest of the elders; he has his own way of accomplishing things."

Roger glanced up at the moon through the branches, inhaling deeply the sharp evergreen scent and the richer smell of moist leaves. "You seem relieved."

"I am! You can't imagine how glad I am to have this whole mess off my hands."

"Just like that?" said Roger, irritated at her readiness to dump her trouble with Sandor onto him. "What will you do now, run away again?"

Sylvia gave him a tolerant half-smile. "You can't goad me into throwing another temper tantrum at you. My guardian said I should have known better than to overreact to your confused behavior, so I'm going to be reasonable if it chokes me."

"Thank you," he said acidly. They resumed walking.

"As for leaving, he thinks I should, right away, but I can't take the idea of – well, yes, running again. So I'll hang around for a few weeks first. After that – well, I passed through a quiet little town near Albuquerque where I could really enjoy living. I may try that for a year or two."

Exasperating as she was much of the time, Roger felt let down at the thought of losing Sylvia's company again. "Well, I wish you luck."

"I have a special reason for staying here the next couple of weeks. I could go back to the Nevada headquarters for this, but somehow I don't want to accept anybody at random for my first time."

"What are you getting at?" He noticed Sylvia's aura fluctuating, and her scent held a musky undercurrent he hadn't sensed before. Was she ill? From the remarks she'd dropped, Roger thought vampires were immune to disease.

"I have something to ask you." She paused, turning to face him. In the silence between them the rustling of hidden animals and the chirps of crickets stirred the air. "Damn, this is hard to say. Any other male of our kind would take it as a routine favor, but you grew up with human beliefs about body functions."

"For all you know, I'm not your kind. Did it occur to you that your Lord Volnar might want to get rid of a human being who endangers your race by behaving the way I do?" Roger had not formulated the theory this way before, but now that he did, it sounded chillingly plausible.

Sylvia shrugged off the suggestion. "I'll worry about that later. The point is, there's no one else in Maryland except Neil, and I'd rather die." She reached up to twist a spray of leaves off a tree branch. "What I'm getting at is that I'm about to enter my first estrus. I recognize the symptoms I was taught about. It'll hit soon, within a week at most."

Stunned, Roger said, "You're asking me to –"

Sylvia nodded. "Mate with me. You don't have to worry about pregnancy, because the first heat period is never fertile. I've got to have somebody, I won't take Neil, and better you than a human male – I *like* you."

He cut her off. "Out of the question. Look, Sylvia, even if I didn't have – stuffy as it may sound to you – moral reservations, I don't –" he evaded her eyes. "I told you haven't been capable of ejaculation for almost twenty years."

"Oh, don't worry, that's normal. If you really are one of us, you will be when the time comes."

Flushing with embarrassment, Roger didn't pursue that point. Sylvia's nails grazed his cheek, coaxing him to meet her pleading gaze. Sensing what it cost her to make the request, he didn't have the heart to refuse outright. "I'll think about it. I can't make any such decision until I know more about this race you claim I belong to."

That answer contented her for the moment. Declining her invitation to hunt, he left her gliding among the trees, nostrils flared, every sense extended in search of warm-blooded prey.

ROGER STARED IN shock at the second page of Monday morning's paper. The headline shrilled, "Vampire Killer?" What-ever sense of well-being lingered from Saturday night's feast instantly crumbled to dust.

"A woman identified as Ellen Soames, age 22, was found dead early Sunday morning on the steps of the Naval Academy Chapel. . . ."

The story went on with the customary sensational drivel about peculiar throat wounds and massive blood loss. Roger skimmed it, thinking of the woman he had left drowsing on the grass near the chapel. She'd been about the right age and had given her name as Ellen. No possible doubt. He hadn't lacerated her neck, much less left her bleeding to death.

He knew who had. So Sandor's call hadn't been a bluff; he meant to pursue his revenge. And an effective one – it occurred to Roger that this crime, unlike the first, endangered him. Someone might remember seeing him with the dead woman.

Roger silently damned his own carelessness. His undisci-plined appetite had thrown another victim into Sandor's clutches. How long would the persecution continue? Roger had a night-marish vision of patients staggering into his office with bleeding wounds several days a week. Neither his career nor his sanity would long survive.

Lingering to mull over the article made him later than normal in getting to work, but Britt intercepted him anyway. While he poured a cup of the double-strength coffee Marcia had made for him, in a pot separate from the weaker brew the two women favored, Britt said, "I lucked into a pair of tickets for the Bach Meistersingers at St. Anne's Sunday night. Want to go with me?"

"Very well." He'd done so once before and enjoyed the music, as well as enjoying Britt's company entirely too much.

"And relax, I won't bite," she whispered, following him into his office.

He guessed the tickets were partly a pretext for Marcia's benefit. Sure enough, as soon as Britt had shut the door behind her, she changed the subject. "I heard about that patient of yours who was attacked Friday," she said without preamble. "Terrible thing, especially hitting so close." He heard more speculation than sympathy in her voice.

"How did you hear?" So far as he knew, the police hadn't released Alice's name to the local media.

"I have a friend in the State's Attorney's office," Britt said. "And have you seen this morning's paper? Another woman was assaulted the same way over the weekend – only that one died."

"I don't want to discuss it," Roger growled, pretending to be engrossed in unpacking his briefcase.

"Well, I do," Britt said, leaning against his desk, arms folded, "and who better to listen than you? I have some ideas on the subject that might interest you."

"I doubt it." Confound it, why wouldn't she take rudeness for an answer?

"Did you know there were two similar killings in Baltimore within the past ten days?"

Roger flinched. Now that she mentioned it, he recalled noticing headlines about such crimes. "I try to avoid reading that sort of thing."

"They present some intriguing angles."

He raised his eyes to hers, strongly tempted to use the hyp-notic force he'd sworn never to inflict on her. "Can't you grasp that I don't find the incident pleasant to dwell on?"

"No use evading it," she said. "Physician, heal thyself. I pre-scribe a long talk over lunch."

If he didn't agree, she would give him no peace and might become actively suspicious of his reluctance. "All right, lunch. Now, I have a patient in ten minutes. Will you please let me get to work?"

IN THE UNGLAMOROUS milieu of a bargain steak house, Britt unfolded her speculations while Roger nibbled halfheartedly at what the menu optimistically called prime rib. "As soon as I saw the report about the murder on the Academy, I remembered those Baltimore crimes. The m.o. is too similar for coincidence."

"I never suspected you had such low tastes. This is worse than dabbling in the occult."

"Insults won't sidetrack me, so don't bother," she said, etching a grid in her swordfish filet with the fork tines.

"Your hypothesis is that it's the same criminal. What about it?"

"This morning I called my classmate from Johns Hopkins in the State's Attorney's office and blackmailed some information out of him." She hesitated before adding, "Off the record and confidential, of course."

"Of course." Roger felt a tingle of excitement along his nerves, despite the threat to his own security.

"My friend says the name `vampire killer' isn't just some journalist's fevered fantasy. All the wounds were made by human teeth, only not quite human. There are anomalies."

"What are you getting at?"

"What would you say to fractures on some of the victims, apparently made by bare hands, but requiring abnormal strength? Or some unidentifiable organic compounds in the saliva found in the wounds?" She gleefully speared a chunk of fish and savored it while waiting for his reaction.

Roger kept his voice even, though anxiety squeezed his lungs. "Sorry, I can't bring myself to contemplate the facts with your enthusiasm. I prefer to view this kind of pathology from a distance – in textbooks."

"But is it pathology?" He gave her a sharp look. "Think, Roger! There are only two possible explanations. Either the at-tacks were made by a psychopath, a blood fetishist, possibly one who imagines himself to be a vampire, or –"

"Well? What's your alternative?"

"Are you ready for some extreme Jungian mumbo-jumbo?" She

leaned toward him across the table. "A real vampire."

He struggled to disguise his alarm as indignation. "Come on, Britt! This time you can't be serious."

"As Hamlet says –"

"And don't quote that tired line about 'more things in heaven and earth.' How can you possibly support this ridiculous notion?"

"The post mortem findings I mentioned –"

"Inconclusive," Roger said.

"But highly suggestive," she retorted. "Oh, I don't mean a walking corpse. Something anomalous and unknown to science, though. And I'm determined to meet this 'vampire.' My friend will give us first crack at whatever consultant work the State's Attorney needs done. If the criminal is what you think, just a Jack the Ripper variant, he'll make a once-in-a-lifetime case study. And if he really is a unique mutation or even something inhuman –"

"What would you do? Administer a battery of Rhine tests for clairvoyance?" The vision of Britt running standard psychological tests on a caged vampire struck Roger as almost humorous. If anyone could do it, she could. He wondered what Sandor would see in the Rorschach cards.

"Don't you understand?" Her eyes shone, her lunch forgot-ten. "Vampirism implies much more than paranormal abilities. It implies immortality. Can you imagine what it would mean to live for centuries as I am now? No aging, no mental decline, perpetual growth and discovery?"

"Britt, don't you see that if vampirism were a fact, it couldn't be like that at all?" He inwardly shuddered at the thought of Britt putting herself within reach of Sandor's claws and teeth in search of nonexistent "immortality." "If vampires existed, they'd have to fit into the natural order. Their life span wouldn't be transferable. You might as well expect a mosquito's bite to give you the power to fly."

"We'd never know without investigating, would we? And I'd give a lot for that reward." Shoving her plate out of the way, she leaned on her elbows, gazing into his eyes.

"As an investigator, your blatant bias disqualifies you. You *want* this nonsense to be true – God knows why – so you over-interpret a few ambiguous data."

"Humor me anyway," she said. "I can't help wondering whether Alice had a special reason for coming to you, other than just happening to be in the neighborhood. Can you shed any light on that?"

How did Britt strike so close when she was shooting blind? No wonder she'd developed an interest in parapsychology; her own intuition verged on ESP. Formulating a reply, Roger felt as if he were crossing a turbulent stream on slippery rocks. "She has always been difficult. Because of the radical mismatch between her and her family – her father and brother, particularly, vacillate between overprotection and criticism – she's become overly dependent on me. They don't understand her; I do. You know how common it is for a lonely patient to fantasize a unique relationship with her therapist."

Britt nodded impatiently. "What I'm most anxious to find out is whether Alice told you anything about her attacker that she might have forgotten to mention to the police."

Roger returned Britt's intense gaze and lied. "Not a word. She was barely conscious."

"Nothing? One of the paramedics thought he heard her say something about 'glowing eyes.'"

Pain lanced through Roger's forehead. "Probably delirious."

"Well, I had to ask," she sighed.

He tried once more to make her see reason. "Look here, Britt, even if there were real vampires with contagious immor-tality, would you want to live for centuries on those terms? Avoiding the sun and subsisting entirely on blood?" The question reminded him of the inadequacy of the meal he was trying to eat, and he disgustedly pushed it aside.

She said with a half-smile, "There could be compensations."

ALL AFTERNOON Britt's thoughts drifted from her patients' dreamwork and behavioral quirks to her lunch conversation with Roger. Curse the man, why did he react so negatively to the sub-ject of the murders? Britt had trouble believing that Roger's attempt to keep her away from the topic sprang solely from the trauma of a patient collapsing in his living room.

Shutting her office door behind the last patient of the day, Britt smiled at the memory of Roger's skittishness that night at her apartment. She mentally relived their brief kiss, reinforcing her determination to demolish that wall he hid behind. What underlay that ridiculous argument about mixing professional and personal relationships? He had no homosexual tendencies; of that she was certain. He hadn't reacted to the kiss like a man who wasn't interested, but rather a man who was scared silly. Of what?

Britt paused for a quick visit to the office suite's washroom. She stared at her green eyes in the mirror. *Of me? Come on, he's not the type to run screaming in panic from a strong woman.* On the way out, she snatched a carton of yogurt from the miniature refrigerator wedged beside the sink. Instead of going home, she planned to brave the beltway traffic for a visit to the University of Maryland in College Park.

Half an hour later, creeping along I-95, she reviewed her speculations about the murderer. She'd told Roger the gist of everything her informant had been able to give her on such quick notice. The killings in Baltimore, however, spanned only a short time. Where had the criminal been before that? She doubted the man's homicidal urges had erupted out of nowhere less than a month ago. Possible, sure, but unlikely.

At the University library Britt intended to skim newspapers from major cities over the past year. The only way a killer this flamboyant could avoid capture would be by changing his loca-tion frequently. She hoped to find a geographic pattern.

Jolted out of her reverie by a pickup truck jumping in front of her, she gritted her teeth and pumped the brakes. One of the few drawbacks of living in a small city like Annapolis was the lack of a major university. The Naval Academy and St. John's College didn't subscribe to the wide selection of newspapers she needed to consult. She took a bite of yogurt and wiped her forehead with her napkin. To make the drive worse, the bug's transmission had taken to emitting an ominous squeal. Maybe Roger had a valid point about her buying a new car.

Entering the cool library was a relief. Britt quickly disposed of the past few days' papers and resorted to the microfilm room to plough through back issues. Soon her eyes ached from focusing on the small screen. If libraries no longer had space to store most periodicals in hard copy, why couldn't they invent a more comfortable way of reading the stuff?

In a few minutes, though, she forgot her discomfort when she stumbled across a suggestive murder report from Albu-querque. With an indrawn hiss of excitement, she scribbled the date, place, nature of the wounds, and the victim's vital statistics. The discovery energized her to keep searching. The task was made more difficult by having to hunt through the entire first sec-tion of each paper. In most American cities, alas, brutal murders weren't uncommon enough to hit the front page.

After a couple of hours, in which she covered New York, Los

Angeles, Las Vegas (bingo!), and D. C. (another hit), among other locations, she leaned back in the chair, rubbing her eyes. A fast scan of the Boston *Globe*, and she'd call it a night. Soon enough the library would throw her out anyway; it must be near closing time.

*Now, why did I leave this one for last? My partner would chortle over that revealing quirk.*

It took her only a couple of minutes to find the most recent of the Boston deaths, about the same time Roger had moved to Annapolis. A teenage boy, slaughtered in the Public Garden. Did that fit? All the other cases she'd noted had involved female vic-tims. Britt scrolled back a week. Her drooping eyelids snapped wide open.

"Serial Murder Suspect Escapes – One Officer Dead, One Wounded."

In sizzling haste she devoured the account of the fight in which a lone man, caught off guard in his apartment, had broken the neck of one policeman, both arms and five ribs of another. The last sentence of the article pulled her up short. She reread it three times before it sank in. "A psychiatric consultant assisting the investigation, Roger Darvell, M.D., was questioned about the crime's 'vampire' aspects and refused comment."

*He would, wouldn't he!* And then, after the numbness of sheer surprise wore off: *That snake in the grass! He's holding out on me!*

But why? What possible reason could Roger have for not volunteering the fact that he'd worked with similar crimes so recently?

Maybe he was guarding information he'd received from a patient in confidence. Offhand, Britt couldn't think of any other motive.

*If he weren't so heart-stoppingly sexy, I'd probably strangle him,* she thought while inserting a dime to print out the relevant page from the *Globe*. True, most woman, at a casual glance, might not attach the word "sexy" to Roger. Britt, though, felt a quiver of warmth somewhere below the waist at the memory of how those gray eyes looked at her when he thought she didn't notice. *None of that! He still deserves a slow and painful death for keeping me out of this!*

Should she tell him her findings right away? Packing her notes into her briefcase, Britt decided to wait a few days for further developments. *Give him plenty of rope to hang himself!*

TUESDAY NIGHT Roger got another call from Sandor. Despite having heard the outlaw's voice only once, he recognized it at the first word. "Thanks for the treat Saturday night, Darvell."

Roger fought the impulse to hang up instantly. The longer Sandor talked, the more likely he'd let some useful remark slip. "What do you want now?"

The voice oozed with counterfeit friendliness. "Why, Doctor, I want to meet you, of course."

"I can't imagine any advantage in that." Roger considered and shelved the idea of setting up a rendezvous with police in ambush. If Sandor shared Sylvia's psychic talent, he would sense the threat and retreat before they had any chance of capturing him – either that, or strike out in murderous rage, as he had in Boston. *If I do try to trap him, it has to be some way that won't endanger innocent people.* "I simply want you out of this area."

"Not a chance. I like it here, and I figured we could hunt together." The mockingly cheerful tone infuriated Roger. "I could use you for an ally, once you learn a few things. I wouldn't mind having a cousin to guard my rear."

"Don't be ridiculous."

"Wrong answer, Darvell." Sandor's voice hardened. "You don't like your prey dropping dead the minute you turn your back? Well, better get used to it – unless you join me. Put a personal ad in the local paper when you're ready. I'll be waiting. And, by the way, I'll have a surprise for you tonight." He hung up.

Roger let out the breath he'd been holding. Stretching out both hands, he watched them tremble with suppressed anger. *This mustn't go on!* He glanced at the dark window. On the nights Roger didn't take human prey, would Sandor abstain or simply find a victim of his own? Probably the latter, for if Sandor's habits were like Sylvia's, he couldn't go two or three weeks without human blood, as Roger did. Nevertheless, Roger knew that every time he dared to satisfy his craving, he would blame himself for causing another death.

The phone jangled at Roger's elbow. Snatching it up, he snarled, "What now?"

A bewildered male voice said, "Dr. Darvell?"

"I apologize, I expected someone else. How can I help you?"

"This is Detective Lieutenant Hayes of the Annapolis Police Department. Dr. Loren suggested I call you."

"Oh?" Roger's chest tightened with renewed apprehension. He doubted this call concerned some unrelated matter. Britt was determined to get embroiled in the murder investigation.

"She's assisting us with a psychological profile of the suspect in these recent serial killings, and she requested that we bring you on board. Would you be willing to help us out?"

"Certainly." Much as Roger loathed the idea, he couldn't allow Britt to run rampant through the investigation without keeping an eye on her. Why was the detective calling him at home to make this request, though?

"Fine." Hayes cleared his throat. "Doctor, I hate to spring this on you, but the reason I called is that another body has just turned up. I invited Dr. Loren to get a look at the victim *in situ*, and I thought you might want to do the same."

*Good God, no!* "Yes, that might be helpful." If Britt would be there, Roger knew he couldn't stay away.

"It's at the Navy stadium, west parking lot." Hayes added dryly, "Just follow the flashing red lights."

## Chapter 10

AS PREDICTED, Roger had no trouble finding the crime site. The dome lights of three patrol cars and an ambulance splashed garish color over the stadium parking lot. The moment he stepped out of his car, the sickening smell of clotted blood hit him. Breathing shallowly through his mouth, he waited for Lieutenant Hayes to break away from the knot of officers huddled around the lump of flesh next to the tall chain link fence surrounding the stadium.

A slender man with a bushy brown mustache and a weak chin, Hayes walked over to introduce himself. "Dr. Darvell? Thanks for getting here so fast. The victim is a black female, age around thirty, unidentified. There's no blood on the pavement under her, so the M.E. thinks she was killed elsewhere and brought here."

"How long ago?"

"Probably dead no more than half an hour." Hayes shook his head in disgust. "Freshest we've found so far." He lit a cigarette. Roger edged away, upwind.

His eyes drifted toward the corpse, outlined in chalk, being photographed by a petite policewoman with a cap of short gray curls like steel wool. At her elbow, Britt was talking to a nondescript middle-aged man in civilian clothes. Roger wrenched his gaze back to the detective. "How did her body happen to be discovered so soon?"

"Some kid in a sports car taking a short cut through the lot. We recorded his statement and sent him home." Hayes cleared his throat, apparently his standard preamble to a difficult remark. "I guess you might as well have a look."

With a nod of greeting to Britt, Roger approached the body. The woman, barefoot, wore the remains of a robe and nightgown. Good Lord, Sandor must have seized her in her own front yard – or her own house! Through the shreds of the gown, Roger glimpsed lacerations on both breasts. The hole in her throat exposed the larynx and esophagus.

Roger knelt down for a closer examination. The photographer began, "Don't touch –"

"I know," he said. Blood spotted the woman's ripped night-gown and the bosom of the robe. The collar of the robe, how-ever, was dry and unstained. *Didn't waste a drop from the throat wound, did he?* Roger's stomach lurched at the thought.

He felt Britt next to him. Standing up, he gladly turned toward her, away from the thing on the ground.

"Roger, this is Dr. Rizzo, from the Medical Examiner's office," she said, indicating the man she'd been conversing with.

Rizzo, dressed in gray slacks and a green polo shirt, his gray-streaked black hair combed forward over a bald patch, shook hands with Roger. "Evening, Doctor. These crimes are like nothing I've seen in this area before – thank God."

"One expects such things mainly in large cities," Roger said. "And with good reason, I'd think. He can't keep this up for long in a place like Annapolis without getting caught."

"We hope." Rizzo thoughtfully smoothed his hair. "Your associate has been telling me about similar cases, elsewhere, that she tracked down in newspaper files."

"She did?" Roger gave Britt a sharp glance. Her face revealed nothing.

"Yesterday," she said. "I'll tell you all about it later." She turned to Rizzo. "Tell him about the fractures."

"Like the Baltimore murders?" Roger said. "And – and the previous two in Annapolis?"

"From superficial examination, I'd say both this victim's arms are fractured," said Rizzo, "and possibly the left leg, as well. Of course, I won't be able to give you any specifics, such as whether the injuries were inflicted before or after death, until the autopsy."

Britt said, "Dr. Rizzo is going to send us a copy, along with copies of the post mortems on the other two victims." To Roger's relief, she started walking away from the fence; he and Rizzo trailed along. "He's also going to check into getting us the reports from the Baltimore murders."

"We need all the help we can get," said Rizzo. "The systematic application of forensic psychology is still pretty new, as you know, but I personally put a lot of faith in it."

Roger wondered if Rizzo always lectured at length on the obvious, or only in stressful circumstances.

"I think I've seen enough," said Britt. "How about you, Roger?"

*More than enough!*

After Rizzo gave them a longwinded farewell and returned to his work, Roger walked Britt to her car, just outside the circle of reddish light. Not for the first time, he noted how poorly illuminated the stadium lot was. "I don't feel one bit like sleeping right now," she said, unlocking the VW. "How about coming over for a couple of hours to talk about all this?"

*Don't tempt me!* In his present state of turmoil, Roger didn't trust himself alone with Britt. He needed a long, strenuous walk in the night air, followed by a cold shower and a glass of milk. "Not now," he said. "Give me time to sort it out. Besides, we have insufficient data to work with. We'll get together after we've read the M.E.'s reports."

He sensed Britt's reluctance to suspend the discussion. Was he only imagining that she observed him with even keener curiosity than usual? After watching her get into her car and drive away, he rejoined Lieutenant Hayes. *If I don't mention the Boston cases to him,* Roger thought, *it'll come up later, and he'll wonder why I didn't volunteer the information.*

"Lieutenant, there's something you should know," he began. "I consulted with the Boston Police Department in a very similar series of crimes. . . ." He summarized his involvement, then mentioned Sandor's escape and gave Hayes the name of Lieutenant O'Toole as a contact.

Glad to have that revelation over with, Roger strolled to the far edge of the lot, bordered by Farragut, a residential street lined with quietly expensive old houses. He still felt too agitated to drive. He wondered if his nervousness were solely due to the call from Sandor and the sight of the murdered woman. *Well, what else could it be? Turning paranoid on top of everything else, are we?*

Roger sniffed the humid air, thankful that the breeze blew toward, not from, the stadium. His skin prickled as if ants crawled on it. He felt – watched. The same feeling he'd had the night Sandor had attacked Alice. He turned his head, surveying the unlit parking lot.

There – a flash of red. Somehow Roger knew he hadn't glimpsed a cigarette tip or a passing car's taillights. Glowing crimson eyes – like Sylvia's.

*Sandor?* It would be typical of the killer to gloat over the carnage almost within view of his pursuers.

Without another second for thought, Roger burst into a run. He charged across the parking lot to the corner where he'd seen that red glint, out of sight of the police contingent on the other side of the stadium. A living aura shimmered into focus.

The man stood his ground like an effigy carved of stone. Roger lunged at him. His fingers, curled like talons, reached for the man's neck.

The other warded him off with contemptuous ease. An instant later, Roger lay flat on his back on the strip of grass beside the street.

The wind was knocked out of him, and the pain of being slammed against the ground reverberated through his bones. In a spasm of rage he clawed at his opponent's throat. The other man pinned his arms to the ground. Roger stared up into silver eyes whose centers glowed red. That observation, combined with the cool skin temperature and the strength that held him immobilized, left no doubt.

*My God, Sylvia was telling the truth! There are more of them!* Until this moment, despite the weight of evidence, at gut level he hadn't believed her claims.

And this – this vampire did not match her description of the renegade.

Roger forcibly slowed his breathing. "You must be Volnar."

The other released him and stood up. "Yes, Roger, I am Anton Volnar."

Roger got to his feet, his ears still ringing from the shock. "Hell of a way to introduce yourself."

"I wanted to observe you from a distance first – and you did attack me." Volnar displayed no anger. In fact, probing for the vampire's surface emotions, Roger touched blankness.

"Well, I don't intend to apologize. However, I'm glad to meet you." He surveyed Volnar – slightly taller than Roger's own six foot four, with black hair, iron-gray at the temples, curling back from a domed forehead, and an aquiline profile. Except for being clean-shaven, he closely resembled Dracula as described by Stoker, even to the eyebrows growing together. "But damned if I'll call you 'Lord Volnar,' like Sylvia."

Volnar said with a thin smile, "Call me 'Dr. Volnar,' if you wish. I have a perfectly legitimate medical degree, even if slightly out of date."

They started walking toward the dark concrete bulk of the stadium. "Out of date?"

"Earned in Paris, mid-nineteenth century."

Two months ago, Roger would have scoffed at that offhand remark. Coming from this creature, it sounded like plain fact. An incautious movement made him wince from his bruises. Volnar noticed.

"I won't apologize either. But you needn't put up with the discomfort. Don't you know how to shut off pain?" Without waiting for an answer, he grasped Roger by the shoulders, ignoring Roger's instinctive recoil. "Turn your attention inward – trace the affected nerves – yes, like that."

The glow of Volnar's eyes made Roger's head swim. *He's hypnotizing me!* Roger forced himself to look away, and the night refocused around him. He sensed Volnar had permitted that moment of resistance; Roger's own strength couldn't have severed the link. The soreness, he noticed, had disappeared. To think he'd worked that operation on his patients many times, for symptoms such as headaches, and never thought of applying it to himself.

"Good enough for a first attempt," said Volnar. "We have much to discuss, but this isn't the place. I'm staying at a hotel on West Street, a block from downtown. Follow me there, and we'll talk." Without waiting for a reply, he got into a rental car parked nearby and started the motor.

*Arrogant devil,* Roger grumbled to himself. *If Sylvia's hero-worship is typical, he probably gets ample encouragement.*

Roger was prepared to put up with a lot for straight answers. He started his own car and followed, as ordered. He found a space on the street a block away from the hotel, while Volnar pulled into the parking garage. As Roger got out of his car, he noticed a fresh breeze. A cold front was moving in, with a promise of autumn temperatures and rain to break the humidity.

When they met in the lobby, the vampire led the way to a second-floor room, where he paused to listen at the door before unlocking it. He projected no awareness of danger; the act seemed to be a routine precaution.

Without bothering to switch on a light, Volnar directed Roger to one of two chairs flanking the table near the window. The room was a double, with suitcases and a briefcase on the extra bed. From a suitcase Volnar produced a bottle of Cour-voisier.

Roger watched guardedly, wondering if, forewarned, he would find that strength quite so irresistible. Volnar said in a tone of quiet amusement, "Don't try. It would be a waste of energy, as well as the time we should spend answering your questions." His eyes raking Roger up and down, he announced, "You need a drink."

Roger accepted the brandy, incongruously served in a stan-dard motel toothbrush glass, with an ungracious mutter of thanks.

"That should take the edge off," said Volnar, "and render you capable of rational conversation."

Roger flushed. He did feel the need for blood, damn it, and it made no sense. After Saturday, he shouldn't have felt the craving for close to a week.

"What's the matter with you?" said Volnar with that same irritating trace of amusement.

"Nothing. I shouldn't need –" He sipped the brandy. "I don't enjoy discussing it."

"Well, I won't waste time catering to your sensibilities. After the stress you've undergone tonight, including exposure to fresh blood, naturally you want to feed." He didn't comment further on Roger's distaste for the blunt language. "We'll deal with that later. What would you like to know?"

The dozens of questions spinning in Roger's head receded into the background. Before he realized what he intended to say, he blurted out, "I want to know what you're going to do about Sandor."

Seated in the other chair, Volnar took a thoughtful sip of his drink before answering. "What do you expect me to do?"

"According to Sylvia, you hold a position of authority in your group. Isn't it your job to stop Sandor from killing, if only to protect your secret?"

Volnar's eyebrows arched as if in surprise at Roger's on-target analysis. "Quite right. Indiscriminate, conspicuous killing attracts attention. How do you expect me to catch him?"

"Confound it, from the way Sylvia talks, you're some sort of blasted demigod! You're telling me you can't find him, as reckless as he is?"

Volnar held up a conciliatory hand. "There's no need to ex-cite yourself, Roger. Episodes like this are always self-limiting."

"Episodes? Is that all this string of pointless deaths means to you?" Roger cut his tirade short, uncomfortably conscious of how his outburst sounded against Volnar's cool control.

"As a matter of fact, I'm catching a plane for London in a few hours. Neil's twin sister, the only person he is likely to listen to, presently lives in England. If I can find her, I hope she may be in contact with him and can persuade him to turn himself over to our Council of Elders."

"Persuade? That's your solution?"

"We'll discuss `solutions' later. Why don't you begin at the beginning and tell me about your acquaintance with Sylvia and your clash with Neil? Omit no detail. We have time."

The sudden change of emphasis jolted Roger into relative calm.

"Didn't Sylvia tell you? Or haven't you talked to her? Does she even know you're in town."

"No, with so little time to spare, I wanted to devote my full attention to you," Volnar said. "I spoke to her by phone last night, and she told me parts of it – from her viewpoint. I want yours."

Beginning at Mrs. Bronson's party back in August, Roger narrated the high points of his friendship with Sylvia and the tangle of events that had followed. He omitted only the more intimate moments, especially that night she had tried to drink from him; that incident was too agonizing to relive.

When he wound down, gulping the brandy to soothe his dry throat, Volnar stared at him for half a minute before saying in a cold, measured voice, "Do you realize how close to catastrophe you came, how many times?"

"I think so," Roger said, bristling at the contemptuous tone.

"I doubt it. If you'd had any inkling of what it meant to betray one of your own, you wouldn't have considered doing so. Didn't Sylvia warn you about that?"

"She mentioned it. I stand by what I told her then – I see no reason to shield a murderer."

Volnar let that pass without comment. "Furthermore, your dietary habits need revision. By abstaining so long between donors, you set yourself up for impulsive acts that lead to disaster."

"I don't intend to be careless," Roger said.

"Good intentions don't suffice, in your present state of ignorance."

"Look here, sir –" The honorific spontaneously slipped out, despite Roger's indignation.

Volnar overrode him. "I'll give you as much instruction as I can tonight. It's not the ideal situation, but it will have to do. Later you should spend a few weeks at our headquarters in Nevada, meet some of the others."

"Nevada? Oh, yes, Sylvia mentioned that she grew up there."

"Off and on. Even solitary predators sometimes need the company of their own kind. A benefit you lacked all these years."

"What are you talking about?" Roger burst out. "Damn it, I don't believe –"

Volnar leaped up from the chair. "You don't believe what you are? Well, I'll show you." He grabbed Roger's arm. Roger bared his teeth in a snarl, then relaxed when he remembered the futility of his earlier resistance. He allowed Volnar to pull him to his feet and guide him to the dresser.

"There," said Volnar. "Throw away your preconceptions, open your eyes, and look!"

Side by side with the older man, Roger gazed into the mirror. The room still lay in darkness except for street lights shining through the window. In the reflected image, Volnar's eyes glowed red like smoldering embers. And so did Roger's.

Roger lurched back to the chair. He sat with his head bowed on his hands until Volnar gave him a refilled glass of brandy.

"You actually avoided noticing that, all these years."

Roger looked up, to find Volnar seated opposite him again. "I don't make a habit of staring into mirrors in the dark." He congratulated himself on the steadiness of his voice. "How can I be – what you are? I don't have Sylvia's range of powers."

"Listen carefully. I am going to tell you a story." Volnar got out a pack of cigars and offered them to Roger, who empha-tically refused.

"I'd expect you to be immune to nicotine addiction."

"I am," Volnar said. "Therefore I can indulge without fear of consequences." He clipped the end of his cigar, lit it, and moved his chair next to an open window. "Now, pay attention." He took a couple of thoughtful puffs. "Consider a nonhuman species living secretly in the midst of *Homo sapiens*. These creatures are phenomenally long-lived – virtually immortal, unless destroyed by dismemberment or cremation. They have a variety of talents that would appear supernatural to the average mortal. But they also have weaknesses, such as sensitivity to sunlight and a highly restricted diet. Where their existence is believed at all, they are feared and loathed.

"A female of that race lived in a French village in the nineteen-thirties. She 'fell in love'" – Roger could hear the quota-tion marks – "with a human male. Now, erotic liaisons between the two species are not uncommon, even those lasting for some time. But deep attachment on the part of the – vampire – is rare. Some of our people were outraged when Claudette actually married her human lover. They thought she debased herself by making such a contract with an ephemeral. Among us marriage does not exist, because our females are sexually receptive only once every few years, and fertile even less often. When it became known that Claudette had not only committed herself in this unprecedented way, but had entered estrus and allowed herself to conceive by an ephemeral, some of the elders demanded that she be ostracized.

"As her advisor, I argued on the other side. Though legends told of such conceptions, none had been confirmed within living memory. The scientific possibilities were boundless. I maintained that if the pregnancy came to term, the offspring should be nurtured and carefully watched. So I kept in touch with Claudette, and she did indeed give birth to a live infant with mingled traits of both vampire and human. Certain indications – aversion to sunlight, rapid healing from minor abrasions – suggested the dominance of vampire genes.

"There were complications beyond our control, however. The war's effects reached even the remote village where Claudette and her husband lived. Suspicion, taken to paranoid lengths, became the norm. Anyone who seemed peculiar was at risk. What had once been outmoded superstition became plausible again. Claudette knew she was suspected of vampirism and placed the child in the temporary care of her husband's cousin, with instructions to contact me in case of disaster. The couple planned to flee the country, picking up the infant at the last possible moment. Before they could get away, they were caught by the local populace and murdered."

Roger was stunned by this dry recital. "My parents."

"Exactly," said Volnar. "This was 1940, and you were slightly over a year old. I got you out of France and found a middle-aged, childless couple delighted at the chance to adopt a 'war orphan' on my terms. One condition was that you keep the name you were originally given."

"Why?" Roger said. "It made things even more difficult for me." His birth certificate read "Roger Sean Gallagher Darvell." Until high school graduation he had used "Gallagher," his adopted parents' name. In college he'd begun to hyphenate the two. After his father's death, in a small gesture of rebellion, he had switched to the simpler alternative of "Darvell" without the hyphen.

"I see you're using your birth names now, however," said Volnar. "By the time your parents were murdered, you'd had fourteen months of life to get accustomed to 'Roger Darvell.' It isn't unusual for our children to remember experiences from that age. I didn't want you confused by suddenly having your name changed."

"Kind of you. Too bad you didn't give a second thought to all the rest of the confusion."

Ignoring the sarcastic tone, Volnar said, "Did you remember anything of your pre-Boston life? When I brought you to the United States, you were already speaking three-word sentences in French."

"No, no memories of infancy." Something did spring to mind, though. "Interesting – when I studied French in high school, it seemed to come naturally to me, as if I'd heard it before." He resorted to the brandy again to cushion the shock of Volnar's "story." "So I actually had."

The elder vampire nodded. "I'd hoped that keeping your ori-ginal name might trigger more substantive memories, help you realize your true nature when the time came. Worth a try, even though it didn't work." He drew deeply on the cigar. Even with the window open, its smoke made Roger feel suffocated. "I kept watch over you, from a discreet distance, until you completed your medical training. Thereafter I heard nothing until Sylvia met you."

"You engineered that?"

"Only in the sense that I introduced her to Mrs. Bronson," said Volnar. "I expected Sylvia to encounter you, but she was quite honest in claiming to know nothing about your background. I needed to witness your reactions to each other, untainted by any prior knowledge on your part."

"But what was the point?" said Roger impatiently. "Why wasn't I brought up by – as you put it – my own kind?"

"An experiment," said Volnar. "We wanted to see how much about yourself you would discover on your own, how well you'd adapt to human society without direct guidance. We needed to know whether a human-vampire hybrid was viable in a social as well as a physical sense."

"Experiment!" Roger stalked across the room, refilled his glass, drained it without pausing for breath, and glared at Volnar. "Good God, if you knew how many times I've contemplated suicide, thinking I was some kind of psychotic –! What gives you the right to experiment on human lives?"

The older vampire regarded him coldly. "You aren't human, remember? I am your advisor – guardian and mentor, you would say – just as I was your mother's. I'm also the oldest of our race, the head of our Council of Elders."

Roger poured himself another shot of brandy. "How old?"

"Older than you could imagine. I've outlived most human civilizations."

"I'm supposed to believe all this on the strength of your word?"

Volnar's eyebrows arched. "Why would I bother to lie to you?" The top layer of his mental shield dissolved, allowing Roger to glimpse his sincerity.

*Unless he's so powerful he can project a lie,* Roger thought. With only Sylvia to judge by, how could he know what Volnar might be capable of? "If you're unimaginably ancient," he said, "I suppose you've come here to offer me the wisdom of the ages."

"That is a human concept. We adopt all cultural elements from the societies around us – including language. We're prag-matists. Philosophy, like art, literature, science, and technology, is *their* specialty."

"I don't necessarily accept seniority and brute force as valid reasons for you to hold the power of life and death over me," Roger said.

Volnar seemed more amused than outraged by his defiance. "Young man, you have two choices. Either accept my authority, or be cut off from our people. You won't be persecuted – as long as you do nothing to attract dangerous attention – but no one except other outlaws will associate with you. And believe me, you wouldn't like most of them."

Thinking of Sandor, Roger believed that. He sat down, poised on the edge of his chair. "What does accepting your authority entail?"

Volnar laughed softly. "Nothing onerous or degrading. When I give direct orders, I'll expect obedience, but they'll be rare, and always for your own good."

Roger wasn't precisely reassured, remembering how, in childhood, he'd reacted to commands delivered "for his own good." But if the alternative was to be cut adrift from his mother's race, he could swallow his pride. "I accept, then – provisionally. Only because I do want to learn what I am."

"I've seldom heard a more halfhearted pledge of loyalty," said Volnar. "Good enough – if you were too submissive, you wouldn't be one of us. I acknowledge that I may have misjudged in your case, carried the experiment too far. Perhaps I should have told you the truth earlier. When your adoptive father was killed, all doubt about your status was removed."

Roger shifted position irritably. Why must the man speak in riddles? Drinking from the almost forgotten glass in his hand, he said, "What do you mean?"

"You were in the car as well; you almost died in that accident. Or so it appeared. What do you remember?"

"About the accident itself, nothing. But they told me I shouldn't have survived the crash to begin with," Roger recalled. "I was comatose for over forty-eight hours, and except for the EEG all vital signs ceased. Permanent damage was expected, if I ever regained consciousness at all. Yet when I did, the attending physician said I looked as if I'd been healing for weeks."

Volnar nodded. "Not a typical human pattern, is it? The incident confirmed that you inherited your mother's nearly indestructible constitution and her rapid healing ability. Therefore, almost beyond doubt, her extended lifespan. Have you ever had an infectious disease?"

Roger's awestruck silence answered the question.

"You see, while you share some outward characteristics of *Homo sapiens*, essentially you are a vampire."

"Why must you use that word? Can't you come up with anything more accurate and less – vulgar?"

"As I told you, we borrow our language from the human population we live among, and of all the terms available, 'vampire' fits us best. It is, in fact, the most 'accurate' – for you as well as the rest of us."

Hearing the word applied to him by this dominant figure forced Roger to face the implications head-on. "You're saying I may live – how long? Forever?"

"For millennia, at any rate, assuming your capacity for healing is a reliable indicator."

"You don't really know, though," Roger said. "You don't know anything about hybrids."

"So far, observation suggests that you are typical of our species, except for your inability to transform, which Sylvia mentioned to me – and minor details such as your greater tolerance for sunlight and ability to consume solid food, which are actually advantages. You should live on indefinitely unless your carelessness gets you killed first. You can't even starve to death. You'd simply lapse into suspended animation until a food source became available."

Roger tried another drink of the Courvoisier and found it was making him queasy. He set the glass on the table. "Suppose I'd never discovered my – special needs – on my own? You had no right to abandon me."

"How did you discover those needs? How old were you?"

"The first stage must have occurred in my early twenties," he began. "I discovered that when I was – intimate – with young women – 'heavy petting,' in the argot of the decade – I no longer needed masturbation to be satisfied. In fact, I'd become incapable of ejaculating." He felt himself blushing but forged on, over-riding his self-consciousness. "Their passion satisfied me by itself. That just fortified my growing conviction that I was abnormal."

"You never suspected it signified something more than simple deviance?" Volnar asked.

Roger irritably shrugged off the question, similar to the ones Sylvia had frequently badgered him with. "How could I? The possibility didn't exist in my consciousness. As far as I could see, I'd become impotent for no reason whatever. I didn't seek treatment; the prospect was too humiliating.

"After that my development remained static until I finished medical school and entered residency. You probably know that a future psychotherapist has to undergo analysis himself. That brought on my crisis. For months previously I'd been – unwell." Roger felt his neck and shoulder muscles tighten at the memory of the blood-drenched nightmares and the constant, gnawing hunger that no amount of raw steak appeased.

"On top of that change, the twice-weekly sessions with Dr. North were an almost unbearable strain. I censored everything I told him, naturally, but maintaining the censorship was stressful in itself. Trying to compensate by siphoning increased amounts of energy from my off-duty companions – of whom I didn't have many – didn't help. North was bright enough to suspect I was holding out on him, and he insisted on hypnotizing me.

"I agreed, confident I could override his will." He recalled his brief contest with North, no battle at all, culminating in his swallowing up the therapist's resistance like a shark engulfing a minnow. The small conquest had quenched Roger's superficial psychic thirst while activating a deeper layer of appetite whose object bewildered him.

"Five minutes into the session, I had him in deep trance. Wondering what to do with him, trying to concoct a screen memory to make him leave me alone from then on, I stared into his eyes, absent-mindedly fingering his wrist." Roger heard his own breathing quicken as he relived the moment. "Instead of planning my strategy – I'd never tried such comprehensive mind-control before – I found myself listening to his heartbeat and respiration, background noises I usually filtered out. I'd long since pigeonholed that ability to hear sounds other people couldn't as more of a nuisance than an advantage."

Volnar took a long drag on his cigar. "With all that going on, how could you still assume you were an ordinary man?"

Roger thought of the webs of rationalization he'd woven to keep himself from falling to pieces. "Those abilities could have been a delusion. Since I didn't dare mention them to anyone else, I had no reality test. Now I caught myself enjoying the sound of North's heart and the tactile sensation of the pulse in his wrist. Suddenly I realized I wanted to lift his hand and touch my lips to that spot.

"I'd long suspected my mental balance was shaky, and this bizarre urge seemed to confirm that. While the analytic part of my mind was reviewing cases I'd read, searching for one that matched my symptoms, I was already raising his hand to my mouth. The office walls seemed to close in on me – my senses contracted to that point where my lips touched his skin. Warm, damp, salty –" The memory made him salivate. He took a long swallow of the brandy. "I certainly didn't bare my teeth on purpose. I didn't know my incisors had grazed the skin until I tasted – God, I couldn't believe what I was doing. It disgusted me, but I couldn't stop with that rush of energy flooding –"

"Enough," said Volnar. "Don't be so graphic. You are upsetting yourself."

"I went lightheaded, saw sparks behind my eyelids. Like lightning bolts in a night sky. Believe it or not, the first thing I thought of was epilepsy. *Petit mal* does manifest itself in peculiar ways. On the other hand, I could hardly have suffered that for years without noticing. I considered alternative explanations the whole time I kept drinking. Defense mechanism – if I didn't think about the act, it wasn't really happening. When I finally surfaced and checked my watch, almost twenty minutes had passed. Good thing the man was healthy for his age. I wasn't up to concocting an elaborate tale for him. I gave him a generalized suggestion that I was mentally sound and he didn't need to waste time with me."

"You started late," said Volnar. "Most of us acquire our psychic talents in our early teens – as you did, didn't you? – but start needing human blood soon thereafter, around sixteen."

"Children don't?" said Roger. He'd had trouble visualizing an infant or toddler feeding on a human adult.

"Of course not," Volnar chuckled. "Babies are born with two needle-like teeth – the only time we have those absurd rattlesnake fangs beloved by Hollywood – to feed on the mother's blood as well as her milk. You didn't, thanks to your human half. At weaning, three or four years old, we lose the fangs and switch to raw meat, milk, and animal blood."

"Makes sense," Roger said. "Growing children would need the calories in solid food."

"In early adolescence the ability to digest it disappears, when we lose our wolf-like incisors and canines, to be replaced by a more human-appearing set for drawing blood inconspicuously. It's a good thing you didn't undergo those changes, or you could never have passed for human."

"I'm still baffled about the way you manipulated me. Why this 'experiment,' leaving me to flounder through those develop-mental stages alone? Why did you care whether a hybrid was `viable'?"

"Quite simply," said Volnar, "because we aren't replacing ourselves. Long-lived predators have to breed slowly in comparison to their prey, to avoid overrunning the food supply, but in recent centuries our low reproductive rate has become a crisis. Females more often than not go into estrus without conceiving. The incidence of miscarriages has increased, too."

Roger set down the brandy and stared at him. "You're looking for new blood, aren't you?"

## Chapter 11

HE WINCED AT his unintentional pun. "You think human DNA might revitalize your gene pool."

"Exactly." Volnar smiled as if pleased at his quick comprehension. "Some of the elders consider it contamination, but I've overruled them. Including the ones who make derogatory re-marks about `lap dogs pretending to be wolves.'"

Roger felt his chest tighten with anger. Though he wasn't sure he wanted to be a wolf, he didn't care for the proposed alter-native.

"Some of them," Volnar continued, "cite the fable of the Ugly Duckling, which they think ends on a note of unwarranted optimism. What kind of a swan could the creature become, crippled by a barnyard fowl's conditioning?"

"Are you deliberately trying to goad me?"

"Only preparing you," Volnar said, "for the hostility you're sure to encounter sooner or later. Not that it's universal. Most of those who know about your existence either tentatively approve or are indifferent."

"The nay-sayers have a point," Roger said. "Do you happen to have read Mark Twain's *Pudd'nhead Wilson?*"

"Actually, no."

"Two boys are switched in infancy, half-brothers, the son of a slave woman and the son of the mistress of the house. When they reach adulthood and the truth is revealed, the young man who's grown up thinking himself a slave suddenly becomes the master's heir. One might expect a Cinderella conclusion, but that doesn't happen. The slave turned master proves utterly unfit for the station to which he was born."

"You don't have to apply that pessimistic tale to yourself. You've done better than that."

"Oh, have I? Not from my viewpoint." Roger took a deep breath, then coughed when he inhaled cigar smoke instead of fresh air. "How can you stand that blasted thing?" He wondered whether the smoke was a test of his willingness to accept Vol-nar's domination. When he'd cleared his throat, he said, "What you've made me is a misfit among both vampires and my human peers."

"On the contrary, you've done remarkably well, considering how you were forced to `flounder,'" Volnar said. "Not unlike Tarzan in Burroughs' novel, who, after being reared by apes, as an ape, taught himself to read and eventually functioned not only as a civilized man but as an aristocrat of the most civilized nation on earth."

"A pulp fantasy," Roger said. "Real-life feral children more often become mental and emotional cripples."

"That didn't happen to you, however," said Volnar, "so I suggest you stop wasting energy on resentment."

"But I haven't turned out like Tarzan. More like a badly socialized puppy."

"In what way?" said Volnar.

"Well, I understand that if you take a puppy away from its mother and litter mates too soon, it doesn't know how to behave like a dog. On the other hand, if you leave the separation too late, the pup can never fully adjust to life with a human master. Either way, you have a maladjusted dog."

"It's true that there are critical periods in our childhood and adolescence – times of imprinting, as with ducklings. The adaptability of young vampires is a double-edged weapon."

Roger stood up, too restless to hold still. "Sylvia has a fear of religious objects – that's the kind of thing you mean, don't you?"

"Yes. Her advisor was too lax. She was exposed to excessive human influences. She almost thought, in her mid-teens, that she *was* human. Then she drifted the other way and picked up a cluster of absurd superstitions about her nature."

"Then I'm not the only child whose upbringing you people royally fouled up." He simmered with tension, half tempted to take a swing at Volnar just to discharge it.

"Learning how you've dealt with your highly specialized problems may help us avoid mistakes with future generations." Volnar rested the cigar in an ashtray and strode to Roger's side. "Don't let anger blind you to the possibilities, young man. This stage is only the beginning. The next is to breed you with a female of our species."

Roger jerked away from the elder's outstretched hand. "What? Do you think for one minute I'd consider that? Creating another child to suffer what I've gone through?"

"He or she wouldn't suffer the 'identity crisis' you've had," Volnar said, walking over to pick up his unfinished cigar. "The child will know his or her nature and destiny from the start. I'll serve as its advisor myself."

"All the more reason why I'd run miles to avoid the whole thing."

"Nevertheless, I do expect you to consider it," Volnar said. "I've contacted a young woman, born in the 1880s, who has proven her fertility. She conceived more than once but miscarried each time. With you as the sire, perhaps a pregnancy might –"

"Not interested," Roger cut him off. "I can't condone any more of your damned experiments. And what makes you think this woman would accept being forced into mating with a – a halfbreed?"

"Not forced! Our women choose their own mates, subject to veto by the elders, to prevent inbreeding. I've already explained your background to her, and she is enthusiastic."

"She may like the idea of being a reproductive machine for you, but I don't!" He almost wanted to rush out of the room and drive away, but the need to learn as much as he could stopped him.

"Juliette doesn't fit that description in the least. She teaches English at the College of William and Mary in Virginia and writes historical romances under a *nom de plume* – far from a mindless breeding machine. However, she does want a child, and her next estrus is due fairly soon. Think it over."

"I don't need to think," Roger said, baring his teeth. "I'm absolutely sure that I don't want to serve as sperm donor to a woman I've never met in support of a project I don't believe in."

Volnar said, "Aren't you curious, if nothing else?"

"What do you mean?"

"Many of our males live out their first thousand years – or more – without once being chosen to mate. This may be your single chance to experience fully consummated genital sexuality."

The notion disturbed Roger, though he couldn't say why; he certainly felt no physical urge for the act Volnar alluded to. "You keep mentioning estrus, as if vampire females went into heat like –"

"Dogs? Wolves?" Volnar's lips quirked in amusement. "They do, and male vampires can consummate the sexual act only when stimulated by a female in heat. Mating lasts through an entire night of repeated copulation. If an unwanted conception occurs, the woman can mentally compel her body to eject the embryo." He became more serious. "Not that this problem comes up very often anymore. We do need your genes, Roger. Your potential hybrid vigor."

"I don't want to discuss it." Suddenly he recalled his recent conversation with Sylvia and the heady scent she had begun to emit. "Wait a minute – you wouldn't suggest that I breed with Sylvia, would you?"

"Certainly not. Did she invite you to?" At Roger's nod, Volnar said, "Mate with her recreationally, if you wish, but breeding isn't an option. She's too young for motherhood. The first estrus is almost always barren. And she is too young emotionally, as well. She's hardly out of adolescence."

"From the standpoint of knowledge and experience as a vampire," Roger said bitterly, "so am I."

"You have a half-brother who believes I've treated you abominably," Volnar said. "If I hadn't absolutely forbidden it, he would have intervened long ago to give you that knowledge."

Surprise at this new revelation sidetracked Roger from dwelling on his anger. "Sounds like an intelligent man. I want to meet him."

"You will, in good time. However, you've probably seen him

without knowing it. I daresay you watch vampire movies?"

"And read the books," Roger said, "idiotic as most of them are. I hoped to get some sort of perspective on my – condition."

"Well, your brother is Claude Darvell, the actor."

Roger sank into the chair, felled by sheer astonishment. "The horror film star? Good Lord!"

"Not that I approve. Claude calls it a 'purloined letter lifestyle' – hide in plain sight. It could only work in a peculiar cultural climate like the present." Volnar shook his head. "He also speaks in a silly-ass-Brit dialect like something out of P. G. Wodehouse; he claims it's his way of appearing harmless. Altogether, a thoroughly irritating young man."

To Roger, irritating Volnar sounded like a worthwhile pursuit. He approved of his half-brother, sight unseen. He conjured up a mental image of the Anglo-French actor he'd observed in several low-budget films – tall, lean, pale, dark-haired, sensual, like a cross between Lord Byron and a young Christopher Lee. No telling how much of that gaunt, broodingly handsome look came from makeup, of course. *Probably a lot less than I ima-gined!* "It never crossed my mind. The name isn't that uncom-mon." An unpleasant thought struck him. "Doesn't Sylvia know who Claude is? She must have suspected a relationship. Why didn't she say anything to me?"

"Because that would have betrayed his secrets without his permission. She's a wild young creature, but she does follow the basic rules. Now that I've given him permission, your brother will get in touch with you. The sibling tie is the most important family relationship we recognize, the only one that remains strong in adulthood."

Acid welled up in Roger's throat. "If it's so damned important, why didn't he get in touch with me a long time ago?"

"Because, as I told you, I forbade it. He's about two cen-turies older than you, but by our standards, that is still young. He knew better than to violate my orders."

Roger leaned back and closed his eyes. Emotional overload, combined with the smoke and too much brandy, gave him a stabbing headache.

Volnar surveyed him as if evaluating his condition and assigning a grade of D-minus. "You're in worse shape than I realized. How often do you feed? From human donors, that is."

Roger evaded the older man's steady gaze. Did he have to be so confoundedly direct?

"Come, now, Roger, a physician shouldn't overreact to a simple diagnostic question. As your advisor, I have not only the right but the duty to ask."

"Every two or three weeks."

He had the dubious satisfaction of getting a reaction out of his advisor – outraged astonishment. *"Three weeks?"* Volnar was actually speechless for a moment. Then he went on, "I withdraw my criticism of your behavior. It's surprising you are able to function at all. Even considering your mixed heritage, abstaining for that long is insane. I'd estimate that you need human blood at least once a week. What in blazes were you thinking of? If you can call it thinking."

"It seems obvious," Roger said stiffly, "that the lower the frequency, the less chance of exposure."

"Up to a point, yes, until you run into the range of diminishing returns. Don't you see that your exaggerated caution may lead to a condition in which you couldn't help committing some reckless act? You are without a doubt the most thoroughgoing idiot I have ever had the misfortune to advise."

Volnar checked his harangue and added more calmly, "You defeated your own purpose. Moderation, young man, moderation." He put the room key in his pocket. "Come along, we're going for a walk. Staying inside and watching you writhe in agony is an uncomfortable way of spending the night."

The suggestion appealed to Roger. Outdoors, the breeze would dissipate Volnar's cigar smoke. They took the stairs rather than the elevator and set out at a brisk pace up West Street away from Church Circle. They walked past restaurants, art galleries, and boutiques toward the more commercial section of town.

Volnar spoke in a low voice that would have been inaudible to human ears a few feet away. "You're ignorant of the risk you were taking. Vampires have been known to go mad from being too long deprived of human blood. In situations where sufficient animal prey is available to keep the body from falling into a protective coma – I've seen the results, and they are appalling."

"How was I to know?" said Roger impatiently. "How long is too long?"

"The optimum interval is forty-eight to seventy-two hours. Preferably no less often than twice a week, and even in your special case, certainly no less than once a week."

*Easy enough to say,* Roger reflected. *Where does he expect me to get this endless supply of victims?*

Volnar continued in a lecturing tone, "In addition to milk and blood, we require psychic energy – 'life-force,' if you will. That is what makes frequent access to human prey essential. One could, of course, live entirely on human blood, but that would be wasteful and hazardous. If the physical need for bulk nourishment is supplied by the vital fluids of lower animals, the quantity taken from human donors can be quite small. Quality and frequency are more important."

Though Roger had figured out most of this on his own, he was glad to have his empirical findings confirmed. The information was of no help on a practical level, however, and he said so to Volnar.

"Your problem, young man," said Volnar, "is that you refuse to come to terms with what you are. You now have no excuse to deny that you are a vampire." Roger winced at the pulp-horror word. "You see, that's precisely my point. Your morbidly hyperactive conscience has flogged you into the belief that if you deny your nature most of the time, fulfilling its demands only when absolutely driven, you are somehow less guilty. Well, I intend to knock those spineless evasions out of you if it kills you."

"If I tried that kind of reality therapy on my own patients," Roger said, "I'd find myself up on malpractice charges."

"That's better," Volnar chuckled. "Now channel some of that fight in the proper direction. Your present behavior pattern is suicidal. If you're that eager to die, at least do it in some way that doesn't endanger the rest of us."

"I don't want to die," Roger said. He realized that the state-ment was unequivocally true for the first time since he'd begun preying on human victims.

"Wonderful," said Volnar dryly. As they walked on in silence, he continued puffing on the cigar. After a while he said, "If you're serious about that resolve, begin by correcting the problem that is distracting you at this moment."

Embarrassed, Roger avoided his piercing stare.

"You're doing it again," Volnar said. "What are you feeling right now?"

"Principally annoyed with you." If, in the vampire subcul-ture, "advisor" was partially equivalent to "therapist," he had to put up with this prying. But he didn't have to pretend to like it. Besides, Volnar could doubtless read his emotions like large print.

"Principally?" said Volnar sharply.

"Why do you insist on my verbalizing it?" Roger demanded. "Do you get that much pleasure out of raking me over the coals?"

"It is not a pleasure at all. I do this because it's what you require. I'm trying to help you, you blasted idiot." His voice held no kindness; Volnar reminded Roger of certain doctors he'd known during his internship, who viewed both patients and medical students as unavoidable nuisances and feebleminded as well. Roger, to his mild surprise, found the edge of contempt in Volnar's tone bracing.

"All right, damn you, I'm thirsty!" he burst out. Glancing around to see whether any other pedestrians were close enough to hear him, he lowered his voice. "And I wish you'd quit harping on the subject." He calmed himself and examined his sensations. "I shouldn't be; I fed only five nights ago. And the truth is, my system is so upset after what I saw tonight – and what Sandor threatened me with – that I'm not sure I could take the opportunity if it were offered."

"You will force yourself, then," said Volnar, discarding his cigarette. "I'm taking you out to dinner."

"You've had a destination in mind all along?"

"Certainly." They passed the public library, set back from the street on a broad lawn, and turned into the residential streets behind it. "Earlier tonight, I spoke to one of the hotel's clerks going off duty. I determined that she lives alone and ordered her to leave her bedroom window open – none of which she consciously remembers, of course."

"You're going to take the chance of entering a house?"

"The donor will not wake. And if we exercise reasonable caution, neither will anyone else."

Roger thought the plan was riskier than anything he'd ever done, but his thirst left him in no mood to argue.

"I assure you, the risk will be negligible." Volnar stopped in front of an small box-shaped house with tall hedges and a red brick facade with white siding. "Can you do this?" he said in the same prison-yard whisper he'd used earlier. And he shadowed himself. But in Volnar's case it would be more accurate to say he vanished. Even Roger, knowing where and how to look for him, perceived only a faint shimmer from his aura.

"Not that well," said Roger. He demonstrated his best effort.

"All right," said Volnar. "More than enough to deceive any casual passer-by." He veiled himself again, as did Roger. They slipped behind the hedge and glided silently around the corner of the house. Roger followed the ghost of Volnar's presence, which became easier to detect with practice, to the rear of the property. Volnar prowled around the backyard, listening at windows and sniffing the air. Finally, dropping the invisibility, he stopped to push up a screen. The window itself, as predicted, was already open.

Roger still had doubts, but when Volnar climbed over the sill, he couldn't do much except follow. They were in the bedroom of a young woman barely out of her teens, clothes scattered on the floor, the bureau and dresser buried under mounds of cosmetics and magazines. Bookshelves near the open closet door held an assortment of stuffed animals, paperback romances, and trilogies of the Tolkien-clone type. The air was thick with cologne and powder, overlaying the muskily sweet perfume of the girl's body.

She lay curled on her side in a double bed, an extra pillow hugged to her chest. Long, black hair streamed over the sheets, lending her a romantic appearance that probably would have been dispelled in seconds if she'd awakened and spoken. But ap-parently Volnar didn't intend for that to happen. "Are you planning to – to take her asleep?" said Roger. "That's practically rape. When I have to do it this way, at least I wake them up first."

Volnar arched an eyebrow at him. "Is that how you appease your overactive conscience?" He pronounced the last word like the name of a disease. "By deluding yourself that half-conscious participation equals willingness? When you feed on your patients, they are in hypnotic trance, are they not?"

"Well – yes." On reflection Roger had to admit that there wasn't much difference from the victim's point of view. But for the predator – "You can't get much satisfaction from someone who's completely out of it."

"One of the first sensible comments you've made," Volnar said. "The solution is simple, however. Inducing REM sleep is easy, and passion experienced in a dream is no less intense than in a trance." He moved to the bedside and placed a hand on the girl's forehead. With a small sigh she turned on her back. Volnar stroked her hair and ran his fingers along the curve of her jaw. Roger noted the flicker of her eyelids that indicated the dreaming phase. To his heightened senses, the throb of her pulse made the air of the room vibrate. He watched Volnar turn the sheet down to her waist, revealing a low-cut cotton nightgown whose thin material didn't conceal the swell of her breasts and the dark peaks of the nipples.

Roger took a step closer, fighting dizziness. A sharp glance from Volnar warned him off. "Privilege of rank?" he whispered hoarsely.

"Yes, if I choose to exercise it," said Volnar, abstractedly caressing the girl as if in no particular hurry. "You'll find, however, that I am doing you a favor." Roger hadn't the strength to challenge his advisor; he sank into the nearest chair and watched. Volnar showed no sign of acute need. His strongest emotion, as he bent over the victim, seemed to be cool appre-ciation.

When he pierced her skin, the sharp scent of fresh blood cut through the heavy air of the bedroom. Roger's stomach con-tracted painfully. Anticipation sent a bolt of electricity from his parched throat straight to his groin and made the cilia in his palms bristle. The bloodlust, though it combined both hunger and thirst, was more than either. The tormenting promise of satisfaction set his nerves thrumming.

Only two or three minutes passed before Volnar withdrew. Roger could detect no change in him other than a slight decrease in tension and a subtle brightening of his aura. "She's well under now," he said. "There is no chance of her waking. And I believe you are thoroughly prepared."

True, watching Volnar had roused Roger's appetite beyond control. As if entranced himself, he sat on the edge of the bed and leaned over the girl. Blood still trickled from the tiny incision in her neck. Ordinarily he would have spent several minutes mesmerizing the victim, to ensure that his kiss would bestow pleasure instead of pain. That work had been done for him. Nevertheless he did linger for a few seconds, savoring the emotions that stirred in her dreaming mind and her body's unconscious response to his touch.

A few seconds were all he could endure. He lay across her, acutely aware of the warmth of her skin, even through layers of clothing. He feasted on the rich taste of blood, mingled with salt and a trace of talcum. Tingling heat radiated from the point of contact, where his lips clung to her throat, through every cell. Wave after wave of sensation surged over him. He hardly noticed the sleeping girl's climax, except as an additional ripple of pleasure in the flood of ecstasy. He lay submerged in it for a timeless interval.

A firm hand on his shoulder brought him out. With a snarl he turned on Volnar, who said mildly, "Ten minutes should be quite enough." Roger became aware of discrete sensations again – the tang of blood in his mouth, the moist smoothness of the girl's flesh, the varied textures of her gown and the bed covers, the humming of insects through the open window, the breeze fluttering the ruffled curtains. He stood up – and staggered with vertigo. A natural effect of being pulled abruptly out of that warm scarlet fog.

"Sit down for a moment, and you'll soon recover," said Volnar. As usual he spoke coldly, the dispassionate diagnostician.

Roger obeyed, still feeling as if he were floating. He gradually settled back to normal and processed Volnar's remarks. "Ten minutes? You *timed* me, for God's sake?"

"You wouldn't want to drain her to the danger point, I suppose, and I had no intention of allowing you to. Do you deny that it was – adequate?"

Roger didn't have to consider that question for long. "Of course not. More than 'adequate.'"

They left just as they'd entered, Volnar closing the screen on the way out. No one lurked nearby to observe their departure, not even a police car on patrol. A cool drizzle fell as they headed back toward downtown.

"Won't she notice the wound on her neck?" Roger asked a block later. He'd wondered about this problem before but hadn't thought to discuss it with Sylvia. "Even though it's small, how will she explain it to herself? Suppose it jogs her memory about you, somehow?"

"You do worry entirely too much, young man," the elder said. "Not likely, since an enzyme in our saliva causes small bite marks to heal within a day or two and prevents infection, as well. Besides, I took the obvious precaution of commanding her not to notice."

Yes, it was obvious, and Roger felt annoyed with himself at not thinking of it before.

On the way back to the hotel Volnar didn't smoke; ap-parently tobacco served him as a substitute for the real thing. After a while he said, "Make sure you never get into that con-dition again. That is an order."

"I'd be happy to obey – sir – but how do you suggest I arrange it?"

"You seemed to have learned to manage discreetly, for the most part," Volnar said. "But on occasion you do need fully con-scious cooperation. That's what you are starved for."

"I'd think revealing our true nature to victims would be the last thing you'd approve of."

"That is not necessary," said Volnar in a tone of over-strained patience. "Have you thought of patronizing prostitutes?"

Roger found the idea distasteful and said so.

"Of course, one has to be careful of tainted blood. Though you're immune to disease yourself, I daresay your scruples would balk at becoming a carrier. But you should be able to discern any traces of sickness and avoid it."

"I'm supposed to tell them I want to bite them and suck their blood? Isn't that a little too – exotic – for most ladies of the evening?"

Volnar laughed softly. "You don't have to be quite that explicit. The important thing is that they know you don't require penetration, which means less work for them. Your paid partner may not realize exactly what you're doing to her, but she'll enjoy it and get well compensated, which should silence your moral qualms."

"I'll consider it," said Roger. The cold calculation of Vol-nar's approach repelled him. *Oh, exploiting patients is so much better, is it?*

"Another advantage – there's no risk of emotional involvement, always a hazard when a personal relationship exists between predator and prey. That was Sylvia's downfall."

"She didn't make that clear," said Roger. "I can understand her attraction to that boy, Rico. The way she described it, his passion must have been – incredibly seductive. But enough to keep her returning to him when it threatened her safety?"

"You really don't understand, do you? You haven't experienced that kind of obsession yet. It wasn't a purely emotional attachment; she was addicted to him. The usual consequence of returning again and again to a preferred donor. And if there's a certain psychic compatibility, one can become 'hooked' after two or three encounters." Sensing Roger's polite skepticism, he added, "Oh, it will happen to you eventually; you may as well accept that. Just try to arrange that when it does, the donor is someone you can enjoy on other levels besides the obvious."

"You talk as if arranging all these ideal conditions were as easy as – as buying a case of wine."

"Simply take the precaution of varying your targets, never using the same donor more than once or twice over a long period of time. It's a genuine physiological phenomenon, and you must not underestimate its force. You have read *Carmilla*, no doubt?"

Roger nodded.

"You'll recall the author's remark that `the vampire is prone to be fascinated with an engrossing vehemence, resembling the passion of love, by particular persons. . . . it will, in these cases, husband and protract its murderous enjoyment with the refine-ment of an epicure, and heighten it by the gradual approaches of an artful courtship.' I'm not sure where Le Fanu obtained his information, but except for the word `murderous,' he is accurate.

"I mention this," Volnar continued, "to impress upon you the perils of such an association. If you want to comprehend what Sylvia experienced when her young pet was killed, imagine the discomfort you were enduring earlier tonight. And imagine, further, that it can be relieved by one donor, and only one. If that donor suddenly becomes permanently inaccessible –"

No wonder Sylvia had behaved irrationally at times! "Discomfort" must be a ludicrously mild word for what she had suf-fered. Roger wished he'd shown her more sympathy.

Volnar said, "There is another duty I must perform in order to function as your advisor. We need to establish a telepathic rap-port. It will be for instructional purposes, not quite the same as the bond you share with Sylvia."

"Sorry, I don't quite understand," said Roger.

"You have exchanged blood with her, haven't you?" Volnar asked. "She implied so to me."

Roger had an uncomfortable feeling that the answer he had to give wasn't the one his advisor wanted. "Well – she let me drink from her."

"You *did* reciprocate?"

"She tried that, but I wouldn't allow it."

"Wouldn't allow –" Volnar was speechless for half a block, this time with anger. "Dark Powers! Have you any idea what you've done? No wonder she overindulged with that boy and got driven out of Boston! If you'd behaved with ordinary courtesy, she might still be there."

"And all those victims of hers Sandor killed, hounding her across country –" Just what he needed, a fresh load of guilt.

"The custom of our people," said Volnar icily, "to establish a bond between mentor and pupil, or to express affection, is a *mutual* exchange of blood."

"Then why didn't Sylvia tell me?" Roger lengthened his strides, wishing he could run away from Volnar's unpleasant truths. "It's hardly something I could be expected to figure out for myself."

"Couldn't you?" said Volnar in a thoroughly unforgiving tone. "You've treated her like a victim – an inferior. I'm surprised she let it go on as long as she did. She must be fond of you; the Creator alone knows why. But she has too much pride to spell out what your presumed affection should lead you to do spontaneously."

"Damn!" After a short silence Roger said defensively, "She might at least have been clearer about what it meant to her." Again he recalled the one time he had tried to fulfill her wish. "No, that's dishonest. She practically begged, and we did attempt it – once. I couldn't go through with it."

"Why not?"

"Feeling her – inside my brain –" Roger felt as if the memory were suffocating him.

"But that's the point of it. In such an exchange you can read the thoughts, share the sensations of your bonded partner, whether vampire or human."

"Oh – then Stoker was right."

"Yes. A single encounter will suffice for you and me. There's no time to explain verbally all you need to know about your nature, so I'll have to transmit the information by osmosis, so to speak."

"What? You expect me to –" Well aware that he would be dominated in that exchange, Roger shrank from the thought of getting that close to the older vampire, even once.

"Why did you suppose I brought up the subject?" By now they had reached the hotel. In the second-floor corridor Volnar again made a brief visual, auditory, and mental scan of the area before unlocking his door. Inside, stale smoke pervaded the air despite the open window.

They sat in the twin armchairs and stared at each other for a moment. "I see you're going to be difficult," said Volnar. "You deserve punishment for exploiting Sylvia, but that's not why I am insisting on the union."

"I know – for my own good."

Volnar ignored the sarcastic tone. "Aside from the fact that it's standard policy, it really is for your own good to overcome this reluctance. Without the bond, it would be practically impossible for me to teach you the skills you need. And I certainly couldn't do it in a single night, much less in the half hour or so we actually have. Also, there will be future occasions when you'll have use for this kind of rapport, so you shouldn't be afraid to initiate it."

"I'm not afraid." Roger settled more comfortably in the uninviting chair. The contentment of satiation was catching up with him. He wished Volnar would be quiet and let him rest.

"What word would you choose? Your inability to open to anyone, even in the most limited and controlled way, hints at paranoia – to an extent dysfunctional even for us." Volnar's tone softened a degree.

"Understandable, of course, in view of the iso-lation you've endured all your life." His voice seemed to fade into the distance.

"Wake up!" Volnar snapped.

"I'm listening."

"There are hours left until dawn," Volnar said. "I suppose you don't sleep properly, either. Well, the sooner we get this over with, the sooner you can rest."

Roger tensed, his drowsiness vanishing. "Right now?"

"The less time you have to brood on the prospect, the less you'll resist, and the easier it will be on you."

Roger sifted through what Volnar had said in the last few minutes. "You mentioned conveying skills. Sylvia is convinced I can learn to shapechange, as she does. Can you –?"

"Teach you that?" Roger felt Volnar fingering the upper-most layers of his mind. After a moment of silence, Volnar said, "No, I sense no vestige of that ability in you. You must realize, as a hybrid you inevitably have certain limitations. On the other hand, in some ways you are more flexible, less vulnerable, than the rest of us. Now, we'll proceed with your initiation."

## Chapter 12

ROGER DIDN'T CARE for being shoved around like a chess piece, yet he found a certain security in the way Volnar projected an illusion of absolute control. "Very well, I'm ready." *At least, I know I'll never be any readier.*

"If you'd grown up among our people, we'd have forged this bond as soon as you reached adolescence," Volnar pointed out. "You are magnifying the process into something far more unpleasant than it is. I intend to show you at once – shock treatment, if you will – that what you consider the worst is nothing to fear."

He stood up, looming above Roger. "I suggest you unbutton your collar." Having done so, Roger gripped the arms of the chair, exerting all his self-control to keep from lashing out as Volnar bent over him. Fighting would be undignified as well as useless. He made up his mind to submit to this invasion – once.

Volnar touched his neck, then drew back. "You are making this unnecessarily difficult. If you don't relax, you are likely to feel pain. You do know how to relax?"

Roger unclenched his hands, exhaled a long breath, and deliberately forced the tension out of his muscles. Volnar leaned over him again and nipped his throat without further preparation. For an instant Roger felt as if he were being sucked down into a bottomless whirlpool. When he clutched Volnar's arms, the old vampire's hands clamped on his shoulders, immobilizing him. Roger tried to scream, but no sound came out. He felt the pressure of Volnar's mind bearing down on him. He couldn't fight that crushing weight. He deliberately went limp, physically and mentally.

As soon as he relaxed, he realized nothing but his own terror had produced that sensation of being drawn into the abyss. Volnar's touch proved to be as cold and remote as his speech. He drank briefly, and Roger felt no loss of energy.

"You appear to have survived that," Volnar said dryly. "Now we reverse the process." He rolled up his left sleeve. "If you prefer to take from the neck, I'll allow it."

"This will be fine," said Roger. The less intimacy, the better. He sank his teeth into Volnar's arm, wishing he could inflict pain on the other man, if only for a few seconds. But Volnar didn't recoil. Roger did not expect any tangible benefit from this exchange. The interspecies polarity that enabled human blood to nourish him was not present; there wasn't even the sexual polarity that had made drinking from Sylvia pleasant, if not precisely satisfying. Yet he did get something from the cool, alien flavor of Volnar's blood – a tantalizing sense of ancient power, hovering just beyond his reach, there for the taking if only he could imbibe enough.

When the old vampire would have pulled away, Roger grasped more tightly. Volnar allowed it for another minute or two. Underlying the coolness of Volnar's flesh and the metallic taste of his blood, Roger also sensed the heat of his own lips and tongue on Volnar's skin, the tickle of his breathing on the hairs of the other man's arm.

*Impossible – I'm feeling through his senses.*

He felt the top layer of Volnar's mental barricade drop. Inside his skull he felt his advisor's exploratory probe, like the fingers of a surgeon preparing to make an incision. Roger struggled to cast out the invader. He might as well have tried to uproot an oak tree.

Volnar's voice spoke inside his head: "Why do you fight? The bond is complete. Neither of us can break it."

Roger felt a surge of vertigo. "Are you saying you'll be inside my brain forever?"

The ghost of a dry laugh. "Not at all. That would be equally distasteful to me. We can initiate and end communication at will, and in any case the rapport works only over short distances. A deeper union would require repeated exposure." The tone of the mental voice hardened. "Now, brace yourself. This part will be strenuous for both of us."

A tornado roared through Roger's head. He groped for an anchor, anything to help him stand against the whirlwind. He had no defense. It shattered his consciousness into a million fragments. Images crashed over him with the force of a tidal wave. Moonless nights, far from any human habitation, illuminated only by the haloes of living creatures' auras. Flying on currents of air above mountain peaks barren except for snow-swept rock. Sprinting through a chill desert night to spring on a coyote and rip out its throat. Stalking through the darkness shrouded in the illusory forms of wolf, panther, giant bat. Gazing into the eyes of an entranced woman who begged to open her veins and share her life-essence. Not one woman, but hundreds. Blood, rivers and oceans of it.

He was drowning –

The overbearing presence became fainter. Roger woke to awareness of his own thoughts. Scraps of information whirled in his brain like autumn leaves lashed by a hurricane. He opened his eyes, realizing that his lips were still pressed to Volnar's wrist.

Volnar pulled away. "That's more than enough. This is only a token exchange, remember?"

Dizzy and nauseated, Roger bowed his head on his hands. "What *was* that?"

"As I explained, that was the only way I could convey everything you need to know quickly enough. An information dump, so to speak."

"I don't know anything," Roger muttered. "It's all – chaotic."

Volnar laid a hand on his shoulder. "The confusion will pass quickly. The knowledge is lodged in your unconscious. The facts will sort themselves out, and when you need a piece of information, it will rise to the surface."

"Telepathy," Roger said. "Verbal transmission of thoughts. I don't believe it." He leaned back against the chair, waiting for his head to stop spinning.

"You do have a habit of skepticism, don't you? Actually, for extended conversation, telepathy is less efficient than speaking aloud. However, in some situations it can be very useful."

"I'm impressed," Roger said. "I wish Sylvia had explained this to me."

"Worth the ordeal?" said Volnar with a hint of derision.

"For once, yes."

"Some gaps may remain. You can, of course, call me when you need further advice or clarification." Volnar took a business card from his pocket and jotted several numbers on it.

Accepting the card, Roger noticed that the seasick feeling had almost vanished. "I can imagine what the psychological community would make of that – exchange. Especially the researchers who are already interested in extrasensory powers." He thought of Britt, with a fleeting image of "initiating" her into a telepathic bond. *If I think that's a good idea, I really am out of my mind.* "Listen, Volnar, the age of superstition is long gone. Why don't you people declare yourselves to the scientific com-munity? Your species and the human race could share infor-mation that would benefit all of us."

"I'm astonished at your naivete." Volnar paced to the window, turned, folded his arms, and glared down at Roger. "Do you seriously believe the human authorities – no matter what a few scientists might recommend – would react well to a group of nearly immortal predators in their midst? How many ordinary people would relish the idea of donating their blood to sustain 'monsters'?"

"Surely it wouldn't have to be like that, not with proper preparation and – well, public relations work."

"Public relations experts can accomplish only so much against primal fears. Do you want to spend your life on a reservation? The American Indians haven't fared very well in that arrangement, have they?" When Roger tried to speak up, Volnar overrode him. "More likely, we'd be locked in zoos, or worse, laboratories. Those who weren't exterminated on sight."

"I find that hard to imagine, not with the current attitude toward endangered species. Many natural predators are admired nowadays – killer whales, Siberian tigers, timber wolves –"

"May enjoy the protection of what some people derisively call 'tree-huggers.' The whales, tigers, and wolves, if they could talk, would doubtless take a dim view of their situation nevertheless."

"Is this why you objected to my reporting Sandor to the police?"

"Objected? Young man, no vampire in his senses would have considered doing what you did. If Sandor is caught and examined, or worse yet killed and dissected, the survival of our whole race would be jeopardized. That's far more important than the premature deaths of a few ephemerals."

"Damn it, Volnar, I can't accept that!" Roger leaped to his feet. "I will not dismiss human beings as – as game animals. I will *not* be like you."

Volnar shut him up with a cold stare. "I mentioned that I was your mother's advisor. Therefore I was bonded with her and shared her death."

"Then why the hell didn't you stop it?"

"Had I not been hundreds of miles away at the time, I would have." Volnar's mind locked onto Roger's. . . .

Roger found himself in the cellar of a nineteenth-century stone house on the outskirts of a small French village. That fact seeped into his consciousness as background information, while in the foreground his thoughts were submerged in those of a wo-man lying on a wide bed covered with sheets of white linen, in a paneled room of that cellar. He shared the panicked racing of the woman's heart as the fog of sleep cleared from her eyes.

A man holding a kerosene lamp stood over her. "Wake up, Claudette! For God's sake, you must –" He spoke in French, which Roger understood without being fully aware of the translation process.

Claudette sprang up and grabbed the man's arm. As her nails dug into the skin, the man winced but did not pull away. "What is it, Raoul?"

Raoul's aura radiated barely suppressed terror, punctuated by the smell of fear on his damp flesh. "They're breaking in – they'll kill you."

Tossing her hair back from her face, Claudette released the man's arm and smoothed the rumpled robe she had slept in. "It's you I'm afraid for, my love. Our kind take a lot of killing." A sullen mutter, swelling to a low roar, assaulted her ears from the floor above. "If you stay here while I confront them, they may not find you."

"Don't be absurd!" Anger flared up in Raoul, blotting out his fear.

The vision blurred, then re-formed in a parlor overstuffed with an eclectic mix of furniture and knickknacks from the Empire period on, which Claudette's eyes darted over unseeing, as familiar background details. Men brandishing a variety of weapons – some makeshift, such as hatchets, some on the level of the World War I cavalry sword an old man in a corner held in an *en garde* posture – clustered around Claudette and Raoul. A boy who looked barely twenty trained a shotgun on the woman. Claudette felt suffocated by the stink of terror and hate.

Her husband flung himself upon the boy with the gun. "Raoul, no!" Claudette shrieked. The blast ripped through Raoul's chest. The pain seared Claudette's flesh as well. An instant later it ceased, chopped off with the cutting of the link that bound her to her mate. She saw, rather than felt, the ax blade that severed Raoul's head.

She fell off a precipice into a black abyss, into an unnatural darkness her night vision could not pierce. Only the scent of her lover's blood, already cooling in death, wrenched her back to the crowded room. A dozen hands closed on her flailing limbs. She fought with all her inhuman strength, her teeth and claws gouging any flesh that came within reach. The taste of blood scorched her mouth. She howled like a rabid wolf, heedless of revealing her inhumanity.

But no matter how many she felled, they kept coming. At last she lay flat on her back, each arm and leg pinned by three or four assailants. The old man with the sword thrust a crucifix into her face. Baring her teeth, she snarled at him. A muscular fellow loomed over her. Almost before her eyes focused on it, the stake plunged between her breasts.

She felt every centimeter of the agony that tore through skin and cartilage to puncture her heart. And still she remained conscious, keening her anguish, to watch the sword sweep down. Its edge, dulled by time, lacerated her neck but did not bisect the spine. She felt the killers' horror when her eyes continued to stare up at them, and tortured ululations gurgled in her throat. She smelled smoke just before a hatchet extinguished awareness with her life. . . .

Roger struggled back to the present as if swimming against twenty-foot surf. Volnar's mind still lay wide open to him. A rush of agony, centuries, millennia of it, washed over him before Volnar slammed the gates shut.

Tears burned Roger's eyes. He refused to let them fall. "Damn you," he whispered. A sharp pain in his chest gradually faded. He realized he had collapsed on the bed. He carefully sat up, becoming aware that the subjective drama had taken only a few seconds of objective time. He returned Volnar's stony gaze. "Have you no compassion?"

"A human virtue" answered Volnar. "One they seldom practice." Aloud he said, "I had to convince you of that, and time is too short for subtlety. Are we agreed that the millennial dawn of interspecies cooperation is not at hand? Good – I trust you won't commit any further indiscretions like betraying one of our kind to human 'justice'?"

Roger subdued his anger and spoke coldly. "Are you saying that Sandor should be left free to slaughter innocent people?"

With an impatient wave of his hand, Volnar said, "The matter of 'innocence' is irrelevant. My point is that allowing Neil to be captured would expose our entire race to carnage that would reduce the depredations of one outlaw to insignificance."

"So all you're going to do about it is look for his sister and hope she knows where he is? Not to mention whether he'll even listen to her. You're the Prime Elder; you're supposed to be practically omniscient. Don't you have any way of tracking a single 'outlaw'?"

Volnar said, "Ordinarily his advisor could. However, his case is anomalous. At the onset of puberty he refused to bond with the woman chosen for his advisor, as he should have. According to her, Neil acquired his psychic gifts abnormally late, almost seventeen. Then they flooded upon him in full strength, substituting a fresh terror for his fear that he would never develop into adulthood. He ran away from his advisor and tried to teach himself. She's washed her hands of both Neil and his sister."

Roger felt a twinge of unwilling sympathy for the sadistic killer. "I can imagine how difficult that must have been."

"From what I've heard about Neil, I suspect his perception has remained duller than normal. If he needs violent emotion to get the nourishment the rest of us absorb from more subtle stimuli, that would account for his obsession with pain and horror."

"Very well, he has problems," Roger said. What a challenge Sandor would pose for a psychoanalyst! "That makes him more dangerous, not less. But as long as he doesn't expose your secret to the world, the people he kills mean nothing to you." He tried to stand up, making his head reel all over again.

"You're in no condition to drive." Volnar gathered brief-case, suitcases, and other personal property as he talked. "You need to rest and assimilate what I've poured into you. I'm checking out now and going to the airport. I'll turn in the key, but the room won't be disturbed until the maid shows up tomorrow morning. You stay here until you feel less agitated."

Though he hated to accept a favor from Volnar after being assaulted with the memory of Claudette's murder, Roger had to agree. He doubted he could walk to his car without staggering, much less drive.

"And keep me informed," Volnar said as he paused at the door, luggage in hand. "No matter what you think of me personally, that is what an advisor is for."

He stepped out. Roger heard the door latch click shut. A wave of exhaustion swamped him. He wanted nothing more than to sink into oblivion. For the first time in months, he felt tired enough to sleep during the night. At the last minute he remem-bered to set his wristwatch alarm for five a.m. Despite his confusion and anger, a pleasant thought struck him. Once he gave Sylvia the profuse apology he owed her, they would be able to talk. Now that he knew the truth, they had so much to discuss. He fell asleep with a vision of the two of them hunting and feasting together in the woods behind his home.

ELECTRICITY SIZZLED along Sylvia's nerves. In the post-midnight darkness under the trees behind Roger's townhouse complex, she paced back and forth, rubbing her arms. Despite the dryness in her throat, she knew it wasn't blood she needed. That wouldn't quench the fire at her core.

Why wasn't Roger home when she needed him? If she didn't get in contact with him in time, whom else could she turn to? *Why did I have to be so stubborn?* If she'd gone to Nevada as soon as the symptoms began, her advisor or the Prime Elder would have arranged a mate for her in plenty of time. Instead, she'd counted on the chance of catching Roger off guard. *Stupid!* If sexual desire did this to human beings, no wonder they be-haved so irrationally! Imagine spending one's whole life in the throes of this agony!

No, human sexuality couldn't be like this. From touching the minds of her donors, Sylvia knew their passion reached an unbearable peak only in the last few minutes before climax. It didn't maintain this intensity hour after hour. She shivered as her erect nipples brushed against the fabric of her blouse. She wanted to strip off her scratchy, binding clothes and run naked through the woods.

*I may have to take an ordinary man. And they're so limited!*

Swift footsteps broke the cycle of her thoughts. She whirled to face the sound. She caught her breath at the sight of the man threading his way among the trees.

"Good evening, Sylvia – or morning, I guess. Don't tell me you were planning to give yourself to the halfbreed?"

She hated the way her heart raced at the sound of his voice. "What are you talking about, Neil?"

"Your friend, the doctor. It took me a while to find out, but a few of our people still talk to me. The ones who know homo saps are just food. The ones who gag at the thought of mating with them." He glided closer to her. She felt a rush of warmth between her legs. "You didn't know the doc's father was human?"

For an instant Sylvia forgot her discomfort. "No, I didn't, and neither did he. That explains a lot."

Suddenly Neil's arms wrapped around her. His heartbeat and breathing thundered in her ears. "Well, now that you do, you wouldn't want to waste yourself on him, even if he were here. Isn't it a good thing I just happened to show up?"

"Do you expect me to believe that?" She squirmed feebly, helpless against the assault of his strength and her lust, and felt the pressure of his erection. "What are you doing here?" A spasm of arousal, deep inside, fought against her contempt for him.

"Followed you from the motel. I wanted to talk to you anyway – and now it's more than talk." He moved one hand upward to grasp her by the hair. "I've had enough of you hanging around with the halfbreed. Whose side are you on?"

"No side – I'm neutral," she gasped. "All I want is to be left alone.

I was planning to move on soon anyway."

He grinned, the rotten-meat odor of his breath hitting her in the face. She wondered whether he slept in an abandoned building or even on the ground under a layer of brush; he didn't seem to have paid any attention to personal hygiene for a long time. "Think I'd let you get away with that, little one? Neutral, hell! If you're not on my side, we're enemies. Now I know you didn't turn me in -- but how can I trust you not to help the doc against me, if you don't give me some sign?"

"What?" she breathed. Much as she loathed the man, she caught herself wiggling against him, aching for closer contact.

"Easy. Remember what fun we had hunting together, before you got squeamish? You join me again. And we'll start with a private celebration." His other hand kneaded her buttocks. Her rebellious flesh responded with another gush of hot liquid.

"No." She could manage no more than a feeble whisper.

"Everything but your mouth says yes. And if you have a baby – sure, I know it's almost unheard-of, the first time, but if – we can be untraditional and bring it up our own way."

*What a grotesque idea*, Sylvia thought. Imagine a baby trained in Neil's way of life – just the revenge against the elders his warped mind would hatch.

Neil's fiery eyes taunted her as he gripped her head, his fingers tangled in her hair, and tore her bermuda shorts down the front.

Sylvia's struggles did no more than entertain him. Though male and female vampires differed less in size and strength than human men and women, Neil was unusually large for his species, as well as older than Sylvia. Deep within, also, she knew she wasn't fighting him with her full strength.

He shoved her onto her back, hard. She scarcely noticed the shock of hitting the ground. Through her blouse his nails raked her shoulders and breasts. She felt his beard rasping her cheek, then his teeth scraping her collarbone. She let out a choked cry. He unzipped his pants. The feel of his hard shaft against her belly made her skin ripple, inside and out. She clawed at him, scenting the pungent odor of his blood, yet her legs involuntarily opened to his thrust.

"Are you going to scream? Be my guest."

She didn't. The townhouse complex was too close, and the taboo against drawing human attention was too deeply ingrained. She would endure Neil's violation – *stop lying to yourself, girl, you'll enjoy it!* – until he exhausted his lust and left her alone. *And if I do get pregnant, by some impossible fluke, I'll kill it!*

But she did sob tearlessly under her breath when he pounded into her – sobbed with shame at the ecstatic convulsions that racked her body.

Six mutual orgasms later, the sobs escalated to shrieks when his teeth ripped into her throat.

A WHITE SQUARE on the foyer carpet caught Roger's eye. What remained of his well-fed contentment wilted like a pricked balloon.

He focused his infrared-sensitive vision on the piece of paper. No heat traces, so the message had been delivered at least fifteen minutes ago. He knelt to pick up the note. A whiff of the metallic odor he associated with vampires drifted to his nose. Sylvia? No, he would recognize her scent. As hesitantly as a child creeping alone into a dark room, he unfolded the paper.

Welcome home, Darvell. I left something for you in the woods behind your building, unless somebody else has removed it by now. Go about a hundred yards due north.

-- N. S.

*DEAR GOD, not another body!* Crumpling the note and shoving it into a pocket, Roger dashed to the back door, unfastened chain and bolt with shaking hands, and raced into the woods. By now the drizzle had grown to a light but steady rain. Once he got a few yards under the trees, he didn't need Sandor's directions. The smell of death overwhelmed the fragrance of sap and pine needles.

Roger slowed to a brisk walk. He did not want to see this. He knew, though, that he had to check out the site before the police examined it. The murderer might have left evidence that implicated Roger.

No patch of heat served as a beacon to guide him, but the white of her face and the red smears from neck to groin snared his vision. All warmth had long since seeped out of her flesh.

Roger fell to his knees a couple of feet from the corpse. *Sylvia!* His head buzzed as if from a concussion. Still mercifully numb, he leaned closer, careful not to touch the blood-soaked leaves around the body. Her blouse and shorts had been ripped to shreds, as had the skin beneath. She lay on her back with arms and legs splayed wide apart. Something was wrong with the angle of her neck.

Good God, he'd torn off her head!

*So she can't regenerate.* Roger's numbness yielded to nausea. He turned and staggered through the underbrush, managing to get well away from the murder site before vomiting. Long after his stomach emptied itself, he crouched on all fours, retching up his anguish. Eventually the dry heaves gave way to sobs. Vampires, Sylvia had once told him, didn't cry tears. Roger hadn't inherited that limitation. Tears scorched his eyes and cheeks, choking him until he almost got sick all over again.

Exhausted at last, feeling as if he'd ejected every drop of fluid in his body, he scooped pine straw over the mess on the ground. Even now, he had the presence of mind to realize he mustn't leave evidence. He trotted unsteadily back home.

The first thing he did was to tear the note from Sandor into tiny scraps and rinse them down the garbage disposal. Next he sat down in the living room to think.

Clearly Sandor intended Sylvia's death as a warning. He was closing in, destroying a person important to Roger, as well as sending the signal that he had no compunctions about killing one of his own race. Roger knew he had to report the murder. Waiting for it to be discovered by someone else could lead to awkward questions.

Another problem came to mind – an autopsy on Sylvia might provide data that could endanger the vampire community. How much did vampires differ, on the gross anatomical level, from *Homo sapiens*? It couldn't be helped; he had no reliable way of concealing the body. *Anyhow, I owe the vampire community damn near zero!*

He went into his office and dialed Lieutenant Hayes' home number.

"Dr. Darvell? Surprised to hear from you. Something wrong?" said the detective's sleep-thickened voice.

"Yes." Roger paused to force his breathing under control. "I was away from home overnight, visiting with a friend from out of town. When I got back, I went for a walk in the woods, as I often do." His neighbors would confirm that habit, if any suspicion arose.

"In the rain?"

"A little rain doesn't bother me – it's refreshing." He swallowed hard. "It seems a – another friend of mine who's been staying in the area for a few weeks stopped by while I was gone. I found her – back there –" To his shame, he couldn't finish the sentence.

Hayes' drowsy voice shifted gears to professional crispness. "I'll be right over."

## Chapter 13

ROGER ENDURED an agonizing Friday at the office, avoiding Britt for fear she would notice his distress and comment on it. On top of the shock of Sylvia's murder, stray fragments of data from Volnar's "download" floated into his consciousness like bubbles rising to the surface of a pond. He returned home that night to the head-splitting jangle of the telephone.

When he picked it up, Volnar said with no preliminary greeting, "Sylvia is dead."

Roger swallowed a mouthful of acid and said, "How did you know?"

The elder's voice drilled into his ear like an ice pick. "Through our bond. In her death pangs, she won the strength to call out to me. I couldn't go to her. I was in the air above the middle of the Atlantic."

"I didn't think the – bond – reached that far." His lungs felt squeezed so that he could hardly breathe.

"Ordinarily not. That was her death cry. But if you had shared a bond with her, you could have heard her thoughts – her pain."

"Damn you, Volnar –" A wave of faintness swept over Roger. He collapsed into the desk chair.

The voice continued implacably, "You might have sensed the danger in time to cover those few miles and save her."

"You're blaming me for Sylvia's death?"

"Neil Sandor attacked her because of you, did he not?"

"Yes." *What the hell do you expect me to do about it now?*

Volnar answered the unspoken question. "Neil has murdered one of our own people. He is now under sentence of death. He's in your territory, your responsibility. If you have the chance to destroy him, you are ordered to do so. And do your best to ensure that the corpse is not autopsied."

"You seriously think I can –"

"So far, his sister refuses to be found," Volnar said. "Since you are his target, he'll eventually come to you. When he does, you must deal with him. I assume you don't want any more deaths on your damned human conscience." He hung up, leaving Roger racked with anger and grief.

AFTER TIPTOEING around the issue, Lieutenant Hayes, persuaded by the same hypnotic pressure that convinced him of Roger's innocent-bystander status, yielded to his demand for a copy of Sylvia's autopsy. The report was hand-delivered Sunday morning just as Roger got home from early Mass at St. Mary's in downtown Annapolis. Postponing sleep, which he dreaded for the dreams it would spawn, he shut himself in his home office to study the file immediately.

The familiar medical terminology made reading it less of an ordeal than he'd feared. He told himself that the extent of the butchery shouldn't have surprised him. Clawing Sylvia's torso, biting her throat, and breaking her neck before tearing off her head were typical of Sandor's *modus operandi*. The Medical Examiner didn't hazard a guess as to what weapon had performed that last operation. *He'd never suspect Sandor did it barehanded,* Roger thought.

One surprising element, though – she had been raped.

That must puzzle Hayes, since the murderer had raped none of his other victims. Roger understood, though, when he recalled Sylvia's plea for him to mate with her. She'd been entering the first stages of estrus. It must have peaked Friday night, when Sandor waylaid her.

*She asked for my help. If I'd given her what she wanted –!*

He refused to let himself break down again. Shutting off the incipient flood of grief, he scanned the rest of the post mortem. So many anomalous details – Sylvia's digestive tract, her blood type, the shape of her teeth – blazoned her strangeness. Roger hoped that, given the human reluctance to believe the impossible, the police would ascribe the oddities to some obscure congenital deformity.

*Do I care whether the vampire species is exposed to public view? If so, why?* His anger over the way Volnar had treated him still simmered. Yet he couldn't deny an impulse to shield his own kind. Volnar expected him to destroy the renegade for the good of their race. How the devil was he supposed to accomplish that?

He recalled Sandor's request for a meeting. Much as Roger hated the idea, he decided to place that personal ad. What he would do when he met his antagonist, he hadn't figured out. He composed a brief message: "N. S. – All right, let's talk. Call me at home. – R. D."

Monday morning he phoned in the ad to the Annapolis *Capital*, paying extra to have it set in oversize type. That done, he arrived at work fortified by an illusion of accomplishment.

He found Britt waiting on his office couch.

As soon as he'd shut the door, giving them privacy, she sprang to her feet and said in a low, rapid voice, "Hayes gave me all the details of what happened Friday night. Roger, why didn't you tell me? Why the *hell* didn't you tell me?"

He shrank from the blast of emotion she hurled at him. "I knew the detective would fill you in. My giving you the same information would have been redundant."

He felt her harden in response to his coldness. She stepped up to him, so close he felt the heat of her body. "You know perfectly well I'm not talking about the case. Hayes mentioned that she was a friend of yours – that you found the body. Why didn't you call me?"

Through the sunglasses he still wore, Roger stared past her, over her shoulder, to avoid meeting the blaze of her green eyes. "He had no right to give you that information."

"Don't waste my time with irrelevancies. Whether he should have mentioned it or not, he did." She clasped Roger's upper arms, her nails denting the fabric of his jacket. "Take off your glasses and *look* at me."

He reluctantly did so. When he looked her in the face, the intensity of her grief for him – *for him!* – awoke the agony he thought he'd buried.

"Roger, why didn't you let me know? I thought we were friends."

He gave her the partial truth, that he had never thought of asking for her support. "I've lived alone all my adult life. I'm not accustomed to sharing my problems."

His remote tone made her back off. "Haven't you heard, Roger? That's what friends are for."

MONDAY'S MAIL included an envelope postmarked Los Angeles. A glance at the signature gave him a small jolt. Volnar's mention of Claude Darvell, Roger's half-brother, had slipped to the back of his mind. The letter read:

*Mon Frere,*

I'm delighted to be "allowed" to contact you at last. Don't let Fearless Leader get to you. True, we have to obey direct orders from him, but that "Council of Elders" is simply a collective label for all our people who've outlived their first millennium. It actually meets only twice a century or less. We're anarchists at heart; the only reason we have a Council at all is in self-defense against those teeming hordes of gregarious homo saps.

Did Fearless Leader give you the standard cautionary lecture about "addiction"? I daresay he didn't mention the positive side— that if an ordinary feeding is like a decent French claret, an exclusive relationship is the equivalent of Dom Perignon. Having one ephemeral who's fully aware of what you are and can't wait to bare her throat for you every time you meet is not necessarily a *bad* thing, *n'est-ce pas?* Think I wouldn't rather have that than a succession of vampire groupies who only want their fantasies fulfilled for one evening? Well, sometimes, depending on the phases of the moon.

If any problems crop up that you don't want to discuss with Volnar, give me a ring. I'm usually in Los Angeles or Big Sur, sometimes London or Geneva.

    Good hunting –
    Claude

AT THE BOTTOM of the page were four telephone numbers. The message had obviously been written before Claude learned of Sylvia's death. Roger decided that if Claude didn't share her high opinion of the Prime Elder, he liked his newfound brother already. He wrote a reply, summarizing his recent experiences and even mentioning Britt.

When he received no call Tuesday night, Roger guessed that Sandor was still playing games, determined to make Roger "squirm" again. He didn't know how long he'd be able to stand the waiting.

To make matters worse, the next morning Britt once more lay in ambush for him, this time with a folded newspaper in hand. The evening classifieds.

As soon as the door was shut behind them, she marched to his desk and slapped it with the paper. "Tell me about this ad of yours in the crab wrapper."

He returned her hard stare. "What ad?"

"Don't try to give me a runaround! The initials have to be yours. I don't believe in coincidences of that magnitude."

"You're studying the personal ads? What next, supermarket tabloids?"

His sarcasm didn't deflect her. "They provide intriguing glimpses into the human psyche. I notice you don't deny it."

"Why should I? You've made up your mind." He remained standing, hoping she'd take the hint and leave.

"What's it all about? What do you know that you aren't telling the police? Not to mention me."

"There's nothing I can tell you."

Britt leaned across the desk. Her excited heartbeat thundered in his ears. "I didn't get around to filling you in on my library search for similar crimes in other cities. I ran across an outbreak in Boston this August. And guess who the *Globe* mentioned serving as a consultant to the police?"

Roger gripped the edge of the desk to keep from flinching visibly.

"Do you know who the killer is?" He felt her insistence as a wave of tangible pressure. "What's the problem? Patient confi-dentiality?"

Let her think that. Any alternative theory she might concoct would be worse for him. "I can't talk about it."

"Then at least let me in on whatever you can. When you meet the man, let me come along – or introduce me to him later. You know how much I want to be part of this!"

He went cold with alarm. "Out of the question! If such a contact took place – and I stress *if* – it would be too dangerous for you."

She transfixed him with an icy glare. "Why for me and not for you? Don't be sexist." Tapping the desk with the folded newspaper, she said, "Get this straight – I won't be left out."

Alone, Roger brooded over whether anything would happen for her to be left out of. Perhaps Sandor had insincerely proposed a meeting just to torment him.

Wednesday evening, though, the anticipated call came.

"Well, Doctor, are you ready to deal? I'm glad to see you showing some sense."

Roger schooled his voice to a dispassionate flatness. Fortunately the caller couldn't read his emotions over the phone. "Your excesses are threatening both of us. I won't have my hunting grounds spoiled."

"No guts, no glory, Doc."

"Why don't you come to my townhouse tonight, and we'll discuss it in detail?"

A laugh rumbled over the line. "Do you think I've survived for almost a century by strolling into the tiger's lair? We'll meet on neutral ground, or not at all. What do you say to tomorrow night in the Tawes Garden, near the sundial?"

"Next to the footbridge?" said Roger. "All right. What time?"

"It'll be full dark by nine, and the place should be deserted."

"Agreed," said Roger. The caller immediately hung up.

Now Roger had to face the question he'd postponed, what to do with the killer when they met. He considered and dismissed the notion of a police stakeout. The carnage in Boston, when they'd tried to arrest the vampire, remained vivid in his mind. Roger mulled over a vague plan to use a blend of blackmail and threats to pressure Sandor into leaving Maryland. *Yes, I'm supposed to destroy him, but how, when he's probably stronger than I am?*

He reviewed the weapons available to him. Garlic was out, as toxic to him as to Sandor. Showing up with a sharpened stake or a high-caliber pistol would destroy any pretense of peaceful negotiation. A cross might work against Sandor. Self-taught and mentally unstable, he might well share the religious phobia common to many young vampires. And despite Sandor's boasts, by vampiric standards he was very young.

*But so am I!*

RAPED. AT HOME Tuesday evening, Britt pored over Sylvia LaMotte's autopsy report. Because of that deviation from the pattern, Lieutenant Hayes conjectured that Sylvia's death was unrelated to the serial murders. Britt knew better. She had no doubt that the criminal had violated and murdered Sylvia to get at Roger.

*Why didn't he tell me about her?* Britt asked herself for the hundredth time. That lack of confidence still hurt. Maybe she was wasting energy, trying to develop a personal relationship with Roger. *No, I won't give up yet!*

Had he known all along that Sylvia was, to say the least, physiologically peculiar? Britt reviewed the post mortem results, vividly illustrated by the M.E.'s stark black and white photos of fractured cervical vertebrae and lacerated thoracic tissue. "The cause of death," read the pathologist's concluding opinion, "was decapitation by an unidentified instrument. Mechanism of death was severing of the spinal column between the third and fourth cervical vertebrae, accompanied by massive hemorrhage. Manner of death was homicide." Classic defense wounds on the forearms showed that Sylvia, unlike the other victims, had fought back.

Even the killer's dentition, judging from the bite pattern, raised questions. Britt lingered over the other anomalies. For instance, the large volume of seminal fluid recovered from the victim's vagina. The M.E.'s staff had presumed gang rape, until their tests pointed to a single source. Doubting the results, they'd arranged for DNA analysis. As for the dried blood under Sylvia's nails, it didn't type consistently. Nor did the victim's own blood. Contaminated samples, operator error? Britt had her doubts.

What would Roger say, she wondered, if she drew his atten-tion to Sylvia's oddly shaped molars, only two pairs in each upper and lower jaw instead of the normal three or four? Or the short intestinal tract? Or the unidentified compounds in the victim's saliva, resembling traces left in her wounds by the attacker's mouth? When Britt had suggested to Roger that the killer might not be human, she had been indulging in a flight of fantasy. Now it seemed downright plausible. But she didn't intend to reopen the subject with Roger until she found out how much he knew.

*Damn the man, I'm going to make him trust me whether he likes it or not!*

With some reluctance she put away her files on the murder cases. She needed to get plenty of sleep, for she had plans for the next evening or two. She only hoped she hadn't missed her chance tonight. She gambled that Roger and the unknown killer couldn't have gotten together this promptly.

Wednesday evening she borrowed a friend's car, drove to Roger's neighborhood at the fall of twilight, and parked around the curve where she could barely see the front of his building. She watched for hours, keeping herself awake with tapes on the cassette player and making two quick dashes into the woods to relieve her bladder. Roger's Citroen did not leave the parking lot, nor did she notice any visitor walking up to the door she had identified as his. At one a.m., yawning and battling leg cramps, she gave up and went home.

Had her stakeout come too late? Could Roger have made contact already? Or perhaps it was a waste of time watching the house at night; her associate could set up a meeting on his lunch hour. Well, he wouldn't be able to evade Britt's diligence in that case; he virtually never went out at lunchtime, so if he did, she'd know something peculiar was up. For that very reason, she con-sidered a nocturnal meeting more likely.

Stifling the protests of her aching muscles and drooping eyelids, she determined to try again Thursday night.

By Thursday night Roger still hadn't devised a concrete plan for dealing with Sandor. For freedom of movement he dressed in casual slacks, a short-sleeved sport shirt, and soft-soled shoes. He tucked a rosary into his breast pocket. That weapon might give him a slim edge over the enemy.

After dark he drove past the Navy stadium and across Taylor

Avenue into the parking lot between the angular, concrete and smoked glass District Court and Department of Natural Resources buildings. He took care to leave his car in deep shadow where it shouldn't attract notice. Though the Tawes Garden was open at no charge all the time, nobody visited it at this hour. While locking the Citroen, he heard footsteps on the pavement, crossing from the stadium. Whirling around, he scanned the shadows. He strained his ears. Silence. Whomever he'd heard must have veered in a different direction.

He catfooted around the building to the garden, an unfenced panorama of trees, shrubs, and other plant life illustrating the various Maryland ecologies. The night felt crisp and cool, pleasant to him though a little chilly for most people. Behind him something stirred the bushes. Again he stopped to listen. Nothing. The wind? A dog? He sniffed the air, but the slight breeze blew from ahead of him. He followed the path around the pond, eliciting a rustle and a quack from a pair of sleepy ducks in the reeds. When he crossed the footbridge, the open, grassy area next to the sundial was still deserted.

Could Sandor be responsible for the faint sounds he'd heard? Speaking the man's name in a cutting whisper brought no response.

He scanned the silent garden for the outlaw vampire's ap-proach. Blast it, where was Sandor? Did he plan to break the appointment, keep Roger guessing?

Suddenly a sense of presence impelled Roger to look up. A winged shape spiraled down toward the clearing.

*Good God, the man's not only a sadist, he's an arrogant, reckless idiot!*

The vampire landed on the grass and melted into human form. "Good evening, Dr. Darvell," he said. Sandor proved to be a broad-shouldered barbarian with shaggy, copper-red hair and beard. His bushy eyebrows merged over the bridge of his nose. He wore jeans with no shirt or shoes. A cloud of carrion stench enveloped him.

"Are you out of your mind, traveling that way in a populated area?"

"Sounds like the voice of envy to me," Sandor said. "A half-breed can't shapechange, right? Too bad." He whirled around, alerted by a sound under the pines. Roger heard a gasp of astonishment, followed by the ragged sound of nervous breathing.

Britt stepped from beneath the sheltering trees.

*Of all the harebrained, reckless –! She followed me!* "Britt, you fool –" Roger stopped abruptly.

Sandor bared his teeth in a wide grin. "You know this woman?"

"Run!" Roger cried.

He knew the futility of that command. Even if Britt had tried, she'd have been no match for Sandor's inhuman speed. Roger broke into a run, trying to intercept Sandor, but the pure-blood out-sprinted him. In a blur of motion Sandor surged across the intervening space and grabbed Britt. Dragging her into the open, he faced Roger with Britt pinned against his body. One hand clutched both her wrists, while the other grasped her neck above the open collars of her loose blouse and denim jacket.

Recovering from the initial shock, Britt said mildly, "You don't have to hold so tight. I've been wanting to meet you."

"Then you've got your wish. But if you don't mind, I'm taking no chances."

"Let her go," said Roger, taking a few paces closer to the pair.

"Watch your step," Sandor said, his clawed fingers stroking Britt's chin. "Surely you don't think you could get to me before I could rip open her jugular?"

Roger read fear in Britt's aura, but she gave no outward sign of it. "You don't need her. I'll vouch for her silence, and we don't want the distraction."

"Oh, yes, we do," Sandor grinned. "She's just what I needed to complete this little party – a hostage for your good behavior. She means something to you, doesn't she?"

Roger cursed himself for so obviously revealing his concern for Britt. "What do you have in mind?"

Sandor glanced up at the sky and back toward the silent office buildings. "Getting out of this exposed spot, to start with." He turned and hustled Britt ahead of him into the pine grove. Roger followed. Sandor shoved Britt down on a bench and sat beside her, giving her arms a gratuitous wrench at the same time. She set her jaw and didn't accommodate him with so much as a whimper.

His right hand still lingering on her neck, Sandor said, "Now that we're more comfortable, we can have a little refreshment and talk over our differences."

Britt's face lit up with amazement that momentarily can-celed her fear. If they ever got out of this, Roger didn't know how he could possibly deal with her. "Look, Sandor, I don't want –"

"Don't give me that, Darvell. I can sense your thirst the same way you sense mine."

What Roger felt emanating from the murderer, though, was not simple appetite like his own, but a violent lust that revolted him. He said wearily to Britt, "Now are you convinced? You won't get immortality from this sociopath; you'll get yourself killed."

"I'm convinced of that," she said, her voice steady, "but not that he's typical of the breed."

"Quiet!" Sandor tightened his grip on her wrists, not forget-ting to watch Roger. He favored Britt with a caricature of a smile. "So you want the vampire's kiss? I haven't had one like you in a long time. It'll be my pleasure to grant your desire – and you'll sure as hell get more from me than from the fangless freak, here." In fact, Sandor didn't have fangs, either, except in his trans-formed shape, but the insult registered loud and clear.

Beyond caring what the renegade said to or about him, Roger interrupted, "Will you stop wasting time? I came here to negotiate, not –" He couldn't say it, not about Britt.

"Right. What kind of deal are you offering?"

"The only deal I'll make with you is that you get out of my territory – right now. If you leave this county – no, better make that the state of Maryland and the D.C. suburbs – I won't pursue."

Sanders barked a laugh. "Don't you think I can see when you're lying? The only way I can be safe from you is to make sure you're in as deep as I am. Now, you listen to my terms. We're going to become partners. And you'll start by sharing this one with me."

The image of Britt writhing in the outlaw's clutches, blood spurting from her torn throat, hit Roger like a blow to the pit of the stomach. He struggled to mask his reaction from the enemy.

"You want it, Darvell – why don't you admit that?" Sandor's fiery eyes flicked repeatedly from Roger to Britt and back again. "You've been wanting this one for a long time. Well, you can just wait your turn." He drew a curved fingernail down the side of her neck. She winced as a thread of blood, luminous with life-energy, bloomed on her fair skin.

A pang of yearning pierced through Roger's outrage. Britt's eyes met his for an instant, and he thanked God that he saw no fear of himself there.

"You can work up an appetite watching," Sandor continued. "I could make her want it, too – make her beg me for it. But I'm not going to cloud her mind. She'll feel everything when I bite into her. If you've never taken one fighting and screaming, you haven't lived. Believe me, after you've watched that, you'll be ready."

Roger's long-denied desire to possess Britt, not in terror but in mutual passion, surged up, to be swamped by the fear and an-ger that washed over him in frigid waves. Britt, thoroughly frightened now, leaped to her feet. Sandor shoved her down with casual roughness.

Roger was amazed at the intensity of his own rage. The worst, he thought, was the subtext of that emotion – not a chivalrous, "Unhand that damsel, you cad," but a predator's roar of, "Hands off – she's mine!" Forgetting diplomacy, he lunged at Sandor.

The vampire jerked Britt to his chest, facing him, and placed his bared teeth against the side of her neck. Roger saw her cringe, her face twisting with disgust. "Not another inch, Darvell."

Roger stepped back. Britt tamed her revulsion and said quietly, "You don't have to go through all that – what's your name?"

"Call me Neil." His hand still encircled her throat, but not so tightly.

"You were right, Neil, I do want intercourse with a vampire. A real one." Sandor shot Roger a triumphant glance. Did his egoism blind him so thoroughly he couldn't penetrate Britt's insincerity? Good – but Roger doubted her fake submission could disarm Sandor enough to tip the balance their way. "Give me a chance to experience it to the fullest," she purred. "I'm ready to cooperate here and now."

With another gloating look at Roger, Sandor said, "Don't even think of interfering. How long I let her live is entirely up to you."

Roger could scarcely keep himself from rushing the killer, against all reason.

"One thing I'd really like, if you don't mind," Britt said, leaning pliantly against Sandor. "Change back into that – what-ever it was. Giving you my blood would be so much more thril-ling that way."

The breathy appeal was so foreign to the real Britt that Roger wondered how Sandor could be deceived by it. Volnar must have been right about the renegade's defective empathic power. What was she up to? Under her fascinated gaze, the vampire did begin to flow out of human shape. Roger suddenly thought of the ogre in "Puss in Boots," devoured when he let himself be flattered into becoming a mouse. But Sandor's alter-nate form had no such weakness.

Wait – didn't it? Seeing the silver-gray wings overshadow Britt, Roger recalled what Sylvia had told him the first time he'd seen her transform. When the molecules were in flux, a vampire was abnormally vulnerable. The wings, in particular, were hyper-sensitive.

How could he use the knowledge, though? Sandor was still watching Roger out of the corner of his eye, while mouthing Britt's throat. Apparently intent on prolonging the suspense, he hadn't yet bitten her. He did, however, relax enough to let go of her arms, instead grasping her around the waist.

"Beautiful," Britt murmured. "I never dreamed of anything like you." Her slender hands crept up over his shoulders, cares-singly skimmed over his temples and cheeks. A low growl rumbled in Sandor's chest. Nauseated, Roger ordered himself not to look away. Britt was fighting to give him an opening.

Her body molded itself to Sandor's. Then her thumbs dug into his eye sockets. At the same instant, she rammed a knee into his groin.

Roger could have told her that wouldn't disable Sandor. With undescended testicles, a vampire wasn't sensitive in that spot like a human male. However, the shock of the double attack broke the outlaw's hold on Britt. Roger charged at Sandor, at the same time as Britt fell to her knees and rolled out of the way.

Sandor's claws slashed at Roger's right arm. Springing backward, Roger suddenly thought of the rosary in his shirt pocket. He pulled it out and thrust it toward the other vampire.

To his surprise, the enemy actually retreated. "Halfbreed scum – using human weapons!"

"Your crimes give all of us a bad name." Roger heard the rasp of his own breathing as well as Sandor's. A crimson haze blurred his vision.

"'Crime' to you and the rest of Volnar's tame dogs! You think he holds himself to those rules?" Reaching behind him, Sandor ripped a branch off the nearest tree. He swiped at Roger, knocking the rosary to the ground.

Roger attacked Sandor empty-handed. Slipping on the pine needles underfoot, they grappled, Roger struggling to keep his antagonist's claws and teeth away from his neck. Though Sandor's wings quivered with the strain, Roger saw at once that the other vampire was stronger than he. A purely defensive strategy stood no chance.

His peripheral vision glimpsed Britt on her knees, groping on the ground. Damn – if only her eyes could handle the dark like his. Roger focused on Sandor, well aware of the danger of getting distracted a second time. The shimmering wings seemed to mock him.

The wings. Roger relaxed the pressure of his hands, throwing

Sandor off balance for a second. As the killer, with a growl of triumph, closed the gap between them, Roger grabbed both wings near the shoulder blades and crumpled the delicate membrane in his fists.

Sandor let out an agonized howl. Roger was vaguely aware of Britt jumping up, the rosary clutched in her hand. She jabbed it at Sandor's chest. The vampire collapsed, stunned, on the ground.

Staring down at him, Roger noticed a second-degree burn where the crucifix had branded the flesh.

Britt gulped a few breaths and said in a shaky voice, "Interesting psychosomatic effect."

Roger's chest ached from the exertion. He, too, had to catch his breath before he could ask whether she was all right. At the moment he didn't trust his perceptions.

"Sure," Britt said. "I knew that book on how to survive rape would come in handy someday. What do we do now?"

Roger eyed the prostrate vampire, who had resumed human form as soon as the cross had touched him. Sandor's legs jerked.

"Get back!" Roger ordered Britt, plucking the rosary from her hand.

Sandor struggled to his feet. Roger thrust the crucifix at him. Sandor's lips curled in a snarl. Lurching backward, he shifted from human to winged form and back again like a time-lapse special effect. He seemed weak, disoriented. One good blow should knock him out, and then – Roger lunged for the wounded vampire. Sandor spread his wings once more and rose straight into the air. A lupine howl keened from his throat as he vanished above the trees.

Roger staggered to the bench, dropping the rosary, and sat down. "Damn! I botched it – if I'd followed through right away, instead of assuming he was disabled –" Roger recognized the source of his vacilation. If he'd captured Sandor, he would have had to decide what to do with him. Both turning him over to the police and killing him in cold blood presented difficulties Roger wasn't ready to deal with. "I thought I could handle him on my own. I was wrong."

"Your eyes," Britt whispered. "You both have the same eyes."

"Does that frighten you?"

Britt sat beside him. "Of course not. Don't you give me credit for being able to tell the difference between you and *that*?"

The tightness in his chest eased. "You understand why I didn't want to satisfy your curiosity?" He dared to meet her eyes.

They remained steady. "You can count on my silence."

"I trust your discretion implicitly."

Britt flashed him a grateful smile. "I wanted to meet a vampire, and now I've met two – one of whom I've been working with for over a month. I won't do anything to spoil that." She radiated no fear now; her eyes gleamed with excitement, and her cheeks were flushed. *She glows from the inside out,* Roger thought.

"That bastard hurt you." His fingertips hovered near the mark on her neck without quite touching.

"Oh, that? Just a scratch. Doesn't even sting."

"Still, you'd better get it cleaned as soon as possible."

He realized her smile had died as she gazed intently at him. "Roger, are you all right?"

"What do you mean, me?" When her fingers brushed his right arm, he looked down and noticed for the first time that Sandor's initial claw-swipe had connected. On Roger's forearm a long gash still dripped blood. He swayed under a surge of dizziness.

Britt's voice, sounding a long distance away, said, "Lie down before you pass out."

He obeyed. Instead of moving to make room for him, Britt took his head into her lap. He felt her hand fumbling in his hip pocket to extract his handkerchief, which she pressed to the wound.

Recalling one of the techniques Volnar had conveyed to him during their telepathic link, Roger turned his attention inward, focusing on the laceration. He visualized the blood flow receding, platelets teeming to fill the gash, the skin drawing together. The pain faded.

His head clearing, Roger hastily sat up and removed Britt's hand from his arm. She stared in fascination at the wound, which now looked half-healed. "Thank God that's over," he muttered, rubbing his eyes.

Britt didn't even look tired. "Speaking of God, I notice you're immune to that crucifphobia." She handed him the rosary, which he automatically pocketed. "A new symptom for the textbooks – except it won't get into a textbook. Roger, I want to learn everything possible about your species – and you as a unique specimen. Did he mean that 'halfbreed' literally?"

Roger saw no point in evasion. Britt held his life in her hands. "Yes, my father was human."

"Fascinating! Look, Roger, I won't do anything to endanger you, ever. You have my word that nothing you tell me will go any further."

He went lightheaded with gratitude. "Yes, I believe that."

"Sure hate to give up my best-selling book." A half-smile played on her lips. "But a friend is in a different category from a murder case."

He glanced at his watch without really seeing it. "We mustn't stay here. Sandor might not be as badly hurt as he looked. We can't take the risk of his coming back and catching us off guard. Let's get together for a long talk tomorrow." He had to separate from Britt soon, or he'd take advantage of her despite his good intentions. The energy drain of the instant healing exercise, on top of the blood loss, had left him famished. The racing of Britt's pulse made his own quicken. He caught himself staring at the V of her blouse, where a button had come unfastened in the scuffle.

"In layman's terms, Roger, you look badly strung out. You're in no shape to navigate. I'm driving you home."

"Can't leave my car here," he protested. Good Lord, didn't she have any inkling of how hazardous staying near him would be?

"Fine, I'll drive yours, if you'll trust me at the wheel. The car I borrowed will be safe in the stadium lot until tomorrow. We can swing around to pick it up on the way to the office."

"What?" A gray mist thickened before his eyes. He shook his head to dispel it.

She leaned closer to him as she spoke. "I'm spending the night at your place. You aren't fit to be left alone." Why, she was being deliberately provocative! Hadn't the past few minutes taught her any caution?

An almost uncontrollable spasm of hunger racked him. He closed his eyes until it waned, then said, "If you do, I can't answer for the consequences."

"Pretty slow on the uptake tonight, aren't you?" she said. "I'm counting on those consequences. Even without immortality, I haven't changed my mind about wanting that experience – the right way."

"No! The risk to you –"

"What risk?" She clasped his hand, sending a renewed shudder of desire through him. "Come on, I know you aren't like Sandor. I saw how you reacted when he – Well, never mind," she said briskly. "You obviously have similar needs, though, and I owe you something for turning your interview into a disaster." The teasing smile returned. "Besides, I can't stand by and watch a colleague suffer."

He relaxed into the inviting warmth of her aura. "In that case, my dear colleague, I'm honored to accept."

## Chapter 14

IN THE CAR he blanked out for a while. When awareness returned, they were driving across the Severn. Britt said, "Good, you're with me. Feel like talking?"

"I have to," he said. "There are some things you need to know before we go through with this."

"I'll second that. My list of questions is a mile long. Some of the things Sandor said, for instance." She glanced at him before going on hesitantly, "Do your kind sense emotions?"

Amazing, how carefully she must have listened, even with her life in danger. "Yes. That seems to account for the need for human blood. Otherwise animals would do. As it is, they're only good for bulk nourishment."

"It also explains your success as a therapist," Britt said. "That and the hypnotic power. You can't imagine how I envy you, colleague. Can you teach me some of those skills?"

"I'm not sure they're transferable, but I'll do my best." His lips quirked in amusement. "Parapsychology research, colleague?"

"Darn right! And you've held out on me all this time!" she said in mock severity. She turned onto St. Margaret's Road and accelerated to forty. "Hypocrite! – you said you didn't believe in the supernatural."

"But we're as much a part of nature as you are. Anyway, I suppose even dragons and unicorns, if they existed, wouldn't seem supernatural to themselves."

She lapsed into thoughtful silence until they turned onto the winding lane where Roger's townhouse was located. "That night Alice Kovak was attacked, you had a date with her."

His chest tightened. "Yes," he admitted.

"Preying on patients is radically unethical."

Trust Britt to view the matter from a skewed angle! She didn't say a word about preying on anyone else. "It doesn't happen often. And I've done them no physical harm."

Britt pulled into the condominium parking lot and shut off the motor. "Psychological harm?"

"Not that I've noticed. They don't remember, and I don't make a habit of repeating it with the same person. Well – until Alice." *Why am I defending myself? Britt is absolutely right; I have no excuse.*

"I still don't like it." She made no move to get out of the car. "Whatever you do, professionally, reflects on me. I can't condone exploitation of patients in my practice."

"I'm not arguing the point. I know it was wrong; I did it because I was desperate."

"Who knows, maybe we can discover an alternative. How often do you need to –?"

"Once every two or three weeks," he said. "Not quite enough, but I function on it. The fluid volume is small."

Curiosity danced in her eyes. "How much?"

"Well, I don't measure it!" The spasm of irritation faded. "Sorry, I'm damn near exhausted."

She hastily handed him the car keys and unbuckled her belt. "Of course you are. I'm the one who should apologize. Let's go in."

Only the relief that washed over him at being safe behind locked doors told Roger how much anxiety he'd still been repressing. Britt watched in amusement as he secured the chain and both deadbolts. "A touch of paranoia?"

"In my situation, it's a survival trait." He poured two glasses of sherry and sat with Britt on one of the twin couches that faced each other in front of the fireplace. A single low-wattage lamp cast the only light.

"You drink alcohol," she said. "Bela Lugosi was off base. Then you won't mind it in my blood?"

Her coolness in discussing the subject amazed him. "Not in moderation. Listen carefully, Britt – I won't do this without a full disclosure of the risks and benefits. I want your informed consent."

"You sound like a cigarette carton. Fine. Tell me what's hazardous to my health. Anemia?"

"Not from one or two encounters," he said. "If it's repeated too often at close intervals, that could hardly be avoided. Weakening of the immune system can go along with it, leading to frequent minor illnesses. Proper nutrition can offset the effects of blood loss, and I'm told that with plenty of other nourishment, the vampire needs to take very little from the human partner." He took a sip of the sherry. The over-sweet taste made him a little queasy.

"Go on," Britt said. "So it's a matter of quality, not quantity?" He sensed excitement in her, with a trace of nervousness. The fine hairs in his palms quivered in response.

"That's right." Imagining the "quality" of feasting on Britt's vibrant energy made his jaws ache. "A healthy donor can compensate for the blood loss and energy drain. Other risks are more significant."

"Such as?" She leaned closer to brush her fingertips over his half-healed wound. He shifted away from her touch, unable to repress a visible tremor.

"A long-term donor loses her appetite. Something to do with the mild anesthetic we secrete. But the appetite loss is supposed to be a temporary phase; if one makes the effort to eat well, normal interest in food returns." He struggled to organize his thoughts, focus on everything she needed to know. The vermilion glow of her aura, pulsing in time with her heartbeat, undermined his concentration. "However, there's a permanent metabolic speed-up. You'd lose weight, though not dangerously. You'd also become abnormally photosensitive."

"That could account for some of the superstitions about vampires' victims becoming vampires."

The quickness of her mind delighted him. "No doubt. But the major negative side effect of our – venom, if you will – is addiction."

Britt leaned forward again, abandoning her drink on the coffee table. "Really? Does a tolerance develop?"

"No, in that sense it's a fairly benign addiction. No increased dose is required, and the euphoria doesn't diminish over time. In fact, it may get more intense."

"Interesting." Her pulse accelerated. Roger didn't dare probe the exact nature of her excitement, whether scientific ardor or something more personal. By now his control was so precarious that he was afraid to touch her.

"The – the vampire also becomes addicted. A powerful psychological dependence. Or so I've been told. The truth is, I only learned about my background a few days ago."

"Then you've never had that kind of attachment?" Britt said. The question seemed to hold strong interest for her.

"No, I haven't dared return to a single donor – oh, hell, victim – more than twice. Too much risk of discovery." He felt Britt's pleasure in that answer. Could he hope that she'd offered herself out of some stronger motive than curiosity?

"You mentioned benefits, too," she prompted.

He watched her take a sip of sherry and thoughtfully lick the corners of her lips. Did she guess how she was torturing him?

"Enzymes in our saliva are supposed to guard against cardiovascular problems, cancer – minimize the outward signs of aging –" He could hardly think straight, much less deliver a physiology lecture. "Understand, all this applies only to long-term donors."

Britt said, "You're telling me that, contrary to the movies, a single encounter with a vampire isn't likely to have any lasting effect at all. And a long-term relationship isn't necessarily bad."

He nodded. "Is there anything you'd like to ask?" Silly question. "I mean, anything that can't wait?"

Her tone became more serious. "Sandor made certain comments about you – about your feelings for me. Were his observations accurate?"

The pulse pounded in Roger's head. He recognized the feeling as sheer irrational panic. Somehow he managed to say, "Yes, completely."

Britt slumped back against the couch, relaxing into a broad smile. "Well, thank goodness! I didn't really like the idea of being just a snack – any more than I see you as just a parapsychology experiment. Next question: Where's your shower? I'm a mess."

He stood up, dizzy with relief at her open desire for him. Now he recognized part of her excitement as sexual, which solved the quandary that had been buzzing in the back of his mind – whether to complete the act here or invite her upstairs. "Good idea," he said. "You can use the one in the upstairs hall. I'll meet you in the bedroom whenever you're ready."

He carried both their glasses up with him and got out a towel and a terrycloth robe for Britt. On the way he switched on the thermostat; Britt might feel chilly on an October night without central heating. While she was busy, he showered in the bath attached to his bedroom. By the time he'd dressed in shorts and his royal blue lounging robe, doubts nibbled at him again. Could Britt actually feel as much enthusiasm as he had imagined? Had wishful thinking made him misinterpret her emotions?

And what would she think of the rather garish decor he'd begun to use as a setting for these encounters? He hesitated in the act of spreading an emerald green satin cover on the bed. (Crimson would clash with Britt's hair.) After all, she was far from just one more encounter.

*Stop dithering, Roger! As a demon lover, you rate about a one on a four-point scale. Better take lessons from Claude's movies.*

After a moment's thought, he decided the atmospheric touches might amuse her. He went ahead and lit the mildly scented candles.

Finally Britt emerged from the guest bathroom. When she halted at the bedroom door, he feasted on the sight of her, with her copper-gold hair tumbling around her shoulders just as he'd fantasized. The terrycloth wrap clung to her lean curves, revealing more than her office wardrobe ever did. The vision made his head spin. Fortunately for his self-control, she broke the spell by bursting into delighted laughter. "Oh, colleague, what is this? Dracula's House of Ill Repute?"

"It is a bit overdone, isn't it?" he said. "The – atmosphere – is supposed to enhance the emotional component of the – exchange."

"Relax, colleague, I love it." She sat beside him on the edge of the bed, picking up her glass and giving him the other one. "Are you saying you feed on emotions?"

"Exactly. That's why a conscious, participating donor makes such a great difference."

"Don't worry, I fully intend to participate. Only you'll have to give me some hints; I've never done this before."

Her flippant tone eased some of his nervousness. "This is a first for me, too. I've never – taken – from anyone who knew what I was. I've always had to put them into a trance, or at least blur their memories afterward."

She placed her free hand gently on his. "The isolation must be – difficult." The sympathy that emanated from her warmed the very marrow of his bones. She drained her drink and said more lightly, "Don't you dare even think about fogging my memory. I plan to concentrate on every detail. Come on, finish your sherry. Maybe it'll reduce some of your inhibitions."

He set the glass on the nightstand. "No, my threshold for alcohol is higher than yours –" He trailed off as she stared at him in mock fascination. "The hell with this! If you want uninhibited, you'll damn well get it! I'm ravenous – and I want you desperately!"

Her eyes widened in shock when he pushed her down on the pillow. He dove for her throat. His teeth barely touched the tender skin; just in time, Britt's muffled gasp brought him to his senses.

He drew back with an effort that left him shaking.

Wrapping her arms around his neck, she said, "It's all right, you just startled me. Don't stop."

Humbled by her fearless offering, Roger forced himself to lick the smooth curve of her neck with his customary gentleness. He kissed the thin scratch, then moved a few centimeters over to taste unmarred skin.

With his upper body pinning hers beneath him, he felt the hammering of her heart, the expansion and contraction of her lungs. Britt's excitement built more rapidly than he'd expected. Within a minute or two her passion had so inflamed his that he couldn't hold back. He nipped her flesh and lapped the trickle of blood in a slow, caressing rhythm.

The ecstasy drowned all discrete perceptions in a single delirious rush. Vaguely he noticed Britt clutching his shoulders, writhing, arching her back. He shifted position to cover her body completely with his, giving her the contact she demanded. He almost blacked out when the explosion of her climax hit him.

She clung to him, trembling, until her passion exhausted itself. Immediately Roger broke contact, though his body screamed for more. If he didn't stop now, he feared he might go on drinking forever.

He lay on his back, Britt's head pillowed on his left arm. Applying direct pressure to stop the scant flow of blood, he said, "I apologize – I don't usually behave that – precipitously. You hurried me, with your infernal teasing."

"The hell I did!" With a lazy smile she rubbed her head against his shoulder. "Oh, colleague, don't look so distressed. I'll think you didn't like it."

He hugged her close. "But I wanted to give you the kind of experience you must have anticipated. I didn't mean to rush."

"Well, the night isn't over yet. Anyway, I have no complaints." She slipped her hand inside his robe to rub his chest. "Is it my imagination that your skin is measurably cooler than mine?"

Good grief, she'd probably go on making scientific observations at the foot of the guillotine! "No, that's accurate. My normal body temperature is around ninety."

"And you aren't perspiring." Britt was; he wanted to lick the salt from her damp forehead but didn't trust himself to stop there.

"We have a more efficient temperature control mechanism than you. It takes a lot more exertion than this to make me sweat visibly. It evaporates so rapidly you don't notice it."

After a few minutes' silence, during which Britt tickled his chest hair in a tantalizing way that he didn't have the will to make her stop, she said, "You surprised me. Oh, I don't mean when you swooped down on me that way. I mean I didn't expect it to be so – sexual."

"Our libido is less – diffuse – than yours. Everything focuses on the taking of blood."

"An entire species with an oral fixation! How Freudian!" She added more seriously, "What about conventional sexual intercourse?"

Roger's chest tightened. He couldn't start lying to her now. "I'm incapable of it. Vampires breed very seldom, and I'm nonhuman in that respect." Would she withdraw because he couldn't satisfy her?

Britt, however, showed no sign of disappointment. "Then taking blood is like an orgasm for you?"

"It *is* an orgasm, indescribably more intense than the standard model. I share your climax and amplify it – my satisfaction depends on yours."

"Interesting. I've been wondering since the day we met how you'd be in bed, but I never imagined it like this." Her open hand skimmed up and down his chest like stroking a cat. He wished he knew how to purr.

"You *what*? Why on earth didn't you – assert yourself – sooner? You're supposed to be a hard-line feminist."

She dissolved into a fit of laughter. Recovering, she said, "How could I make advances, the way you advertise your fear of intimacy? It was hard enough getting you to go out to lunch once in a while. Besides, if you can read emotions, why didn't you pick up on my interest and save us all this trouble?"

"I've gone to great lengths to keep from getting close to you – avoided touching, barriered myself against your emotions. I – desired you too much to stand that kind of temptation." Confessing his feelings to Britt wasn't as hard as he'd expected. "That accounts for my occasional discourtesy toward you."

"Occasional! Roger, I love your gift of understatement." Her nails grazed his chest. "You know what turned me on about you first?"

He surprised himself by attempting a joke. "If it wasn't my irresistible vampire magnetism, I have no idea."

"It was the `Haavuhd' accent. Gives me chills – I could listen to you talk for hours."

"From my viewpoint," he said dryly, "you have the accent."

"It's pure Baltimore, hon," she said in an exaggerated drawl.

"That's one piece of culture shock I had to adjust to when I moved here – supermarket clerks I'd never met before calling me `hon.'"

She raised her head and looked at him quizzically for a second, before snuggling into the curve of his arm again. "You shop at the grocery store?" She answered herself, "Silly me, of course you must. Aside from all the non-food supplies, I've seen you drink milk. Not to mention those vanilla diet shakes at lunchtime. I always wondered why; you sure don't need to lose weight." She ran a hand over the taut muscles that covered his ribs.

"As you've noticed, I can't eat most solid foods. Never have been able to."

"Did you drink blood all your life? I can't imagine how your adopted parents would've dealt with that."

"Good grief, no." The things they had been required to deal with were bad enough. "It started during my internship. I began having dreams of blood. Tried to analyze them out of existence by myself – not exactly something I wanted to mention to the hospital staff, when I was trying to get into a psych residency. I'd wake up with erections, but I'd lost the ability to – ah – relieve the pressure –" To his dismay, he blushed. "I tried to convince myself the craving was not what it was. I became quite adept at self-deception."

"I bet you did," said Britt. "When did you finally figure out what you needed?"

"Well, it came to a head during my training therapy." He narrated the same experience he'd told to Volnar the previous week.

"You fed on your training therapist? Oh, Roger!" She burst into helpless giggles. When she recovered, she said, "By the way, why are you lying here half dressed?"

"For one thing, I can't move while you're immobilizing my arm."

Britt sat up and untied her wrap. "Well, I'd like to look at you, please. You can look, too, if you want." She leaned over to hang the robe on the bedpost.

Roger was pleased that her professional neatness carried over into her personal habits, but at the moment he was captivated by her bold sensuality. Her nakedness gave him the incentive to remove his robe and shorts. He'd never had any reason to share that intimacy with a donor before. To his distress, he reddened under Britt's direct gaze.

"Maybe you aren't interested in looking?" she said.

"Where did you get that idea? Just because the visual stimulus isn't primary doesn't mean it has no effect." Her full, firm breasts, flat abdomen, and long legs embodied the perfection he'd always imagined her to possess.

She knelt beside him on the bed. "Sit back and relax; I want to get a hands-on sense of our differences." He humored her, plumping a pillow behind him and leaning against the headboard. Britt's fingers encircled his wrist, while her other hand explored his jawline.

"If you're counting my pulse," he said, "you won't get an accurate reading. Contact with you distorts the results."

"Why, colleague, is that a compliment?" He stiffened as her fingertips played at the corners of his mouth. "Don't be so tense, Roger. Won't you let me examine your teeth?" He obligingly bared them for her. "No fangs."

"Not necessary. The incisors and canines are razor-edged." She ran her index finger along the front teeth, hazardously close to that cutting edge. He flinched. "Don't – I might –"

Her hand moved to his shoulder. "It's all right, I trust you."

"If I accidentally drew blood, I wouldn't be able to stop. You – tempt me – too much."

"Trust yourself, colleague," she said earnestly, her eyes holding his. "I know you'd never hurt me." She let go of his wrist to trace the inverted triangle of hair on his chest, down to where it tapered to a point at his navel. "Unusual pattern of hair growth. And it's like silk – mmm."

He tensed again when she fondled his genitals. He reminded himself that she wouldn't find anything shocking or abnormal; his anatomy was human there, even if his responses weren't, quite. "Interesting," she murmured. "But you said you didn't –"

"The fact that I don't focus on genital sexuality," he said, struggling to keep his voice steady, "doesn't mean I feel no sensation there. Thirst makes my entire body sensitive. A network of capillaries doesn't recognize fine discriminations." He guided Britt's free hand to his chest, letting her skim over the taut nipples.

Hers, too, were fully erect. Her aura showed darker pools of heat at breasts and groin. The intoxicating scent of her arousal made him lightheaded. In her warm handclasp he felt himself hardening. "You're still – thirsty?" she said. He nodded, not trusting his voice.

He captured her caressing hand, hoping for a distraction from his mounting excitement. A mistake – with the ball of her thumb she sketched spirals on his palm. "Little hairs," she said delightedly, "just like in the legends. What are they for?"

"They register heat, electricity, magnetism, air pressure – something like a cat's whiskers." Objective discussion had lost the ability to cool his ardor, continuously fueled by her seductive touch.

"If they're so sensitive," she said, "how can you stand to grasp objects?"

"It only reacts to light touch. Firm pressure overwhelms the nerve endings and has no effect." Unlike her relentless tickling.

"Fascinating." She bent over to flick her tongue across his palm.

"Britt, I wish you wouldn't do that."

"Why? Don't you like it?"

"Too much," he groaned.

"I'd like to kiss you," Britt said matter-of-factly. "May I?"

In answer, he tangled one hand in the luxuriant hair at the nape of her neck, pulling her close. When her lips touched his, though, he allowed the kiss without returning it.

The disappointment in Britt's eyes almost shattered his self-control. "Come on, colleague, I'm sure you can do better than that!"

"I can," he said. "But it might provoke me into – renewing my demands." His teeth were tingling; the cilia in his palms bristled with the need to touch her heat and softness.

"Good," Britt said. "I want to find out what it's like when you aren't hurried." Again she pressed her mouth to his. The invasion of her tongue shattered the last of his resistance. Gathering her into his arms, he drew her down beside him.

"Britt, are you sure?"

"Hard to convince, aren't you?" She lightly bit his shoulder. "Yes, I'm sure I want to make love with you."

He buried his face in her hair, astonished at the sudden tears that stung his eyes. "Is that what you call it?"

"What do you call it?" she said.

"Nothing, usually. I try to think of it as little as possible."

Britt pulled back to stare into his eyes. "I hope that will change from now on."

He kissed her again, feasting on her passion. In leisurely exploration, his lips wandered over her neck, shoulders, and breasts, while she retaliated by nibbling everywhere she could reach. Her mouth and hands set him on fire. His heartbeat raced in sync with hers. This time he lavished on her the attention she deserved, and neither of them had any complaints.

AT FIVE A.M. Roger glanced up from the journal he was reading to drink in the sight of Britt stretched out asleep on his bed. She'd resisted her fatigue as long as possible, eager to question him. They'd talked for hours, until he had finally persuaded her to rest, around one. Since then he'd been relaxing in an armchair across the room, simultaneously watching her and reading.

A ripple of the sheet drew his eyes. Britt rolled over and looked at him. "Aren't you sleepy? Come lie down."

The invitation reminded him of how exhausted he really was. And now dawn was near enough to let him sleep. He lay next to Britt, and she curled up with her head on his chest. Another first – he'd never shared a bed with anyone before. Enfolded in the warmth of Britt's aura, he sank into the welcoming darkness almost at once.

A subjective instant later, he woke with Britt's voice ringing in his head: "Roger, wake up!"

Her anxiety shrilled in his ears and sent his pulse rate soaring. He snapped fully awake. Britt was bending over him.

"Take it easy, colleague," she said. Noticing that he was squeezing her wrists painfully hard, he let go.

"Sorry. What's wrong?"

She looked embarrassed. "Nothing, I guess. I couldn't find any vital signs – you scared me."

"*I* scared *you*?" His adrenaline jolt was ebbing now. "You nearly shocked me into cardiac arrest, waking me that way. Didn't I explain that for vampires deep sleep is actually suspended animation?"

"Being told and witnessing it are two different things." Kneeling on the bed, she let her unbound hair sweep across his chest. "Let me make it up to you."

"I've drained too much energy from you already." Besides, sated to the point of intoxication, he wanted most to go back to sleep. A glance at the bedside clock told him that wasn't an option.

Britt extended her arms in a catlike stretch. "I don't feel drained – I feel wonderful. I'm really a morning person anyhow."

"I've noticed," he said dryly. Her habit of bounding into the office, obscenely cheerful, at nine a.m. was one of the minor trials of his life. "Truthfully, colleague, I'm not sure I'm –"

She filled in the gap his hesitation left. "Up for another round? I'll fix that."

Wasting no more time in argument, Britt worked over him with her teeth and nails. When all his nerves were humming with the delicious torment of her caresses, she lay on top of him. He felt as if his skin burst into flame at every point where their bodies touched. At the moment of her climax, she offered her throat to his kiss. He needed only a taste to drown in her ecstasy.

Her panting breath hot on his shoulder, she said, "Roger, that's so – I'm at a loss for words!"

"You? Then I've accomplished the impossible."

She stirred enough to nip his earlobe. "You've done some

thing, anyway. I almost never have multiple orgasms."

So he had managed to give to Britt, as well as taking from her. That knowledge lent a piercing sweetness to his pleasure. "It's a completely new experience for me, too. After last night I realize I've been – starved – for the past twenty years."

She kissed him lightly on the cheek. "How do you feel now?"

"Drunk, with none of the unpleasant side effects. Sleepy. Speaking of which, why did you wake me? Surely not just to indulge our mutual appetite?"

She sat up and scowled at the clock. "I have to get dressed for work, and I figured you'd want to call Marcia and tell her you won't be in."

Roger reluctantly sat up, too. "Why would I do that?"

"You've had a rough night. You need to sleep it off."

"You've had an equally stressful night, and I don't see you planning to stay home." He walked over to the closet and picked out a suit. "I've never skipped a day for that reason, and I don't plan to start now. Rather like the heavy drinker who claims he's not an alcoholic because he's never missed a day of work."

Laughing, Britt headed for the guest bathroom.

After they'd showered and dressed, and Britt had fueled up with orange juice and Instant Breakfast ("If I'm going to spend nights here regularly, you have to get something to eat in this house," she admonished him), he drove her to the stadium for the car early enough to give her time to rush home and change clothes before office hours. Just before parting from him, she said, "I'd like you to make me a promise, Roger. No more patients."

He felt a flutter of anxiety beneath his diaphragm. "I'd like to assure you that it won't happen again. But I've made that resolution before and failed."

"Maybe with my help, you won't fail."

What she implied thrilled and yet frightened him. "Britt, serving as my only source of – nourishment – could be dangerous for you."

"Let me worry about that."

As much as he wanted to evade the issue, he knew he had to speak up before he lost his nerve. "You must understand – I would never force you, physically or mentally. If I make that promise, I'll be placing myself completely in your hands."

She gave him a quick, firm hug. "We'll discuss it later."

He got to the office long before either Britt or Marcia, of course, and spent the time drinking coffee to wake up and reviewing case files to reroute his train of thought. When Britt arrived half an hour later, he made a point of staying out of her way. He didn't feel ready to handle their new relationship in the work setting. Despite this careful avoidance, her presence seemed to seep through the walls and permeate the very air he breathed. Only when occupied with a patient could he forget what he'd shared with her. Replete and tired as he was, stray wisps of memory still had the power to stir his appetite.

*What's the matter with me? I shouldn't feel acute hunger for nearly a week.* He recalled Volnar's longwinded lecture about "addiction." So the Prime Elder hadn't been exaggerating, after all. *Damn, I'm really hooked. In one night, hooked, netted, and trapped. And I love it!*

Fortunately for Roger's equilibrium, these reflections were cut short by the arrival of Alice Kovak. This would be her first session since the attack, whose only outward sign remained a gauze square taped to the side of her neck. Roger's preternatural sight discerned the paleness of her aura, marred by scattered dark blotches. After soothing her into relaxation on the couch, he asked how much she remembered of the assault.

"Still nothing," she said. "Except his eyes – like flames. I don't want to remember."

"That's understandable," Roger said from his position near the head of the couch. "But we've discussed before how much worse it is to evade such memories. The unknown, the repressed, is always more frightening than the reality. When you're ready, you will remember what you need to." In this case, of course, he meant to screen her recollections so that she wouldn't dredge up anything to implicate him.

"He keeps after me – calling me –" she murmured.

"Threatening phone calls? Have you reported this to the police?"

Alice shook her head impatiently. "Not on the phone – in *here.*" She tapped her forehead. "I hear him calling inside my brain. I don't remember what he looks like or anything else, but I know it's him."

"Alice, how could he do that? Reality test – he isn't superhuman." Except that he was, of course, and her perception could very well be based on fact. *If Sandor is trying to lure her into his clutches, it's my fault.*

In an unexpected spasm of energy, Alice sat up and twisted around to clasp his wrist. "I do remember one thing – how you took care of me when I got to your house. You saved my life."

He kept his voice even, suppressing the impulse to shake off her touch. "You saved your own life. You should be proud of the courage and presence of mind you displayed."

"If you hadn't been there for me –" She didn't let go. "I wish I could pay you back somehow." She started to put her other arm around Roger's neck.

His total lack of response surprised him. A few minutes ago he'd been feeling twinges of thirst for Britt.

*For Britt – not for anyone else. This girl leaves me cold.*

He gently unfastened Alice's hands and maneuvered her back to her seat on the couch. "We've talked about this before, too. You don't actually feel a personal attraction to me." No, she felt an unnatural fascination – the aftereffect of the one time he'd fed on her.

She huddled sullenly in a corner of the sofa. "Yeah, sure, transference. You have a label for everything, don't you?"

"Do you resent that?" Drawing her out, he led her through the rest of the fifty minutes. Her insistence that her attacker, the man with glowing eyes, was stalking her, "calling" inside her head, preyed on Roger's mind. He was grateful to usher the girl out of the office at the end of her session.

In the ten minute break, he flipped the yellow pages to "Florists" and ordered a dozen red roses for Britt. *I must be losing my mind, but I'm enjoying it.* The gesture was little enough to show his gratitude. No signature; he ordered the card to read simply, "Thank you." His newfound "addiction" didn't feel like enslavement; rather, Britt had freed him from the whims of his body. Two weeks ago, a casual touch from a female patient would have sent him into an emotional tailspin.

At lunch he considered taking a forty-five minute nap, as he sometimes did, but decided against it. In his fatigued condition, waking up after that short a time would feel worse than not sleeping at all. About ten minutes into the lunch hour, Britt knocked on his door.

## Chapter 15

HE WARILY WATCHED her stride over to his desk and sit on the edge of it. "Well, now I know why you stay in every day at noon," she said. "And to think I worried that you weren't eating properly."

"You were right," he said, "but for a different reason." After a glance at her, he forced his eyes back to the case file he was annotating. "Anything in particular you wanted?"

"To thank you for the flowers. They made Marcia's day. Now she can needle me about my secret admirer for the next week or two."

"You're very welcome. Now, we really should get back to work, shouldn't we?"

He felt her stiffen at his coolness. She straightened up and backed away a couple of paces. "I was thinking of offering you lunch, but I gather that isn't a good idea."

"Here? Certainly not."

He didn't realize how harsh he sounded until she stalked to the door. "Britt, wait."

She turned to glare at him.

"Forgive me – I sense every nuance of your emotions so keenly, I forget you can't read mine. I'm trying to keep my distance because if I touched you, I couldn't –" He hated admitting his weakness.

Britt let go of the doorknob and walked back to the desk. "I see. For a minute I actually thought you regretted last night."

"Never that! But this isn't the place."

"I have to agree," she said. "Would you like me to come over again this evening?"

Heat flooded him. He could hardly restrain himself from leaping up to embrace her. "Yes. And the promise you asked for – you have it."

Her eyes gleamed. "You won't regret that. I won't give you time to miss them! Your weekends are going to be fully booked from now on, colleague."

Listening to her through the walls a minute later, as she puttered around her office, he caught the sound of humming. Since Britt's musical style was best described as off-key monotone, it took him a while to distinguish the tune. When he did, his weariness melted away.

She was humming the James Bond theme, "Nobody does it better...."

AFTER HE'D finished putting away the groceries he'd bought on the way home, Roger showered and dressed, then sat down in the living room with the *Wall Street Journal* to wait for Britt. That diversion kept him occupied less than five minutes. Instead he got up and paced. Britt had promised to come over at six thirty, and he'd never known her to be unpunctual. Since that time was still half an hour away, he had no right to worry yet.

But he did worry, every second she was out of earshot. The fact last night's pleasure had temporarily wiped out of his mind haunted him: Sandor hadn't minded butchering one of his own kind to strike at Roger. Therefore he would doubtless be thrilled to destroy Britt for the same reason. He knew Britt's importance to Roger, and she had no way to protect herself.

*Good God, why did I ever let her go home alone?*

By the time Britt rang the doorbell, Roger's fear for her had grown to an icy knot in his chest. He practically dragged her inside. Slamming the bolts into place, he said, "Confound it, what took you so long?"

She looked puzzled by his harsh tone. Holding up her left wrist, she said, "My watch says six thirty. Is yours fast? Roger, what is the matter with you?"

"I should have followed you home; we shouldn't have separated."

A small frown appeared between her eyebrows. "I don't like the sound of that, but we don't have to discuss it standing in the foyer, do we? I'd like to put my things down somewhere." She carried her briefcase and an overnight bag in addition to her heavy shoulder purse. She had changed out of her tailored pantsuit into slacks and a Johns Hopkins T-shirt.

Roger carried the overnight case upstairs. Coming back down, he found Britt curled in a corner of the office couch, briefcase on her lap. "You're prepared to stay the night, I see," he said. A detached part of his mind registered amusement at his awkwardness, as if this situation weren't commonplace for a middle-aged bachelor in this liberated decade.

"Possibly the weekend," said Britt, "depending on how soon we get sick of each other. We both like our privacy."

"True. At the moment I'm more concerned that I won't want to let you go, not that I'll be eager to throw you out. Staying close to me for too long could be hazardous for you." He sat down on the other end of the couch, torn between the need to hold her and the fear of repelling her with his voracious demands.

"Horse hockey," said Britt cheerfully. "I plan on being here for you every weekend, and more often if you like."

"Of course I'd `like.' That isn't the point. I'm used to abstaining for two or three weeks straight, and I get along perfectly well."

She greeted that claim with a ladylike snort. "Some snakes go without eating a year at a time, but I doubt they like it. Every weekend, colleague. I intend to take proper care of you, so you might as well resign yourself."

"Yes, Doctor." Maybe he'd learn to restrain himself in the face of her seductive willingness. Perhaps after the first few encounters, her mere presence in the room wouldn't make him lightheaded with desire. And perhaps the entire Delmarva Peninsula would slide into the Chesapeake Bay tomorrow morning.

"Last night," she said, "I got some idea of the strain you've been living with. Now I understand what you meant about having trouble working in hospitals. How did you ever get through your residency? The emergency room must have been sheer hell for you."

He nodded. "It didn't stop when I became a psych resident, either. I got called down to the ER for consults several times a week."

She said with a half-smile, "Traumatic amnesia cases – attempted suicides – little old ladies who can't remember what year it is – paranoid street people punching out paramedics, spitting on interns, and bleeding all over the trauma room floor – oh, yeah, *those* psych consults."

"Yes, I imagine Johns Hopkins and Mass General aren't too different in that respect."

"What about your surgical rotation? That must have been even worse."

His lips twitched with amusement at the memory of an incident that had been far from funny at the time. "My first day in the OR, I passed out."

Britt squeezed his hand. "Oh, boy. How long did it take you to live that down?"

"Actually, it worked to my advantage in the long run. I had a reputation for being too `perfect,' enjoyed showing up the other residents on rounds. The only reason they tolerated my company was that I was always eager to take other people's night shifts. I overheard one of the nurses, later that day, saying maybe I was human after all."

She leaned against his shoulder. "I wish I'd been there."

He hugged her lightly, fighting the impulse to pull her into a closer embrace. "No, you don't. Nobody liked me very much. Hell, *I* didn't like me. I was an arrogant, introverted, anxiety-ridden, self-absorbed workaholic."

"Not one bit the way you are now, huh?" she said, deadpan.

He stared at her blankly for a second, then laughed. "You can't have had too easy a time in training, yourself. Women weren't that common in our specialty back then."

Britt shrugged. "Sure, I put up with the usual garbage – anatomical specimens in my locker, groping from the male residents, snide comments from professors who thought I should get married instead of taking up a spot that really belonged to a man. It was all part of the standard `be twice as good to be minimally accepted.' Thank Heaven things are changing."

"Did you consider getting married?" He wasn't sure whether he really wanted to know; the thought of another man touching her elevated his blood pressure instantly.

"I went with another resident during the last couple of years," she said. "We were never formally engaged, but it was understood. Until he accepted an appointment in the midwest, without consulting me first, on the assumption I'd just drop all my plans and tag along after him." Britt shook her head. "That killed it. A month later, I couldn't believe I had ever considered spending my life with him."

"Shall I hunt him down and kill him for you?" Roger said. In response to her laughter, he added, "On second thought, the idiot did me a favor." Britt poked him lightly in the chest, a gesture that did nothing to steady his pulse. He put a few inches between them and resolutely shifted the conversation to a neutral topic. "Have you eaten? I stocked up on supplies for you."

"Yes, that's what I went home for, among other things. I've also taken my shower and so forth, so we can spend all evening, uninterrupted, on these reports." She tapped the briefcase. "Or until the lack of sleep knocks me out, anyway. Since med school I've lost the art of pulling all-nighters."

Roger didn't need to be told that she'd just bathed. Her natural fragrance, blood-tinged and combined with a hint of soap and powder, did unfortunate things to his concentration. Unable to resist the temptation, he moved over and put his arm around her shoulders again.

```
        Barnes & Noble Booksellers #2608
              795 Citadel Drive East
              Colorado Springs, CO 80909
                    719-637-8282

STR:2608 REG:004 TRN:2403   CSHR:Hannah I

BARNES & NOBLE MEMBER      EXP: 10/25/2015

Dark Changeling
   9780759900967          T1
   (1 @ 14.95) Member Card 10% (1.50)
   (1 @ 13.45) Item Cpn $ (11.45)
   (1 @ 2.00)                         2.00

Subtotal                              2.00
Sales Tax 11 (7.630%)                 0.15
TOTAL                                 2.15
CASH                                  5.00
CASH CHANGE                           2.85

MEMBER SAVINGS                        1.50


             Thanks for shopping at
                 Barnes & Noble

101.34C                     10/15/2014  02:30PM
```

CUSTOMER COPY

products purchased at Barnes & Noble College bookstores that are listed for sale in the Barnes & Noble Booksellers inventory management system.

Opened music CDs/DVDs/audio books may not be returned, and can be exchanged only for the same title and only if defective. NOOKs purchased from other retailers or sellers are returnable only to the retailer or seller from which they are purchased, pursuant to such retailer's or seller's return policy. Magazines, newspapers, eBooks, digital downloads, and used books are not returnable or exchangeable. Defective NOOKs may be exchanged at the store in accordance with the applicable warranty.

Returns or exchanges will not be permitted (i) after 14 days or without receipt or (ii) for product not carried by Barnes & Noble or Barnes & Noble.com.

*Policy on receipt may appear in two sections.*

## Return Policy

With a sales receipt or Barnes & Noble.com packing slip, a full refund in the original form of payment will be issued from any Barnes & Noble Booksellers store for returns of undamaged NOOKs, new and unread books, and unopened and undamaged music CDs, DVDs, and audio books made within 14 days of purchase from a Barnes & Noble Booksellers store or Barnes & Noble.com with the below exceptions:

A store credit for the purchase price will be issued (i) for purchases made by check less than 7 days prior to the date of return, (ii) when a gift receipt is presented within 60 days of purchase, (iii) for textbooks, or (iv) for products purchased at Barnes & Noble College bookstores that are listed for sale in the Barnes & Noble Booksellers inventory management system.

Opened music CDs/DVDs/audio books may not be returned, and can be exchanged only for the same title and only if defective. NOOKs purchased from other retailers or sellers are returnable only to the retailer or seller from which they are purchased, pursuant to such retailer's or seller's return policy.

"You look beautiful."

Britt made a tut-tut sound. "Now you're hallucinating, on top of everything else. In this baggy old shirt, with my hair all over the place? Come on!"

"I approve of your hairstyle," he said. "May I?" He drew her into his arms, burying his fingers in the silken mass of her hair, inhaling its clean scent. He soaked up her warmth like desert earth absorbing rain. For the moment he needed nothing more.

After several minutes she pulled back, her fingers laced behind his head, to meet his eyes. "Colleague, have you considered seeking treatment for this hair fetish of yours?"

He immediately removed his hands.

"Idiot, can't you tell when you're being teased?" With a tantalizing scrape of her nails along his cervical vertebrae, she let go of him. "Most men are hair fetishists. But you can't use it to distract me from that rattlebrained remark you made when I walked in. What's this 'we shouldn't have separated' stuff?"

"Every minute you're alone, you are in danger." Again the weight of anxiety settled on Roger. "Sandor knows I – care for you. Attacking you would be his next logical step."

"Are you saying you want to protect me?" He heard no tender gratitude in her voice. Her eyes glinted dangerously.

"Of course I do, damn it! I put you at risk in the first place! Why do you think I was so determined to keep you away from this case?"

"If you think I'll stand for that, you're seriously out of touch with reality." She retreated to her end of the couch, lifting the briefcase onto her lap again. "I chose to get involved, and I bear my own risks."

Roger swallowed the protests that sprang to his lips. He should have known Britt would react this way, and a bigger fool than he was would recognize that pursuing the argument would just alienate her. "At least promise you won't take any more stupid chances?"

"Like following you last night?" She granted him an apologetic half-smile. "I won't do anything else without consulting you, if you'll promise the same. All for one and one for all." She offered her hand.

"Illogical – there are only two of us." Clasping her hand, he said, "I agree – no more secrets." He amended, "As far as I can live up to that without betraying other people's secrets."

"Great, we can go over the files on the case again – honestly, this time." Though her voice held no reproach, Roger flushed with shame. She flipped her briefcase open. "Got anything to show me?"

Digging a folder out of the file cabinet, Roger laid it on the broad cherrywood desk. "Reports on the Boston murders. Not that they'll tell you much you haven't already surmised."

Britt pulled up the chair from the computer table and spread out her materials. "And you can look over my notes on the local crimes, tell me how close my guesses came. Colleague, much as I hate to draw attention to my human imperfections, I can't read in this light." The curtains, as usual, were closed.

With an apology, Roger switched on the hanging lamp above the desk, to cast a cozy glow over the work space.

Leaning on her elbow and opening the topmost of her files—the autopsy report on Sylvia, Roger noticed – Britt said, "You know, last night I actually managed to forget about all this."

"So did I." He couldn't keep the pain that stabbed through him out of his voice.

"If you start feeling guilty about that," said Britt, "I'll be strongly tempted to bonk you over the head with your *Physcian's Desk Reference*. How is self-flagellation going to help your friend?" Her bracing tone softened. "Are you ready to talk about her?"

"Yes." He struggled to blank out the image of Sylvia's mutilated body. For the first time he saw his eidetic memory as a curse rather than a gift.

"It's none of my business, but – were you lovers?"

"No, I don't think that relationship exists among vampires. They – *we* satisfy our libidinal needs with human partners. Sylvia and I were – close – in Boston, and she blamed me, with perfect justice, for Sandor's persecution of her." Britt's silent invitation drew Roger out and made talking about Sylvia less difficult than he'd expected. "I made several disastrous choices. That's not neurotic guilt, it is simply a fact."

Britt's fingers rested lightly on his. "All right. Listen to the advice you'd give a patient – put it behind you and move on. Learning from your mistakes is one thing; wallowing in them is something else altogether. I don't understand about the rape. You said vampires don't normally indulge in genital sexuality."

"They're incapable of it, except when the female is in estrus. Sylvia was."

"Interesting." Britt's nails tapped thoughtfully on the desk top. "Then maybe it wasn't rape."

"No, in that she probably didn't resist at the crucial moment. On the other hand, I'm absolutely sure she didn't consent." After a minute's reflection, he amended his answer. "In an ordinary rape, would you judge that the victim's orgasmic response made it any less rape?"

Britt's mouth twisted in distaste. "Just the opposite! Why did he decapitate her? Homicidal frenzy? Revenge for trying to refuse him?"

"More than that," said Roger. "He wanted to make sure she was dead. Breaking her neck alone wouldn't have done it."

"Then the legends are true, to that extent?" Resting her chin on both hands, Britt gazed speculatively into the middle distance. "What other methods of killing vampires work? How about the stake in the heart?"

Did she contemplate undertaking Sandor's destruction herself? No, even Britt wouldn't try that singlehandedly; the question had to be purely theoretical. "Only to the extent that a stake left in the body holds the wound open until irreversible damage occurs. Otherwise the vampire's system could regenerate. Besides decapitation, the sure methods are total destruction, such as by fire or explosion, or, at least, destruction of all or most of the brain."

"I see." Britt fidgeted in the wooden chair and rubbed the back of her neck. "I can't tackle this without chemical assistance. Got any coffee?"

"Of course, you know I drink it myself."

"Then bring on the caffeine. Time to get to work."

Roger went to the kitchen to start the coffee. When he came back with a tray bearing the full pot and two mugs, he found Britt hunched over a map she'd spread out on the desk. The greater Washington area, including Baltimore, Annapolis, and northern Virginia. "What's that for, colleague?" He set the tray on the top corner of the desk, off the map.

Britt took a mug in her left hand and continued marking red X's on the map. "Not as much detail on streets as I'd like. I thought we might find a pattern by pinpointing the locations of the killings, with dates. So far it doesn't suggest a thing to me."

Sipping his hot coffee, Roger leaned over her shoulder. "It doesn't suggest much to me, either. They're clustered mainly in Anne Arundel County, which we already knew. What would you expect to notice that the police wouldn't?"

"Not me, you. I hope you can visualize your way into the killer's mind and make something out of this mess." She gestured at the random sprinkle of X's, each with a date jotted beside it.

"Where did you get that idea?" said Roger. "I don't think like a vampire. I was brought up as human and only found out about my mother's race the night before Sylvia died."

"You think more like a vampire than anybody else I know," said Britt, marking the final spot on her map.

"The trouble is, Sandor isn't even a typical vampire," Roger said. "He's a sadistic psychopath with an exhibitionist streak and faulty impulse control."

"And superhuman powers, Lord help us. Still, there are points you can verify. For one thing, you can confirm my doubts about these dates. Aren't there an awful lot of gaps?"

"I see what you're getting at," said Roger, sitting in his swivel chair. "From what I know of Sylvia and – others, full-blooded vampires can't go that long without human prey. These –" he tapped the stack of files – "can't be his only victims."

"Then what does he do between murders? Do you think he feeds without killing when things heat up too much?"

"Maybe." Thinking of Sylvia's habits, Roger said, "Self-indulgent as he is, I'm willing to bet he takes a victim at least every other night. If he could restrain himself, he could even kill them without drawing attention. As you noticed, the wound can be almost invisible."

"Yes – and suppose he chooses victims who won't be missed that much?" An undercurrent of excitement bubbled in Britt's voice. "Street people, other marginal types?"

"He'd have to choose carefully, to avoid people contaminated by drugs or disease."

"Still, he must be doing something like that," said Britt. "Roger, I'll have to backtrack through the newspaper files for incidents along those lines, less conspicuous unsolved deaths. Or maybe suggest that Lieutenant Hayes dig up post mortem reports of that type from Baltimore, Annapolis, and D.C., if I can think of a plausible way to bring it up without mentioning my nutty theory about vampires." She gave Roger a self-mocking grin.

"Your map does suggest one thing," he said. "It reminds us how mobile Sandor is. Whether he's using a stolen car or muscle-powered flight –"

"Would he do that in an inner city neighborhood?"

Roger shrugged. "You saw him. He seems to have some kind of invulnerability complex. However, I consider a car more likely. If so, assuming he doesn't mind spending half the night on the move, we should extend our search over half of Maryland and northern Virginia, or possibly as far as Philadelphia and Richmond."

Britt's shoulders sagged. "You're right, darn it. Zeroing in on his lair doesn't look too hopeful."

"If he has a house or apartment, at least there's a hope of his making a slip that would get him noticed," said Roger. "But that isn't necessarily the case."

Folding the map, Britt said, "Explain that."

"He wouldn't mind foul weather and uncomfortable sleeping conditions as much as an ordinary man would. I suspect he rests in abandoned buildings, a different location every day." Hazardous as that practice sounded, Sandor's unkempt appearance bore out the supposition. "I wouldn't think of doing it myself – one would be totally exposed and unprotected in the daylight hours – but he seems to think he leads a charmed life."

"Then catching him helpless by day doesn't sound promising." Britt drained her coffee and poured another cup. "Let's read through these reports. Maybe inspiration will strike."

They spent the next hour going over the files, exchanging occasional comments. Britt's marginal jottings made it clear how close to the target her guesses had struck. Skimming her notes from big-city newspapers across the country, Roger wondered how he could ever have hoped to keep her ignorant. *Thank God she's on my side!*

At one point she asked, "What about that teenage boy in Boston, right after you left? Any connection?"

"One of Sylvia's – donors," he said. "Another revenge killing." He explained how Sandor had pursued Sylvia from city to city.

After a while Britt scooted over to the computer station to type in a chronology of the dates and a list of common factors from the various crimes, along with additional facts she'd picked up from Roger. "I don't know that I want this in writing," he said.

"Suppress your paranoia, colleague. Stored on disk under a file code nobody but us knows isn't exactly `in writing.' I think better this way." Finished, she frowned at the screen. "Profile of a homicidal vampire," she said. "One more thing – we should watch the papers for reports of UFO sightings, similar weird phenomena."

"I don't get the connection."

"As you said, the other night in the Tawes Garden couldn't be the only time he's risked flying in a settled area. People must catch glimpses of him sometime."

"Yes. Not that we can alert the police to that clue." He poured a cup of coffee, found that it had cooled to lukewarm, and set it aside.

"That's the frustrating part," Britt agreed. She rubbed the back of her neck and stifled a yawn. "Did you tell Lieutenant Hayes about the Boston case?"

"Yes, I wouldn't have wanted him to stumble on it by himself and wonder why I kept quiet."

"If we do manage to track down Sandor, though," she said, "we can't turn him over to the authorities, can we?"

"Unfortunately not. Exposing him could expose all the rest of us." Volnar's orders weighed heavily upon him. "I have to eliminate him without giving away the existence of our kind – and I don't know how."

Saving the file and switching off the computer, Britt winced in discomfort as she leaned back in the hard chair. Roger stood behind her, hands on her shoulders, thumbs at the base of her neck. "Let me help." She relaxed into his slow, rhythmic massage, accompanied by just enough psychic influence to drain the ache from her muscles.

She let her head droop back, resting against his midriff. "Nice," she murmured. "If you could bottle this stuff, the makers of prostaglandin inhibitors would go bankrupt. This is a form of hypnosis, too, isn't it – the way you touch people?"

"Yes." His hands wandered from her shoulders to her upper chest. "Except I've never touched anyone else as – intimately – as I touched you last night."

"And you better not!" Her eyes drifted shut. "Are you trying to seduce me or put me to sleep?"

His breathing irregular from the contact with her, he said, "I haven't decided. Which would you prefer?"

"Depends. Are we ready to knock off for the night?"

"We'd better. You're extremely distracting, colleague."

She rubbed her head against him. "I didn't mean to be."

"In your present condition, you can't help it."

"What condition?" She stood up and began putting away the file folders.

"Haven't you noticed how diligently I avoided you at this point in your cycle last month?"

Turning to face him, she blushed, though her eyes held steady on his. "Why, no, I didn't make the connection. You mean every month you'll know exactly when –?"

"Of course." He clasped her hands. "Forget the files until tomorrow; they aren't going anywhere. You're still in pain, and I want to ease it for you."

"Just backache, cramps, the usual. Did you have something more than a massage in mind?" Freeing her hands, she wrapped her arms around his waist.

His voice rough with leashed desire, he said, "I understand many women gain relief from those symptoms through orgasm."

"Well, it's certainly worth an experiment," she said, her teasing smile erasing the fatigue lines around her mouth. "But – well – it would be kind of messy."

"You think I care?" He could barely restrain himself from sweeping her into his arms and carrying her to bed.

"Most men would."

"Then they're taboo-obsessed jerks." He nuzzled her neck. "Please – you're dealing with a desperate man here."

"Then what are we waiting for?"

Upstairs she insisted on spreading a bath towel on the bed before she would undress and lie down. "I wouldn't think of ruining your satin sheets. Colleague, you really want to –?"

Removing the last of his clothes, Roger sat beside her, bridling his eagerness. "Does that repel you?"

"Not at all. It's just so different from the typical male reaction." With a husky laugh, she opened her arms to him. "Well, if you were a typical man, I wouldn't be here."

He foraged over her body with delicate caresses of fingers and tongue, working his way downward with exquisite deliberation, until she moaned aloud with impatience. When he had her writhing with unrestrained passion, he urged her to her first climax before claiming his reward. Although the taste differed from the blood that flowed in her veins, it was redolent of her passion and satisfied him just as fully.

After her second orgasm she gasped out a question about the soundproofing of the walls. When he assured her, "Completely reliable," her moans segued into screams.

BRITT STAYED all of Friday and Saturday night and a few hours of Sunday night, going home each day. The harmony between her determination to maintain her independence and Roger's lingering need for privacy while he slept pleased him. His rational self rejoiced that they could bask in their mutual passion without chaining each other. The less calculating half of his mind gibbered with fear whenever Britt was out of his sight. He took care to restrain that overprotective impulse in her presence.

After she left Sunday night, he received a shock when he played back the day's messages on his answering machine. Following two calls from telephone solicitors, he heard a voice that he knew and loathed all too well: "Doc, you're probably wondering when I'll come after that woman of yours. I will, and don't you forget it, but not any time soon. I'm giving you plenty of chance to –" A blip in the tape, a few seconds of silence, and the same voice resumed: "You're about to find out how it feels to be hunted."

## Chapter 16

AFTER SOME hesitation Roger told Britt about Sandor's phone message. Recalling what he'd learned about intimacy with a vampire enhancing the human donor's psychic gifts, he recognized that already Britt was beginning to read his emotions with an accuracy greater than chance. He couldn't lie to her, for whenever she sensed him holding anything back, she pounced on it.

"As you mentioned before, we can't report incidents like that to the police, so we're on our own," said Britt the next Saturday morning as they shared breakfast in his dining room. Or, more accurately, she was eating while he watched. She sliced off a corner of her cheese omelette and transferred it to a small plate for Roger. "Do you think you could kill him? Last time, you hesitated."

"And now he's targeted you. Next time, I won't hold back."

"That message he left gives me an idea." She chewed thoughtfully, staring at the opposite wall with a look in her eyes that worried Roger.

"What it tells me is that you've got to be more careful. At least let me pick you up instead of driving over here at night by yourself."

"Don't start that again," she said with an impatient wave of her fork. "If anything, I should go out alone more often, try to decoy him into the open."

"What?" He reached across the table to grip her hand. "Don't even think of that!"

She tugged until he released her. "Stop telling me what to do. Be logical, colleague. Is it better to wait around for him to attack, or set up a confrontation on our own terms?"

"Even assuming he'd fall for an obvious decoy setup," Roger said, "you can't do it because it wouldn't work without my cooperation. And you won't get it."

With a sigh she said, "Oh, all right, I won't try to blackmail you into cooperating."

"And give me your word that you won't try some hare-brained plot on your own."

"I promise – no suicide missions."

Roger took an unenthusiastic nibble of the omelette. "The hell of it is, he intends to work on our nerves with this waiting game, and it's succeeding. We haven't heard of anything that could be attributed to him all week."

Britt nodded agreement. "And if you think I'll give him the pleasure of knowing he's succeeded, by creeping around afraid of shadows, forget it. And I'd still like to know where he gets his meals between murders."

Britt had spent Wednesday evening digging through newspaper back issues again. She'd reported only a couple of dubious deaths that might fit the specifications. "No doubt he's more discreet than we gave him credit for," said Roger. "Don't give up on your idea of flagging reports of weird phenomena, too."

"I haven't," she said. "If I come across any, you'll be the first to know. Must we talk about this all the time? What do you think about getting tickets to the Colonial Players' performance of *Pygmalion* next weekend?"

Roger's pleasure at the thought of Liza Doolittle and Henry Higgins quickly yielded to anxiety. "I don't know whether going out at night would be wise. We can be sure he's watching you –"

Britt leaped to her feet and flung her napkin down on the table. "There you go again! I will not put up with this! I have no intention of living the rest of my life under house arrest!"

Roger hurried around the table to grab her by the arms. She stiffened and shoved at him. He let go, appalled at his own roughness. "Confound it, Britt, I don't want that! I'm simply asking you to exercise ordinary caution."

Unmollified, she glared at him, her chest heaving. "It's more than that – and I want it nipped in the bud right now. You do not own me."

Did his concern come across that way? "I could never think that. If I've given that impression, forgive me." He noted a slight relaxation of the tight line of her lips. "If you want to go to the play, we'll go." Relenting, Britt nestled into his embrace. Lavishing kisses on her, he thought, *This can't go on. How much of this can our relationship stand?*

THE NEXT MURDER victim discovered was a thirty-six-year-old real estate agent in Glen Burnie, up Route Two near Baltimore. Her husband had called hospitals and police, worried when she hadn't come home after showing a house one evening. The woman's body turned up the next morning in a dumpster behind a Seven-Eleven. Her car had vanished. According to Lieutenant Hayes, so had her automatic teller card, which had been used to withdraw the maximum allowable cash within a few hours of her death. *Devious bastard,* Roger thought. *Must have hypnotized her PIN out of her before he drained her.*

The same day, Roger received a letter in a plain white envelope, no return address, postmarked Washington. With no salutation, date, or signature, it read, "How do you like the waiting? How does it feel to wake up every day wondering if I've taken somebody close to you again? Don't worry, I'll get back to that – when I'm good and ready. Don't know about you, Doc, but I'm having a great time. After I've had my fun, we'll get together."

True to his vow of honesty, Roger showed the note to Britt before destroying it. They discussed it in the car Friday night on the way home to Roger's place after the *Pygmalion* performance. "What do you think he means by `get together'?" she mused. "A final confrontation, winner take all? Or does he still think he can persuade you to join him?"

"Does it matter?" Roger said. "If I meet him again, I'll do my best to destroy him." That resolve still held a dreamlike quality. Roger couldn't visualize himself committing premeditated homicide, even in a just cause.

When he parked the car and opened the door for Britt, his eyes involuntarily flickered toward the woods behind the house. No hint of movement, no prickling sensation of being watched. Checking for those signs had become automatic.

Inside, he scarcely gave Britt time to hang up her coat before drawing her into his arms. "Standing up in the foyer?" she murmured, molding her body to his.

"Certainly not." He rubbed his cheek against her hair, savoring its fragrance. "I just need to hold you for a minute." He released his pent-up anxiety in a long sigh. Her blood-heat and the glow of her aura soothed and refreshed him. "Oh, God, you feel so *good.* I wait all week for this."

"It feels great to me, too." She rubbed her hands up and down his back. "This weekend-only restriction was your idea. I'd love to –"

"Absolutely not." Reluctantly he pulled out of her embrace. "If I didn't put some restrictions on myself, I'd never be able to keep my hands – et cetera – off you. Come sit down for a while."

He poured sherry for both of them and left Britt in the living room while he detoured into the study for a velvet-covered box he'd picked up at a jeweler's that afternoon. Her eyebrows arched in surprise when he placed the box in her hand. "What's the occasion?"

"Must there be one? Open it."

She flipped up the lid. Her eyes widened at the sight of the gold chain from which hung a cross set with emeralds. She lifted the necklace out of its box and let it dangle from her fingers, glittering in the muted glow of the lamp at the end of the couch. "Colleague, you make me feel like a kept woman." She wasn't entirely joking.

"No one could mistake a successful psychiatrist for a kept woman." He took the delicate chain from her. "Allow me."

She gazed down at the necklace as he fastened it around her neck. "Seriously, Roger, expensive gifts make me uncomfortable."

"It's part of a long-term strategy," he said, hoping to lighten her mood. "Next I intend to take you shopping to replace that rattletrap you drive."

She flashed a smile. "It's a deal. But this is a whole different order of –" She fingered the cross. "Real emeralds."

"Certainly. To match your eyes, nothing less." He cut her off before she could protest the compliment. "Dear colleague, I enjoy giving you things. Why deny me the pleasure? Besides, this has a practical purpose."

"A jeweled cross? I can't wait to hear it."

"I'm hoping this is one form of protection you'll accept."

"Oh – I think I see."

"Yes," he said. "You saw how Sandor feared my crucifix – feared it so much that it burned his skin. If you'll promise to wear this at all times, I'll worry about you a little less."

"Fine. Anything to mitigate your worrywart tendencies." She kissed him lightly, drawing back before he could deepen the embrace. "Now, how about some more biofeedback practice?"

Britt had proved an apt pupil in controlling her autonomic functions, and she never passed up an opportunity for drill in the technique. "Are you sure you aren't too tired?" Roger said.

"Nice try. Do you expect me to believe that if we went to bed, you'd let me sleep?"

He blushed at her teasing. He knew she sensed his eagerness to drink from her, after abstaining all week. "All right, let's practice."

Britt slipped off the couch to lie face up on the carpet, her arms limp at her sides. She closed her eyes and took long, deep breaths. Sitting beside her on the floor, Roger lightly touched the center of her forehead. He slowly counted backward from ten. By the time he reached "one," she had sunk into trance.

He dropped his voice almost to a whisper. "Britt, I want you to decrease your heart rate by ten beats per minute. Begin now." He silently counted seconds until she'd carried out the command. In less than fifteen seconds she had reached the goal. "Excellent. Now, concentrate on your left hand. Drop the surface temperature of the skin. Very good." He saw her left hand turning paler by the second. Touching her fingers, he felt their coolness, compared to the rest of her body. "That's right. Now I want you to dilate the capillaries and make your hand warm up again."

Watching the immediate result of his suggestion, he marveled at how quickly she'd picked up these techniques. He wondered whether she could learn to suppress pain and bleeding, as he did. He hadn't thought of a way to instruct her in that skill, since he certainly couldn't inflict pain on her for didactic purposes. After they'd run through several more exercises, he counted up to ten to bring her out of the alpha state to normal consciousness.

She sat up and stretched her arms, wiggling her fingers. "I can't get over how great I feel after these sessions." She remembered every detail of the training; Roger kept his word never to blur her memory. "I just wish I could do half so well when I'm fully awake."

"That will come with practice," Roger said. He sat back against the couch, putting an arm around her, and she laid her head on his shoulder.

"What I really want to learn is your empathic perception. Think how much more efficiently I could treat my patients if I could read emotions the way you do."

"We'd have to work on that in public, around other people," said Roger. "I'm not sure how we'd manage it."

"You'll think of something."

"One thing we do have to practice in crowds, no matter what the difficulties," he said. "You must develop enough clairvoyance to know when you're being watched – for your own protection. Fortunately, that's something most people have a touch of anyway."

"But not like you," she said wistfully. "You know, I could really start envying those powers of yours. Invisibility must be a terrific asset sometimes."

She'd been awestruck when he'd demonstrated his ability to cast a psychic veil over himself. "I wouldn't know," he said, nuzzling the tender spot behind her ear. "I've hardly ever used it in any practical context."

"Stop that," she said. "I've just thought of something." She cupped the emerald cross in the palm of her right hand and touched his lips with the index finger of her left hand. "Draw some blood for me."

His tongue flicked her finger. "I beg your pardon?"

"Unless you want me to go get a sterilized needle. Look, this psychic link between us is a real entity in some sense, isn't it? I want to – well, objectify it."

Still puzzled, Roger nipped her fingertip. She allowed him to lick a single drop before she touched the center of the cross and dabbed it with her blood. Then she clasped his hand. "Now you."

Realizing what she had in mind, he bit his own finger and anointed the cross with a token drop of his blood. "You see," Britt said, "now it's not just a piece of jewelry you bought. It contains a part of both of us. If psychic emanations stick to material objects, it's carrying a charge."

"Yes, I see what you mean," he said, lifting her hand to his lips to taste the blood welling from the tiny cut. "I don't know whether that's objectively true or sentimental drivel, but it can't hurt." Seized by a sudden rush of desire, he enfolded her in his arms and kissed her with ravenous intensity. When they came up for air, he said unsteadily, "I'm almost glad you're going out of town Thanksgiving week. The break will be good for us. I want you – so terribly – God, sometimes I'm afraid I'll devour you!"

"Didn't I tell you to trust yourself?" She tilted her head, gazing into his eyes. "I've made you hungry, haven't I?"

"How did you guess, colleague?"

Laughing softly, she said, "Then I'd better do something about it."

*TWENTY YEARS ago I'd have been trying to "cure" him,* Roger thought, watching his last patient preparing to leave at noon on the day before Thanksgiving. Now psychotherapists no longer classified homosexuality as an illness, and Roger's job was to help the young man live with his situation. Lately the patient had been wrestling with the problem of whether to reveal the truth to his parents. Recalling how difficult it had been to conceal his true nature from Britt, Roger sympathized.

"See you next Wednesday, Doctor," said the patient on the way out. "Too chilly for golf today?"

Roger summoned up a dutiful smile for the feeble joke. He didn't use his Wednesday afternoons for anything except catching up on sleep.

Not that he expected to rest very well, as tense as he was with Britt visiting her sister in southern California. Sunday evening Britt would come home, thank Heaven. Only four more empty nights. He exchanged an automatic "Happy Thanksgiving" with the patient and prepared to lock up. *Happy? Not without Britt.*

Adrift in his reverie, Roger turned with a start when Marcia stepped up behind him to say goodbye. "Good afternoon," he said curtly, hoping his jumpiness didn't show too much. The frustration of Britt's absence made him short-tempered.

*And I thought the separation would be good for us!* Good for her, at any rate. Driving through the glaringly bright November afternoon, he smiled at the memory of how Britt had fought his suggestion that she was becoming borderline anemic. She hadn't trusted Roger's perception of the altered taste of her blood and the shade of her aura. Finally they'd borrowed a friend's lab equipment to test her hematocrit, and she'd had to concede.

Aside from considerations of her physical health, the perspective of distance could only benefit their relationship. He hadn't mentioned one more factor, that he felt relieved to have her out of Sandor's range, if only temporarily.

However, he had taken too lightly the problem of lengthy abstinence. Of course he had gone without human blood for two weeks on many past occasions – but those had been before he'd become conditioned to feeding every weekend.

And before he'd learned what real satisfaction could be! Knowing what he was missing made hunger doubly acute. Despite his fatigue and the eyestrain caused by the sun's glare on the Severn, he felt an erotic frisson at the memory of his last night with Britt, the Friday before

Something else he'd overlooked, he reflected as he turned right on the Severna Park side of the bridge, was how strongly he'd come to depend on Britt *between* weekends. Daily contact with her fed his psychic hunger, equally as important as the physical need. During her vacation they had talked on the telephone several times. Hearing her voice without feeling the touch of her mind frustrated him almost beyond bearing – but not enough to make him give up that tenuous contact.

*Four more nights. I can stand anything that long.*

At home he took a quarter pound of ground sirloin out of the refrigerator and blended it with undiluted canned beef broth. He'd run out of frozen blood and would have to stock up at a butcher shop in

Baltimore or Washington soon. He sat in the dim living room to drink his concoction, grimacing at the flat taste.

*I'll have to hunt again tonight.* He'd fed on live animals every night from Sunday on, and the craving had rebounded sooner and harder each time.

*No doubt about it, I'm thoroughly spoiled.* He chugged the rest of the drink. Maybe he could manage a decent few hours of sleep before sunset. More likely, he'd suffer through famished dreams of Britt all afternoon.

Just as he was turning the bed covers down, the phone rang. Stifling a curse, he made himself answer in a politely neutral tone.

"Dr. Darvell, this is Anna Kovak. Alice – I don't know what's gotten into her – she locked herself in, and she says –" Roger heard the woman swallowing sobs between phrases.

*Oh, Lord, not Alice again!* Over the past month, Roger had convinced himself he'd noted signs of improvement in her depression. "Slow down, please, Mrs. Kovak, and try to speak calmly. What is Alice doing right now?"

A voice in the background rumbled, "Let me talk to him, why dontcha?"

Mrs. Kovak said, "No, no, I can explain it to him. Doctor, Alice is locked in her bedroom with my bottle of Valium. She took one pill, and she said – she says she'll take them all if we try to get in. She won't talk to anybody but you."

The background voice, who Roger suspected was Alice's father, put in, "Knew that shrink would be a waste of money."

Mrs. Kovak, her voice shrill but controlled, said, "Can you come over right away, Doctor?"

Roger suppressed a sigh. *There goes the afternoon.* "Very well." While he doubted Alice sincerely meant to kill herself – she'd chosen too inefficient a method – ignoring her cry for attention might lead to a more serious attempt.

Shielded by his broad-brimmed hat and lightweight gray coat, Roger drove back across the Severn and through Annapolis, then across the South River to Edgewater. The area was still largely rural, and the Kovaks' home sat on a wooded waterfront lot almost a mile from the nearest neighbor. They lived in a rambling, elderly house they had converted into two separate units.

Seeing it for the first time, freshly painted, with wrought iron grills covering all doors and windows, Roger reflected that Mr. Kovak's auto body shop must be thriving. He knew from listening to Alice that she lived in one half of the house with her parents, who rented the other side to their grown son, Peter. Farther back on the lot stood a detached garage, and three partially dismantled cars crowded the side yard. Through the trees Roger glimpsed the river, a couple of hundred yards away.

When he got out of the Citroen, a young man wearing a blue work shirt with the body shop's logo trotted up to him. "You the doc? I'm Pete Kovak. About time you showed up."

Peter was a lanky twenty-six-year-old whose black hair curled greasily down his neck. Roger didn't need ESP to guess that the boy shared the elder Mr. Kovak's opinion of "shrinks." With Peter trailing him into the house, Roger greeted Mr. and Mrs. Kovak, whom he'd met once before.

"Any change since you called me?"

Mrs. Kovak, whose faded blonde hair suggested that as a girl she might have looked like Alice, began a reply, to be cut off by her husband. "No, she's still in there. I still think none of this woulda happened if –"

Having no patience for a wrangle about Alice's treatment, Roger interrupted, "Then I'll go right in and talk to her. Where's the bedroom?" He could have found the girl by the noise of her breathing but could hardly advertise that power.

Mrs. Kovak waved vaguely toward the hall. "It's at the very end."

Roger strode to the bedroom door and knocked. "Alice, it's Dr. Darvell. May I come in?"

"Just you. Nobody else." He heard her walk over to unlock the door, then cross the room again.

When he entered, she said in a voice hoarse with suppressed tears, "Lock it." He did. Alice sat on the bed with her legs curled under her, holding the open bottle of capsules.

Roger gave the room a quick once-over. Tidy, even to the stack of books on the floor beside the hutch whose shelves they overflowed. Alice's twin bed was covered with a patchwork quilt that, along with the Rackham fairy tale prints on the walls, contributed to the childlike ambience of her refuge. He didn't risk alarming her by stepping closer right away. "Alice, can you tell me what brought this on?"

"Nothing – everything. I don't know – I went to the mall this morning, because Mamma keeps bugging me about getting out more. I was watching the kids hanging out, shopping with their friends, and it all seemed so hopeless. Doctor, I'm so lonely!" The word ended on a sob.

The popular prescription of busy-ness and sociability for a depressive sometimes backfired, Roger mused. "Let me tell you a secret." Her eyes actually widened with interest at that. No, she wasn't ready to die just yet. "Everyone is lonely sometimes. Controlling your depression will not guarantee perfect happiness. No therapist can guarantee that. Loneliness is a permanent part of the human condition."

*And there I go, lecturing a patient – exercise in futility.* Yet Alice's eyes did spark with response for a second, before she answered in the flat tone of someone stating an axiom, "Easy for you to say. You don't know how I feel."

"Oh, but I do." He could never tell his patients how true that claim was, how his empathic talent picked up every nuance of their emotions. "That's what I was just saying. We all know how loneliness feels." He took advantage of her communicative mood to ease closer to the bed. "Will you give me that bottle?" His eyes enticed and trapped hers.

"I'll give it to *you.*" She put the cap on and held the container out to him.

Roger plucked it from her fingers, slipped it into his pocket, and sat beside her. "How many have you taken?"

"Just one. Just to show them I was serious."

"Were you?" he said evenly. "Do you really want to die?"

"I don't know. If there's another world after death, it's probably as – *nothing* as this one. Anyway, I don't much want to live. I'm scared, Doctor. He calls me – at night – and I dream I'm going to him. Or maybe it's not a dream. He's close by. I know it!"

"He? The man who attacked you?" She nodded. Roger examined her aura, seeking a trace of a vampire's shadow on her. Was she suffering from a delusion? Or could Sandor actually be returning to her over and over, draining her? That gradual approach would be atypical of him. Yet Alice looked pale and weak enough to support that assumption.

She clasped Roger's hand. "You're the only person who makes me want to live. Nobody else understands me."

"We've been over this before. You mustn't make me into more than I am." He increased his subtle pressure on her mind. "And keep your voice down. We aren't in the office now. You'll upset your parents."

"Oh, them." The dragged-out weariness in her voice lightened as she said, "I want to talk about you and me. I just couldn't wait for our next session." She rose onto her knees to sway toward him, wrapping an arm around his neck. "You know I – I've got a thing for you. I've told you enough times. Why won't you listen?"

"I do listen. That is my role, not what you're suggesting." He became aware of the rapid flutter of her pulse. Though thin to the point of emaciation – she wasn't one of those women who dealt with depression by overeating – she adhered fanatically to a lacto-vegetarian, high-fiber diet that kept her blood clean. Even now, in her washed-out condition, she would taste good.

"But you're *not* listening," she said petulantly. "You won't believe my feelings for you are real. I hate that!" She delivered the last remark in a vehement whisper, obeying his demand for quiet.

"I believe that you think they're real." True, Alice's overture was an attempt to manipulate him, yet on one level her lust for him was unfeigned. The mounting excitement she radiated mocked Roger's self-control. He caught himself salivating. *I have to make her stop!* "Lie down, Alice, and let's run through your relaxation exercises." She obeyed, half entranced by the mesmeric influence he couldn't keep himself from exerting.

Dropping his voice to a level she could barely hear, he cupped her face between her hands and drew his fingers lightly down her temples and jawline to her neck. "Follow my hands, Alice, and as I touch each part of your body, feel the tension flowing out, warmth and healing flowing in. . . ." Conditioned by long practice, she yielded and grew pliant, muscle by muscle, along the path he traced. The treatment wasn't working as Roger had hoped, though. The relaxation drill didn't erase Alice's sexual excitement, but only made it more dreamy and sensual.

*Probably because I don't really want to cool her off.* When he consciously tried to stop arousing her, tension knotted his hands and stirred Alice out of her languor. "I have to go, now that you're feeling better," he said, afraid to make matters worse by continuing the exercise.

"No, please don't," she whispered. Her hands slid up his arms. "My folks won't try to come in here – they're too scared of what I might do. Make love to me."

"That's out of the question. Aside from the ethics, you're a virgin."

She said with a bitter smile, "Right, a twenty-year-old virgin. A freak. That needs fixing, and I want you to do it."

"That isn't a sound motive for sexual experimentation." He hardly heard the words himself, and he knew very well that his hypnotic gaze was telling her the opposite. Against all reason, he reached out to stroke her temples again. "You will remember nothing of this except the relaxation exercises. You will not attempt suicide again. When you awaken, you will be serene, content, at peace." Would the suggestion take? Probably not, considering her past record, but it might calm her down for a few weeks. As for the command to forget, that would work – and did it mean he'd decided to accept what she offered?

*I can't! I promised Britt.*

His animal nature snarled, *Well, Britt isn't here, and I'm starving!* Alice had taken one Valium, not enough to affect Roger. He sensed her health wasn't up to par, as if she might be sickening for a viral infection. At this early stage, though, it wouldn't spoil the flavor of her blood. And he wouldn't take enough to hurt the girl, no more than he had the first time.

As he bent over her, shifting his massage to her neck and shoulders, she embraced him again. The liquid rhythm of her blood, like waves lapping on a sheltered beach, eroded his resistance. Without his conscious will, his hand drifted over her breasts and abdomen to the juncture of her thighs. She thrust against his delicate probe, moaned softly, and went limp.

Her release pushed him over the edge. He drank, watching himself with cold contempt, while his famished senses wallowed in the heat of her blood and her desire. After several minutes he realized Alice was growing weak, though still clinging to him with ravenous lust, and yet he felt no infusion of energy.

*I'm overdoing it – got to stop!*

Shuddering with the effort, he unfastened his mouth from her throat. Alice clutched at him, murmuring, "No, don't stop!" He surrendered. After all, he was giving her pleasure, more than any merely human male could.

*Is that the best rationalization you can dream up? You sound like those vermin who seduce patients on the pretext of curing their inhibitions.* But he kept drinking.

Several minutes later he realized that, although gorged to the point of satiety, he didn't feel satisfied. Her blood tasted little more piquant than a raccoon's or deer's. Whatever he'd grown to expect from the feast wasn't there.

Disengaging, he pressed his handkerchief to the incision until the bleeding stopped. Alice lay entranced, heavy-lidded. Her pale aura screamed Roger's indiscretion.

*Thank Heaven her parents can't see it.* Did the girl need a transfusion? Scanning her aura more deeply and listening to her heart, Roger decided she would recover without one. "Sleep now," he whispered. "Sleep and be well."

In the living room he handed the Valium bottle to Mrs. Kovak. "I suggest you lock these up, or, better yet, get rid of them." She clutched the bottle and nodded meekly. "Alice is resting. When she wakes up, try to persuade her to eat and drink something, but don't badger her. Understand?" He gazed sternly at both the girl's parents in turn. Peter seemed to have retreated to his side of the house, Roger was glad to see.

"Sure, we got it," said Mr. Kovak. "I know she's had a rough time. I'm not about to push her around."

So Mrs. Kovak had somehow managed to calm down her husband. "One more thing," Roger said. "She may still be a danger to herself. I strongly urge you to have her committed for a brief period of observation."

"Put her in a mental institution?" Mr. Kovak said. "No way!"

"But if the doctor thinks –" his wife began.

"Only a three-day period of observation," said Roger.

"I said no! She's not crazy."

Since it was obvious that pursuing the argument would only worsen Mr. Kovak's hostility, Roger turned his attention to smoothing the atmosphere all over again. After delivering the ritual reassurances the couple expected from a physician, he made his escape.

On the drive home the glare of the afternoon sun nauseated him. Rolling down the windows didn't help. By the time he reached his townhouse, his stomach was churning. He dashed inside to the bathroom and disgorged everything he'd drunk.

Afterward, weak with shame as well as nausea, he stood under a cold shower for ten minutes. *What have I done? Risked exposure and broken my word – for nothing!* Good God, had he actually ravished a patient with her parents waiting a few rooms away? But why the violent physical rejection? That had to be more than sun-sickness. Nor could a single Valium upset his system that way.

*Addiction!* So Volnar hadn't been talking about a mere emotional habituation; he meant true biochemical dependence. Roger physically required his lover's blood.

That night he dined only on warm milk, afraid to insult his body even with animal blood. For the first time, he was pro-foundly grateful to receive no long-distance call from Britt.

## Chapter 17

WHEN THE phone rang after 11 p.m. on Thursday, he expected and dreaded to hear Britt's voice. Instead, the caller turned out to be Mr. Kovak.

"We're at the hospital with Alice. She wants to see you – damned if I know why."

Roger didn't take the man's surly tone as a hint that he suspected Roger's misdeed. Mr. Kovak seemed the type who would entertain suspicions of any counselor's motives and competence. "What's wrong with Alice?" He went cold at the thought that she might have collapsed from exsanguination.

"They say pneumonia. She's in intensive care. You coming or not?"

"Yes, I'll be right over." Roger hung up without a goodbye and rushed out.

Pneumonia. Not anemia, thank Heaven, but no less Roger's fault. He'd noticed her less than vibrant condition and had taken her anyway. Weakening her immune system had probably led to the infection. And in her slightly undernourished state, she might die of it.

At the red brick community hospital downtown, in a residential district just off Duke of Gloucester Street, Roger hurried up to the ICU and found all three Kovaks waiting in the lounge. Mrs. Kovak clasped his hand and thanked him for coming. Alice's father and brother looked as if they wanted to blame Roger for the girl's illness but couldn't think of a plausible reason. "Hell of a way to spend Thanksgiving night," Mr. Kovak growled.

Buzzing the intercom, Roger was admitted to the ward and introduced to Dr. Harlow, the resident on duty, a trim young black man whose coffee-and-cream face showed lines of strain. He earnestly delivered an encyclopedic account of Alice's condition, the convoluted technical terminology boiling down to "stable." *Was I ever that young?* Roger mused, keeping his face impassive to hide the weight that instantly lifted from his mind.

"When will she be transferred from the ICU?"

"Tomorrow, probably," said the resident.

"Very good, I'll call to check on her in the afternoon."

"One thing puzzles me," said Dr. Harlow, his frown lines deepening. "Her hematocrit's low, which pneumonia doesn't account for. No symptoms of internal hemorrhage, either. I've ordered a few tests." He detailed them, while Roger nodded agreement, keeping his expression neutral. Once replenished by a transfusion, Alice's blood wouldn't show any signs to provoke further investigation – he hoped.

Finally Dr. Harlow ushered him into Alice's room. Hooked up to the respirator, she could greet Roger only with her eyes. The odor of sickness and disinfectant made his stomach turn over. *The smell of death.* For the first time it struck Roger that although eventually he might be killed, he would never experience this creeping decay. He forced himself to walk to the bed and take the girl's hand. She clenched his, her nails digging into his flesh.

"Easy," he said, stroking her forehead. "I assure you that you'll be all right. You're frightened and uncomfortable now, but that will pass." He stared into her eyes, compelling belief. The grip on his hand relaxed. "Surrender your will to mine. Let me take your pain away." That was the least he could do. He continued to murmur incoherent reassurances while smoothing her damp hair. He felt her breathing ease; the bedside monitor showed a slowing of her heartbeat and a drop in blood pressure. Five minutes later she drifted into sleep.

In the lounge he passed on to the Kovaks Dr. Harlow's assurance that Alice would move to a regular ward the next day. No doubt they'd already been told, but Roger knew in these circumstances people tended to hear only half of what was said and distort the rest. The sadness and fear they projected felt like a block of stone lying on his chest. He repeated, "Alice will be perfectly all right," several times, with variations, exerting hypnotic pressure on each of the three in turn. Mrs. Kovak greedily devoured the reassurance, while the two men lost little of their wariness.

Just before leaving, Roger said, "When Alice has recovered, I don't think it would be wise for me to continue as her therapist. She's developing an unhealthy dependence on me. I suggest we discuss transferring her to Dr. Loren." He wasn't surprised to see Mr. Kovak nod agreement.

Roger retreated before Dr. Harlow could pop up and trap him in another medical consultation. Outside, he inhaled a deep breath of the relatively clean air, considering what he'd recommended to the Kovaks. That course of action couldn't be avoided, which meant he would have to tell Britt the whole story.

*As if I'd conceal it from her anyway!* He would have to call her immediately. No, not tonight; by now it was after nine in California. Tomorrow evening. He felt guilty relief at postponing the confrontation.

After one the following day, he called the hospital to check on Alice. As predicted, she had recovered enough to move out of the ICU. Roger said a silent prayer of thanks. At least he'd have a modicum of good news to pass on to Britt.

He flipped through his address book to her sister's number. After he'd stared at it long enough to memorize it several times over, even without his eidetic memory, he admitted to himself that he didn't want to confess his transgression over the phone. The complicated, painful situation didn't allow that kind of handling. He had to tell her face to face.

*Sunday night. I'll tell her then.*

On the other hand, suppose she phoned him earlier? How could he carry on a normal conversation while keeping that secret? Could he wait for her return home?

That night, after hours of postponement with every scrap of busywork he could devise, he still vacillated between the two equally threatening alternatives. In the dim cave of his study, he glared at the phone as if it were a vicious beast ready to pounce. He picked up and replaced the receiver twice before admitting he hadn't the nerve to make the call.

He needed advice, and he'd rather grope through the fog forever than appeal to Volnar. Instead he dialed his brother Claude's Los Angeles number.

In a heavily British accent, Claude said, "It's delightful to hear from you, little brother. Damn shame about Sylvia, though."

"Did you know her?"

"Not really. Ran into her a couple of times." Over the line, Roger heard cloth rustling and the phone being moved, as if Claude were settling for a long conversation. "I knew that blighter Sandor was a blot on the landscape, but I never thought he'd go that far."

"Were you acquainted with Sandor?"

"Only by reputation. Crossed paths with his twin, Camille, a couple of years ago. She hung about with those white-faced young people who dress in black and write poetry that doesn't scan – said they made for good hunting – but she seemed sane on all other subjects." In a more sober tone, he added, "Except for defending her scum of a brother, but that's to be expected. Sibling loyalty."

A sudden onslaught of anger squeezed Roger's throat. "If sibling loyalty is so damned important, what about all those years when I –"

"Don't bare your fangs at me, little brother. I had no choice. Among our kind, age really does mean wisdom and power. Nobody in his senses would defy one of the eldest."

"Meaning Sandor is out of his senses." Roger forced his breathing and blood pressure under control. He hadn't phoned to pick a fight with Claude.

"Hell, that goes without saying."

"Volnar has passed a death sentence on him and expects me to carry it out."

"He would, wouldn't he?" said Claude with a humorless laugh. "I daresay it's meant partly as a sort of test. Are you man enough – or vampire enough – to defend your own territory? That's how he would see it. But surely you didn't call to discuss Neil Sandor?"

"Not directly. I've had a hell of a week, and I need to talk about it, if I'm not interrupting anything."

"An hour ago, you would have been." Claude purred like a cat replete with cream. Roger fantasized about decking him. "But now I'm at your disposal. By the way, how is your lady? Dare I hope she is yours by now?"

"In a manner of speaking," Roger said.

"So you did score. Well done, *mon frere*!"

Roger struggled to leash his temper. "I don't think of Britt in those terms."

"Oh, like that, is it? Then why would you waste time ringing me up on a Friday night? Why aren't you enjoying her company at this moment?"

"She isn't here; she's visiting her sister in Long Beach," Roger said. He flexed the fingers of his left hand, which had been clutching the edge of the desk. "That's what I need advice on."

"And you don't want to discuss her with Fearless Leader. Can't blame you," Claude said. "Fire away. You sound damn near worn out. Been starving yourself while she's out of reach?"

"If I wanted to hear that, I *would* go to Volnar," Roger said, rubbing his forehead. "Britt has been away from home since Saturday morning."

"And you didn't want anyone else. I understand that. I've had that experience myself, a long time ago. Dom Perignon, *n'est-ce pas?*"

"Yes." Roger's throat went dry at the thought.

"Have you bonded with her? They say that's even better – Chateau Lafitte Rothschild, as it were. I admit I've never gone that far with an ephemeral myself."

"No," said Roger. "The idea frightens me." He moved to the office couch, resting the phone on his lap.

"How long have you been intimate with your Dr. Loren?"

"A little over a month."

"She knows exactly what you are, doesn't she? From the way you described her, she wouldn't tolerate unanswered questions."

"That's right."

"And you're still holding back?"

"I don't even know that she'd want the two-way bond. We've never discussed it." Roger plumped a cushion against the sofa arm and lay back on it.

"She's interested in psychic research, isn't she? Have you tried teaching her some of your skills?"

Roger thought of how the process both intrigued and frustrated Britt. "All she's been able to pick up is the biofeedback – controlling her autonomic functions to some extent. And she seems to be developing an empathic talent. She reads my emotions too accurately for chance."

"Of course," Claude said. "Prolonged contact with a vampire has that effect. But you can't teach her most of those skills without the bond. She'd love it."

Memory of his mutual blood-sharing with Volnar scraped on Roger's nerves. Could he face that again, even with Britt? "You don't know her. I'm not sure, myself, how she would react."

"Still, it sounds as if you're getting along swimmingly. So why are you so miserable?"

Roger told him everything that had happened from the moment Alice's mother had called on Wednesday. The rehearsal made the prospect of repeating the story to Britt slightly less formidable.

"So she didn't die?" Claude said in an offensively offhand manner.

"No, the antibiotics seemed to have the pneumonia under control."

"Then you aren't a killer. Your conscience ought to be clear."

The image of Alice in the ICU made Roger queasy all over again. "You don't understand."

"No, old thing, frankly, I don't. I haven't got a conscience, just a set of pragmatic ethics. After all, what else are ephemerals *for?*" After a pause he continued, "Is it because the girl's your patient? You've used patients before, haven't you?"

"Not since Britt and I –" Depression settled like a damp cloud on Roger when he thought of Britt's probable reaction to his behavior. She would rightly insist that the nights of torment he'd suffered in her absence were no excuse.

"Let's see if I have this straight," Claude said. "A twenty-year-old girl threw herself at you, and being half-starved, you didn't resist very hard."

"Not starved. I'd gone without for only four and a half nights."

"Sounds like hell to me," said Claude, "but then you have that half-human streak, old chap."

"I should have exercised better self-control." Roger recalled his shock when he'd pulled back from Alice's limp body and realized how much he had overindulged. With the metallic tang of her blood lingering in his mouth, he'd still felt empty. "The worst of it is, I knew she wasn't well. But since it wasn't serious enough to spoil the – the flavor, I ignored the signs."

"Unwise of you, but understandable in the circumstances. Now she's recovering, so all's well – except that you're agonizing about what your Dr. Loren will say when she finds out. You're afraid to confront her?"

"That's essentially correct." Roger wished Claude wouldn't use such a flippant tone.

"You're a fool as well as a coward, old thing."

Roger felt too near exhaustion to bother resenting this remark. "Because I have scruples about violating a patient?"

"That's beside the point," Claude said. "Because, given your Dr. Loren's attitude on the subject, you risked losing the kind of relationship few of us find even once in a century."

"Spare me the lecture; I've delivered it to myself a hundred times." He rubbed his eyes, stinging from the fatigue of five days without proper sleep. "And stop calling her my' Dr. Loren. After this weekend, she may not be."

"Was the girl worth it?" said Claude.

"You know the answer to that. It wasn't much better than animal blood. Worse, in fact, since it made me sick."

"You do have a severe case," Claude said, his voice radiating genuine empathy. "You're thoroughly fixated on your friend. And you care about her, don't you? Enough to want her around even when you aren't thirsty?"

"Of course." What kind of selfish hedonist did Claude take him for? Or was that mind-set the vampire norm?

"Not that I'm any expert," said Claude, "but this sounds an awful lot like that thing ephemerals call love."

"I haven't even begun to think of that." A dull ache was building in his forehead.

"In all seriousness, I think you should consider bonding with her. It would minimize or eliminate any chance of future misunderstandings. And they say the depth of the union is – indescribable."

Roger shifted uneasily on the couch. "The question is academic, since she probably won't care to speak to me again."

"You know, you could simply not tell her what happened."

Roger retorted in a blaze of indignation, "Lie to her? Don't be obscene!"

"Calm down, *mon frere*. I'm convinced of your commitment. Isn't it about time you tried convincing her?"

Roger sat up, his hand spasmodically tightening on the receiver. "I can't explain all this to Britt over the telephone."

"Then you must do it the moment you see her. However, I'd give her some advance warning that all isn't well; don't spring it on her out of the blue." He chuckled. "Hell, any magazine advice columnist could have told you that."

Roger's head ached. He felt as if he were being backed into a corner. "Perhaps you're right."

"Of course I am," said Claude. "Given the condition you're in –"

"Good Lord, is it that obvious?" Glancing down to check his free hand for any sign of a tremor, Roger caught himself clenching it into a fist in his lap. He uncurled his fingers.

"To another vampire, blatantly so, even over a long-distance line. I don't think you've got much to worry about; your friend won't care about anything other than relieving your obvious distress."

Roger's throat went dry at the image of Britt's tall, slender body in his arms, her green eyes gazing into his, offering herself. "I can't count on that."

"Considering the alternative, what have you got to lose? *Au revoir, mon frere.*"

After breaking the connection, Roger stared at the telephone for at least five minutes before lifting the receiver again. He dialed Britt's sister's number in Long Beach.

After he'd endured the embarrassment of asking a pre-teenage boy to call Dr. Loren to the phone, Britt came on the line and said, "Colleague, it's wonderful to hear your voice! I wasn't expecting a call so soon before I'm due home." The delight in her greeting momentarily silenced him. "Why do I get the idea that you're feeling underloved and underfed?"

The teasing tone brought her image vividly to mind – her sparkling green eyes, her fair redhead's skin, her magnificent titian hair. "That's true, but it isn't why I called."

"I'm glad you did. I miss you."

"That's entirely mutual." How could he possibly work up the nerve to tell her what he needed to?

"Have you been getting any rest?" she said.

"I've tried."

"Meaning you haven't slept well since I left." The concern in her voice brought a lump to his throat. "Dreams?"

"Too many." He'd explained to her how little REM time he required, so she understood the significance of excessive dreaming. "The kind that make me miss you even worse."

"Then let me give you a visualization to tide you over. I'm lying on the bed upstairs in Hal and Darlene's room, in a Navy housing unit in San Pedro," she said, dropping her voice to a sensual murmur. "I'm looking out the window toward the ocean and Catalina. At least, I could see Catalina in the daytime. Right now all I see is dark water with a streak of moonlight. What are you doing?"

"Sitting in my home office talking to you."

She laughed. "Oh, Roger, you're so literal-minded." He heard the creak of bed springs as she shifted position. The sound made his heart race. "There's something I wanted to run by you, anyway. Darlene's pedigreed Siamese just had kittens, and she offered to give me one. She'll have him shipped to me by air when he's old enough. I had to ask you about it, though."

"Why? Your cat, your house." He relaxed a trifle at the conversational reprieve.

"Would it be safe for me to have a pet when you're around all the time?"

"Well, I won't eat it for breakfast in a fit of absent-mindedness!" After weeks of intimacy, did she think he was that dangerous?

"Silly, that's not what I mean at all. I'm asking whether he would be too afraid of you or too hostile to adjust."

"Oh." Roger's annoyance was replaced by a pang of sadness at the thought of Katrina. "No, if the animal grows up in close contact with me, he won't mind."

"That's great. Now, your turn, why did you call?"

He took a fortifying breath. "I need to talk to you about an important matter that's come up, as soon as you arrive home Sunday."

Alarm crept into Britt's voice. "Not another murder?"

"No, nothing like that. It has to do with a patient, and it does need immediate attention." His nerves twitched under his skin; they felt as raw as if she could sense his deception over the three-thousand-mile gap.

Her voice lightened again. "Oh, I see. You're getting desperate, and you want to be sure I'll come right over for a bite."

Desperate? She was all too right about that. "Colleague, I wish you wouldn't talk that way over the telephone."

"Stop being paranoid, Roger. I'm alone with the door closed. Anyway, if Hal or Darlene overheard, they wouldn't give it a second thought. Now, can't you tell me anything specific?" "I would rather wait until Sunday. It's too involved to go into right now." Surely she could hear the dishonesty in that excuse.

Sounding puzzled, Britt said, "All right, colleague. I'll drive right over to your place after I get home. I would have anyway. Goodnight, then."

SATURDAY AFTERNOON he went to confession. This time he had no need to exaggerate his contrition. For this sin, he was heartily sorry for his offense and sincerely intended amendment of life. *If it's not already too late!* The priest's absolution and the imposed penance did little to lift Roger's spirits. He wanted Britt's forgiveness more than God's. *And if that's blasphemy, I suppose I've added a few more years to my term in Purgatory.* Early morning mass on Sunday didn't help much, either. He hardly needed the reminder from the Epistle for the First Sunday in Advent that "love does no harm to a neighbor."

When Britt called Sunday night to say that she'd just arrived from the airport and would be over within twenty minutes, Roger almost yielded to panic and told her to stay away. All that stopped him was the certainty that she would ignore any such request. Only one fact mitigated his anxiety about confessing to her – Alice had bounced back quickly from the pneumonia and had gone home that morning.

Roger prowled from kitchen to study to living room, seething with impatience. When he considered a shot of brandy to settle his nerves, his stomach knotted in protest. Perhaps some warm milk? No, only one thing could appease his thirst now.

He lost track of how many minutes passed before the doorbell rang. Through the wooden barrier he heard Britt's heartbeat and breathing. When he opened the door, both quickened in anticipation. One level of his mind automatically registered her clothes – tapered slacks and an emerald-green pullover, no bra – and the way she wore her hair, in a long ponytail as a compromise between her dress-for-success chignon and the unbound wildness that delighted him. But the deep pink of her aura and the intoxicating scent of her clean, healthy flesh overwhelmed his senses.

Britt waited for him to latch, bolt, and chain the door, then opened her arms to him. Her wounded expression when he drew back without touching her almost destroyed his resolve.

"Colleague, what's wrong?" she asked.

"We have to talk first." He led the way into the living room, and waited for her to settle on one of the twin sofas.

He sensed Britt struggling to suppress her anxiety and hurt. "I don't know that you're in any condition to talk," she said. "I doubt you can even think straight. I know you're hungry – why won't you let me take care of you?" She lowered her mental barrier, strong for an ephemeral's, enough to let him feel her eagerness for that sharing.

He hardened his own shield in resistance, painful as the effort was. Though the two of them had no telepathic rapport, Britt had developed enough empathy to sense Roger's withdrawal. She gave up and said briskly, "All right, I'm listening."

Pacing back and forth in front of the bare, cold fireplace, he told her of the past week's events in a brief, dry style, as if reporting any other case history. With no display of emotion, she asked a few pointed questions about the patient's condition. He answered them.

"You expect a full physical recovery, then?" she said.

"I don't anticipate any problems there."

"And what are you planning to do with Alice?" Aside from the tightening of her lips, Britt showed no outward sign of the anger he knew boiled inside her. He heard her pulse racing.

"I'll turn her over to you, unless her parents choose to send her elsewhere," Roger said. "I've told them she's becoming too emotionally involved with me, and I can't do her any more good."

"Well, at least that's the truth!" Britt's calm facade cracked.

"Roger, how could you? Couldn't you control yourself for one lousy week?"

He stopped, spun around to face her. The anger that flooded him took him by surprise; he had to choke it down before he could speak. "I regret what I did. However, I don't think your reaction is quite fair." He wanted to erase the words as soon as they popped out. *Why did I make a stupid remark like that?*

Her aura turned a smoldering red. "Fair! Are you implying that I shouldn't have left? That I have some obligation to chain myself to your side?"

He realized that his visceral reaction had implied exactly that. Good God, what was the matter with him? "Colleague, I didn't say that, nor would I ever –"

"You're implicitly blaming me for your failure. And I thought we'd developed some kind of mutual respect!"

He was tempted to grab her and shake her until she saw things his way. He restrained himself, trembling with the effort. If he touched her, it would be all over. He kept his voice icy. "Does it disturb you so much that I fed on someone other than you?"

Britt sprang to her feet, fists clenched at her sides. "You arrogant – monster! You don't even understand! She wasn't just anyone; she was your patient. And if professional ethics don't matter, you made a promise. You promised *me* you'd stay away from the patients. I thought that meant something!"

He did understand, of course, and heartily agreed with her judgment. Damn, why had he blurted out that reckless, defensive remark? It was too late to explain; Britt was deafened by her indignation. "What are you going to do? Report me to the board?"

"I should. But you know I can't. Damn you, Roger, I couldn't expose you that way." Unshed tears glimmered in her eyes.

He took a step forward, reaching for her. Her heartbeat thundered in his ears. "Don't touch me," she said flatly.

A fresh surge of anger inundated him. *How dare she!* She belonged to him; she was his lawful prey. He could take her here and now, by force, feed on her pain instead of her passion—

*What am I doing?* Though she must have felt the searing rage spewing out of him, she stared him down, as fearless as ever. He stepped back, quivering with leashed emotion. What he'd almost done would have lost her forever.

"Get away from me," she said, blinking back angry tears. "I wish you'd – oh, just change into a bat and fly away!"

He had to get out before he did something unforgivable. "With pleasure!" He stalked out and slammed the door.

He ran blindly along the wooded roads. When the crimson fog cleared from his vision, he found himself approaching Route 50. For once its cacophony of blinking stoplights, the glare from fast food restaurants and used car lots, and the roar of traffic didn't batter his senses. Nor did the night air soothe him. His inner turmoil drowned out all external stimuli. He vaguely noticed a clump of blue-jeaned teenagers, their hands full of paper bags and Coke cups, dodging out of his way. What must they think of a tall, ascetic-looking man storming along the sidewalk with the ferocious concentration of a tiger running down a gazelle?

The comparison snapped him out of his passion-induced trance, and he moderated his pace. Unbidden, the memory of the thin flavor of Alice's blood sprang to mind. How could he have settled for a mere orgasmic robot? He wanted only Britt.

Was it just wanting? What did he feel for her? He confronted the emotions he had so far avoided analyzing. Britt had become his life – and not only because her blood sustained him. He felt that without her warmth he would wither into an empty husk.

Across the street shone the logo of a restaurant highly regarded for gourmet seafood dishes at upscale prices. Roger charged through a crosswalk against the "Don't Walk" sign, darting past the bumper of a Cadillac that screeched to a halt, its horn blaring. He needed to wind down and think over his predicament; why not do it in the traditional spot for such ruminations? Though he'd rushed out without his wallet, he did have loose bills and change in a side pocket.

He walked around to the side entrance of the restaurant and into the cocktail lounge. To his relief, the live entertainment consisted of a pianist playing unobtrusive blues tunes. Roger took a stool at the bar and ordered a shot of Glenlivet, which he gazed at for a couple of minutes without tasting.

Lost in his despair, he didn't register the woman sitting next to him until she spoke. "Not too bad, is he?" She nodded at the piano player. "Better than the deafening rock and roll a lot of bars have." She paused to sip her strawberry daiquiri. She didn't even pretend to wait for a reply to her transparent conversational ploy. "Would you like to dance?"

In spite of his distaste for this public soliciting, Roger allowed himself to be distracted. Anything was an improvement over his own thoughts. Automatically his predator's instinct evaluated the woman, Hispanic, buxom yet slim-waisted, with an upswept coil of glossy black hair. Though the pink in her cheeks came from blusher, her aura pulsed with rosy health. She didn't smell of smoke, drugs, or disease.

With no conscious intent, he snared her chocolate-brown eyes. Her patter trailed off into silence, and she stared at him unblinking. In five minutes he could lure her into the parking lot and taste her blood. The image roused no appetite; nausea welled up in his throat. "Get away from me!"

She jumped at his harsh tone and scurried to a table at the far end of the room.

He couldn't do it. Even when no ethical problem interfered, he couldn't feed on an entranced victim. Not after Britt's vibrant response.

Half-consciously he abandoned his drink, wandered out of the lounge, and headed toward home. *Do I love her, then?* Despite his lifelong study of human emotion, Roger still hadn't settled on a definite meaning for that word. Used in so many irreconcilable ways, it might as well be semantically null. He recalled Claude's litmus test for "love": "Do you still want her around when you aren't thirsty?"

By that criterion, Roger – cared – for Britt. He couldn't bring himself to use the more emotionally charged word. After all, as she'd justly accused, he hadn't even cared enough to resist temptation after giving a solemn promise.

Across the street near McDonald's, a teenage boy walked past wearing a T-shirt that read, "If you love something, let it go. If it returns to you, it is yours forever. If it doesn't return, hunt it down and kill it." *That's what I almost did.*

What now? Leave Annapolis, as he'd left his Boston practice?

*Some example of caring that would be! She's right, Dr. Darvell, you are a self-centered monster.* No matter how she justifiably scorned him now, she needed him financially. The only honorable course, Roger decided, would be to stay as her partner, behaving with distant professional courtesy. If the anguish of seeing her daily without touching her half killed him, so be it. That was no more than he deserved.

He plunged into the woods again, crashing through the underbrush and seething with frustration. Dead leaves and pine needles rustled under his feet. When he slowed down, it was only from reluctance to go home and discover Britt had left. Flickering over his surroundings, his eyes registering the bluish auras of insects and the still paler haloes that surrounded live plants. He barely noticed, until the pink aura of a small mammal caught his attention.

His night vision picked out a raccoon waddling across the path several yards ahead. Doubtless used to dining on scraps from suburban garbage cans, the animal showed no fear. It gave Roger a bold glance and kept walking. Saliva pooled in his mouth. His jaws ached with the urge to bite – and here was a legitimate target for his hunger and fury.

Capturing the raccoon's eyes with his own, he forced it to stand paralyzed until he crept close enough to grab it. He flipped the limp animal onto its back and plunged his teeth into the sparsely-furred belly. Hot blood gushed, almost too fast to swallow. Roger gorged in a frenzy, dropping the corpse only when the arterial spurting ceased.

Although not exactly satisfied, he felt in control again. If Britt hadn't left, he wouldn't have to face her halfmad with need. He accelerated to a brisk trot. When he reached the town-house complex, it occurred to him, with a flash of grim amusement, that he had let a guest throw him out of his own home.

To his surprised relief, Britt's car was still there.

## Chapter 18

He paused, hand on the doorknob, listening. Britt was still in the living room, her breathing ragged. He heard her leap up when he opened the door. She hadn't bothered to lock it – damn careless.

When he emerged from the foyer into the living room, she stood in front of the fireplace waiting for him, her shape outlined by the pulsing glow of her aura. She had started a fire in the hearth. Though her eyes were pink-rimmed from crying, her challenging "Well?" was crisply controlled.

"You should have locked the door," he said, halting a few yards away. "You should take better care of –"

"Your property?"

The word stung, for it cut too close to his occasional impulses. "Never that, colleague. I simply want you to exercise reasonable caution. Sandor hasn't given up on us. He seems to be harassing Alice Kovak."

"She did mention that." Britt's voice held no shade of emotion. All that gave Roger hope was the absence of open hostility. She stared at him in the dim light of the fire and the single lamp he'd left on. "Whose blood?"

He hadn't realized how disreputable he must look. "Raccoon. Excuse me, I have to clean up."

He retreated to the bathroom. In the mirror he found a streak of drying blood on his chin. A few dead leaves clung to his clothes, not to mention raccoon hairs on his shirt. *I'm surprised she didn't run screaming for her car.* He tasted not only blood but the fur he hadn't been able to avoid. He brushed his teeth, washed his face and hands, and grabbed a clean shirt from the bedroom.

In the living room, Britt was still pacing. At a gesture of invitation from him, she sat stiffly on the edge of one of the couches.

He sat opposite her, forcing himself to meet her eyes. "I was afraid when I got back, you wouldn't be here."

"And I was afraid that if I left, you might not follow me." She almost, but not quite, smiled. "I overreacted. Oh, there's no excuse for what you did, but blowing up at you won't help. And I didn't quite mean all those things I said."

"Listen, please – I deeply regret breaking my word, and considering the disastrous consequences, I think you can count on its not being repeated."

She folded her arms and said warily, "I accept that."

"I won't desert you professionally, and if that's the way you want it, our future—associatio— need not be any more than professional."

Her stiff pose melted along with the ice in her voice. "Oh, Roger, I don't want that! I don't want to end our relationship; I want to fix it."

"So do I." He packed all the sincerity he could into the words, without violating her by hypnotic coercion.

"Then why are you sitting over there?" Her voice quavered, and her cheeks reddened from emotion as well as the fire.

He joined her on the other couch. "I'm afraid I won't be able to hold back – that if I touched you, I'd try to influence you."

"I trust you that far." She clasped one of his hands in both of hers.

"What can I do to convince you that I won't repeat this –" "Mistake" was a flabby, self-serving word. "That I won't violate my promise again?"

"Listen, Roger, I can't be your conscience." Her voice hardened again. "You have to straighten up and fly right for your own sake, not just for me."

"I know that." What he didn't know was how. Only his union with Britt stood between him and the life he'd led for nearly two decades. He squeezed her fingers, relaxing his grip when she winced. "I don't have just professional ethics to motivate me. I've got the memory of how completely – inadequate –" Her heartbeat accelerated, making him lightheaded. "Britt, I don't want anyone but you."

She caught her breath in a gasp. "Roger – I had no idea."

"What?"

"Touching you, like this, I can feel it – feel your hunger. I never suspected – you feel *hollow.*"

"You can actually pick up my sensations?" Why should he be surprised? Her empathic talent had increased steadily over the past several weeks.

"In *here.*" She laid a hand over her diaphragm. "Hunger – thirst – oh, Lord, it feels like you're dying."

"Far from that! I'm used to the craving," he said. "It hits you harder because it's new to you."

"Forgive me, colleague, I've been too hard on you."

Roger relaxed slightly, letting out the breath he hadn't been aware of holding. "Indeed? I came to precisely the opposite conclusion."

"When I yelled at you for not waiting a single week, I didn't understand. I thought it was like – oh, going on a diet, or giving up chocolate for Lent." Her nails dug into his skin. "I never suspected it was like this."

"It wasn't, most of the time. Not until I became used to having you near, basking in your – affection." His head pounded with tension. He didn't know how much longer he could restrain himself from pouncing on her. He disentangled his hand from hers. "Then I suddenly had to do without seeing you every day, touching you, if only for a minute at a time."

"I've missed you, too, physically as well as emotionally. Withdrawal symptoms – you warned me, but I didn't think it would be so literally true. I've been jumpy, couldn't sleep, had no appetite – had to explain it to Darlene as a new variety of PMS." Britt relaxed into a teasing grin that made Roger dizzy with the sudden release of anxiety. "And that's on top of the ordinary, nonpathological symptoms of missing you. First time I've used the vibrator in over two months."

He felt himself flushing at her boldness, even as it delighted him. He wondered – not that it was any of his business – damn, he had to ask. "Did you purchase one on impulse or take it with you?"

"I packed it deliberately. I had a feeling I was going to miss you. A lot. My point is," she continued, "if I felt that bad, how much worse must it be for you? I never came close to understanding that before. No wonder you couldn't resist when that girl practically fell into your lap. I always swore I wouldn't blame you for being what you are, and that's what I was doing."

"A generous attitude, colleague, but you were right. If ordinary men can conform their biological drives to social constraints, I should be able to do the same."

"Nevertheless, I overreacted – and you know why?" She blushed a faint pink. "Because for a few minutes I actually thought you'd been using me all this time – just a convenient food source, and any casual replacement would do as well."

"Britt –" His chest constricted. Any protest would sound hollow. That he could have hurt her so, even briefly –!

"I know that isn't true. I really was jealous, can you believe it?" Again she flashed him a smile. "How does that make you feel?"

"Ashamed," he said.

She held out her hands, palms upward in a tentative beckoning gesture. "You look terrible. I prescribe a hug."

She melted into his arms. The next minute was a blur. His universe contracted to the pressure of her warm body against his, her breath on his neck, the pounding of her heart, her fingers in his hair. He embraced her as tightly as if he could merge his flesh with hers, cell to cell. "Dear God, Britt, I thought I'd lost you!"

"And I was afraid, when I said those horrible things, that you'd think I meant them." Her voice shook. He tasted the salt of tears on her cheek.

"For God's sake, don't cry," he groaned, kissing her neck. He'd been afraid that he wouldn't be able to touch her without ripping into her throat, but within the circle of her aura his hunger receded into the background. Her affection in itself refreshed him.

After a moment he regained enough control to speak without breaking into tears himself. "How long can you stay?" He loosened his hold to draw back and brush a hand over her erect nipples through the clinging shirt. The tiny heat-sensitive hairs in his palm tingled at the touch.

"All night," she said, grazing the back of his neck with her tapered fingernails. "I don't care if tomorrow is Monday; I've missed you too much. You should have heard the way Darlene snickered about my getting a cross-country phone call from a man. She was actually relieved, though – she'd started to think you were a figment of my frustrated imagination. At least now she'll stop worrying that I might be a lesbian."

Roger stared incredulously into her eyes. "She couldn't think that!"

"Not seriously, I guess, but what other reason could a passably attractive woman pushing forty have for staying unmarried?"

Their shared laughter at the absurd notion was short-lived. Within seconds a more urgent emotion overruled it. His intent gaze captured hers. He felt as if he were drowning in her eyes, instead of the reverse. She breathed rapidly through parted lips. "Roger, don't look at me that way – you make me feel faint."

"I can't stop," he murmured. "You intoxicate me. God, you smell delicious!"

"Oh, damn, Roger – I hate to admit it, but I want you so much I hurt."

"*You* hurt?"

Their open mouths met, her tongue darting at his as if she, too, were ravenous. His thirst revived, so fierce his head reeled with it. Terrified of treating her too roughly, Roger broke off the kiss and made himself slow down. He insinuated a hand under her shirt, savoring the heat of her skin. Her desire was so palpable that he didn't need her gasp of pleasure to confirm it. He felt drunk with the fragrance of her arousal.

"Wait." Fighting for breath, he forced himself to stop caressing her. "Britt, before we go any further, there's something I must ask you." Claude's advice sounded better all the time; Roger knew it was the only way to make Britt absolutely sure of his sincerity.

"Uh-oh, you sound serious again. That always means trouble."

The tinge of anxiety in her voice pained him. "It doesn't have to. Feel perfectly free to refuse. I just want to suggest something that will increase the depth of our intimacy, our – openness." He'd discovered that his fear of vulnerability was far less than his terror of any future estrangement. "I'd like you to drink my blood."

"Sounds interesting. Why?"

"Two-way blood-sharing creates a telepathic bond. You'd never have to be afraid of my betraying you again, because you would *know*."

"You mean we could read each other's minds, like in *Dracula*? What Stoker calls the Baptism of Blood?" She sounded enthusiastic rather than frightened.

"Better than that, or so I've heard. The closeness is supposed to be unimaginable." He hesitated to mention the other factor, knowing how she would react. "And also for your own protection."

She frowned. "That again? How so?"

"You need to develop your psychic skills as fully as possible. I realize I can't stay with you twenty-four hours a day, and I see now that it would suffocate you if I did. With your paranormal powers enhanced by that bond, you'd be better able to protect yourself."

Her joy washed over him like a stream of cool water in midsummer heat. "Colleague, I thought you'd never ask!"

He pulled back to stare at her. "You *want* this?"

"I've been wondering about it for weeks. I *had* read Stoker, after all. I just had no idea whether it was really possible."

"Then why didn't you ask?"

Britt snuggled up to him, her head on his shoulder. "What, and scare you away? Think I don't know how afraid you are of revealing yourself to anyone?"

Flushing, he said, "I didn't know it was that obvious – and I shouldn't have reacted that way with you."

"What do we tell our patients? There are no 'shoulds' with emotions. Well? What are you waiting for?"

Her eagerness stirred his passion, which, however, did little to relieve his nervousness. "I'm not sure how to go about it." He raised his left hand to his mouth, preparing to bite the wrist.

Britt clasped his hand. "Not there; it's too impersonal."

"Well, I'm not going to try slitting my own throat with a pocketknife. In my present condition, I'd probably sever an artery. And I keep my nails trimmed too short for self-laceration like Dracula in the novel."

After thinking for a second, Britt said, "Here?" and kissed him on the shoulder.

Roger unbuttoned his shirt and pushed it back from his shoulders, then turned his head to slash the skin where her lips had touched. Though he was immune to the mild anesthetic in his own saliva, the razor-edge of his incisors was too keen to hurt. Britt pressed her open mouth to the trickle of blood.

His first reaction was an indrawn breath of astonishment at the rapture produced by her hot tongue. All his nerve endings vibrated with the electricity of her kiss. The blood seemed to bubble like champagne in his veins.

At the first brush of her naked mind on his, fear drowned his excitement. Memories of Sylvia's devouring emptiness and Volnar's cold probe overwhelmed him. For a moment he struck out blindly, unconscious of Britt as anything but an invading parasite.

Then pain speared him. Not his own pain, but hers. Dimly realizing that he was hurting Britt, he stopped fighting. Instead he slammed shut the door of his mind.

Britt vanished. He found himself in a gray void, falling endlessly. His own silent scream reverberated in his skull.

A gentle caress brushed his icy barrier, like the warmth of her hand. He locked onto that sensation and stopped falling.

"Let me in, Roger. It won't hurt. We can't hurt each other." Thrusting his panic away like a poisonous insect, he opened to her.

He felt an echo of his own fear in her, immediately submerged by a flood of desire. Letting it sweep him away, he tasted a piercing sweetness even she had never given him before.

Gradually he became aware of tasting his own blood through her senses. With his own eyes shut in drugged enchantment, he saw himself through Britt's heavy-lidded gaze. The reversed vision made his head spin; sensing that, she closed her eyes. He felt her mounting passion, the hypersensitivity of her nipples, the tightening in her loins. He couldn't wait any longer; he bent to the sweet-scented curve of her neck and drank.

As their excitement grew, they fed the sensations back and forth to each other in a rising spiral, until Britt reached her peak, crying aloud. Strangely, linked with her, he felt a phantom tension and release in his own genitals – one small part of his pleasure. He shared her fulfillment to a soul-shaking depth he had never dreamed possible. She picked up that ecstasy, and it spurred her to another climax. They continued reinforcing each other, swept away in mutual delirium, until he made himself break away.

When he regained the capacity for coherent thought, Roger "heard" Britt's voice in his head: "So we don't have to see through each other's senses all the time. That's a relief; too much of it could make me dizzy."

Mentally groping, Roger realized that the total union had indeed faded, but that he could reawaken it, or fragments of it, at will. "Yes, being close this way doesn't mean we'll never want privacy inside our own skulls."

"Did you know what it would be like?"

"Dear colleague, I had no idea! If I'd known, I'd have done it weeks ago."

After a moment of amorphous content, Britt said aloud, "We can experiment with telepathy later. It's more tiring than I expected."

"True – forming articulate sentences isn't like that spontaneous –" He could find no words for it. The memory alone fired his ardor anew. "I don't believe this. I don't want to behave like a greedy monster, but – "

"You're still thirsty," she said. "Remember, you can't hide a thing from me now." She was almost purring.

"You did say 'all night.' We've barely started." He longed to enjoy her at leisure, with a clear head. Or as clear as it could ever be, with the flavor of her life on his lips.

Britt's fingers fumbled with his shirtsleeves while he eased off her pullover. She paused to unbind her hair, a red-gold cascade that flowed through his caressing hands. Britt tugged at the one sleeve he hadn't removed yet.

He took over the task. "You know, it would be more efficient if we'd each undress ourselves."

"But not nearly as much fun."

A minute later, both naked, they tumbled onto the carpet. Stroking the silky hair on his chest, Britt said, "Your skin feels even cooler than normal."

"Because I'm famished." He hugged her close, delighting in the fit of her firm curves against him. He wished he could enjoy her with every square inch of exposed skin simultaneously. It seemed that her pulse and his, her breathing and his, kept precise rhythm with the throb of her aura. As a doctor he knew that was impossible, since heartbeat was always faster than respiration, but that was how it felt.

She raked her nails down his spine, making his stomach cramp with hunger. Her fingers then crept between their bodies to fondle him intimately. In return, his hand slipped between her thighs. He found her hot and ready. When she reached climax, he licked the smooth arch of her neck in slow, swirling strokes, without piercing the skin.

After she caught her breath, Britt said, "Why didn't you drink? I hope it isn't something ridiculous like penance."

Something like that, perhaps. "I simply wanted to – give, once, without taking."

"Oh, Roger!" She hugged him, her head on his shoulder. "I don't think of it as taking. I can't stand to feel your hunger. Let me give you what you need."

"We don't have to stay on the floor, you know. The bed is freshly made."

Britt scanned his face with feigned concern. "Are you sure you can hold out long enough to get there?"

With a growl he swept her up in his arms and carried her to his room, pausing only to fling back the satin sheets on the king-size bed before laying her down. When he stretched on top of her, and she wrapped her long legs around his, he sensed her trembling on the verge of another orgasm. The nip of his teeth sent her over the edge. The rich elixir in her veins flowed into him, its healing warmth renewing every cell of his body. With their thoughts entwined as tightly as their bodies, he felt her astonishment at how piercingly sweet her blood tasted to him.

At last, satisfied, he stopped lapping at the tiny incision and laid his head on her breast. "Good?" she murmured.

He stirred to kiss a still-erect nipple. "Need you ask? But too fast

– I'm sorry."

Her fingers tightened in his hair. "Will you quit apologizing! You've got hours to do it over until you get it right."

"Mmm," he agreed with a drowsy smile. "Though I'm not sure that's good for you."

"I've had a week away from you to build up my reserves, and I couldn't stand to hold back."

He ached with gratitude for her ardor. How could he ever have risked such a treasure?

Britt's next remark startled him out of a near-doze. "Roger – you love me."

He opened his eyes. "I do? Are you quite certain?"

"Absolutely," she said, laughing softly. "I know love when I feel it."

"Interesting." After pondering her statement for a minute, he said hesitantly, afraid of the answer, yet longing for it, "And do you love me?"

She buried her face in his neck and giggled weakly until she could collect herself to answer. "I've loved you for ages – I think since the first night we went to bed together."

"Then why didn't you say anything?"

"Without being sure of how you felt? Even we liberated women have our pride."

After a moment's contented silence, he said, "Do you want to get married?"

Britt understood at once that he was asking for information, not making a request. "No, we have no reason to. You don't need a live-in cook and housekeeper, and I don't need financial support. We're both used to living on our own, so why fix what isn't broken? And think of the ghastly things marriage would do to our tax bracket!"

"I agree," said Roger, "primarily because if we lived together, my self-control would be strained too severely. With that constant temptation, I couldn't keep away from you."

She nestled against his side, one arm draped over his chest. "Anyway, we're united at a deeper level than any ritual could accomplish, aren't we? In the sense that matters most, we *are* married."

He held her close, utterly fulfilled and secure for the first time in his life. And yet, recalling the anguish that had torn him less than an hour before – "So this is love," he said thoughtfully. "This is what the poets and novelists glorify, what the sappy popular songs go on about?"

"This is it."

His arms tightened around her. "It *hurts.*"

"Welcome to the human race."

"RECENT STUDIES Of The Long-Term Effects Of Antidepressant medication clearly demonstrate..."

Roger frowned at the flashing cursor on the computer screen. For the moment he couldn't recall what those studies were supposed to demonstrate. This article wasn't going well. He hoped to build some coherent conclusions from the various antidepressant trials he had performed on Alice and other patients. Worries over Sandor's recent low profile distracted him, though. Well aware of what lay behind the renegade's compulsion to kill, Roger knew he hadn't simply stopped.

He wished he could believe Sandor had left Maryland. *No, you don't,* he admonished himself. *Not if it means spending the rest of your life wondering where he'll strike next.* It struck him as ominous that the only sign of the murderer since before Thanksgiving had been the dreams Alice Kovak, now Britt's patient, reported to her – nightmares of rending teeth and crimson eyes.

Roger was also distracted by a vague unease, emanating from Britt, that crept through the lower levels of his mind. For the past week or so, something had been troubling her, separate from their concern about Sandor. Though Roger sensed some problem building toward crisis, she hadn't yet confided in him. Doubtless her preoccupation centered on a patient, and confidentiality prevented her from consulting Roger, except in general terms, without permission. And he wouldn't consider violating her mental privacy.

Still, it was almost impossible to work with her unexplained distress nagging at him. He checked his watch. After ten p.m. on a Thursday night – why wasn't she asleep? The barrier of five miles and the Severn River didn't keep him from sensing her anxiety. Verbal telepathic communication over that distance took more effort, but he decided to call anyway. Even if she wouldn't reveal specifics, she might accept his comfort. He figuratively turned up the gain on his mental output.

"Britt, what is the matter with you?" The texture of the thought came out more impatient than he'd intended.

He sensed hesitation before she replied. "Headache, cramps, backache – the usual."

""The usual" makes you tired and cranky, not anxious. You're holding out on me."

"Not by choice. I can't tell you anything at this time."

"At least you admit there's something to tell. That's better."

"Stop talking as if I'm obligated to consult you on every problem that pops up. If I want your help, I know when to ask." The uncharacteristic outburst reminded Roger of her bodily discomfort.

"I didn't mean to imply that, or to harass you. You know your pain affects me. I wish I could help you with the physical part of it."

Her tone lightened. "You can. Come right over."

He steeled himself against her mental seduction. "Not until tomorrow night."

"This 'weekend only' rule is your self-imposed limitation, not a law of nature."

The deeper their intimacy became, the less Britt wanted to hold back. Roger insisted that their mutual attraction made rules, however arbitrary, essential to preserve her health. He knew how wise they were to continue living apart; constant proximity would have made moderation impossible. "I wouldn't enjoy taking you to the ER and trying to explain why you need a transfusion."

"Well, this weekend that hazard won't exist. I'll probably start by tomorrow night."

Roger looked forward to that. He rejoiced that three nights per month he could enjoy Britt in a mode not only harmless but beneficial. Disturbing images flowed into his mind; he attempted to block them.

Feeling his resistance, Britt undermined it by projecting a sensual fantasy of her own. "I hope you're going to be very hungry this time tomorrow."

"Why do you like torturing me?"

"Because you're so easy to get a rise out of that it's irresistible." She added with a feigned sigh, "Oh, all right, I guess I have an obligation to calm you down. Let's see, I can't suggest that you think of blizzards and snowdrifts. You'd probably *like* that. Think about the boardwalk in Ocean City at high noon on the Fourth of July."

"That's enough to kill anyone's appetite."

"As far as I've seen, *nothing* kills your appetite." The flirtatious overtones disappeared from her mental "voice." "Oops, my phone's ringing. Later, colleague."

Roger turned back to the computer. Unable to concentrate on the interrupted article, he picked up renewed anxiety and agitation from Britt. A tentative overture brought a rebuff; she didn't want to be distracted. Giving up on work for the night, Roger saved his file and tried to settle in the living room with a horror novel (outlandish enough to provide comic relief from his own peculiar adjustment problems), a Bach fugue, and a glass of milk. Stephen King's latest banquet of gore, however, couldn't compete with the subliminal echoes of Britt's unhappiness. Roger actually relaxed when the telephone rang twenty minutes later.

"Yes, colleague? Why are you calling this way?"

"I'm phoning from a police van," Britt said. "It would look kind of strange if you showed up without anybody seeing me call you."

"Police? Where? What's going on?"

"Don't panic yet," she said. "You may need the panic button later. I'm at a patient's home. She's locked herself in with a Luger, threatening to shoot herself or anybody who breaks in."

The news didn't slow Roger's pulse. "She?"

"Alice Kovak."

"Good God, my sins have come back to haunt me."

"Afraid so," Britt said. "She won't talk to me; she wants you. Look, I'll tell you the details when you get here. You know where the house is?"

"I could hardly forget, unfortunately. On my way."

Outside, a weepy drizzle misted the cool night air. In the car he seethed over the prospect of talking Alice out of selfdestruction yet again. *So she's still obsessed with me. How long will I have to keep paying for that?*

After crossing the Severn and South Rivers, then driving through Edgewater to the Kovaks' semi-rural neighborhood, Roger caught sight of revolving red and blue lights as soon as he turned onto their road. The police had done a good job of discouraging curiosity seekers. Aside from family, the only civilians present were a local TV news team. Roger gritted his teeth in exasperation at the sight of the reporters.

He pulled up behind Britt's new car, a forest-green Porsche adorned (or disfigured, in his opinion) by a Red Cross bumper sticker proclaiming, "Blood donors make better lovers." She broke away from the huddle of police officers in the front yard and ran to him, her thoughts welcoming him with the embrace they couldn't physically share in public. "Come on, we'll talk in my car." In the front seat of the Porsche, she said, "Alice resented your turning her case over to me, but I thought she'd worked through that. Obviously I was wrong."

He strove to keep from responding to her distress and thereby augmenting it. "Specifics?"

"She's still infatuated with you," said Britt. "In the past couple of weeks you've been the main topic of every session with her."

"Somehow I'm not flattered."

"Nor should you be." Britt's tone held no shadow of condemnation; she'd forgiven Roger and was concerned only with the patient. "You told me yourself that the attraction isn't personal. But do the aftereffects of a vampire attack usually last this long?"

"Not in a balanced personality. Not without encouragement. But Alice, on top of everything else, nearly got killed by Sandor. No wonder she became obsessed with the only vampire in reach. I'd hoped transferring her to you would cure that."

"Well, it didn't work."

"If I needed any further reason to avoid preying on patients –" He sighed heavily. He'd remained faithful to Britt except for that one lapse, but it only took one. "Colleague, why didn't you tell me this sooner?"

"Aside from the confidentiality factor, I didn't want to worry you."

"Didn't want to worry –!"

"There's worse," Britt said. "She's conceived the notion that you're a vampire."

Roger stared at her, beyond surprise. "I trust you've tried to convince her otherwise."

"Sure. In a non-directive way, naturally."

"Naturally. The hypnosis I used should have blotted out Alice's memory of our encounters, but the unconscious works in mysterious ways." He took a deep breath and opened the car door. "I may as well go talk to her."

Alice's family hovered beside the front walk, as near the house as the police would allow. Roger sensed the layman's awe of a physician emanating from Mrs. Kovak. "I don't know what's gotten into her, Doctor. Last night she got out of bed and disappeared for hours. And now this!" Her wide eyes beseeched Roger for an instant solution.

Resentment from Mr. Kovak and Peter, especially the younger man, scalded Roger. "Can't figure out why she's so set on talking to you," Mr. Kovak muttered. Peter simply scowled.

Roger turned on the father. "You knew your daughter had suicidal tendencies. Where did she get the gun?"

Taken aback, Mr. Kovak retreated a step and said less

belligerently, "My Luger – it was in the top of the closet. Look, I didn't think Alice even knew I had it."

"Haven't you learned she is not a fool? Her introverted personality doesn't mean that she doesn't observe things."

Britt silently interrupted, "This isn't the time, Roger. Ripping into them now is pretty callous."

"You may be right. But I don't have much patience with human stupidity."

"No worse than some examples of vampire stupidity I could mention."

The tart flavor of Britt's rebuke silenced Roger. Unable to bring himself to apologize to Mr. Kovak, he introduced himself to the police officer who seemed to be in charge, a tall, middle-aged black with a Marine-style haircut. The officer gave him a preoccupied handshake and said, "Just a second while I let the girl know you've arrived."

Taking a battery-operated megaphone from a subordinate, he blared, "Miss Kovak, Dr. Darvell is here. If you'll open the door for him, I give you my word nobody else will try to get in."

Silence. After a few seconds, Roger heard the click of the front door lock. He walked onto the porch and took a moment to focus his attention, so that the tumultuous emotions of the spectators faded into background noise. From inside, he felt the girl's anger and fear like a hovering cloud of smoke.

Slowly turning the knob, he inched the door open. "Dr. Darvell?" said Alice's voice, shrill with tension. "Come in."

## Chapter 19

HE STEPPED INSIDE, pulling the door shut behind him and locking it. The room was unlit. Good – Roger's night vision gave him an advantage. Alice could see him by the glow from the street lamp just outside the picture window, but she probably couldn't distinguish details. She sat in an armchair across the room near the television, cradling the Luger. She raised the muzzle as Roger took a step closer.

"Stay back, Doctor. You can sit on the couch."

Moving with exaggerated slowness, he did so. Her appearance as well as her voice showed how distraught she was. Her long, blonde hair was tangled, and her eyes continually darted from Roger to the window and back. Her thin legs, clad in cut-off jeans, were tucked under her, prepared to leap.

He suppressed a surge of annoyance at the sight of her. Her fixation on him wasn't her fault, after all. He had brought it on by his own reckless self-indulgence.

Uncomfortable memories of the second encounter, the one that had nearly killed her, flashed through his mind as Alice held the gun on him. *More dangerous than a bottle of tranquilizers.* He assumed a relaxed pose, arms along the back of the couch, both hands in sight. The air of nonchalance, he hoped, masked his inward stance of taut alertness. "Why did you want to speak to me, Alice?"

"I remember what you did to me," she whispered.

"Oh? What do you remember?" He kept his voice even.

"You sucked my blood."

"Why would I do such an extraordinary thing?" he said in a slightly bantering tone.

"Because you're a vampire – why else?"

"Nobody believes in vampires, Alice. And if they did exist, I couldn't be one. Vampires are destroyed by sunlight, aren't they? You've seen me during the day many times."

She looked unsure for only a few seconds. "Then I guess the sun doesn't kill them. Because I know what you are."

How could one argue with that kind of logic? Nevertheless, he tried again. His main goal was not to change her mind, but to get her off guard so that he could use his inhuman strength and speed to disarm her without injury to either of them. "Come, now, Alice, I don't even have fangs."

"Your eyes glow in the dark," she said.

So they did, a factor he'd momentarily forgotten. "A trick of the light, surely."

"Stop trying to lie," she said, her breath coming fast and shallow as she tried not to sob aloud. "I *remember* your teeth in my neck."

Her words evoked an all too vivid image. Despite his mental revulsion, Roger's body responded. He felt disgusted with himself for salivating like a starving wolf over a creature who could offer him nothing more than he could get from any healthy mammal. How could he have succumbed to this neurotic child after experiencing Britt's mature passion? After a moment's struggle for control, he said in his blandest professional tone, "How do you feel about that?"

"It makes me sick!" she cried. "But then – then I liked it. I wanted you to do it again. Oh, God, I *begged* for it!" She broke down. Yet even with tears streaming down her cheeks, she managed to keep the gun steady and her eyes on the target.

"Have you talked to Dr. Loren about that?"

"She doesn't believe me," Alice gulped. "Nobody does. Except maybe Peter, a little bit. Our grandparents on both sides came over from the old country. They used to tell us stories –" She glared at Roger. "I don't like Dr. Loren. Why'd you make me switch to her?"

"Precisely because of those delusions about me. Surely you can see I could do no good as your therapist in that situation?"

"Why did you leave me to *him?* If I have to belong to somebody, I'd rather it be you."

Roger's stomach cramped at the blend of lust and terror she projected. "Can you tell me whom you're talking about?"

"Him – the man who –" She had to swallow a lump of fear before she could force out a complete sentence. "He called me last night, and I sneaked out of the house to meet him. He drank – the way you did – and then he gave me a message for you."

The hair prickled at the nape of Roger's neck. "For me?"

"He said –" Alice's voice shifted to a croaking whisper – "`Darvell, this girl belongs to me now. If I want it, everything you own can belong to me. Including that lady doctor of yours. So you better reconsider joining my side. Just you and me against the rest of the pack. After I've taken everything I want from you, I'll make the offer again.

Enjoy the wait, Doctor.'" Alice's breathing was jagged.

Trying to capture her eyes, Roger pitched his voice to a hypnotic murmur. "Calm yourself, Alice, you're hyperventilating."

"What do you care? You just want to get rid of me!" She wiped her face with the back of her left hand. Her right, holding the Luger, trembled.

If she was wavering, this might be the moment to act. He could cross the room in a lunge so swift it would be only a blur in her sight. "If you truly believe I've mistreated you, we could discuss it at greater length. Tomorrow at my office would be far more appropriate."

He started to rise, holding out a hand toward her. "You really don't want to upset your family this way, do you?" When she made no immediate threatening gesture, he stared into her eyes, willing her submission to his mesmeric power. For a moment she was caught, melting beneath the force of his gaze. He tensed to spring.

He had overestimated her vulnerability. "No – I won't let you do that again!" Her finger curled around the trigger.

Absorbed in the attempted hypnosis, he couldn't dodge in time. The bullet seared through his right forearm.

Momentarily stunned by the pain and the deafening crack of the shot, he moved at no more than human speed. A sob tore from her throat. "Don't touch me!" She turned the muzzle toward herself and fired again.

As he sprang toward her, an instant too late, he automatically clamped down his mental barrier. Thus he escaped the direct experience of her agony. He reached her at the instant she squeezed the trigger. He clamped onto her wrist just quickly enough to deflect the barrel from her forehead. Instead the bullet drilled into her skull at an angle. Her blood splattered him. He recoiled, choking down nausea. Somehow he remembered to keep his thoughts blocked so that Britt wouldn't pick up his sensations.

Opening a minute crack in his shield, he sensed a blank where Alice's consciousness had been. Probing the body slumped in the chair, one side of her head streaming blood, he heard the thready sound of her pulse. She wasn't dead yet. Breathing shallowly to minimize the effect of the blood smell, he automatically folded his handkerchief and pressed it to the bullet wound.

Battling dizziness, he rushed to the door, opened it, and shouted, "Paramedic, stat!" He dodged out of the path of two emergency techs who sprinted from the waiting ambulance to the house.

To the police officer in charge, he said, "She shot me, then herself. She may live – too soon to tell." He turned to the Kovaks. "I'm deeply sorry." The words carried little conviction, even to himself. Mrs. Kovak collapsed into the arms of her husband, who glowered at Roger over her head.

Roger continued down the sidewalk, shrugging off attempts to support him. Ignoring the clicks and flashes from news cameras, he leaned against the hood of his car. Britt shoved her way through the cluster of uniforms with her medical bag. "You're wounded. How bad – ?"

"Most of the blood is hers. I just got hit in the arm."

"Roll up your sleeve."

As he peeled off his jacket and fumbled with his longsleeved shirt, Peter Kovak stormed up to them. "I'm holding you responsible for this. Both of you." He flicked a glance at Britt, then returned his cold stare to Roger. "Especially you, Darvell. You'll hear from me." With the four splayed fingers of his right hand, he smeared the congealing blood on Roger's shirt – Alice's blood – into an elongated brand. He then marched up to the house, where a uniformed officer blocked the door.

"What do you suppose he has in mind?" Roger said wearily as Britt bandaged his arm. Though she didn't let it show, he sensed her distress at the sight of the entry and exit wounds. Luckily the bullet hadn't lodged in the flesh. A mental nudge from her reminded him to focus on the injury long enough to damp down the pain and start the healing process.

"Probably going to sue us," said Britt with false lightness. "About time we got something for those outrageous malpractice premiums." She snapped her bag shut and said in a lower tone, "Want to come home with me? First I'll have to talk to the Kovaks – you can go ahead and wait for me."

"Thank you, yes," he said, grateful for her offering without waiting for him to ask. He was touched by her consideration for his pride, little though he had left where she was concerned.

He watched Alice being carried to the ambulance, whose red light threw a lurid glow over the scene. Roger recalled a poem he'd once read, which compared that pulsing glow to the spurting of a severed artery.

One of the paramedics intercepted him as he was about to get into his car. "Doctor, you should have that bullet wound checked at the emergency room. I saw what it looked like when you took off your jacket."

"That's totally unnecessary," Roger snapped. His control of his overwrought emotions was rapidly slipping; he had to get out of public view as soon as possible.

"A nine-millimeter bullet drilling through muscle tissue is no joke."

"It isn't as bad as it looks." He tried to summon enough power to make a trained professional believe the lie.

"But you may need additional treatment –"

"Look here, young man, my associate and I are both M.D.'s, and we've already determined that I don't require hospitalization. What I need is to be left alone so I can go home and get some rest." To the policeman who'd just come up behind the paramedic, he added, "I trust you can take my statement tomorrow?"

Given a hard psychic shove, both of them backed off. After setting a time to report to the police station the next day, Roger headed for Britt's apartment.

He waited in the car, head down on the steering wheel, until she arrived to unlock the apartment door. Once inside her living room, she started to embrace him, but he held her off. "You don't want to touch me now." He glanced down at his bloodstained trousers. "These clothes are a total loss. And I need a shower." Though he ached to crush her in his arms, he felt too much self-loathing to inflict himself on her.

"Be my guest," she said, reluctantly moving away from him. "What can I get for you?"

"Something highly alcoholic," he said over his shoulder on the way to the bath attached to her bedroom, already stripping off his torn, blood-soaked shirt.

He stood under a scalding hot shower for five minutes, then ran it on full cold for an equal time. Emerging, he found that Britt had removed his clothes and laid out the blue lounging robe she kept for him. Tonight he was doubly glad of the convenience of storing a few clothes at her apartment; he wouldn't have to wear that outfit again.

Only while toweling dry did he recall that he shouldn't have got the bandage wet. He peeled it off, unsurprised to see that it was no longer needed. The pair of punctures looked half healed, though a muscle-deep soreness lingered. In the next few days, of course, he would have to wear a dressing in public to hide the inhumanly fast recovery.

He found Britt, draped in an emerald and gold caftan, waiting in the bedroom with a triple martini. Good choice – neutrally flavored and high proof. He drank it straight down. "May I have another? This is one time when I wish I could get drunk." He switched off the bedside lamp, leaving the room illuminated only by a pair of tapers she had lit on the dresser. Pacing to the window, he stared down at the dark, empty street.

"You can if you work at it," said Britt, standing close without touching him. "But that's not what I'd prescribe. You need something more substantial. No matter how it looks on the outside –" she touched the wound – "I know you can't finish repairing this without blood."

"I'm not hungry."

"Erase and correct, colleague. You are always hungry; that's axiomatic. What you mean is, you're determined to punish yourself for what Alice did. And I'll bet at least half your guilt comes from your own imperfection instead of concern for her – which makes you feel even more guilty."

"Granted." He slammed his clenched fist down on the dresser. "Damn! I *hate* to fail!"

Britt patted his hand. "Easy, there – if you feel the urge to wreck furniture, do it at your house. In your boundless egoism, have you forgotten that Alice is officially my patient now? I own a hefty chunk of the guilt. Want to fight me for it?"

He was too sunk in misery to respond to her bracing tone. "If I'd stayed more alert or moved faster – For that matter, if I hadn't been so bloody arrogant, relying on my 'supernatural' powers, I might have exercised a modicum of ordinary judgment." He closed the curtains, walked over to the bed, and sat down.

Britt sat beside him, one hand resting lightly on his shoulder. "Delusions of omnipotence. We aren't responsible for anyone else's choice. She had free will."

He gave her a bleak stare. "Oh, really?" He bowed his head on his clasped hands. "She shot herself," he said, "to keep me from touching her."

"Oh, Roger!" He heard tears in Britt's voice and struggled not to break down himself. "You shut me out. You didn't let me share it."

"Believe me, you don't want that memory." He felt chilled, though to him the midDecember temperature outside was merely bracing. "Why am I fighting the truth? I'm a monster. The human genes from my father don't change that."

"Quit being melodramatic! This is just another form of self-indulgence." For once her brisk tone didn't shake him out of his depression. He heard her opening a nightstand drawer and looked up, unwillingly curious. She leafed through a Bible and thrust it into his hands. "There. Read." Her forefinger jabbed the page.

"Psalm 104?" He wondered what she was getting at.

"Verses 20 through 22."

He read, "Thou makest darkness, and it is night, when all the beasts of the forest creep forth. The young lions roar for their prey, seeking their food from God. When the sun rises, they get them away and lie down in their dens." He shut the book and returned it to her. "So?"

"See, God loves nocturnal predators, too."

He smiled faintly at her effort, though it didn't have much effect on his mood. "How does He feel about predators who can't control their bloody damn appetites?"

She replaced the Bible in the drawer and put both hands on his shoulders. "Lie down and let me help you relax." He stretched on his back. Her hands stole inside the robe, massaging his chest, shoulders, and neck. Almost against his will he felt the clots of tension begin to dissolve. "You've had a shock, you've lost blood, and you're in pain," she said. "You need to drink from me."

"Later, perhaps." He still felt no physical hunger, only a fathomless yearning for her warmth.

"I didn't think you came here just to swill martinis and stare at the ceiling."

He reached up to put one arm around her. "I came to exploit and take advantage of you."

"Well, that's what I'm here for." She countered his harsh tone with such aplomb that he almost smiled.

"I don't want to be alone tonight. I want – need – to be held. But I won't be much good to you."

"Let me worry about that."

"The truth is, I feel I shouldn't even be touching you, after what just happened. I don't want to – taint you."

"For Heaven's sake, cut out that tripe." Her fingertips stroked along his jawline, soothing rather than exciting. "If you don't want my blood, let me take from you. At least it will distract you from all this self-pity."

"Yes, of course." That intimacy would make no difference to his physical condition, since the amount she could draw was negligible. Although he could revive the sense of total oneness anytime at will, it remained most vivid when the two of them were actually joined in blood-sharing. The communion refreshed him even when he gave rather than taking.

Britt folded back the robe to bare his chest. With one of her long, sharply tapered fingernails she inflicted a diagonal scratch just below the clavicle. It had taken her a while to learn how to cut deeply enough to draw blood, because she'd feared hurting him. He had eventually convinced her that he found a brief, minor pain like that stimulating rather than discouraging. In this case the frisson along the nerves provided a welcome diversion from the dull throb of the bullet wound.

Blood welled from the incision. She kissed him on the lips, then nibbled slowly down over his neck and chest until she was licking the droplets with mothlike flickers of her tongue. Roger knew most of her pleasure in this act came from sharing his passion. What tasted to him like a full-bodied vintage wine was, to her, just a somewhat salty fluid.

Gradually, as he relaxed and opened up to her growing excitement, the heat of her lips on his skin took its usual effect. At the same time, her hands roamed over his body, stroking his chest in expanding spirals, running her nails up and down the insides of his thighs, playing with his testicles and teasing his penis until it stood at attention.

He returned her caresses, skimming his open palms over her breasts, then massaging her back as she pressed the full length of her body against his. Her warm weight upon him stirred him almost as much as the avidity of her kiss. She sank her teeth into his flesh as she reached fulfillment.

"Better now?" she whispered, still breathless, laying her head on his shoulder.

"Beloved," he murmured into the fragrant cascade of her hair. He preferred not to meet her eyes when using such language, for it still came awkwardly to him. His arms tightened convulsively around her. A moment later he said more calmly. "Yes and no. You've succeeded in distracting me. But now you have to face the consequences."

"I told you that's what you needed," she purred. "Are you sure you're ready?"

"Well – the hairs in my palms are vibrating, my throat's burning, every centimeter of erectile tissue on my body is rockhard, and my damn teeth are tingling so badly I think I'll explode if I can't taste you right *now*."

"Okay, you're ready."

"Don't act so smug about it." He rolled her over on her back and reclined across her. His lips and hands ranged over her body, first through the silky fabric of the caftan, then with no barrier at all. He traced the pathways of her tightly coiled nerves, melting the knots of soreness in her abdomen and thighs. He luxuriated in the double-exposure delight of feeling her sensations and emotions simultaneously with his own – the smooth curve of her breast beneath his hand, the touch of his hand on her skin, the contrast between his coolness and her heat, the delicious tightening in her loins when he kissed her.

About to pierce her throat, he drew back, shaken by the intensity of his thirst. She arched her neck with a frustrated moan. "Dear colleague," he said unsteadily, "how long has it been?"

She gathered her wits to produce a coherent answer. "An eternity. All of four days."

"My God, it seems like years. I'm starving for you."

"That's what I expected," she gasped. "Shock. Trauma. *What are you waiting for?*"

He kissed her throat, thrilling to the leap of the pulse under his lips. "I'm afraid of being – ungentle."

Her nails dug into his back. "Can't you understand that I don't care? Drain me, if that's what you need."

The words stabbed him with the sharpness of a tangible wound. "Don't say that – it terrifies me." His mouth captured hers, then moved down to her neck again. The radiance of her life flowed into him. He bathed in it, oblivious to everything but the blood thrumming in her veins and her passion answering his.

For the rest of the night he didn't allow her out of bed for more than three minutes at a time. He ravished her over and over, urging her to one orgasm after another, driving both of them to exhaustion and beyond. Whenever he relaxed, Alice's image and her parroted message invaded his mind, and he turned to Britt to banish the memory. Far from complaining, she encouraged his frenetic appetite. Clearly she considered this mindless abandon the therapy he needed.

Around three a.m. she fell into a wrung-out, sated sleep, nestled in the curve of his arm. Lulled by the rhythm of her heartbeat and respiration, he drifted in and out of a semi-conscious doze. The candles on the dresser burned down to pools of wax and went out. Just before dawn he coaxed her awake for a final, gentler interlude. When she got up afterward, he was dismayed by her enervated appearance. Nevertheless he pretended to ignore the faintness she tried to conceal.

By now he knew better than to offend her with apologies.

BETWEEN DAINTY nibbles from a granola bar, Britt said, "Bet you didn't see this morning's *Washington Post,* did you?" She unfolded the paper on Roger's desk. They were sharing a private lunch break at the office the day after the shooting. "Looks like our quarry finally got careless again." She pointed at a short article on one of the inside pages.

"Halloween Coming Late?" the headline quipped. The reporter gave a tongue-in-cheek account of a "giant bat" sighted over Rock Creek Park the previous night. As highly colored as the two separate informants' stories were, Roger didn't doubt Britt's conclusion.

"So we know he hasn't left the area," said Roger.

"If we didn't know already, from what Alice told you last night." Weariness from more than lack of sleep shadowed Britt's eyes. Roger wished he had risked her ire and insisted she take the day off.

"There was always the chance he'd given her that message weeks ago," Roger said. "The `bat' seems to settle that point." He frowned at the wrapper Britt was crumpling. "Is that your entire lunch?"

"I had a cup of yogurt and a can of V-8," she said. "Look who's talking. You haven't eaten all day."

"You know I don't need anything. Not after last night." In spite of the worry that preyed on him, an echo of the pleasure they'd shared rippled through him.

"That's a lot of Taurus," said Britt. "If it were true, I'd be too weak to stand up. You do need additional nourishment. If I pour you a glass of milk, will you drink it?"

Roger spread his hands in a gesture of acceptance. As Britt got up to fetch the milk, the telephone rang.

"Lieutenant Hayes calling," said Marcia. "I know you don't like to be disturbed at lunch, but –"

"Put him on," Roger said.

"Doctor, I have bad news," said Hayes with his characteristic nervous cough. "I'm calling from the hospital downtown. Your patient who shot herself died last night. This morning, actually, just before dawn."

Roger leaned back in his chair, willing his heartbeat to slow down. Considering the severity of Alice's wound, he shouldn't be surprised. "I'm sorry to hear that. But where do you come in?"

"She didn't die naturally. I mean, not from the gunshot wound itself." Britt, overhearing, set down the styrofoam cup of milk and stared quizzically at Roger. After a pause, Hayes went on, "Somebody got into the intensive care ward and pulled the plug – unhooked her from the monitors, IV, and so on. Then he – well, this is one of the crazy parts. He cut her throat, severed the left jugular and carotid, with some jagged object, and the M.E. can't figure out what."

*Claws. He tore her neck open with his fingernails – something no human assailant could manage.* Nausea welled up in Roger's throat. When he had it under control, he said, "Why in the name of all that's holy are you just getting around to notifying me?"

"Give me a break, Doctor! I've been here since six thirty, interviewing staff, trying to figure how the perp got in without anybody catching him."

"I apologize," Roger said. "Lieutenant, how *did* he accomplish that?"

"You tell me!"

Roger stood up. "I'll be right over." After Hayes hung up, he switched to Marcia and ordered her to cancel his one o'clock patient.

"Mine, too," said Britt.

"Certainly not," Roger said. "There's no reason for both of us to go."

She scowled at him in frustration. "I don't know if I should let you out of my sight."

"You know how you felt when I treated you that way," he said. When Britt conceded the point with a reluctant smile, he gave her a quick kiss on the cheek. "You'll get every detail, don't worry."

As he was about to leave, Britt said, "Your milk."

Rather than argue with her, he drank it down without pausing for breath.

A few minutes later he rode the elevator up to the ICU at the community hospital. The disinfectant fumes made him wish he had skipped the milk. In the lounge Hayes and Rizzo, the medical examiner he'd met at the stadium, waited for him.

"If this doesn't take the prize!" said Hayes after a perfunctory greeting. "Nobody remembers any suspicious person wandering the halls last night, coming or going. The nurses on duty in intensive care didn't see anyone. In fact, they don't remember a thing from about five a.m. until their relief arrived at six!"

"Don't remember?" Roger echoed. He was beginning to guess how the murder had been accomplished.

"Total blank." The detective shook his head. "I take back every sane thing I ever told you about this case. I think the guy really is a phantom."

"Unless he disguised himself as an orderly or a maintenance worker," said Roger. *More likely he used that psychic veil illusion.* But he couldn't suggest that to Hayes.

"That could explain how he got to the ward without being noticed. Not how come the nurses don't remember what happened."

"Are they still here?" said Roger. "Could I talk to them?"

"The senior nurse on duty is. I let the other one go home. All the patients were transferred to other rooms for the day, and anyhow none of them saw a thing." Hayes smoothed his moustache. "Say, you think he could've somehow drugged the nurses?"

"I didn't notice any signs of that," Rizzo put in, "but I wouldn't rule it out."

Roger asked the medical examiner about Alice's death. The reply added nothing substantial to what Hayes had said. "She seems to have been dead between thirty and forty-five minutes when the morning shift came in and found the duty nurses sitting at their station in a daze. With the carotid artery severed, your patient died instantly without regaining consciousness."

Since Rizzo seemed to expect it, Roger muttered an expression of relief that Alice hadn't suffered. Meanwhile, Hayes had left the lounge and was just returning with a middle-aged nurse in tow, her short-cropped auburn hair fading to gray, her eyes bloodshot behind square, gold-rimmed glasses. The detective introduced her as Mrs. Gifford.

"I'd like to talk with her alone, if I may," said Roger. When the two men had left the lounge, Roger invited Mrs. Gifford to relax on the divan and immediately lulled her into a trance. He viewed her instant submission as ominous in itself.

"Now tell me, calmly, knowing you are completely safe, who came into your ward this morning at five."

Her expressionless voice answered, "A tall man – big man – with deep red hair and a beard. He just – popped out of thin air. For some reason I'd been dozing off. Next thing I knew, I looked around at Kathy, and she was asleep with her head on the desk." A small frown creased the woman's brow.

Roger traced circles on her temples until she sank into tranquility again. "It's all right now. Nothing will disturb you. Tell me what you did then."

Her hands resting limp on her knees, Mrs. Gifford said, "I got up to walk over to Kathy, at the console, and wake her. Then this man – appeared – beside her chair. Something went wrong with my vision. The lights seemed to go dim all of a sudden. And I thought the man's eyes burned, like red-hot coals. He told me to sit down and relax. I felt warm and sort of – liquid – all over. Something told me he shouldn't be there, but I couldn't get excited about that. He told me not to worry, to go to sleep and forget about him." She heaved a long sigh. "I guess I did fall asleep, because the next thing I remember, the day shift nurse was shaking me." Her breathing quickened. "That man – he got to one of the patients –"

Smoothing the tension from her neck and shoulders, Roger said, "You must not worry about that. You aren't to blame. Forget what you saw, and be at peace. I will now count to ten, and you will awaken refreshed. One, two. . . ."

A few minutes later, he lied to Rizzo and Hayes with all the persuasion at his command. "I can't get her to remember anything. I suspect a quick-acting drug, rapidly eliminated from her system. Unless, of course, your suspect hypnotized both of them."

Rizzo greeted that suggestion, as Roger expected, with a nervous laugh. No one could hypnotize two people at the same time that thoroughly, not when the victims were alert and on guard.

*No one human, that is,* thought Roger. Until this incident, he hadn't acknowledged what a deadly adversary even a "young" vampire could be.

Chapter 20

*HE'S PLAYING with us,* Roger told himself for the dozenth time since the disaster at the hospital. The "giant bat" sighting demonstrated that Sandor had lost none of his brashness, and the murder of Alice showed that the renegade hadn't restrained himself out of caution. He could strike at Roger and Britt whenever and however he chose. Roger wondered whether Britt had remained safe because of the cross she wore constantly, or whether Sandor simply wasn't ready to claim her yet.

Furthermore, over the past few days since Alice's death, they'd heard nothing of the Kovak family except through official police contacts. If Mr. Kovak or his son planned to sue Doctors Darvell and Loren for malpractice, they were in no hurry to initiate the process.

Shortly after nine o'clock Wednesday evening, Roger's reading of the *Boston Globe* was interrupted by a twinge of apprehension from Britt. He extended an inquiring telepathic tendril.

"Nothing" she replied. "The phone startled me."

Since she didn't insist that he break contact, Roger listened in on the conversation. To his dismay, the caller turned out to be Peter Kovak. "Dr. Loren, we got a little emergency here."

"Yes, what is it?" No sign of Britt's anxiety crept into her voice.

"It's my mother. She's in real bad shape, hysterical. Dad and I can't calm her down."

"I understood she had been prescribed tranquilizers?"

"Yeah, but she threw them away after – you know." The young man's voice quavered with emotion; Roger wished he could read its nature through this indirect link. "She never got around to refilling it. Look, Dr. Loren, seems to me you owe us. Can you come check on her?"

Of course Britt felt she "owed" Alice's family; Roger knew trying to convince her otherwise would be futile. "Yes, I'll be there as soon as possible."

After she'd hung up, Roger spoke to her: "Colleague, I'm not sure you should make that visit alone at night. And since when do you make house calls, except in a graver "emergency" than this?"

"Come off it, Roger. If you had received that call, you'd be out the door already. You feel more responsible for their troubles than I do."

"Because I *am* more responsible. Besides, I'm better able to protect myself."

Anger flared in Britt's telepathic voice. "I functioned perfectly well for thirty-five years before I met you."

"Granted, better than I did before meeting you." But the prickle of uneasiness along Roger's spine wouldn't go away. "At least let me come with you, for my own peace of mind."

"Are you kidding? The way two out of three of them feel about you?"

While Roger couldn't deny the soundness of Britt's argument, his internal alarms screamed at the thought of her visiting the Kovaks alone. Rationally considered, though, what harm could come to her? Mr. Kovak wouldn't have consented to Peter's calling Britt if they harbored resentment against her. Roger gave up his objections, contenting himself with observing Britt through their mental link.

WHEN BRITT'S car pulled up in front of the Kovaks' house, she saw nothing to justify Roger's qualms. The house stood quiet, with several lights shining in addition to the bare bulb on the porch. Britt walked up and rang the bell on the side occupied by the elder Kovaks.

Peter opened the door and stepped onto the porch. He wore a floppy gray sweatshirt that hung well below the waistband of his commercially faded jeans. "Glad you could make it, Doc." He cast a nervous glance over his shoulder at the dark, wooded back yard.

Listening, her hands stuffed in the pockets of her hooded windbreaker to tame their illogical tremor (blast Roger!), Britt heard no footsteps in the back rooms, no crying. She sensed Roger's inner alarm jangling again. She pushed it to the back of her mind. He had to learn she could take care of herself, and damned if she'd let his overprotectiveness cloud her judgment.

Lightly grasping Britt's elbow, Peter guided her inside and locked and bolted the door with his free hand, then steered her toward the hall. "Thanks for coming. Mom's in their bedroom."

Britt's psychic antennae, fine-tuned by contact with Roger, vibrated at that remark. "Roger, something feels wrong. I think he's lying."

Linked with Roger, she felt his fingers flex as if the young man's neck were within their reach. "Then get away from him – now!"

Before Britt could jerk out of Peter's grip, he pulled a revolver from under his sweatshirt. "Sorry about that, Doc," he grinned. "I made a little mistake. Mom's in Florida. They're visiting her folks – therapy, like – and they won't be back until Sunday. *He* helped me talk them into taking a little vacation."

For an instant Britt's vision dimmed with the shock. *I should have listened to my worrywart colleague.* "He? Who?" No answer. Recovering, she said coolly, "What are you trying to accomplish, Peter?"

"Get moving." He prodded her down the hall to the master bedroom. "I told you I blamed you and the other shrink for what Alice did. It's time to pay up."

When Britt stepped into the bedroom, she noted that it had been stripped down. The sheets had been removed from the double bed, the dressers cleared of all portable objects. A couple of dresser drawers had been taken out altogether. "Give me your purse," the young man ordered.

For a few seconds Britt considered flinging it in his face as a bid for escape. She sensed Roger's relief when she discarded that idea and simply handed over the heavy bag. "This wild escapade won't do you any good. Dr. Darvell knows where I am."

"Great, that'll save me the trouble of contacting him. I want him here." Peter backed out and closed the door, locking it with the click of a deadbolt.

Britt stepped over and gave the knob a ritual tug. "Do they always live this way, or was it arranged just for me?"

"I suspect the deadbolt is new. He seems to have gone to elaborate lengths to get the room prepared" Roger answered.

"Right. There won't be much point in searching the drawers and closets for a weapon. He'd have cleared out anything useful." She could always attack Peter with a coat hanger, of course, if she were fool enough to try such a ploy against a loaded gun. She glanced at the barred window. "And what a lucky break for him that the security grills were already in place."

She plopped down on the bed, surrendering to the shakiness she'd suppressed in the attacker's presence. "I guess there's no use telling you to stay away." Buried under that facade of detached intellect, he hid an alter ego who'd be right at home in the annals of the Round Table. Danger to women seemed to have that effect on men of his generation.

Roger had already collected his car keys – not bothering with a jacket, since the temperature, in the fifties, would feel pleasantly cool to him – and started out the door. "Don't be silly," he told her.

"But, colleague, it's you he wants. I'm just the bait." She walked a bit unsteadily to the attached bathroom to splash cool water on her face. The medicine cabinet stood empty, its mirror door removed, and the toothbrush rack held a plastic glass. "Thorough, wasn't he?" Britt observed.

She fought to keep her head clear of the scarlet fog that threatened to engulf Roger. "If you think I'd consider leaving you to face that maniac alone – well, you insult me." To Britt's relief, he suppressed his anger, its pressure gradually receding.

"If you must come after me, at least take precautions," she urged. Should Roger and Britt not appear at the office in the morning, Marcia would call them at home. He ought to leave word for her.

Thinking over the suggestion, Roger agreed. He erased the message on his answering machine and recorded a new one: "Marcia, if you are hearing this, Dr. Loren and I are being held by Peter Kovak at his home. If we don't contact you by noon, notify the police." By that time police intervention could hardly make matters worse.

Britt followed his reasoning but doubted its validity. "Must you have her wait until noon?"

"I won't risk the law intervening too quickly and endangering you. Confound it, this is a hostage situation!"

"I noticed." She reined her own fear, striving for a detached stance that wouldn't feed Roger's panic.

She felt him chafing at the downtown congestion around Market Circle. After passing through Eastport and reaching Forest Drive, he made better time. As he turned up Route Two toward the South River bridge, Britt addressed him again.

"You're actually coming here alone?"

"You couldn't expect me to bring reinforcements in these circumstances. Aside from the risk to you, how could I possibly explain this situation to the police?"

At that moment the scratch of a key at the door deflected her attention. Peter's head poked in, along with the muzzle of the gun. "Comfortable, Doc? I hope your partner gets here soon so I don't have to call him. Waiting could make me nervous, you know." He waggled the revolver. "You'll never guess what my sister told me about him. Unless maybe she told you the same thing. She said Darvell was a vampire. Can you believe that?"

Groping with her embryonic ESP, Britt couldn't tell, through the murk of his grief and hate, how seriously he meant the derisive comment. "No, I can't, and I don't believe you could, either."

"Yeah? Well, I'm about to find out. *He* told me how to check on it. Maybe your friend's a nut case who thinks he's a vampire. Or maybe he's something worse. Whatever, he's gonna pay."

Alarmed, she passed on the information to Roger. "Peter's serious about punishing you for Alice's death. He more than half believes her vampire stories, and he plans to test the theory on you. Colleague, I don't want you to end up with a stake through the heart."

"I'll try to avoid that."

WHEN ROGER turned onto the winding, sparsely developed road, he went cold with the fresh realization of how isolated the duplex was. Too far from the neighboring houses to be visible, it was also sheltered by the woods that surrounded it on three sides, with the riverbank beyond. He drove further on, parked just around the curve, and walked back. Britt's car, he noticed, no longer sat in front of the house. Peter had thought to hide the evidence.

Before approaching the house, Roger cast a psychic veil over himself. Thus rendered invisible, he glided soundlessly through the neatly trimmed front yard and around to the back. Trees pressed close, leaving only about twenty feet of grass on each side. The dismantled vehicles still occupied the space in front of the detached garage. He noted a sports car in one of the two driveways.

Roger surmised from his previous visit that the master bedroom and bath had to be at the rear of the building. In confirmation, Britt pulled aside a curtain to stare out into the darkness. Though she couldn't see Roger, she doubtless felt his nearness despite the concentration that kept him from calling to her.

Scanning the windows of the room next to her prison, he noted that the drapes had been removed. Strangely, both the bedroom window and the smaller, frosted one that must belong to the bathroom were festooned on the inside with strings of white, bulbous objects.

*Fresh garlic,* he decided. *Good grief, the man really does believe in vampires.*

What was the point, though? Garlic intended to keep Roger out would decorate the whole building, not just two rooms.

Where was Peter? Roger heard no one moving inside except Britt. To search for the kidnapper by extrasensory means, he would have to drop the illusion of invisibility; he hadn't learned to do both at once. Allowing the psychic shield to dissolve, he probed for any life-energy other than Britt's. The back of his neck prickled.

It took him only seconds to sense the man lurking in the trees behind him. As Roger turned, Peter said, "Wasn't expecting you so soon. Don't try anything – vampire." He aimed a flashlight and a .38 at Roger.

*Maybe I should reconsider my opposition to gun control.* Roger held up his hands and surveyed Peter, who wore a silver cross around his neck, gleaming against the sweatshirt. "Don't tell me you've adopted your sister's delusion," said Roger in a conversational tone that he hoped sounded confident. "No sane person believes such things."

"Don't give me that. I just saw you appear out of thin air." He glanced at the woods behind the garage, then back at Roger.

"It's a little dark to be sure what you saw," said Roger.

"Well, I can see that arm from here – not a mark on it, where you were bleeding from a bullet wound last week. Maybe I wasn't sure before, but now I think Alice might've known what she was talking about. *He* explained it all to me." At the mention of his sister, hate flared in his aura. "You're here to pay for what you did to her."

"What do you think I did?"

"We'll talk about how you screwed her over later." Peter gestured with the gun. "Go on – in the house."

Roger contemplated his chances of safely rushing the man. Not good – in Peter's strung-out condition, any threat would goad him into shooting. The thought of taking another bullet filled Roger with an aching weariness. He obeyed the order, saying as he walked ahead of his captor, "What about Dr. Loren? Now that you have me, you don't need her."

"Don't be funny."

*Well, we all know "crazy" doesn't equal "stupid."*

Peter escorted him into the other side of the house and down the hall, shoving him into the master bedroom – judging from the car posters on the walls, the one Peter himself normally slept in. Roger listened to the deadbolt on the outside of the bedroom door snick into the locked position. How long did Peter imagine he could keep two people jailed in his house, even in this location? The window grill looked effective, though; Roger almost wished he had taken his chances with the gun outside.

Like the room Britt occupied, this one, too, had been stripped bare of all useful – or harmful – objects. Here even the closet stood empty, with its doors removed. Not only that, as Roger had noticed from outside, the curtains were gone. Garlic festooned the doorjamb as well as the bedroom and bathroom windows. Between its reek and the excessive heat from the forced-air system, the room stifled him. Experimenting with baseboard vents, he managed to shut off most of the hot air. He still felt queasy from the garlic, though.

Contact with Britt came as a welcome distraction: "I'm not sure letting yourself get captured is such a hot idea" she told him.

"I couldn't leave you alone in the villain's clutches, could I?"

"In the immortal words of Princess Leia, this is some rescue!"

"Colleague, your faith in me is an inspiration."

He heard laughter in Britt's thoughts before she continued more seriously, "Peter really believes it, doesn't he? Crosses, garlic, the whole package."

"I can't imagine how he arrived at that conclusion. He's hardly the imaginative type." Roger scanned the windows. "If he thinks garlic is an impassable barrier, he's in for a shock."

"Not to mention what he doesn't know about you and crosses. That glass looks pretty thick. Could you break it?"

Roger walked over and tapped on the window. "Probably, but what's the point? I couldn't rip out the bars."

"Then we have to trick our way out. Any ideas?"

"Not at the moment. It would help if we were in the same room."

"Right, better chance of dividing his attention. I'll work on it."

Her resolutely optimistic tone touched Roger. "Britt, are you all right?"

"So far, sure. I've dealt with violent patients plenty of times. Nobody can get through residency without that. But I need to rest now; concentrating this way makes my head ache."

They broke contact except for the wordless bond uniting them continuously. Roger prowled around the room, rechecking every detail in search of a weakness. Fifteen or twenty minutes brought him no closer to finding one. Moreover, the aroma of garlic made him feel suffocated. He lay down, closed his eyes, and breathed slowly, turning his attention inward. Britt had fallen asleep, whether from fearlessness or an impulse to withdraw. Either way, he approved of her conserving energy.

Some time later, the key turned in the deadbolt. Roger stood up, instantly alert. Peter stood in the doorway, brandishing the gun. "Stay back, and you won't get hurt – yet."

"How long do you think you can keep this up?" said Roger. "We'll be missed tomorrow, and that threat you made was probably overheard."

"A couple hours of sunlight should be plenty for what I've got planned. And I don't care what they do to me, after I get you for Alice."

"What, exactly, do you accuse me of?"

"She said you're a vampire, and I don't think she was making it up. She couldn't invent stuff as – as dirty as what she told me."

*Little do you know the imaginations of young girls.*

"She said you drank her blood," Peter went on. "I know she shot herself because you contaminated her."

A bit of reality testing seemed in order. "When am I supposed to have done this foul act?"

"September."

"Then why did she wait so long before attempting suicide?"

Peter looked uncomfortable. "I'm not sure about that."

"Then how can you be sure enough to accuse me of being a mythical monster?"

"That's why you're in here," Peter said. "Like I told Dr. Loren, either you're some kind of pervert who bites women, or you're the real thing. When the sun rises in the morning, between that and the garlic I'll have my proof." His voice rasped with hatred. "But that's not the worst. Why'd you have to kill her? Were you that scared she'd tell somebody what you did?"

"What in God's name are you talking about?"

Tears glistened in the young man's eyes. "She was lying there in a hospital bed and you *killed* her – in cold blood! Who else could've gotten in, or wanted to?"

*Good God, he blames me for what Sandor did!* Knowing denial would make no dent in Peter's belief, Roger said nothing.

"For all I know, you might've killed those other women I read about in the papers. If you'd do it to Alice, you could do it to anybody." Peter backed out of the room. Just as the door closed, he added, "Think about sunrise, Darvell."

So that explained the bare windows. Roger did not care to think about how uncomfortable the room, with its off-white walls, would become after daybreak. But if Peter expected Roger to disintegrate into dust at the first rays of dawn, he'd be disappointed.

"He can't expect that," Britt pointed out. "He knows Alice saw you during the day."

"True, but he's hardly thinking rationally."

"What's his plan, I wonder? Get "proof" that you're a vampire, then come on with the traditional stake?"

"Probably. I'm more concerned about what he plans to do with you. After this he can't just let you go, but he can't reasonably accuse *you* of killing his sister."

"As you said, reason doesn't have much to do with it. Never underestimate the power of positive paranoia. He considers me negligent because I tried to convince Alice you weren't dangerous."

"I haven't decided whether to keep maintaining he's deluded or play the vampire role to the hilt."

"The latter, I'd think. He may assume you're more vulnerable than you really are."

Roger tabled the question and inquired how Britt was feeling.

"Fine, honestly. I'm not the one who's stuck in a room decorated in Early Produce Department. I think I'll try to rest again. Captivity is duller than I'd have expected – nothing to read in here but old issues of *House Beautiful.*"

Her thoughts dissolved into an amorphous cloud as she drifted into sleep. Roger spent the next several hours alternately lying on the bed, leafing distractedly through a copy of *Car and Driver*, and pacing off the dimensions of the room. He couldn't sleep at night in any condition other than surfeit or absolute exhaustion. Though he knew he shouldn't waste energy, boredom combined with anxiety made him restless. Britt was right; captivity was numbingly dull.

When she woke up and addressed him again, the first hint of gray was lightening the sky.

"I wonder if Peter's planning to starve us to death," she speculated.

"If he has any sense left, he'll take care of you. He should realize you're the only reason I haven't tried to kill him."

"Roger, you wouldn't" she thought dubiously. "You're too civilized."

"A domesticated wolf is still, at the deepest level, a wolf. It's in the genes. If you were attacked, I'm sure I could get my human half out of the way long enough to react accordingly. As far as I'm concerned, the man deserves death already. He's committed a capital crime."

"What?"

"He threatened you."

"Oh, Roger, stop talking like an idiot." The tenderness in her tone contradicted the words. "You know, in spite of everything, I feel sorry for him."

"So do I, on one level," Roger admitted. "But not enough to let him hurt you."

Britt returned to the immediate practical problem: "I think I can persuade him to put me in with you. The Brer Rabbit trick."

"Please don't throw me in the briar patch?"

"Right. If I don't lay it on too thick, I should be able to make him curious about what terrible thing I expect to happen if we're together." Her tone became lighter. "We wouldn't have to go through all this if you could change into a glowing mist and ooze under the door like Dracula."

"Remind me to work on that. But it would be too late even for the Count; the sun's almost up."

"What time is it?"

He checked his watch. After five. For the next few minutes he watched the gradual paling of the sky and tried to conceal his uneasiness from Britt.

Shortly she told him the kidnapper was unlocking her door. "He's actually remembered to feed me. Looks like a ham and cheese sandwich."

She said to Peter, "I heard thought I heard footsteps through the walls. Do you have Dr. Darvell here?"

Peter held the gun on her. "Why, do you want to see him?"

She pretended to accept the taunt at face value. "Not if there's any truth in what you claim."

"Thought you didn't believe in vampires."

"Not in the sense you mean. But, as you implied, there've been cases of people who imagined themselves as vampires and behaved as such. Maybe – maybe I should have listened when Alice claimed Dr. Darvell drank – attacked her." She feigned disgust with the last sentence.

"We'll find out soon enough," said Peter with a self-satisfied smirk. "It's almost day."

"If he does imagine he's a – a vampire, he might react violently at sunrise. I'm glad I won't be near him then."

Peter gave her a speculative look and withdrew. Roger had little time to compliment Britt on her acting, for soon after Peter locked her door, he opened Roger's. "Getting hungry?"

"On your assumption," said Roger, "if I were, I'd turn into a wolf and rip out your throat. But to answer your question, I'd like a glass of milk."

Peter glanced at the window. "It'll be light soon. I can't wait to see what happens to you."

Roger was mildly surprised when the requested milk appeared a minute later. Still taking no chances, Peter served it in a plastic cup with a Budweiser logo. After watching intently while Roger drained the cup, Peter disappeared again. If he assumed vampires lived solely on blood, he must be confused.

Daylight seeped in through the window. For another hour Roger was able to avoid direct sun by keeping to shadowed corners. Soon, though, the glare began to cause discomfort. He retreated to the bathroom, trusting the frosted glass to filter out some of the rays, but the unrelieved white of the walls and fixtures made the smaller room no better. Roger lay face down on the bed, huddled to expose as little surface area as possible. He wished he had worn a jacket.

When he heard Peter's tread in the hall, he stood up, unwilling to appear at a disadvantage. The kidnapper looked the worse for lack of sleep but smiled at the sight of Roger. "Having fun?"

Roger licked his parched lips and said nothing.

"Make it easy on yourself. Admit what you are, and I'll kill you quick."

"Go to Hell," said Roger. He immediately regretted the lapse.

Peter's grin broadened. "After you, Doc." He relocked the door.

He circled around to the other bedroom to gloat over Britt. "You should see your Dr. Darvell. I think he's weakening."

Roger sensed Britt's heartbeat quickening in alarm, even as she assumed a defiant tone. "He's not 'my' Dr. Darvell. Look, Peter, if you give me some evidence that you're right, I'll be on your side. I wouldn't care to work with a homicidal maniac."

Peter greeted this remark with a skeptical snort and left her alone. She turned her attention to Roger.

"Colleague, how are you, really?"

"Not good. Could be worse, though. The trees do help a little. If only they were closer to the building."

"That lunatic is going too far," she fumed. "We have to do something."

"I am open to suggestions."

The effect of prolonged direct sunlight on him resembled heat exhaustion. His throat felt raw, not from blood-need, but from dehydration. Water quenched the thirst for only a few minutes, after which he had to take another drink. The short-lived relief was almost not worth the strain of getting up repeatedly. Britt maintained wordless contact with him, suppressing her anxiety to offer him comfort.

In about an hour Peter checked on Roger again. Roger made no attempt at concealing his condition this time. Let the idiot classify him as a vampire; the effort to convince him otherwise was getting nowhere. As before, Peter went straight from Roger to Britt. "I think I will let you see him."

"Wait a minute – you don't mean –?"

"The sun's really getting to him," said Peter. "I wonder what would happen if he had a chance to – uh – build up his strength?"

"I can't believe you're saying this," said Britt in a convincing simulation of outrage. "You think he's some kind of blood-thirsty monster, and you want to – to feed me to him?"

"You got it," said Peter. "It's what you deserve, after you wouldn't believe Alice. If you'd listened to her, she might be alive now."

"You're out of your mind!"

"When he bites you, that'll be all the proof I need. You'll be convinced, too, and if you're lucky I might save you in time so you can help me the way you said." He waved the gun. Britt didn't move. Tossing her the windbreaker she'd worn on the way over, Peter grabbed her arm and jerked her toward the door. "Come on, we haven't got all day!"

She tugged and squirmed in his grip. The man was lucky, Roger thought, that Britt was only pretending to resist; she could fight much harder. In the corridor she yielded to the temptation of inflicting a few scratches on Peter's arms. His fingernails dug into her wrist, and he pressed the muzzle of the .38 into the hollow of her throat.

## Chapter 21

"LISTEN, BITCH, I'm through playing. You gonna cooperate?"

Britt gulped and nodded. Peter marched her out the back door and inside the other half of the house. In the hall outside the bedroom he held the gun on her while unlocking the bolt with his other hand. He shoved Britt inside and slammed the door. She pounded on the panel with both fists until he'd turned the lock and walked down the hall.

Roger lay on his back, eyes shaded with one arm, watching her performance. "You can stop now; he's gone."

Britt hurried to the bedside, pushing him back to a supine position when he tried to sit up. The first minute was a rapturous blur. Her hair was straggling down, her blouse and slacks were rumpled from being slept in, and she tasted like ham and cheese. She was beautiful. When she got a good look at him, tears of anger shimmered in her eyes. "Roger, how do you feel?"

He forced a smile and tried to answer lightly. "Well, I'm feverish and nauseated, and my head hurts like the very devil – otherwise, just fine."

"You don't have to violate your human half," she whispered fiercely. "I'll kill him myself." She took off the windbreaker draped around her shoulders and spread it over Roger, then shifted to cast her shadow across his face. "At least I can – as Peter said – help you build up your strength. You aren't going to argue, I hope?"

He smiled wryly. "I'm not arguing. Allow me to point out, however, that physiological processes aren't very intelligent. If I could keep anything down in my present condition, my body would probably respond the way a well-fed vampire's system usually deals with extreme stress – by falling into suspended animation."

"Oh – I forgot about that."

"I don't think unconsciousness would be a terribly useful tactic."

Britt clenched her fists in frustration. "But I can't stand this – I want to help you."

"You are helping. Beloved." His fingertips traced the outline of her face as if seeking reassurance that she was real. "Actually, I'm too sick to feel hunger. But I wish I weren't so thirsty." She looked confused. "Confound the imprecise English language. I mean I'm dehydrated."

"Yes, I should think so! Don't move, I'll get you some water."

He felt an irrational reluctance to let her out of his reach. She was back in almost no time, though. He sat up to drink the cup of water she'd brought, then laid his head in her lap. She readjusted the windbreaker, which helped a little. Her hand, usually so warm, felt strangely cool on his forehead.

"You *are* feverish," she said. "That scares me; you're supposed to be immune to sickness."

"This is a special case."

"We have to get you out of here," she fretted.

"Any ideas?"

She glanced at the door. "I know you can't do anything about the deadbolt, but couldn't you rip the door off its hinges?"

"Probably," Roger said. "Looks like typically shoddy modern construction."

"Then why haven't you done it?"

"Because it would take a little time," he said. "What would our host be doing while all that racket was going on?"

"I guess the same argument applies to breaking the window. Otherwise you'd have done it just to get fresh air. I like Italian food myself, but this is ridiculous." She leaned over in a vain attempt to shade him more thoroughly. "Sorry, it isn't funny."

"And the higher the sun gets, the worse it will be," Roger said.

"Then we have to act soon, before you get any weaker. Say, you can still take him, can't you?"

"Of course." Roger decided acting insulted would demand too much effort.

"It all comes back to the gun," Britt sighed in frustration. "We need to distract Peter long enough for you to disarm him. Could you hypnotize him?"

"Not a chance. He's too wary. If he were immobilized long enough, I might be able to overcome his resistance – in which case it wouldn't be necessary anyway."

After a moment's thought she brightened up. "How about setting the place on fire?" She smacked the mattress, raising a puff of dust.

"In theory, an excellent plan," said Roger. "You have the means to start it?"

"Don't you?"

"No, I didn't bother with anything but my car keys."

"First time I ever wished I smoked," Britt said. "If I did, I'd carry matches in my jacket."

"I smelled cigarette smoke on Peter's clothes," Roger said. "It's possible he may have overlooked a book of matches in one of these drawers."

"True," Britt said. "Can't hurt to look."

"And after we get him in here?" said Roger. "He's still the one with the weapon."

"Can't you just try wrestling it away from him?"

"Not when a bullet meant for me could hit you. And I don't care for the idea of being shot twice in one week, either."

"Too bad he cleared out all the deodorant and aftershave and so forth. Squirting something in his face would slow him down. All we have is water."

"I'd prefer sulfuric acid myself," Roger said. When Britt started to get up to search for matches, he clasped her hand. "Colleague – beloved – if we don't get out of this –"

"Don't be silly," she said. "Of course we will. You have superhuman powers, remember?"

He fixed his eyes on hers, silently conveying what words could express only in part. "I love you, Britt."

"I know," she breathed. "Don't look at me that way when you can't follow through."

"I wish I could have been more for you."

"Stop using the past tense!"

"Very well," he said in the same solemn tone. "I wish I could be all you need. You've often complained of my inhibitions. If I had a sort of Bela Lugosi flair –"

"Lugosi is overrated. Now, if you looked like Frank Langella –" Dropping the pretense of frivolity, she lay across him, her face hidden on his chest, and said in a rapid, fierce whisper, "Stop being obtuse, Roger. I didn't fall in love with a fantasy of vampirism; I fell in love with *you*. I love everything about you, even the traits that drive me up the wall."

"That isn't logical." He knew they had to stop before they drove each other into hysterics. He held her away from him. "We can indulge in emotional displays later. You were going to look for matches."

"Right." Brushing tears from her eyes, Britt rearranged the jacket over him. At that moment they heard the deadbolt click.

Britt leaped up. Too late – Peter, opening the door, caught her in the act. If nothing else, Britt's jacket covering Roger made the situation clear.

Frowning, Peter swept the gun from Britt to Roger and back again. "You'll help me, huh? Sure!" He gulped rasping breaths between phrases. "You were in it with him all the time."

Britt folded her arms and glared back at Peter. Roger discarded the jacket and sat up.

Peter's weapon hand jerked convulsively. "Hold it right there!" He turned the muzzle toward Britt. "You – get over here."

"I'm getting fed up with taking orders from this kid," she told Roger.

"In the circumstances you haven't much choice." He tried to bridle his anger at his own helplessness. Encouraging her to fight would be unpardonably reckless.

Britt slowly walked over to stand in front of Peter. "So the lady doc and you have a thing going, huh?" the young man said to Roger. "Great – just remember what'll happen to her if you get any ideas about jumping me. What you did to Alice – I can't do the same to your woman, but there's something else almost as good."

His meaning hit Roger harder than Alice's bullet had. Britt's stifled gasp made her comprehension plain. "Steady, colleague," she told Roger. "He still has the gun. Maybe when he lets his guard down, we'll have a chance."

Roger choked back his rage. If Britt could maintain her self-possession under that threat, he could do no less.

Peter prodded Britt's midriff with the gun. "Lay down!"

"Certainly. Where?"

"On the floor." His chest heaved. "And I didn't say you could talk."

Britt lay flat on her back on the braided rug in the center of the room.

"Get the pants off," Peter said. Roger stood up. Their captor hadn't forgotten him, though. "I told you not to move!" Roger didn't sit down again, and the young man didn't insist.

Britt unzipped her slacks and wormed out of them without getting up. "Haven't had much practice at this, have you?" she said.

A deep flush spread over Peter's face. "Shut up!"

Roger silently told Britt, "As much as I hate to say this, you'd better try not to antagonize him."

Peter's left hand fumbled with the fly of his jeans. Somehow he managed to keep the gun trained steadily on Britt at the same time. Roger resisted the impulse to close his eyes. Britt's fear and disgust reached out to him. For an instant he felt an urge to flee, block out her sensations. How could he bear to feel her being violated?

Shame at his cowardice swept over him. He mentally embraced her. He felt her thighs roughly shoved apart as Peter knelt between them. The attacker's thick fingers hooked the elastic of her briefs and tugged them down. Britt stared fixedly at the man's nakedness. That bewildered Roger; he'd expected her to shut out the sight.

"Can't risk missing any chance," she told him. "I have to stay alert."

Her heart raced. Involuntarily she cringed when the tip of the erect organ brushed her inner thigh. "Roger, help me!"

Somehow Roger knew it wasn't physical help she wanted. He opened his mind to her, to the innermost depths, and felt her delving down to grasp what she needed. Fueled by Roger's strength, she cast every atom of her fear and loathing at Peter like heat from a flamethrower.

He reeled, though not quite losing his balance. His erection wilted instantly. With his left hand he slapped Britt hard across the mouth. The blow cut her lip.

Her sudden pain and the scent of her blood threw Roger into a frenzy. He sprang toward Peter, forgetting the gun until he heard it go off. He lurched to a halt.

BRITT'S VOICE sounded in his head: "It's all right, I – deflected – his hand. He missed."

She kneed Peter in the diaphragm and rolled away from him. The young man stumbled to his feet and waved the gun wildly between his two targets.

Roger saw all this through a red blur. Rage intoxicated him as blood never had. Some rational corner of his mind recalled what he'd been taught about projecting illusions, and his anger grabbed that knowledge and channeled it like high-voltage electricity. He charged at Peter, pouring his power into the visible incarnation of his hate. Ravening tiger, flame-spouting dragon – no image could be too terrible to express what burned in him.

He never knew what his opponent saw. Peter dropped the gun and stood paralyzed as Roger swooped down on him. Roger's nails – Peter may have seen them as the claws of a lion, the talons of a monstrous bird of prey – gouged the young man's throat. Blood fountained from the gash.

Roger picked up the man and flung him at the window. It shattered. Good, some fragment of Roger's humanity noted – the cuts from glass shards would obscure the scratches on the neck. The body rebounded to the floor and lay still.

Abruptly Roger's surroundings snapped back into focus. Britt was scrambling into her clothes. Peter lay in a puddle of blood, his body heat already seeping away. Suddenly the smell of fresh blood, sickeningly mingled with gunpowder and garlic, hit Roger. He staggered into the corridor and leaned against a wall.

Britt put her arms around his waist. "I believe you enjoyed that."

"Immensely." The realization of what he'd done struck him. He had gone berserk, like a monster from a nineteen-forties horror film. The man had invited death, all right; what devastated Roger was finding himself possessed by his fury, killing by instinct, almost by reflex. How could Britt stand to touch him?

His vision grew fuzzy again. "I think – I'd better sit down." He lowered himself to the floor. Britt knelt beside him, cradling his head on her breast. She displayed not the slightest revulsion. She behaved as if a neurotic half-human vampire were all she wanted in a lover.

Gray patches gathered before his eyes. Somewhere outside he heard an amplified voice demanding Peter's surrender. "Oh, damn, I told Marcia to wait until noon," he said. Then he fainted.

WAKING UP IN the back of an ambulance gave him a bad few seconds of disorientation. Britt's mental touch stabilized him. Minutes later he was an unwilling guest of the community hospital's emergency room. Odors of sickness and disinfectant choked him, while his head pounded with a barrage of negative emotions from every side. Fortunately Britt was there, never letting go of his hand except when a doctor or nurse insisted.

In a curtained alcove they fended off medical personnel while answering the questions of a bewildered Lieutenant Hayes. "I have to admit you two keep my life interesting," said the detective, leaning against a vacant bed while a nurse took Britt's blood pressure.

Britt described how Peter had summoned her. She bent the truth by claiming to have phoned Roger before driving to the Kovaks' place. Roger then took up the narrative. Both glossed over the exact way in which Peter thought the two doctors had mistreated Alice. Instead they stressed the young man's belief that Roger had committed the murders.

"That was really something," the detective said, thoughtfully smoothing his moustache, "the way you threw Kovak into the window. Broke it."

"Violent emotion sometimes confers unusual strength," said Britt. "Adrenaline, you know." She wiped at the smear of blood on her chin.

"The guy must have been a certifiable nut case," the detective said. "Garlic all over the room! What was he afraid of, vampires?"

"Perhaps," said Roger at his blandest.

Confronted by nothing but uninformative variations on the same answers, the detective tucked his notepad away and said, "I don't think you have to worry about criminal charges. Straight-forward case of self-defense." Yet Roger glimpsed uncertainty in his eyes.

"But don't leave town?" said Roger.

Hayes returned his wry smile. "Not for a few days, anyhow. I'm sure somebody will be in touch with you." He shook hands with both of them and left.

A resident tried to persuade Britt of her need for a tetanus shot. She rejected it, along with antibiotics and a list of lab tests. Roger was equally emphatic in convincing the ER staff that his collapse had resulted from nothing worse than fatigue and hunger. That argument elicited an offer of orange juice, which he refused. His stomach would certainly revolt if subjected to that abuse. The resident walked off muttering to himself. Doctors traditionally considered other doctors the worst possible patients; why violate the stereotype?

While Roger and Britt signed themselves out at the ER desk, a counselor from the rape hotline descended on them. Giving Roger a dubious glance, the woman pressed her card on Britt, appearing puzzled that Britt didn't show interest in her support. Roger admired the way Britt collected herself enough to say in a courteous tone, "I appreciate the offer, but we need to go home now. I'll be sure to call you later if I want someone to talk to."

Roger felt an irrational twinge of jealousy that she might want to share her pain with anyone but him.

"Of course I don't. But that's no reason to be rude to the woman. Her group does good work."

At last free to go, Roger learned that Britt had talked Lieutenant Hayes into having his car brought to the hospital parking garage. She had driven her own, since she had no physical injuries. Outside, the temperature was dropping. Roger had overheard the ER staff mentioning snow predicted before midnight.

The two of them went straight to Britt's apartment and showered together. Neither one found any erotic stimulation in this activity; emotional and physical exhaustion blotted out all other feelings. They lay together on Britt's bed, the room converted into a dim cave by the heavy drapes. Hard to believe it was only about noon. Britt reclined on one elbow, looking down at Roger.

"You did kill him."

"Yes."

"How do you feel about that?"

The memory of the past few hours rushed in upon him. Fury welled up like bile in his throat. "God, I wish I could bring him back to life and kill him again – slowly!"

"That kind of thinking is counterproductive." Suddenly Britt began to tremble, clinging to him, silent tears streaming down her cheeks. Roger found himself crying, too.

When they'd calmed down, he said, "When I – attacked – what did you see?"

"You, of course." She sounded puzzled. "You, defending me. What else?"

"Peter saw – I don't know what. A monster."

Britt hugged him tighter. "That was in *him*, not in you."

"I'm not so sure about that. I *wanted* to terrorize him. I wanted to rip him to shreds. Britt, I killed a man." Speaking the words aloud made the act real to him for the first time. "Not in rational self-defense. In a fit of rage."

"Reality test, Roger. Would you feel guilty if you'd had a gun and shot him to protect me?"

"Probably not, at least not in the same way." A dark wave engulfed him. "But you don't understand. I *enjoyed* it."

"I was cheering you on, so what does that make me? That adrenaline surge is a human thing. So is the drive to strike back at somebody who hurts you. It has nothing to do with your vampire half."

"The way I felt, I could have torn him limb from limb and gloried in it." The memory didn't stir any echo of that berserk exultation. Nausea roiled in the pit of his stomach.

"Did it make you hungry? Did you want to drain him?"

"Good God, no!"

She laid her head on his chest. "Then your anger might have been sinful, but it was a human sin."

"There's one big difference. No ordinary human being can do that much damage without a weapon. What if, the next time, it's an ordinary mugger? Or someone who scrapes my car in the parking lot? Or simply a man who looks at you the wrong way? Do they deserve instant death, too?"

Britt heaved a deep sigh. "How different is that from a combat vet or a body-builder or a martial arts expert? We all have to learn to curb our instincts. Your problem may not be quite the same as other people's, but it doesn't make you a monster. Or absolve you from listening to your superego, for that matter."

The cold lump in his chest began to thaw. "It would be easy to use the `monster' status as an excuse, wouldn't it? I don't suppose you've changed your mind about serving as my super-ego?"

"No, thanks, I decline that nomination. And Jiminy Cricket is otherwise employed." She stroked Roger's jaw and teased the corners of his mouth. "Enough, this is too soon to think about it. Do you need to–"

He felt no appetite, only a yearning to sink into the enfolding shelter of her love. "I thought – I didn't think you'd want to be touched."

"You call that thinking?" she said with mock severity. "I know the difference between rape and love."

"Really, I can't, not so soon after – that. And you shouldn't. We both need sleep more than anything. Do you need help relaxing?"

She nestled into the curve of his arm. "Not now."

SLEEP THREW HIM back into that locked room, with his eyes burning from the glare of the sun. Britt lay supine on the floor; this time, though, her arms and legs were immobilized, chained to wooden pegs driven through the rug into the floorboards. She arched her back like a bow, keening her terror and pain. Roger strained to rise from the bed and release her. Like a stake through the heart, the sun pinned him down.

Peter Kovak stood over Britt, straddling her. He aimed the revolver at her chest. It fired. The deafening crack plunged Roger into darkness.

HIS EYES SNAPPED open. Britt, curled against him, trembled and gasped. When he touched her shoulder, she opened her eyes and stared blankly for a second before waking to full awareness.

"Oh, man." She swiped a hand across her face. "Nightmare. You, too?"

He nodded.

"I'll bet it was the same one." She stretched, then rested her head on his shoulder. "An unwanted side effect of the bond that I never would've expected."

"Nor I." His breathing slowed to normal. "I'm almost afraid to go back to sleep, not if it does that to you. To both of us."

"Something else is bothering you," she said. "Besides committing manslaughter and worrying about a homicidal vampire lurking somewhere out there."

"Oh, you don't think that's enough?"

"You know I can sense when you're not leveling with me," she said.

"If so, I'm not conscious of it myself." Under the gentle pressure of her attention, he mulled over the images swarming in the back of his mind. One that he hadn't expected drifted to the surface. "Good Lord, I didn't realize –" His lungs tightened. *I can't tell her that. It's too petty.*

"What is it, Roger?"

"It's ridiculous. I don't even want to mention something so trivial and self-absorbed, compared to what you've been through."

"You might as well," she said, tracing circles on his chest, "because I won't leave you alone until you talk."

"While your life was in danger, I realized how I've – deprived you – destroyed your chance for normal love."

"What!" She brought her unprofessional shock under control. "Explain yourself, and don't give me any nonsense about home, family, and the patter of little feet. That would be illogical, even for you, since you know I had my tubes tied a month before we met. I have no desire to get pregnant at age thirty-five-plus, and if I ever wanted children after all, I'd adopt."

"There's one other significant thing an ordinary man can give you that I can't." He drew a deep breath and forced out the next words. "What Peter tried to do – he could hurt you that way, and I can never give you –"

"Oh, Roger!" Britt's hands massaged his temples, coaxing him to relax. "I've told you over and over that I don't miss it."

"So you have, and I know you're sincere – or think you are. Nevertheless, that doesn't prove you don't, on some level, feel cheated."

"Why me, Lord?" Britt muttered. "Why couldn't I have fallen for some nice, straightforward, simple-minded man of action, like my brother-in-law?" She laid her head on his shoulder again. "I didn't realize that particular omission bothered you so much."

"Nor did I, until a crisis made me aware of it," Roger admitted.

"The obvious remedy is to take direct action and correct the omission," Britt said.

"You know I can't –"

"No, I only know you believe you can't. Why?"

"I've explained to you that I've been incapable ever since I started–"

Her hard stare cut him off. "There's that rigid mind-set of yours again. You are unique. Stop limiting yourself to preconceived categories."

"Don't you always remind me that it does no good to lecture a patient?"

"All right, I got carried away. But why do you insist that your vampire genes make you incapable of penile-vaginal intercourse? The assumption is completely untested." She raised her head to look into his eyes. "Isn't it?"

"Well, yes."

"Then let's test it."

"Is that what you want? Now, after – all that?"

"I certainly wouldn't object," she said. "I'd love for you to get my mind off – all that. Wash away the taste of it."

He gave her a fierce hug.

"But right now I'm just the therapist. The point is, would it help you? Would it defuse any of this exaggerated guilt you're hauling around?"

The thought of sharing that intimacy with Britt excited him more than he would have expected. "If you think it's possible, I'd be glad to try."

"It's easy to find out. You role-play the patient, and I'll ask you the same questions I'd ask an ordinary man being treated for sexual dysfunction, to decide between sending him to a urologist or the Masters-Johnson clinic."

"Well, this is infinitely preferable to your office couch," said Roger as her nails skimmed lightly over his chest. "Fire away."

She sat up and drew his head into her lap. "Do you have morning erections? Or whatever the equivalent should be called."

"Yes."

"Any sensation associated with it?"

"No."

"Do you have psychogenic erections?"

"No, I need direct physical contact." After a moment's thought, he revised his answer. "Except where you're concerned. The touch of your mind has the same effect as the touch of your hand."

"Do you masturbate?" She wasn't as unembarrassed as she tried to appear; her cheeks turned pink.

"When you were out of town, I tried it for the first time in over a decade. After twenty minutes with no relief in sight, I decided it was a pointless exercise in frustration." He absent-mindedly rub his head against her thighs. "You already know most of this."

"But I have to pretend I don't. You're the patient, remember?" Her hand wandered down to his genitals.

"If you treated your patients this way, you'd lose your license."

"You don't ejaculate at all?"

"No – and that you do know."

"But you don't miss it, do you? You have orgasms, very intense ones. I know that from experience."

Growing impatient with her casual caresses, he lifted her hand to his lips and nuzzled the wrist where the pulse throbbed.

Difficulty in breathing made her voice less firm when she spoke again. "I don't miss it either. Since I can't get pregnant, it's irrelevant anyway. What we want is penetration, not the mechanics of a particular kind of orgasm."

"You think we can achieve – penetration?"

"Why not?" She resumed fondling him. "You obviously have erections sufficient for intromission – I've seen plenty of hard evidence for that." She gave the "evidence" a firm squeeze.

"Colleague, spare me the dreadful puns!" He wasn't so foolishly possessive as to question where she'd gained the experience to judge so confidently. Of course a beautiful woman in the prime of middle age wasn't untouched. Roger felt gratified enough knowing that she'd had no one else since before they met.

"If you were a human patient," she said, "I would remind you that you have perfectly normal erectile responses. I would diagnose ejaculatory incompetence. However, since you aren't a typical human male, for you it's not dysfunction; it's perfectly normal. So why are you giving yourself hell over it?" Shifting his head out of her lap, she lay on top of him and nibbled his shoulders and chest.

"Is this part of the therapy?" he said, running his hands slowly up and down her back. The smoothness of her skin sent electricity quivering through the cilia in his palms. His dormant lust awoke with blinding intensity.

"Sure. You've heard of sex surrogates?"

"I can't think of you as a surrogate anything – you are unique." He wanted to touch her everywhere at once, to merge with her, immerse himself in the tidal rhythm of her blood. "Beloved, I wouldn't want you to feel rushed, but I think I'm in danger of expiring from thirst in the next thirty seconds."

"Physiologically impossible." She scooted down and nipped the inside of his thigh, threatening his already precarious control.

"Two minutes, then. Three at the outside. That's not fair; I can't reach you this way."

"Then you just have to suffer." Her tongue flicked over his erection, then up his abdomen and chest to tantalize each of his nipples in turn.

He groaned aloud and tightened his arms around her. "Please – now."

She eased out of his embrace, but only to lie on her back. "Like this," she said.

Hesitantly he moved on top of her. "You don't mind my weight?"

"You never worried about that before." She wrapped her arms around him. "Don't feel obligated if you don't want to."

"Oh, God, you know I do!" She opened to him, and he plunged into her as smoothly as if they had rehearsed the maneuver a thousand times. Instead of submerging himself in the sharing of her perceptions, he held a slight distance to savor his own sensations to the fullest. He had touched and tasted her moist heat over and over, yet this intimate embrace seemed an entirely new feeling.

"Don't try to move," she whispered. "I just want to hold you." Her legs twined around his. She gasped and cried out his name. The imminence of her climax sent his desire spiraling out of control. Tasting the sweetness of her blood, he wondered on some detached level if all women, at the moment of fulfillment, pulsed inside with such ardent strength. It didn't seem possible.

When she began to rock her hips, he moved slowly, then faster as her thrusts accelerated. She spiraled into a second climax, drowning his doubts in ecstasy.

At last he rolled on his side, bringing her with him. Her cheeks, he found, were damp with tears. He kissed away the drops, reminded, in a low-key, unstimulating way, of what he'd just drunk from her veins. "And you said you hadn't missed it."

"I hadn't, in the abstract," she said. "I'm just sorry I waited so long to have it with you."

"Are you ready to go back to sleep?" He no longer feared losing himself in unconsciousness.

She stifled a yawn. "Sounds like a great plan."

Holding her, he allowed himself to sink into oblivion. The release of tension freed the deeper layers of his mind to process the data that his earlier anxiety had buried.

Hours later, he dreamed again. This time he stood in the back yard of the Kovaks' house, with Peter's gun trained on him. When Peter glanced toward the woods, Roger followed that look. The garage caught his attention. In the dream, he noticed what hadn't registered in real time. The windows in the front of the large door were covered by dark curtains.

The dream-landscape showed him something that hadn't been there at all, before. He glimpsed a red gleam under the trees at the rear of the lot. The dim shape surrounding the twin points of crimson expanded, darkened, until it became the outline of huge, batlike wings.

Roger woke more smoothly this time. Sitting up, he gazed down at Britt. She stirred and opened her eyes. "I remember what Peter said," she murmured.

"Yes," Roger said. *"He* explained what happened to Alice. *He* taught Peter how to deal with me."

"It seemed farfetched that Peter would suddenly start believing in vampires, didn't it?" said Britt, leaning on one elbow. "Sandor got to him. Sandor has been watching that family for weeks – Alice said he 'called' her. I think he's taken to sleeping in their garage. Isolated, protected from sunlight, perfect for a homeless vampire. And Peter's parents were so distraught he could've easily kept them from discovering him."

"Yes, he's old enough to have at least that much control." Roger visualized the renegade lurking under the trees, watching Peter imprison both of them. "He manipulated the boy into dealing with us. Punish me by hurting you, possibly killing you—" He choked down his anger. This was no time to let emotion cloud his intellect. "Then disable me, after which Sandor could take his time finishing me off."

Britt's eyes shone with dawning excitement. "Yes, I think that's exactly what happened."

"If he went dormant at sunrise, slept out the day in the garage," said Roger, "he may be there at this moment."

## Chapter 22

ROGER ROLLED OUT of bed and started pulling on his discarded clothes. "It's not full dark yet. If I hurry, I have a chance to catch him off guard."

"You mean 'we,' don't you?" said Britt, dangerously quiet.

"I don't want you anywhere near him!"

"Roger, you aren't thinking straight." She covered her face in a gesture of mock despair. "And why should that surprise me? Look, if we separate, you can't protect me. Suppose he decides this is the perfect time to pay me a visit?"

Roger paused in buttoning his shirt. "Damn, you have a valid point."

"Thanks ever so much." She threw back the covers and reached for her underwear. "All for one and one for all, remember?" She scrambled into her clothes, hanging the emerald cross pendant around her neck.

Minutes later, they were in the Citroen heading for the Kovaks' place. The predicted snow flurries had begun, without enough accumulation yet to make the roads slippery. Roger wore only a light jacket, while Britt was bundled in the full regalia of winter coat, scarf, fur-topped boots, and gloves.

"At least promise you won't take any idiotic chances," he said as they drove across the South River bridge. "If I ask you to stay out of the way, for God's sake listen to me."

"I'll use my best judgment," she said. "I won't do anything dumb." He had to be content with that much of a concession.

At the Kovaks' he again parked around the curve out of sight of the house. Dusk was already deepening to nightfall as they walked up the driveway. Roger considered activating his psychic veil, but since he couldn't shroud Britt as well, he decided not to bother. The snow, he hoped, would keep traffic to a minimum, so no one would notice their trespassing.

The house was dark, the forensic team long since finished. Yellow crime scene tape stretched across the front porch. Britt stared at the garage, a dim hulk to her human eyes. "You think he'll still be there?"

she silently asked.

"The police wouldn't have any reason to search the garage, so he may well be." Roger guided Britt to the shelter of a tree at the edge of the yard. "I'm going to check for signs of life. Stand here and don't move. Please."

Britt conveyed reluctant assent. Stepping off the gravel driveway, he stalked silently around the garage. The windows in front were still curtained. The small side door, too, had a dark cloth over its grimy window. Roger stood motionless and listened. Holding his breath, he heard a slight breeze in the branches, Britt's lungs inhaling and exhaling the frosted air, and the nervous racing of her heart. He filtered out those sounds and focused on the garage. There – another set of lungs and the ponderous rhythm of a slower heartbeat.

*He doesn't sound dormant.* Roger eased closer to the side door. A rustle of movement within alerted him just in time. He backed up several rapid paces. He heard Britt's feet on the gravel, tiptoeing across the driveway to stand just behind him. "Damn it, I thought we agreed –"

The door flew open, and Neil Sandor leaped out. Catching sight of Roger, he slammed to a halt on the threshold.

His eyes smoldered. With a teeth-baring grimace he said, "What's my line here? 'We meet again, Doctor'? And about time, too." Roger felt the outlaw's eyes crawl over him and linger on Britt. "Come inside and sit down, both of you. We need to talk."

Conscious of Britt behind him, so close her breath warmed the back of his neck, Roger said, "We can talk here. You come out." He'd be a fool to give up his maneuvering space.

Grinning as if he guessed Roger's thoughts, Sandor swaggered to within two yards of the couple. He wore jeans and a red plaid flannel shirt, to which clung the odor of decomposed blood. A sign of mental deterioration, Roger thought; healthy predators practiced fastidious cleanliness. The outlaw's hair and beard had grown into a wild tangle. His eyebrows formed a single bristling thatch; his fingernails were long, curved talons.

Roger's stomach lurched. *So this is what a feral vampire looks like!* He swallowed hard.

Sandor noticed the reaction. "Don't like what you see? Masks off – this is what we really are. This is what you are, half-breed."

"No. I am not like you." He took an involuntary step backward. "We do not have to be ravening beasts."

"Why so timid?" said the other. "The way you're guarding your pet, I'd think you're expecting me to do something – impulsive."

"Considering your treatment of Alice, what should I expect?" Roger said. "Not to mention Sylvia, one of your own kind."

Sandor's derisive smile vanished. "I had good reasons. One of which was to get your attention. I don't stand for any young cub screwing around with me."

"After living over a century, you haven't learned any more refined language than that?" said Roger. Why didn't Sandor attack? If he was stalling in hopes of getting Roger to lower his guard, two could practice that strategy.

"Why, Doctor, you sound downright hostile. You're expecting me to start a fight, aren't you? That's not what I want."

"Oh? What do you want?"

"To give you one more chance." Sandor, bold as always, made no attempt to shield his emotions. He radiated no anger, yet below the surface simmered impatience – and something else? Hunger?

Yes. As far as they knew, he'd gone weeks without a violent kill, which he seemed to require for satisfaction. Britt, also sensing the vampire's need, projected hope. Could they use that urgency against him, Roger speculated? Unlikely that Sandor would fall for another mock seduction, nor would Roger allow Britt to risk herself that way.

"Allow, hell!" she silently retorted. "I guess you're right, though. Still, he's hungry and you're well-fed; that should give you some advantage."

The outlaw, watching them and apparently encouraged by their silent attention, continued, "Join me, Doctor – oh, hell, let's dispense with the titles and surnames. They're human conventions, anyway. I'm Neil, you're Roger. Help me hit back at the Council. You don't owe any more to Volnar's pack than I do."

An unwilling surge of sympathy rippled through Roger. "Rejecting them was your own choice."

Neil assumed a relaxed stance, his hands stretched out, palms up, in a parody of appeal. "Do you mean to say you *like* rolling over and playing dead for the elders, bowing your neck to those stupid rules?" Every word evoked an answering spark in Roger. "They accommodate the ephemerals' culture too much. They expect us to act human, instead of claiming our rightful heritage."

The last sentence shredded the tenuous web of sympathy he'd begun to weave. "You forget, I *am* human," Roger said.

"No, you're not!" Neil's voice dripped contempt. "You just

happen to look like one. But you're not a real vampire yet, either. Volnar won't let you be one. Face it, how much has he actually taught you?"

Roger's resentment of Volnar boiled to the surface. He struggled to recall the positive dimensions of their telepathic exchange. "There wasn't time. He transmitted as much as he could. I recognize his motives, even if I have – problems – with his methods."

Neil shook his head in disgust. "Roger, you're so bloody naive. Did Volnar give you one solid reason to trust him? Didn't he keep that mental shield of his locked and barred every second, except when it suited *his* purposes?"

Roger couldn't deny that argument. Young and inexperienced as he was, Volnar could have deceived him with impunity.

Britt's thoughts entwined with his, like a firm handclasp. "Careful, Roger, don't let him confuse you. To him you're just a weapon against the others. He wants to warp their prize genetic experiment."

"Let me teach you." Neil's coaxing tone would have fooled anyone who couldn't sense the cynical manipulation beneath it. "Let me show you what our life should really be like."

"Oh, like yours? Lurking in the shadows, lairing in holes like a wild animal?"

"Freedom, Roger." Neil grinned, running his tongue over his lips. "Do you enjoy being domesticated all that much? You had a taste of the real thing recently, didn't you? You killed that boy."

"You influenced him, didn't you?"

"Sure, I've been watching him. Who do you think convinced him Alice was right about you being a vampire? I tried to make him forget our conversation, think it was his own idea to scrag you and the lady doc."

"You should have tried harder," Roger said. "He remembered enough to betray your presence here."

Neil waved away that fact as irrelevant. "So how did you like it – the kill?"

The image of Peter's lifeless body twisted Roger's guts. He kept his voice even. "Not at all."

"Because you aren't used to it. Come on, admit you got high on it. For a few seconds, didn't you feel that ultimate thrill?"

A rush of heat suffused Roger. The taste of that instant when he had cast aside his human veneer, let his darker self possess him, flooded his senses. For a moment he yielded to the delirium, a crimson mist gathering before his eyes.

Britt's hand on his shoulder cleared his brain. Neil's pleasure in that momentary weakness struck him like a poisoned arrow. "I reject that," said Roger. "That is not what I choose to be."

Neil edged closer. "Get thee behind me, Satan?" he mocked. "Have you considered that maybe you can't transform because you've never let go, never immersed yourself in your true nature? Come with me, Roger – let me teach you to shed those human limitations and glory in feeding the way you were meant to feed – and you can learn to fly."

Ambushed by the memory of Sylvia soaring over the tree-tops, Roger felt a pang of yearning as sharp as blood-thirst. *No, it's impossible; Volnar said I had no trace of that talent.* But why assume Volnar told the truth? *Even if he didn't, would I change myself into a rabid wolf, exiled from human and vampire society both, just for the power to fly?* Such considerations felt arid in contrast to the promised reward. Neil's eyes scorched him like live coals.

For an instant Roger had actually forgotten Britt. Now she edged around him to stand at his side, facing the renegade. "My, how altruistic you're becoming, all of a sudden." Her voice sounded unnaturally loud in the snow-muffled darkness. "So you just want to help Roger claim his true heritage? You want to help him grow into a proud, wild animal, roaming free under the moon, a lord of the night?" The melodramatic words rang with scorn. "Horse feathers! You're running scared. You don't like having to sleep with both ears pricked, waiting for someone to sever your head from your body. You want a companion to share the risk."

The shot hit home. Neil bared his teeth in a snarl.

Unafraid, Britt pulled the cross out of her coat and clutched it. "Not only that, you're getting lonely. Your recent behavior pattern makes that obvious. You need somebody you can dominate, so you don't have to admit to yourself how badly you need companionship. First you tried Sylvia, a young woman barely mature. And now you're trying to suck in Roger. You think he's a pushover because he's not only young, he's half human. Well, if you think that –"

In the midst of this speech, the outlaw's aura deepened to a lurid violet-red. Rage emanated from him like hard radiation. His face shed its human facade, dark velvet fuzz sprouting on the cheeks, the ears elongating to points, the teeth sharpening. "Shut up!" he cut her off in a thick growl. He swayed toward Britt, then rocked back on his heels. "Can't you see what she's done to you?" he said to Roger, the words barely comprehensible. "She's weakened you. She's prey, damn it – share her with me –"

Neil's involuntary transformation shook Roger to the depths. A vampire out of control, submerged in madness, posed a more frightful threat than one simply driven by lust and malice.

Britt held up her cross, which seemed to shine from within. "Think again, Neil. You can't touch me while I have this, can you?"

Fury overwhelmed the vampire's fear of the cross. Emitting a howl devoid of any trace of rationality, he lunged at Britt. Roger blocked him.

The renegade's claws dug into his shoulders, shredding his jacket. Neil panted in his face, sickening him with a stench like decayed meat. Roger threw his weight against the other vampire. They slipped on the light coating of snow and rolled together on the gravel of the driveway.

Roger shifted his grip to claw at Neil's throat. His opponent fended him off. Roger heard the grinding of the other's teeth. Flipping Roger onto his back, Neil snapped at his throat. Roger flinched away, rammed a knee into his adversary's groin. With the whiplike dart of a striking snake, Neil scored a gash on Roger's neck. Only Roger's instinctive recoil kept the wound superficial.

Taking advantage of Neil's instant of complacency at this achievement, he raked his nails across Neil's cheek, then shoved the other vampire off him. Roger sprang to his feet. The scent of blood, his own and the other's, made his head reel. He felt drunk. With a roar he charged at Neil.

In a blur of flailing limbs, the enemy grappled with him. Somehow they kept their footing as they struggled. Again and again Neil's teeth scraped Roger's neck and collarbone. In a second of clarity, Roger thought, *I taste almost human – and he likes it!* He let his arms go limp, throwing Neil off guard. When the purebred vampire closed with him once more, he dodged, then bit into Neil's throat.

The chilled-metal flavor scalded Roger's mouth like acid. Gagging, he didn't anticipate the blow that rammed into the pit of his stomach. Neil followed up with a swipe of his talons down Roger's chest.

Staggering, Roger glanced down at his ripped shirt, the red slashes across his ribcage. Neil drove a fist into his jaw. Roger fell to the ground, pain screaming through his nerves. *As if his claws were tipped with poison!*

No, that searing pain wasn't wholly physical. He was feeling the other vampire's agony, too, amplified by the berserker rage. Roger slammed down his mental barrier. *Damn bloody monster, stay out of my head!*

Neil landed on him with crushing force. Roger's skull hit the ground so hard he almost blacked out. The grip of Neil's hands around his neck jolted him to full awareness. *He's going to kill me, like Sylvia.* In some corner of his mind Roger knew he should be able to control the pain that left him writhing helplessly, the blood flow that drained his strength. But he couldn't summon up that power. He needed all his energy to bar Neil's sensations from his consciousness.

Blackness thickened before his eyes. *God! Is this death?* Through a crack in his barrier he felt a gentle probe. *Get out!* Then a fragment of awareness returned. It was Britt whose touch he felt.

"Roger, don't let him do this to you. If you fight the contact, you're playing his game. He's more terrified of the bond than you are! Use that!"

Britt's strength flowed into him. Though he knew she stood several yards away, through some doubled vision he saw her kneeling beside him, pressing the luminous cross into his hands. *Yes! Neil enjoys pain – let him experience what real pain is!*

Roger grabbed tightly onto the burning agony in his chest and channeled it into the renegade vampire's clutching fingers. The cross Britt held, which Roger mentally grasped in union with her, blazed with their shared love and pain. He drove that energy up Neil's nerves and veins to the vampire's heart. Momentarily their three hearts throbbed in unison, racked by the same torture. Then Neil, his limbs twitching with convulsions, collapsed on Roger.

Roger heaved the quivering body off him. Rolling Neil on his back, Roger knelt on the vampire's chest. Out of the corner of his eye Roger glimpsed Britt crouched on the ground, hugging the cross to her breast. To his heightened senses the symbol radiated a green glow that bathed all three of them in a halo of palpable light.

Roger charged into Neil's mind, smashing the remnants of the other vampire's shield like a house of cards. "So you like to feed on pain? You don't know what you're talking about! You're a coward; you've never opened yourself to the full range of your victims' emotions. You picked and chose what you wanted, as if humanity were a buffet. Well, you're about to find out what you've been missing!"

Whatever fragment of rationality Neil still possessed cringed in terror. Roger ignored it. Instead he laid himself wide open to memories he'd tried to annihilate. First he embraced the image of Sylvia begging him to merge with her. He flung at Neil the panic of her mind invading his, the anguish she'd felt when he'd cast her out. Like a raw wound, worse than the gash in his chest, Roger relived her sorrow for Rico, her sadness at leaving her home, wandering as a fugitive. He opened himself to her yearning to mate with him and her distress when he'd refused, abandoning her to Neil's violation. Roger then disgorged his own sick horror at discovering her mangled corpse.

Whimpering like a maimed animal, the vestigial scrap of Neil's consciousness curled into a ball in the center of his skull. The feedback of the pain tormented Roger almost beyond endurance. An electric current of renewed energy flowed into him. Britt. He resumed the attack.

"Neil Sandor, you're the one who doesn't know what it's like to be a fully functioning vampire. Our relationship with our donors is meant to be symbiotic. You've cut yourself off from half of what you were created for – crippled yourself!"

A gasp of resistance: "So you think you do know?"

*Do I? Didn't I trap myself in a stereotype of vampirism as rigid as his? God, what a fool I've been!*

"Yes. Brought up as human, I can look at our existence from a fresh viewpoint. I can see what it ought to be." Roger cast himself back to the night when Alice had collapsed at his door, on the verge of death. He drowned Neil in the terror she'd felt that night. "Did you drink deep of this? Or just taste it and run away?"

He then force-fed Neil those hours he and Britt had spent as captives in Peter's house. Roger enveloped the other vampire in the miasma of hate, fear, and grief that had hovered around Peter like a fog over a swamp. The vision of Peter's fixed stare, eyes red-rimmed from weeping for his sister, his hair and skin clammy with sweat, his hand squeezing the revolver, sprang to life. And then the moment of his death, his head crashing into the window.

"I didn't kill him for pleasure," Roger told Neil. "I knew how he felt. I know what it is to face losing a person who means everything to me." He revived the terror of the void that threatened to engulf him when Peter aimed the gun at Britt.

Neil shriveled like an undersea creature washed up on the sand at high noon. A ratlike screech: "Get away from me!"

Roger shrugged off the feeble spasm of resistance. "Hardly. I have the strength now. You are weaker because you're alone. I have an ally."

"Your pet!"

"No. She provides for me out of love. Something you'll never know."

*Unless you choose to reach out.* Roger didn't bother projecting that thought. He knew the renegade would never take that risk. "You've seen too many sensational movies, picked up distorted ideas of what we should be. You believe that nonsense about satanic autonomy. The fact that we're solitary predators is only part of the truth. The blood-bond sustains us. Without it, we wither away."

Roger visualized the emerald cross, refulgent with light that pulsed like a heartbeat, in his grasp. He extended it toward the other vampire. "Take it. Let it heal you." The radiance burned Neil like sunlight.

With a last despairing wail, what was left of Neil Sandor fled into the darkness.

The world heaved as if racked by an earthquake. When Roger's vision cleared, he was lying on the ground next to Neil. Probing, he touched no sentience. He heard no hiss of air in the lungs, saw no expansion of the chest. A few seconds of concentrated listening, however, brought the stutter of a feeble pulse to his ears. Before second thoughts could rise up to sap his resolution, Roger clamped his hands around the renegade vampire's neck. With a single twist he broke the spine.

Panting as if he had run across town on foot and battled for hours instead of a few minutes, he staggered to Britt and leaned over her. She lay face up, her eyes closed, still holding the jeweled cross to her breast.

He touched her, both physically and mentally. He felt nothing.

Heaving a sob, he gathered her into his arms. He felt himself falling into blackness. For a timeless interval it deafened and blinded him.

What drew him back was the flutter of her heart against his chest. She was only unconscious, not – not gone. He carried her to the car and laid her on the back seat. Crouched beside her in the cramped space, he rested both hands on her head. "Britt– wake up." He whispered to her and simultaneously spoke inside her mind. Nothing. He hadn't realized how deeply he'd drained her life-force to fuel the attack.

"Dear God, Britt, why didn't you stop me?" He plunged into her mind.

Again the void swallowed him. He had never seen darkness before, only the luminous gray other people called "dark." But this time he would not yield to the emptiness. He clung to the certainty that Britt lived – somewhere. His eyes strained through the blackness until he glimpsed a tendril of light. He floated toward it. He grasped it like a golden thread to guide him through this labyrinth.

For the place had now become a maze, no longer a featureless darkness. He traced the thread through tunnels like the corridors of a dungeon in a Gothic tale, their stone walls coated with frost. At the center of the labyrinth he found Britt lying on a bed of stone; around her hung icicles glimmering with an internal blue light of their own.

One segment of his mind knew this was not a real place, only an imaginary construct to help him lure Britt out of her retreat. He thought, *How archetypal can you get? She would love this!*

He stepped through a veil of cold that resonated in his bones like a musical note pitched too high for mortal ears. Britt looked and felt like a statue of ice. He pressed his lips to hers.

At first he felt no response. With a dim idea of restoring the life-force he had taken, he bit his lip to warm her cold mouth with his blood. He poured his soul into a plea for her to waken. An echo of her normal vitality answered him. He fed it, lavishing his energy upon her, nourishing her as she always nourished him. He felt his heart beat with hers, his life flowing into her as if they shared a single bloodstream.

Abruptly he found himself in the car, holding Britt and kissing her. He discovered he actually had bitten his lip, and somehow his teeth had scratched Britt, too, for he tasted her blood mingled with his like a sacrament. Except for the abysmal fatigue that weighed upon her, she felt normal to his psychic touch.

"Beloved, can you forgive me –"

"Don't!" She placed a finger on his lips. "I did what I wanted to do – what we had to do."

He strapped the seat belt around her and got out his car keys. "You're so cold – I have to get you home."

With a faint smile at his solicitude, she said, "I appreciate the thought, but we aren't finished yet."

He arched his eyebrows interrogatively.

"Sandor," she said. "You only broke his neck, didn't you?"

Roger understood at once. Hurrying back to the Kovaks' yard, he found the renegade's body where he had left it, dusted with a fine layer of snow. He lifted it over his shoulder and carried it away from the garage, into the woods. What now? Though he knew he had to finish the job, he couldn't bring himself to decapitate Neil. The thought of dismembering a body – even Neil's – as Sylvia had been dismembered revolted him.

Besides, if the body were found, that mutilation would attract more official interest than a less exotic murder would. *Excellent excuse, Roger,* he chided himself. But it did have the merit of truth. A further complication came to mind: If at all possible, he must make sure the body was *not* found, at least not until it decayed too far for reliable autopsy results.

He recalled what he'd been told about total destruction of the brain. Without giving himself further time for reflection, he opened the side garage door with a handkerchief wrapped around the knob and rummaged among the tools for a suitable blunt instrument. Sledgehammer – perfect. Hefting the weapon, he returned to the apparent corpse. Roger's stomach churned at the thought of what he had to do. He ordered it to shut up. *There's no consciousness here. Think of this as wrecking a machine.*

He raised the hammer and slammed it down on the other vampire's skull.

After one glance at the crushed ruin, Roger averted his eyes. Apparently Neil's system had shut down, withdrawing into suspended animation, for the blood only oozed instead of splashing. Swallowing nausea, Roger used his foot to turn the body face down. *I can't leave this half-finished!* He repeated the operation on the brain stem. To make absolutely sure, he swung the hammer again – and again – and again –

Sick and shaken, he finally stopped the battering and steeled himself to take one more look. Good enough – the vampire could not possibly retain enough intact neural tissue to guide regeneration.

Grasping the body by the belt, he lifted it just high enough to prevent drag marks on the ground. The awkward grip made his arm ache by the time he reached the riverbank, but he couldn't stand the thought of touching the corpse any more than necessary. He ripped off Neil's shirt, wiped the handle of the sledgehammer, and looped one sleeve of the torn garment through Neil's belt. After knotting the shirt to secure it to the belt, Roger tied on the hammer. He forced himself to work carefully instead of rushing through the job the way his revulsion tempted him. The knots mustn't come loose; the body had to settle to the bottom of the South River and stay there.

He gave the hammer one last swipe with the handkerchief, which he then stuffed in Neil's jeans pocket. Heaving a deep breath, Roger lifted the body over his head and flung it as far into the river as his inhuman strength allowed. It sank with a dull splash. With luck, by the time someone discovered the corpse, if ever, decomposition would preclude any questions about its species or the cause of death.

Snowflakes continued to fall, lightly but steadily. *Please, keep up long enough to hide the footprints and the blood.* Luckily, there wasn't much of that to worry about. Back at the house, he used a spray of pine needles to brush snow over the stain on the ground. Fortunately, if the police paid a return visit, they would have no reason to search the grounds for traces of Sandor. They didn't know he had ever been there.

Waiting in the car, Britt sat up in the back seat, her face strained and tight-lipped.

"You didn't watch that, did you?" He was appalled at himself for not raising a mental barrier against her.

"I needed to," she whispered. "Witness. Let's go home."

He drove to his place on automatic pilot, thankful for the instincts that enabled him to negotiate the sparse traffic with only a fraction of his attention. The snow was growing thicker by the time they reached the townhouse. Breathing a prayer of thanks, he led Britt inside, helped her out of her wraps, settled her on one of the paired couches, and covered her with a blanket.

"Why here?" she murmured.

"Because I want to take care of you."

"Okay." Her eyes drooped shut.

Though he hated to leave her, even for a minute, he had to scrub his hands before he could bear to touch her again.

Returning to the living room with a brandy-laced glass of milk for Britt, he found her lying face down with her head pillowed on a cushion. She turned sideways to look at him as he sat beside her. He ran his hand down her back, eliciting a faint ripple of response.

"Hold me," she whispered. He pulled her into a sitting position and drew her close, chest to chest. Her skin felt as chilled as his. She began weeping quietly into his neck.

"Don't, beloved, you'll make me cry, too."

She drew a shivering breath. "Why should we deny ourselves a natural catharsis?"

So he cried with her until they were both exhausted. Some time later they half-reclined on the sofa, with Britt nestled into the curve of his arm, drinking her spiked milk. "I put you through that with him," Roger said. "Forgive me – I never meant to drain you that way."

She gave him a hard squeeze around the midriff. "Stop

apologizing! Face it, colleague, we're a team."

"Do you think I did the right thing?"

"WE," SHE CORRECTED. "We made the only acceptable choice."

"I killed again."

"You executed a man who'd been sentenced to death. According to vampire ethics, you did exactly right. Do you have any regrets?"

He searched his thoughts. "No. Not this time. No thrill of victory, either. Just relief."

"Then we did the best we could in the circumstances. The police will have an unsolved case, but the murders will stop. That's the important thing. No choices are perfect."

"I think I agree with you."

"Wonderful," said Britt with a trace of her usual astringency. "About time you started listening to me."

The peace he felt surprised Roger. Only by drawing on both vampire and human traits had he managed to deal with the threat. His two sides did not undercut, but enriched each other.

Following his thoughts, Britt said, "Satisfied that you aren't a monster? Anyway, if you are, you're *my* monster."

He settled gratefully into the shelter of her embrace. "I think I can live with that."

~ The End ~

## Margaret L. Carter

Margaret L. Carter read DRACULA at the age of twelve, and it changed her life. The resulting interest in horror, fantasy, and science fiction led her to become a writer, meet her future husband, and pursue degrees in English literature. A lifelong vampire fan, she earned a Ph. D. from the University of California, Irvine, with a dissertation that included a chapter on DRACULA.

She edited DRACULA: THE VAMPIRE AND THE CRITICS (1988), the first anthology of essays on Stoker's novel, and compiled THE VAMPIRE IN LITERATURE: A CRITICAL BIBLIOGRAPHY (1989). She also edits a semiannual fiction zine, THE VAMPIRE'S CRYPT. Her stories have appeared in various fanzines and anthologies, including several of Marion Zimmer Bradley's "Darkover" volumes. Margaret's first novel, SHADOW OF THE BEAST, a werewolf tale (also set in Annapolis, where she currently lives), appeared in 1998.

She and her husband, a Navy Captain, have four sons, two grandchildren, and an assortment of cats.

Visit Margaret's web site at:
http://members.aol.com/MLCVamp/vampcrpt.htm

Printed in the United States
30596LVS00001B/9